CITY

OF THE

DEAD

Also by Daniel Blake
Thou Shalt Kill

CITY
OF THE
DEAD

DANIEL BLAKE

G

GALLERY BOOKS
New York London Toronto Sydney New Delhi

G

Gallery Books
A Division of Simon & Schuster, Inc.
1230 Avenue of the Americas
New York, NY 10020

First Gallery Books hardcover edition July 2012

GALLERY BOOKS and colophon are trademarks of Simon & Schuster, Inc.

For information about special discounts for bulk purchases, please contact Simon & Schuster Special Sales at 1-866-506-1949 or business@simonandschuster.com.

The Simon & Schuster Speakers Bureau can bring authors to your live event. For more information or to book an event contact the Simon & Schuster Speakers Bureau at 1-866-248-3049 or visit our website at www.simonspeakers.com.

Designed by Kyoko Watanabe

Manufactured in the United States of America

10 9 8 7 6 5 4 3 2 1

Library of Congress Cataloging-in-Publication Data

Blake, Daniel
  City of the dead/Daniel Blake.—1st Gallery Books hardcover ed.
    p. cm.
  1. Detectives—Pennsylvania—Pittsburgh—Fiction. 2. Pittsburgh (Pa.)—Fiction.
—Fiction. I. Title.
  PR6069.T345C58 2012
  823'.914—dc23
                                        20110
43780

ISBN 978-1-4391-9762-2
ISBN 978-1-4391-9765-3 (ebook)

To Jenie and Jeremy Wyatt,
top-drawer parents-in-law

Prologue

December 26

The sea ran back down the beach.

Franco Patrese felt the warm sand between his toes and smiled. There might be better places to be in the world right now, but none sprang to mind. It was sunny and hot, he'd spent the last six nights with an English girl who had the dirtiest laugh and nicest smell of anyone he'd ever met, and the most strenuous task he faced today was sorting out the precise sequence of swimming, sunbathing, lunch, beer, and sex.

Exactly two weeks ago, Patrese had sat in a Pittsburgh hospital room and listened to a murderer's confession. It had been the culmination of a case that had consumed him for months and taken with it much of his faith in human nature. Exhausted and traumatized, he'd searched online for last-minute holidays, and ended up among the palm trees here in Khao Lak.

The first week had been an open-water diving course—a refresher course, in Patrese's case, as he'd done a lot of diving in his youth but hadn't been for a few years now. It was there that he'd met Katie, the English girl currently asleep in his beachfront hotel room. They'd dived to reefs and wrecks, swum with Technicolor rainbows of marine life: cube boxfish dotted in yellow and black, nudibranchs of solar orange, shrimp banded in Old Glory red and white.

Now Patrese had another week in which to do the square root of nothing. For the first time in months, perhaps longer, he felt—well, not exactly happy, given everything that had happened back in Pittsburgh, but certainly carefree. Tension was leaching like toxins from his body with every day that passed.

He kept walking toward the sea, waiting for the next wave to roll up the sand and lap around his ankles like the licking of an eager puppy.

The water continued to retreat, almost as though it were playing a game with him. Through one wave cycle, then another, and still it receded.

Patrese's brain was so firmly in neutral that it took him a few moments to realize how unusual this was.

In the shallows, swimmers laughed in amazement as the water drained around them. Tourist canoes were left stranded on ropes suddenly slack; beach vendors picked up fish writhing on the sand. Patrese heard questioning voices, saw shoulders shrugged. No one had ever seen such a thing, it seemed.

He had.

A Discovery Channel program, he thought, or maybe National Geographic. They'd reconstructed a historic earthquake—Lisbon, that was it, sometime in the eighteenth century—with CGI effects, talking heads, and a narrator whose voice was set firmly to "doom." The program had shown many of Lisbon's residents fleeing to the waterfront to escape fires and falling debris in the city center. From the docks, they'd seen the sea recede so far and fast that it had exposed all the cargo lost and wrecks forgotten over the centuries.

And after that . . .

"Tsunami!" Patrese shouted. "Tsunami!"

A couple of people looked curiously at him. Perhaps they thought he was calling for a lost dog. A lobster-colored Englishman in a black-and-white soccer shirt clapped and began to sing. "Toon Army! Toon Army!"

A posse of Germans were twenty yards away. Patrese ran over to them.

"Move! You've got to move!"

"Hey!" One of the Germans clapped him on the shoulder. "Chill out, man."

"There's a tsunami coming!"

"Tsunami?"

"Tidal wave."

The Germans looked out at the ocean. The water was a carpet of azure as far as they could see.

"I don't see no tidal wave," said the shoulder clapper.

They all looked at Patrese with a sort of benevolent wariness, clearly bracketing him as slightly demented but probably harmless.

"It's coming, I tell you," Patrese insisted.

"Whatever you're on, man, can you give me some?"

"Please leave us alone now," said one of the German women.

Patrese opened his mouth to say something else, but the Germans were already turning away from him. He kept moving, telling everyone he could find: Leave the beach, go inland, get somewhere high. Some people packed up their stuff without a word and did what he said. Some ignored him or feigned incomprehension. Some, the smart ones, took off to other parts of the beach and began to spread the word.

A white crescent on the horizon now, awesome in its grace and beauty. For a moment even Patrese stood spellbound, watching as the crescent began to grow.

Then he ran.

Behind him, the tsunami reared up, an angry cobra of seawater. It flipped a fishing boat over and swallowed it whole. Urgent voices surrounded Patrese, a dozen different languages and all saying the same thing: *Move, run, keep going.*

Katie was standing at the entrance to the hotel, wearing one of Patrese's T-shirts over her bikini. Her hair was tousled, and her eyes were still bleary with sleep.

"What the hell's going on?" she said.

Patrese grabbed her without breaking stride. "Move. Come with me."

"Franco, what the fuck . . . ?"

"Just do it!" He had to shout to be heard above the roaring.

The tsunami smashed through the swimmers who hadn't managed to get ashore in time and raced up the beach with murderous intent. It was every monster from every nightmare bundled together and made real; surging into the hotel, devouring whole rooms in seconds, tearing husbands from wives and children from parents.

Water all around Patrese and in him, holding him up and dragging him down. Water does not strive. It flows in the places men reject. Chest and spine pressed vise tight and harder still, a balloon expanding from within. Bubbles around his head and ringing beyond heart thumps in his ears; air, life itself, scurrying away into mocking oblivion. The camera's aperture of consciousness closing in, light shrinking from the edges, dim through flashes of jagged crystals. Thoughts slowing, panic receding, resignation, acceptance, dulled contentment, blue gray flowing around, sounds gone, and this is how it ends, this is it, just let go and slide away, like falling about in a green field in early summer.

Then suddenly the water went out and the air came in; coughing, spluttering, frenzied inhaling, man's reflex to survive. Patrese opened his eyes and saw that the tsunami was gone, pulling itself back out of the hotel and down the beach. Bodies spun like sticks in the surge. Patrese felt a wall at each shoulder, and realized he'd been pinned in a corner, facing away from the beach. Blind chance. Anywhere else in the room, he'd have been swept straight back out to sea.

From the dining room upstairs came voices, giddy and shrill with relief. Patrese climbed slime-slippery steps and looked around the room. Two dozen people, he reckoned: the quick ones, the lucky ones.

Katie wasn't among them.

I t could have been very romantic. Private room in one of the city's most expensive restaurants, hard on the shore of Lake Pontchartrain. Just the two of them: him handsome in a swarthy, weathered way, not quite yet ruined by the years; she with skin the color of barely milked coffee under an orange-and-black madras headdress. They wouldn't have been young lovers, that was for sure, but it was anyone's guess as to exactly how old they were: They weren't the kind of people to keep their original birth certificates. The best estimates put her somewhere in her late fifties and him half a decade older. Whatever the truth, they weren't saying.

It could have been very romantic, were it not for the four men who stood outside the private room—two of them hers, two his, all of them armed—and were it not also for the FBI surveillance van that sat at the far end of the parking lot, listening in through the microphone attached to the underside of the wine bucket. The Bureau had guessed the room would be swept for listening devices before the diners arrived, but not after that. They'd guessed right. Now all the listeners needed was something incriminating; something they could hear and, even better, something they could record. These were two big fish, and the Bureau desperately wanted to net them.

The male fish was Balthazar Ortiz, a senior member of Mexico's Los Zetas drug syndicate. Los Zetas were somewhere between a faction of the Gulf Cartel and a private army of their own. The organization was full of former Mexican special forces soldiers like Ortiz, and they were ruthlessly good at what they did. Los Zetas had sprung two dozen of their comrades from jail somewhere in Mexico a couple of months back; they'd killed the new police chief of Nuevo Laredo six hours after he'd taken office.

And *she* was Marie Laveau, one of the kingpins—queenpins?—of the New Orleans underworld. In particular, she was Queen of the

Lower Ninth, a hardscrabble district perched at the corner where the Mississippi met the Industrial Canal. The Lower Ninth, uneasy by day and terrifying by night, reeked of poverty and drugs. It was overwhelmingly black, of course; that went without saying, that was just the way it was in this city.

The original Marie Laveau had lived in New Orleans in the nineteenth century, and had styled herself the Voodoo Queen. A hairdresser by trade, she'd also claimed to be an oracle, an exorcist, a priestess, and much more. For every known fact about her life, there were a hundred myths. So, too, with this one, the current Marie Laveau. She claimed to be not just a descendant of the original but the very reincarnation of her. She also styled herself the Voodoo Queen, but with the proviso that the spirit of the Voodoo Queen was immortal; she was only the temporary guardian of it.

Marie gestured across the shimmering darkness of the water. In the distance, headlights slid along the Lake Pontchartrain Causeway, the twin-span interstate bridge that connected the city to the north side of the lake.

"The second Marie Laveau—daughter of the original—she was conducting a ceremony on the lake when a storm came up. Swept her out into the middle of the lake. She stayed in the water five days. When they found her, she didn't even have exposure."

Ortiz nodded. "Shall we get to business?"

Marie sighed, as if his lack of interest in small talk was somehow discourteous. "If you like."

"Now, I don't know how you did it before, with my, er, predecessor . . ."

"Just like we're doing it now."

"Good. That's good."

"Round about this time, every year. See how the arrangement's gone the past twelve months, see how we want it to go for the next twelve."

"Okay. And the arrangement; how is it for you?"

"The arrangement's not the problem."

"Then what is the problem?"

"You."

"Me?"

"You. You're the problem."

The folds of Marie's green kaftan seemed to shift and rearrange themselves, and suddenly she was holding a Magnum Baby Eagle pistol with an extended barrel to accommodate the silencer on its end.

Ortiz just about had time to look astonished before Marie shot him straight through the heart.

Interlude

P atrese stayed in Khao Lak for three weeks after the tsunami. Every day of those three weeks, from before dawn until after dark, he worked with a frenzy born of knowing one sure thing: that once he stopped, he'd never start again.

He helped carry corpses—one of them Katie's—to warehouses stacked to the ceiling with coffins, body bags, and cadavers. He helped dig through rubble with his bare hands, dragging bodies out into the open and off for whatever dignified burial their families could give them. He helped pin photographs of the lost and missing on walls; he listened to the impotent bewilderments of each newly arrived wave of relatives. He helped pile debris into trucks, and helped drive those trucks to landfill sites. He helped aid workers hand out food, helped doctors distribute medicines, helped hammer up walls and roofs for makeshift shelters.

He helped everyone but himself, knowing that he could wait.

And at the end of those three weeks, he suddenly knew it was time to go. There were more people helping with the reconstruction than were needed, and they were beginning to get in one another's way. Hardened professional aid workers were scorning fresh-faced Western volunteers as "disaster tourists"; locals were chafing at soldiers who ordered them around.

The night before Patrese left, he was taken to see Panupong Wattana. Wattana was five foot two on a good day, always immaculately turned out in what seemed an endless rota of lightweight suits, and he'd been around Khao Lak pretty much every day since the tsunami: giving interviews to the world's media, glad-handing those unfortunate souls who'd lost everything, and generally strutting around like some latter-day Napoleon. As far as Patrese could make out, Wattana was a hybrid of politician and businessman. Clearly, the two roles were seen as complementary, even indivisible. Equally clearly, the concept of a conflict of interest was a very remote one around these parts.

"The great Stakhanovite!" Wattana exclaimed, clasping Patrese's hand in both of his own. "I have heard much about you; the American who works like a Soviet!"

Patrese mumbled something noncommittal about just doing his bit.

"Come, come, Mr. Patrese. You are too modest, and we all know it. I just want to thank you on behalf of the people of Khao Lak, of Takua Pa district, of Phang Nga province, of Thailand itself . . ."

Patrese half wondered whether Wattana was going to keep on, much as he had addressed envelopes when a child: name, street, city, country, earth, galaxy, universe.

". . . and to tell you that if you ever need anything in America, three of my sons are there, and I've instructed them specifically to do anything you ask."

"Where are they based?" Patrese asked, more out of politeness than a genuine desire to know.

"Johnny's in Baltimore. Tony, New Orleans. Mikey, San Diego."

Johnny, Tony, Mikey—damn, Patrese thought, they sound more Italian than I do.

"Well, I'm in Pittsburgh, but if I ever go visit any of those places, I'll be sure to look them up."

The Bureau might not have caught Marie discussing anything concrete about her drugs business—the "arrangement" she'd spoken about could have meant anything—but they'd gotten something better: audio evidence of a murder. The cough of the silenced pistol hadn't been loud enough to carry outside the room, so neither Marie's bodyguards nor Ortiz's had heard; but it was clearly audible on the surveillance tape.

Backup had been there inside three minutes; barreling through astonished diners into the back of the restaurant, shouting at the bodyguards not even to fucking think about it, and into the private room, where Marie was sitting calmly across the table from a very dead Ortiz.

The surveillance might have been a Bureau operation, but the murder squarely and clearly belonged to the New Orleans Police Department. Homicide detective Selma Fawcett took charge of the investigation. Selma—named after the Alabama city of civil rights movement fame—was black, which didn't make her a minority in the NOPD, and female, which did.

Short of actually catching Marie with a smoking gun, this seemed to Selma pretty much as clear-cut as cases went. Marie was so guilty, she made O.J. look innocent.

Under Louisiana law, murder in the first was reserved for killings with aggravated circumstances. Since none of those circumstances applied here—there'd been no kidnap, rape, burglary, robbery, and the victim hadn't been a member of law enforcement—Marie could only be charged with second-degree murder, which in turn meant the maximum sentence she could receive was life rather than death.

That suited Selma fine. She'd seen firsthand what Marie's kind of drugs did to people, and if the last, best option was putting Marie inside till the end of her days, then that would have to do. Selma was less keen on the fact that the second-degree charge allowed Marie to be released on bail—$500,000 bail, to be precise—but since there was little Selma could do about that, she tried not to let it bother her too much.

The world and his wife grandstanded on this one. The Bureau trumpeted the success of their surveillance operation. The police department pointed to the speed of their officers' response and the efficiency of their investigators. The assistant district attorney took personal charge of the prosecution. Even the state governor himself went on television to restate Louisiana's commitment to drug-free streets. Impressively, he even managed to get all that out with a straight face.

Marie said she wanted a quick trial, as was her right. She also said she wanted to defend herself. This, too, was her right. She started to keep a tally of everyone who quoted to her the maxim about a man who is his own lawyer having a fool for a client.

The trial date was set for late June, and pretty much everyone who came across Marie said that, for a woman facing the prospect of life imprisonment, she seemed about as concerned as someone putting the cat out for the night.

It was ten below freezing when Patrese arrived back in Pittsburgh, and the welcome he got at police headquarters wasn't a whole lot warmer. He'd worked there almost a decade, he'd always thought of himself as fairly popular, yet pretty much not a single person asked how he was, said it was good to have him back, suggested they go for a beer. They must have known about the tsunami: Even the most inward-looking of America's TV networks couldn't have ignored it. They just didn't seem to care.

Patrese knew why, of course. The case that had so consumed him had also accounted for his partner, Mark Beradino. Beradino had lost his career and more because of it, and since Beradino had been a legend in the department, and since the department didn't like to see a legend brought low, they'd looked around for someone to blame. Patrese was clearly that someone. That this was unfair—Beradino had brought all the bad luck and trouble on himself—was irrelevant. A scapegoat, a sacrificial lamb, had been sought, and Patrese was its name.

There'd been a time, perhaps as recently as a month ago, when Patrese would have said, "Screw you all," and put up with it until people came to their senses. But as he walked through the endless institutional corridors, catching snatches of discussion about the Steelers' upcoming championship game in Foxborough, he realized that he simply couldn't be bothered. He'd just spent three weeks among people who really had lost everything. The static he was getting now seemed so petty in comparison.

He found an empty meeting room and dialed his old college buddy Caleb Boone, now in charge of the FBI's Pittsburgh office.

"Franco! Man, am I glad to hear from you! Been trying you for weeks."

"Caleb, you want to grab a beer?"

"No."

"No?"

"No. I want to grab many beers."

Patrese laughed, relieved. "I believe that's the recognized international signal for a serious FatHeads session."

"I believe it is. Seven?"

"Sounds good. And listen, we can talk about this more when we're there, but I was wondering . . . I was wondering if the Bureau has any vacancies. For a cop."

"Vacancies? In the Pittsburgh field office?"

"No. In any field office *apart* from Pittsburgh."

The FatHeads session indeed turned out to be serious; seriously liquid and seriously long. Patrese stumbled to bed sometime nearer dawn than midnight, and trod gingerly through the next day as a result. He was just about feeling human again by the time he went around to his sister Bianca's for dinner, and for a few hours lost himself in the uncomplicated and riotous warmth of her own family's love for him; her briskly efficient doctoral clucking, her husband Sandro's watchful concern, and the endless energy and noise of their three kids.

"Here," Bianca said suddenly, as they were washing up. "Meant to give you this."

She reached up to the highest shelf and pulled down a small jar. There was some kind of fabric inside, Patrese saw. It looked old and frayed.

"What's this?" he said.

"It's your caul. I found it while packing up Mom and Dad's stuff." Their parents had been killed in a car crash a few months before.

"Funny thing to keep around the place."

"Mom, what's a caul?" said Gennaro, Bianca's youngest.

"Some babies are born with a membrane covering their face and head."

"Yeeuch!"

"Not 'yeeuch,' honey. It's perfectly natural; it's just part of the, er, the bag that holds babies inside their moms' tummies. Uncle Franco was one of those babies. And having a caul is special."

"Why's it special?"

"Lots of reasons. If you have a caul, it can mean you're psychic . . ."

"I wish," Patrese muttered.

". . . or you can heal people, or you'll travel all your life and never tire, or—"

Bianca stopped suddenly and clapped her hand to her mouth.

"What?" Patrese said.

She spoke through her hand. "It doesn't matter."

"Tell me."

She took her hand away, put it on his shoulder, and looked him squarely in the eye.

"It means you'll never drown."

Boone called as Patrese was driving back home.

"This a good time to talk, buddy?"

"Er . . . sure."

"You okay? You sound a little, er, distracted."

Patrese glanced at the caul jar on the passenger seat. "No. Just driving."

"Okay. You asked about the Bureau? Got a name for you: Wyndham Phelps."

Patrese laughed. "Sounds like someone from *Gone with the Wind*."

"Good Southern name. I told him all about you, and he wants to meet with you."

"Where's he at?"

"He heads the field office in New Orleans."

Part One

July

The jury was coming back in today; Marie was certain of it. And that meant she could leave nothing to chance.

She took six white candles, stood them in a tray of holy water, and lit them. Then she took twelve sage leaves, wrote the name of one of the apostles (with Paul standing in for Judas) on each leaf, and slipped six into one shoe and six into the other. This was so the jury would decide in her favor.

She dabbed court lotion on her neck and wrists, just as she'd done every day during the trial. She'd made the lotion herself, by mixing together oils of cinnamon, calendula, frankincense, and carnation, and adding a piece of devil's shoestring and a slice of galangal root. This was to influence the judge and jury.

Finally, she took a white bowl piled with dirt. The dirt she'd gathered herself, with her right hand, from the graves of nine children in the St. Louis Number One cemetery. She placed the bowl on her altar, facing east, between three white candles. Then she added three teaspoons of sugar and three of sulfur, recited the Thirty-fifth Psalm, asked the spirits to come with all their power to help her, and smeared the dust on the inside of her kaftan. This was so the court would do as she wished.

She was ready.

The sidewalk outside the courthouse was packed: crowds four or five deep, pressing against hastily erected barriers and watched by police officers who shifted uneasily from foot to foot in the oppressive heat. The gathering felt more like a street party than a demonstration. People passed food to one another, creased their faces in laughter. Clearly, Marie wasn't the only one convinced she'd be acquitted.

The trial had lasted only a week. Marie's defense had been simple: Ortiz had killed himself. The "problem" she'd referred to on the surveillance tape was his carrying a gun: She'd seen it on his waistband as he'd shifted position. Then he'd brought the gun out and, before she'd even been able to react, he'd shot himself. As to *why* he'd done so, she had no idea. But then, the burden of that proof wasn't on her, was it?

She'd brought in witnesses who testified that she funded many amenities in the Lower Ninth. Folks got in trouble with their finances, she helped them out. Folks got beaten up by the police, she helped them out. She pointed out that she'd never been convicted of anything in her life, not so much as a traffic offense, and yet the Bureau was bugging her like she was bin Laden or John Gotti or someone.

She was representing herself, she said, so the jury—most of them people of color like herself, just trying to make their way in a world stacked against them—could see what she was really like. No smartass lawyer twisting her words for her. The other side could do that all they liked, but not her, not Marie Laveau, no sir.

It had been pure theater. And now it was time for the curtain call.

The courtroom itself was so full it seemed almost to bulge. People fanned their faces and tried to stay as still as possible: The aging municipal aircon system was nowhere near up to coping with a couple of hundred excited metabolisms.

An expectant murmur fluttered off the walls as the jury took their seats.

Judge Amos Katash, who looked like the older brother of Michelangelo's Sistine God and was clearly relishing every moment of this performance, shuffled some papers and cleared his throat. "Would the foreman please stand."

A gray-haired woman with reading glasses on a chain around her neck got to her feet, glancing at Marie as she did so.

In the gallery, Selma closed her eyes. Like every cop, she knew the old adage about the foreman never looking at the defendant if they're guilty—and as Selma had maintained right from the start, Marie was as guilty as anyone she'd ever come across.

"Have you reached a decision?" Katash asked the foreman.

"Yes."

"And is the decision the decision of you all?"

"Yes."

"In the matter of the State of Louisiana versus Marie Laveau, do you find the defendant guilty or not guilty of the murder of Balthazar Ortiz?"

"Not guilty."

Pandemonium in the courtroom; a dissonant vortex of triumphant whoops, frantic applause, tears and outraged shouts. Marie smiled and waved daintily, as though she were on the red carpet at the Kodak Theater. Selma pinched her nose between thumb and middle finger as she shook her head in disbelief.

Fourth of July, and New Orleans was hotter than a fresh-fucked fox in a forest fire.

Patrese took a sip of daiquiri and pinched at his shirtfront, trying to peel it away from his skin.

"Hell, Franco," laughed Phelps, "you look like a water cannon's been using you for target practice. Know what it is? Thick blood. All those steel-town winters have given you sludge in your veins. A couple of years down here, the stuff'll be running through you like water, and one hundred degrees won't even make you sweat. Till then, my friend, make like us locals. *Laissez les bons temps rouler.*" He clinked his glass against Patrese's and gestured around the party. "Quite something, huh?"

It sure was, thought Patrese. White-suited waiters glided between the guests, proffering champagne here, stuffed lobster claws there. Three barmen shook and mixed every cocktail Patrese had ever heard of and plenty he hadn't. A string quartet floated Haydn under the hubbub of conversation and laughter. Exotic fish glided endlessly around ornamental ponds.

New Orleans held fast to the old ideals of high society. Anybody who was anybody spent their Fourth of July here, at the Brown House, a steep-gabled, Syrian-arched monument to Romanesque Revivalism. No matter if you wanted to go to your beach house or visit with family, when you were invited to the Brown House, you went. It was the largest house in all of New Orleans, and it was owned by the city's richest man.

Who was, as usual, nowhere to be seen.

St. John Varden's Gatsby-like absence from his own parties may have been because he preferred to work, because he found other people tedious company, because he wanted to enhance his mystique, or all of the above. Only he knew for certain, and he wasn't telling.

Patrese had been in New Orleans only a few months, but that was long enough to realize Varden was everywhere and nowhere. The logo of his eponymous company sprouted across the city like mushrooms after rain; his name bubbled up in quotidian conversations, an eternal presence in the ether. But he appeared in public only once a year, at the company's AGM, and if you wanted a photo of him, it was the corporate brochure or nothing.

In contrast, his son—St. John Varden Jr., universally known as Junior—was working the guests with practiced ease. In another era, he could have been a matinee idol, all brooding hazel eyes, jet-black hair, and olive skin. As it was, he'd been a proper war hero. Purple Heart in Desert Storm, Silver Star in Bosnia, and finally the Medal of Honor in Afghanistan; the first living recipient of the award since Vietnam. He'd left the army and announced his intention to go into politics. Eighteen months before, he'd become governor of Louisiana in his first attempt. Massachusetts had the Kennedys and Texas the Bushes: Louisiana had the Vardens.

"Here," Phelps said, "let me introduce you to a few people."

Phelps's wife had filed for divorce earlier in the year and gone to live with her new lover in Mobile, so Patrese was his plus one today. There were plenty of other people Phelps could have brought—hell, half of Patrese's new colleagues at the FBI's New Orleans field office would have killed for the chance—but Phelps, lord of that office, had chosen to ask Patrese, the outsider.

There'd been protests; whispered and civilized, perhaps, but protests nonetheless. Patrese wasn't a Southerner. Worse, he hadn't even been a Bureau man until a few months ago.

All the more reason to show him how we do things down here, Phelps had said; and that had been that.

Patrese shook hands and repeated people's names back to them when they were introduced, the better to remember who was who. He already recognized Marc Alper, the assistant DA who'd prosecuted Marie Laveau and was now putting a brave face on the verdict: "You can never predict juries." Here was a chief justice, here someone high up in City Hall, here a golfing store magnate, all full of back-

25

slapping bonhomie, safe and smug in the knowledge that if you were in here, you counted for something.

All men, Patrese noticed, and all white. The absolute top jobs— mayor, DA, police chief, pretty much everyone barring Phelps him-self—might have had black incumbents, but to Patrese the dark crust seemed very thin, like a pint of Guinness in negative.

"And this," said Phelps, his voice rising slightly as though in an-ticipation of a drum roll, "is Cindy Rojciewicz."

Patrese knew she'd be a knockout even before she turned, just from the reactions of everyone around them. It was like something from the Discovery Channel: the males puffing their chests out, the females bristling and snarling with affront.

"Hiii," said Cindy, in a voice that suggested she'd spent more time than was healthy smoking filterless cigarettes and watching Marlene Dietrich films. "Wyndham's told me a whole heap about you." She winked. "All good, of course."

Such an obvious lie, Patrese thought. Why, then, was he so flat-tered?

Raven hair, cobalt eyes, and a dress that straddled demonstrative and slutty might have had something to do with it, he conceded.

With every wife in a five-yard radius practically dragging their husbands away by the hair, and Phelps excusing himself with a pat on Patrese's shoulder—he could hardly have made it more obvious if he'd winked and given a thumbs-up—Patrese suddenly found him-self alone with Cindy.

She nodded toward his shirt. "Spill something?"

"Sort of."

"You wanna come inside and freshen up?"

"Come inside? You *live* here?"

She laughed. "I wish. I'm Mr. Varden's PA. I know my way around."

"And he won't mind?"

"Jeez, Franco, it's a house, not a darn museum." *Houshe, musheum*; she was drunk, Patrese realized.

Drunk, sexy as hell, and inviting him inside. A good Catholic boy might have made his excuses. A lapsed Catholic, never.

"Then let's go," he said.

She walked a pace in front of him. He kept his eyes above her waist for at least a second. A triumph of willpower, under the circumstances.

They dodged a couple of waiters and went in through a pair of French doors. It was much darker now that they were out of the sun, and Patrese blinked twice as his eyes adjusted. Cooler, too. He gave a little shiver as the sweat began to dry.

Cindy was holding a door open. "Over here."

He caught a tendril of her scent as he walked past. It was a library, air heavy with leather and walls paneled with wood the color of toast.

She closed the door behind her.

"You can freshen up in a second, Franco. But first, I want to . . ."

He was already moving for the kiss as he turned back to her.

". . . say there's something terrible going on," she blurted.

Their lips had almost touched before he realized what she'd said. He pulled back and looked at her, almost too startled to be embarrassed.

"I need to tell someone about it," she said. "I need to tell *you*."

"But you've never even met me."

"Exactly. *Exactly*. Everyone here knows everyone. Tell one of them, you tell the whole bunch. Might as well take out a personal in the *Times-Picayune,* you know? But not you. You don't know anyone here, not properly. Not yet. You're not"—she grabbed for the word, missed, found it with a snap—"*tainted*."

Cindy was talking fast but coherently; the strange lucidity of the drunk whose brain can only focus on one thing at a time, but does so with the precision of a laser.

"Okay," he said. "Then tell me. What is it?"

"Too big to tell you now. Too complicated."

"Just give me an idea."

"Oh, God . . . Sacrifice."

"Sacrifice?"

"Sacrificing people."

"*What?*"

"I've got documents. Evidence. I need you alone, not with"—she waved an arm vaguely toward the window—"all that boo-yah going on out there. And I need to trust you. Maybe I won't, next time. Maybe I'll have got you all wrong."

"But you've just told me—"

"I've told you nothing. Not yet."

A shadow fell across the strip of light at the bottom of the door. Patrese and Cindy watched it pause a moment, then disappear.

"So," she said, "you interested?"

"I told you already. Yes."

"Good. Can't meet tomorrow—we're out of town all day."

" 'We'?"

"Mr. Varden and me. Wherever he goes, I go. You free Wednesday? After work?"

"Sure."

"You know Checkpoint Charlie's?"

"Esplanade and Decatur, right?"

"A man who knows his bars. Always a good sign. Eight o'clock? Don't get out of work much earlier, I'm afraid."

"Eight's fine."

"Good. See you then."

She opened the door, and they stepped out into the corridor.

She studied Patrese's face. He wondered if she was going to kiss him after all.

"Noah," she said. At least that's what it sounded like to Patrese. *Noah.*

She walked back out into the light.

The office had a weekend feel to it. Half the staff had taken an extra day or two around the holiday itself, and so Patrese found himself with a morning uninterrupted by the usual round of meetings and briefings.

If he was going to go through with this, he wanted to get it right. In the few months he'd been with the Bureau, he'd been struck most of all by the scale on which things were done. Resources were ten times what he'd been used to in the Pittsburgh PD. Cases were larger and more intricate, focusing on serious criminals rather than the lowlifes who formed the staple of every Homicide cop's beat. Hell, even the agents' suits were better, their shoes shinier.

He pulled from the shelf the Bureau's *Manual of Investigative Operations and Guidelines*—MIOG, as it referred to itself, with the usual inability of any bureaucracy to resist an acronym—and found section 137, "The Criminal Informant (CI) Program."

"Worse than having no human sources," the text began, "is being seduced by a source who is telling lies."

Typical Bureau, Patrese thought; assume the worst, right from the get-go. But he took the point. He didn't know the first thing about Cindy, and until he did, his default would have to be that she was yanking his chain unless specifically proven otherwise.

> Failure to control informants has undermined costly long-term investigations, destroyed the careers of prosecutors and law enforcement officers, and caused death and serious injuries to innocent citizens and police.

This, too, Patrese knew full well. He'd run informants in his days on the Pittsburgh Homicide beat, usually gangbangers in between prison sentences who'd have sold their grandma for a hit of crack and lied as easily as they breathed. Smart lawyers picked government cases apart on technicalities, the perps walked free, and heads rolled; sometimes figuratively, sometimes literally.

Cindy was, potentially at least, a different kettle of fish altogether. Whether that would make her easier or harder to control, Patrese had no idea.

Informants must be classified according to one of the following 12 categories: Organized Crime (OC); General Criminal (C); Domestic Terrorism (DT); White-Collar Crime (WC); Drugs (D); International Terrorism (IT); Civil Rights (CR); National Infrastructure Protection/Computer Intrusion Program (NI); Cyber Crime (CC); Major Theft (MT); Violent Gangs (VG); Confidential Sources (CS).

White-collar crime, Patrese presumed, given Cindy's position, though he couldn't help but feel the categories were pretty arbitrary. Where did violent gangs end and drugs begin? Couldn't major theft also be organized crime?

The FBI considers the following factors in determining an individual's suitability to be an informant:

1. Whether the person appears to be in a position to provide information concerning violations of law that are within the scope of authorized FBI investigative activity.

He had to presume that Cindy was in such a position, or else she wouldn't have come to him in the first place. As Varden's PA, she must be privy to vast swathes of information, much of it private and sensitive. Tick that.

2. Whether the individual is willing to voluntarily furnish information to the FBI.

She'd approached him, hadn't she? Not the other way around. Another tick.

3. Whether the individual appears to be directed by others to obtain information from the FBI.

Unlikely. If Varden wanted to find out something from the FBI, all he had to do was ask Phelps. In any case, Patrese had been a cop, if not an agent, long enough to recognize the moment in an investigation when a suspect, snitch, witness, whoever, started asking questions rather than answering them.

4. Whether there is anything in the individual's background that would make him/her unfit for use as an informant.

Patrese didn't know the first thing about Cindy, of course; not even her surname. Something Polish, it had sounded like when Phelps introduced them, but he couldn't have repeated it, let alone spelled it.

He Googled "Varden," found the company Web site, and dialed the main switchboard. Best not to announce his interest too clearly, he thought.

"Good morning, Varden Industries."

"Hi," he said. "I'm calling from FedEx. We have a package for someone in Mr. Varden's office, but I'm afraid the surname's illegible. It's a Cindy someone."

"That would be Mr. Varden's PA, sir. Cindy Rojciewicz."

"Spell that for me, please."

"Certainly, sir. R-O-J-C-I-E-W-I-C-Z."

"Thank you. The courier will be 'round later."

Patrese hung up, logged into the National Instant Criminal Background Check database, and entered Cindy's name.

No matches.

Then he Googled her.

Turned out her father was a congressman. Roger Rojciewicz,

Republican, and therefore known in Washington as 3R. He represented Louisiana's first congressional district, which comprised land both north and south of Lake Pontchartrain, including most of New Orleans's western suburbs and a small portion of the city proper. And he seemed quite the big shot: chairman of the Congressional Subcommittee on Energy and Water Development, and a member both of the Subcommittee on Homeland Security and the Committee on Appropriations.

No surprise how Cindy had gotten her job with Varden, then.

About her personally, Patrese found much less. Nothing helpful there, either. She was pictured on a high-school reunion Web site, and she'd written condolences on a tribute board to a teenager who'd committed suicide. Every other appearance she made on the Web was Varden-related, and pretty anodyne at that: job applications, media inquiries, and the like.

He wondered if he'd have been so keen to find out more about her without an official excuse, and realized that he already knew the answer.

5. Whether the nature of the matter under investigation and the importance of the information being furnished to the FBI outweigh the seriousness of any past or contemporaneous criminal activity of which the informant may be suspected.

See above, Patrese guessed.

6. Whether the motives of the informant in volunteering to assist the FBI appear to be reasonable and proper.

This was key. Informants tend to be motivated by one or more of MICE: money, ideology, compromise, ego. Cindy's behavior the previous day had suggested ideology more than anything else. She'd used the words *terrible* and *tainted,* as though whatever she wanted to tell him was some great moral wrong that needed righting.

But there could be—in Patrese's experience, there usually was—more to it than that. Informants never had just one reason for snitching, and the reasons they did have were rarely static, but rather waxed and waned in importance as an investigation progressed.

Points seven through ten were all things Patrese would find out only once the investigation had begun: whether they could get the information in a better way; whether the informant was reliable and trustworthy; whether the informant was willing to conform to FBI guidelines; and whether the FBI would be able to adequately monitor the informant's activities.

Point eleven concerned legalities of privileged communications, lawful association, and freedom of speech. One for the lawyers to argue over. All billable, of course.

12. Whether the use of the informant could compromise an investigation or subsequent prosecution that may require the government to move for a dismissal of the case.

Patrese thought for a moment. He wasn't aware of any current investigation that this could compromise, but that meant nothing. He was still the new kid here, and if he knew anything, it was that what he didn't know far outweighed what he did.

Perhaps he should ask Phelps about this.

Perhaps he should talk to Phelps, anyway.

Cindy had told Patrese not to tell anyone, hadn't she?

Actually, he remembered, she hadn't. She'd said, "Tell one of them, you tell the whole bunch," but that wasn't the same thing, not at all.

And she must have known that if she involved Patrese, she'd be involving Phelps, too, sooner or later. She'd hardly expect Patrese to run something like this without the knowledge of his own boss, and if she did, she was clearly deranged, and therefore by definition not worth bothering with.

Patrese dialed Phelps's extension.

"Hi, Franco."

"Hey, Sondra." Sondra, Phelps's secretary, was the longest-serving employee in the entire New Orleans field office. Phelps was the tenth Special Agent-in-Charge for whom she'd worked. She liked to joke that she was the Crescent City's own version of the Queen of England; her prime ministers might come and go, but she was always there, though admittedly a little older and grayer each time around.

"Is the *gran queso* there?" Patrese asked.

"Franco, I keep telling you, you're in a French city now. *Grande fromage*. And no, he's not around. He's out of town today."

"Tomorrow?"

"Tomorrow he's here, in the city, but not here, in the office. Conference down at the Convention Center. You wanna call him, you want me to put you in the diary for Thursday, or is it anything I can help with?"

Patrese toyed for a moment with the idea of telling her about Cindy. Sondra might not have been an agent, but she'd probably give better advice than the rest of them put together.

But Cindy was Varden's PA, and when it came to Varden, Patrese already knew, treading carefully was the order of the day. He didn't want to involve Sondra with something that wasn't her problem; nor did he want to ring Phelps and get a snatched few minutes on the phone. He wanted to ask Phelps his advice face-to-face, talk through the options with him one by one.

But he couldn't do that before he'd seen Cindy.

The hell with it, Patrese thought. He'd keep the rendezvous, commit himself to nothing, and brief Phelps when it was done. If Phelps chewed him out, so be it.

"Thursday morning's fine," Patrese said.

"Great. He's got fifteen minutes at ten. That do?"

"That does nicely. Thanks."

Patrese hung up and stared out of the window. The view was hardly *National Geographic*: the parking lot out in front of the building, and the traffic rumbling along Leon C. Simon. He needed another couple of pay grades to get one of the higher floors looking out the back over Lake Pontchartrain.

He turned his attention back to the manual.

The single biggest mistake an agent can make in his relationship with the confidential informant is to become romantically involved.

Spoilsports.

Patrese was there a quarter of an hour early. The moment he walked in, he was glad he'd changed between leaving work and coming here. Collar shirt and flannel pants would have marked him a mile off as a stiff trying to unwind, but with a faded Pitt T-shirt and battered jeans, he blended right in.

Checkpoint Charlie's is located pretty much right on the spot where the French Quarter fades into Faubourg-Marigny, which is to say, right on the spot where most tourists turn on their heels, because their guidebooks mark the edge of the Quarter as the edge of the known world, with bohemian Faubourg one of those uncharted territories on medieval maps emblazoned with the warning *Here Be Monsters*.

Patrese ordered an Abita and looked around. It was somewhere between a biker bar and a college hangout; pretty empty at the moment, but doubtless hopping in the small hours, even hotter and sweatier than it was already, if that were possible.

A blackboard announced live bands later that night. Somewhere to his left, pool balls clacked against each other. A ceiling fan moved lazily overhead.

He'd tried to work out a hundred times how to play this, and still had no clear answer. But sitting here, listening to other people's laughter, Patrese decided just to go with the flow; trust his instincts, take it from there. Cindy had called the meeting. Let her make the running.

Eight o'clock came and went.

He wasn't especially bothered. New Orleanian attitudes about time are pretty loose; not surprising, perhaps, when half the city's bars are open around the clock.

Maybe Cindy had been held up at work. Maybe she was plucking up courage, which around here usually involved a couple of daiquiris. Maybe she was playing hard to get; make him wait, establish her terms.

There was a fire station right across the street, and a bunch of firemen were sitting out front, admiring the girls who walked past. Most of the girls seemed happy to admire them right back.

Eight-thirty.

Patrese would have called, but he didn't have Cindy's number. She hadn't given him her cell. If she was still at work, Varden would be there, too, so she wouldn't be able to talk. He could see if she was in the phone book, but that might appear too creepy, finding out where she lived and calling her.

He was hungry. The menu said that Checkpoint Charlie's burger and chips were famous as far as Berlin—Berlin, Germany, not Berlin, Connecticut—which made him laugh, so he ordered that, medium rare.

A dark-haired girl came in. For a moment, Patrese thought it was Cindy, but she was too tall, and not nearly as attractive. She had a bag of laundry slung over her shoulder, and he watched with mild surprise as she walked straight through the bar and into a Laundromat out back.

What a great idea. Separating lights and darks would be much more fun with a few tequilas inside you. Why had no one else ever thought of that?

Unlike some people, Patrese didn't mind sitting in a bar on his own, but only if he'd gone there alone to start with. Waiting was something else entirely. He dropped his shoulders, told himself to relax.

"Here you go, baby," said the waitress, setting his burger and another Abita down on the table.

The menu was right; the burger was well worth its international fame.

Nine o'clock.

She wasn't coming; he was sure of that now. An hour late meant no-show, even in New Orleans. The disappointment surged in his throat. He'd really wanted to know what she'd found so terrible.

And to see her again, too, of course.

Sirens out front, the endless two-tone urban sound track. A cop car streaked by, an ambulance hard on its tail, pushing through behind before the traffic could re-form.

The moment the clock ticked nine-thirty, he paid the check and got up to leave.

"Do you have a phone book here?" he asked, so suddenly it surprised him.

"Surely." The bartender nodded toward a pay phone in the corner. "Should be one right there. Probably covered in graffiti by now. Everyone's a comedian, you know?"

The directory was indeed there, and it was indeed covered in graffiti.

Patrese flicked through to the R's.

Rojciewicz, C. Only one of them. An address on Spain Street, five minutes' walk from the bar. Presumably why she'd chosen it as a meeting place in the first place.

Patrese entered the number into his cell and walked outside while it dialed.

It rang eight, nine, ten times. No one home.

He was about to hang up when a woman's voice answered. "Hello?"

"Cindy?"

A slight pause—and call it years of experience, call it having been on the other end of this plenty of times before, call it whatever, but in that moment, Patrese knew what the woman's next words were going to be, and that having to say them was one of the worst things in the world.

"Are you family?" she asked.

Bee-striped tape, rotating blues and reds, radio chatter, stern-faced cops, neighbors crowded wide-eyed and soft-voiced; the tropes of a homicide scene, unvaried from Anchorage to Key West. Patrese felt at home; he knew his way around such places.

He flashed his Bureau badge, ducked under the tape, and went inside. The building was a nineteenth-century town house subdivided into condos. Cindy's was on the top floor, and Patrese was sweating by the time he reached her apartment door.

Not just from the heat, either. No matter how many times a man inhales the rank sweetness of death, he never becomes used to it, not really, not properly. Especially not in the sauna of a Louisiana summer.

Selma appeared in the doorway. She was half a head shorter than Patrese, and her eyes blazed with an anger that he instinctively thought of as righteous.

"Who the heck are you?" she snapped.

He showed his badge again. "Franco Patrese, from the—"

"I can see where you're from. The Federal Bureau of Interference."

"Hey, there's no need for that."

"No? How about Freaking Bunch of Imbeciles? You like that one better?"

"Listen, I'm here because—"

"Yes. Why *are* you here? Picked it up on the scanner and had nothing better to do? Let me tell you something, Agent Patrese. We, the NOPD, are perfectly capable of solving homicides all by ourselves, you know? It's not like we don't get enough practice. So don't call us, yes? We'll call you."

Patrese recognized Selma from coverage of the Marie Laveau trial, which meant he knew why she was pissed at the Bureau. Marie had managed to cast doubt on the legality of the Bureau's surveillance procedures: technicalities, sure, but things the Bureau should have made certain of to start with. And that doubt had played well with the jury. It might not have made *the* difference, but it had certainly made *a* difference.

So Patrese didn't blame Selma. In any case, he'd been on the other side of the fence himself, and he knew that, even without high-profile trial fuckups, pretty much every police force in the land resented and envied the Bureau in equal measures. It was a turf war, simple as that, as atavistic and ineradicable as all conflict. The turf caused the war, and there would always be turf; therefore there would always be war.

"I was supposed to meet her tonight," he said.

The woman cocked her head. "You the one who called just now?"

"Yes."

"You a friend?" She said it in a tone that suggested disbelief that Bureau agents would ever have friends.

"Business. She, er, she said she had something to tell me."

"Like what?"

"I don't know. She never showed. Now I know why."

"This something—you think it was important?"

"I'm certain it was."

"I mean, was she the kind of person who'd know something important?"

"You don't know who she was?"

"Sure I do. Cindy. Cindy Rojciewicz."

"That name doesn't mean anything to you?"

"We've only been here a half hour or so." The police car and ambulance he'd seen, Patrese thought. "We're still getting things straight. You want to stop messing around and tell me?"

"She was St. John Varden's PA. And her dad's a big-shot congressman."

The woman puffed her cheeks and blew through pursed lips. "Sheesh." She stuck out a hand. "Selma Fawcett. Homicide."

"I used to work the same beat."

"Not around here. I ain't never seen you."

"Back in Pittsburgh."

Selma narrowed her eyes. "Patrese, you said? Mara Slinger? That the one?"

Mara Slinger. The case that had wrecked him. "That's the one."

She thought for a second. "Okay, Agent Patrese, here's the deal. You go in there, you take a look around, tell me if you see anything that might . . . I don't know. Anything. Anything that might help you, anything that might help me. But you don't touch, you don't take pictures, and most of all, you don't forget, not for a second, that this is my scene and you're here on my say-so. You understand?"

"I do. Thanks."

"Good. And I'm sure I needn't tell you this, but . . . it's not pretty in there."

"It never is."

"No. But this one really, really isn't."

Selma wasn't wrong.

The one saving grace was that it hardly looked like Cindy anymore. Her vibrant beauty had drained away with the blood that was *everywhere*—spread out in oily slicks on the floor, dripping from tables, and splashed in patterns of arterial fury across the walls. It seemed impossible that anybody should have had so much blood in them.

Cindy was lying on her back in the living room, naked. Her left leg was gone entirely; cut clean through, high on the thigh. Much of the blood must have come from here, Patrese thought, where the killer had sliced through the femoral artery.

Something had been left in place of Cindy's leg. With all the blood, Patrese had to peer closer to see what it was. When he did, he made an involuntary start backward.

A snake.

A rattlesnake, to be more precise, and clearly as dead as Cindy was.

As far as he could make out, her other leg and torso were untouched.

Not so her face. A mirror had been smashed into her forehead with an ax head.

Patrese liked to think he'd seen his fair share of the unusual, the warped, and the downright depraved, but this was right up there— rather, right down there—with anything else in his experience. No psyche he'd ever come across, even the most damaged, could have done something like this.

Cindy's right arm lay crooked across her chest. Patrese looked for injuries.

Nothing.

In particular, no defense wounds, where she'd tried to fight off her attacker.

But the spatter patterns on the wall indicated she'd been alive when her leg had been severed. Arteries didn't pump out huge pressurized waves of blood when their owner was dead.

Alive and passive meant unconscious, with or without sedation.

Patrese walked through the condo, dodging the crime-scene officers in their hazmat suits. It was small, two rooms masquerading as four; a kitchenette with an outside door off the living room, a bathroom off the bedroom.

Aside from the living room, there was no blood. Cindy had been killed where she lay.

Patrese went into the bedroom. It was where he always headed at a crime scene. People tend to keep the truly revealing things about themselves in the bedroom, as it's where they're most vulnerable. Sleeping or making love, that's when defenses are lowest; that's when people are exposed, flayed, softened.

In the top drawer of Cindy's bedside table, Patrese found, in order, a pack of rubbers, a folded square of paper that he knew would contain cocaine even before he opened it, and an envelope of what turned out to be nude photos of her. Amateur shots, probably taken by a lover and printed off of a computer. They weren't exactly hardcore, but nor were they the kind of snapshots you took to pharmacy developers.

When he looked up, Selma was standing in the doorway.

"What do you reckon?" she asked.

He rubbed his eyes. "Where do you want me to start?"

She gave a wan smile, the first he'd seen. "Ain't that the truth."

He showed her what he'd found.

"Quite the party girl," she said. Her voice was flat, unimpressed. "Pathologist reckons she's been dead twelve hours, give or take. Hard to tell, it's so hot in here."

Pathologists estimate the time of death according to the cadaver's temperature, working on the principle that the body loses a degree or two every hour postmortem, but a room as warm as this one would skew the readings. Body temperature is ninety-eight degrees Fahrenheit, give or take. New Orleans summer, no aircon, and windows closed, presumably to keep the smell from escaping—the room certainly felt about that hot.

"Twelve hours dead means she wouldn't have gone into work today."

"Yup."

"She was PA to the richest man in the city. She didn't turn up without explanation, he'd have wanted to know why."

Selma nodded. "Last call made from the apartment phone was eight-thirty this morning. We dialed the number. An office extension, now on voice mail."

"Calling in sick?"

"Could be. The voice-mail message is an electronic one, no name given, so we won't know who it belongs to till tomorrow morning."

"But if she called in sick herself, she was either being forced to, or she must have known her attacker and had no idea he'd come to kill her. If her attacker called in pretending to be her—"

"—her attacker must have been a she."

"Yes. But even then . . . You work with someone, you know their voice. You can't just call up and pretend you're someone else. So she let her attacker in. There's no forced entry, is there? And he made her call her office—"

"—or it was a lover, and they were going to have some fun together."

"The neighbors see any men come around?"

"One last night, around ten o'clock. But he left a few minutes later."

"Description?"

"Vague. Black. Six foot, hundred and eight pounds."

"Could be half the guys in this city."

"Exactly."

"And no one this morning?"

"Not that no one saw."

Patrese thought for a moment. "The kitchenette has an outside door. Where does it go to?"

"I haven't checked."

They went back through the living room, where the crime-scene officers were bagging Cindy's cell phone for evidence, and into the kitchenette.

Patrese pushed down on the handle of the outside door with his knuckles, so as not to confuse the fingerprint testers.

The door swung gently open. Unlocked.

Patrese looked out. Fire escape, running down into the rear courtyard. He turned back to Selma.

"Fifty bucks says that's how he got in."

"I don't gamble."

He looked at her. She was serious. He held up his hands. "I didn't mean to offend."

"Accepted. Now, tell me. The snake. Why?"

"Is this a test?"

"I'm asking your opinion. That's all."

"Okay. The snake—well, evil springs to mind, doesn't it? The serpent in Eden. Forbidden fruit. Temptation. That kind of thing."

"Pretty much my thoughts, too. The leg?"

"Well, if we're still looking for the obvious imagery—'If thy hand offends thee, cut it off.' That's somewhere in the Bible, no?"

"It is indeed."

"A hand, I could understand. But a leg . . . why would you cut off a leg?"

Selma shrugged. "I don't know. The mirror? The ax head?"

"Those, I have no idea."

"Again, me neither. So I'm not even going to theorize, you understand? I'm going to wait for what Forensics says, and turn every corner of Cindy's life upside down, and see what comes of that. The data never lies."

"Do you disapprove?"

"Of what?"

"Of her. Of Cindy. Photos. Drugs. Sex."

"What makes you say that?"

"You didn't look too thrilled when I showed you the photos. You don't gamble. I'm guessing you're a—you're a woman of faith."

"She's dead, Agent Patrese. What she did when she was alive doesn't matter."

"That's what Homicide cops always say."

"Maybe. But I happen to believe it's true. Everyone's equal above the ground, and everyone's sure as heck equal beneath it. I've handled cases of murdered whores and murdered nuns, and I've given as much to one as to the other. I've given it everything I've got. You don't believe me, you walk out of that door now and never come back."

The air was already warm and heavy when Patrese met Phelps at seven A.M., three hours ahead of schedule. Though traffic was already building on the I-10 ramp a couple of blocks away, the lobby of the New Orleans Police Department headquarters was quiet at this time of morning and they could speak undisturbed.

Hoping that being in public would save him from getting chewed out, at least for the time being, Patrese told Phelps as quickly and succinctly as he could what had happened: Varden's party, Patrese's research, Selma at Cindy's apartment.

"Good work, Franco," said Phelps.

Patrese bit down on his surprise.

"I should have called you," Patrese said, knowing like every law enforcement officer that two layers of butt-covering are always better than one, "but like I said, I wanted to meet with you in person first . . ."

"Franco, I said don't worry about it." Phelps's teeth were bright white when he smiled, as though he'd run a coat of paint over them. "You showed initiative. I like that in my agents. And now we've got an 'in,' right from the get-go."

"That's just a fluke."

"I don't care. You learn to take credit for things you didn't intend, then you'll really start going places in the Bureau. Like I said, we've got an 'in.' Doesn't matter how or why, just that we have. The NOPD doesn't much care for us—"

"I got that impression."

"—and if they can freeze us out, they will. But not here. Well done, young man."

A cop in uniform appeared. "Special Agent Phelps? Agent Patrese?"

"That's us."

"If you'd like to follow me?"

They rode the elevator to the third floor in silence. The cop took them as far as a meeting room, enjoined them both to have a good day now, and left.

Patrese and Phelps stepped inside the meeting room. Selma was already there, prettier and younger than Patrese remembered from the previous night. Then again, no one looked their best at a murder scene. Especially the victim.

Next to Selma was a heavyset man whose mustache and temples were shot through with sprays of gray. Both detectives got to their feet. Southern courtesy was always on show, Patrese thought, turf war or no.

"Wyndham." The man shook Phelps's hand.

"Ken. You know Franco Patrese?"

"Not had the pleasure." He shook Patrese's hand with a grip that was just a touch stronger than necessary. "Ken Thorndike. Deputy chief of police."

Selma nodded at Patrese, and they all sat down.

"We got coffee and beignets." Thorndike nodded toward the sideboard. "Just about the only inedible beignets in the city, but that's budget cuts for you. Blame Nagin."

Ray Nagin was the mayor, a black man who'd gotten twice as much of the white vote as he had the black. Only in New Orleans.

"Okay," Thorndike continued. "Won't keep you long, 'cause there's lots to do. First off, this is our case till otherwise proven. Clear?"

"That depends on what the deceased wanted to discuss with Agent Patrese," Phelps said. "It could be interstate, it could be international . . ."

"Then you can go through the usual channels, when—if—that transpires." Thorndike made it sound as though the slower and more congested those channels were, the better he'd like it. "But till then, this is homicide, pure and simple. We don't even know if her rendezvous with Agent Patrese and her death are related."

"Hell of a coincidence if they aren't," Phelps said.

Thorndike glowered at Phelps, and Patrese realized what the two of them reminded him of: a corporate executive and a union boss, negotiating industrial action with ill-disguised antipathy. Phelps's hair was swept back, and his cuff links glittered even in the dull strip lighting; he was probably the only man in the entire city who wore long sleeves in the summer. In contrast, Thorndike's hands were rough, and his nose sat slightly off-center; the legacy of at least one break, possibly more.

"Listen, Ken," Phelps said, and even to Patrese it sounded slightly—deliberately?—patronizing. "Varden's her boss, her daddy's a congressman. We have to tread carefully, we all know that."

"That don't make them above the law. And I know Detective Fawcett is *very* keen on that."

"No one's saying it makes them above the law. But this is different from dealing with a two-bit hooker out in Desire."

"Shouldn't be," Selma said.

"Maybe. But it *is*. And the Bureau can help you here."

"Yeah?" Thorndike raised a skeptical eyebrow. "If it's the kinda help you gave us with Marie Laveau, we'll take a pass. Thanks anyway."

"Bring us in, and it shows those men—Varden, Rojciewicz—how seriously we're taking it."

" 'We'?"

"We. Law enforcement, not any one agency. Strength in numbers. Shows them we're doing everything we can to solve the case."

There was an unspoken agenda here, too, of course; unspoken because it was both delicate and blindingly obvious. Those closest to the deceased are always prime suspects. In Cindy's case, that meant that either her boss or, God forbid, her father might be involved, especially, perhaps, if they were part of whatever Cindy had wanted to tell Patrese about.

She'd chosen Patrese because he was an outsider. In contrast, you didn't get much more inside than Varden or Rojciewicz. So if they were innocent, they'd be reassured that everything was being done to catch the killer. And if they weren't, then they'd be worried. And worried people make mistakes, sooner or later.

Thorndike thought for a moment, and then turned. "Selma? This is your case. You want Bureau help or not?"

She looked at Patrese a beat before answering.

"Help, yes. Agent Patrese was a cop till not so long ago. He can't have totally gone over to the dark side yet." She smiled, but Patrese knew she was serious. "Command, no. We work together, we share information, but my word goes. Yes or no?"

Growing up with two sisters had made Patrese a good judge of which battles were worth fighting and which weren't. This was the latter, he knew. It wasn't an opening gambit; it was a one-time offer. Better for him, and for the Bureau, to be inside the tent pissing out.

"Yes," he said.

She stood up. "Good. Then let's get to it. We've got an incident room already set up. There's a spare desk in my office. You can use that."

Phelps and Thorndike were also on their feet.

"Can you give us a minute, Selma?" Patrese said. "I'd like a word with Mr. Phelps."

"Fine. I'll be outside."

"What's on your mind, Franco?" Phelps said once Selma and Thorndike had left the room.

"Don't take this the wrong way, but . . ."

"Okay. Now I know what you're going to ask."

"You do?"

"Yup. 'Cause in your position, I'd ask exactly the same thing. I go to Varden's parties. I'm in contact with him. Heck, I might even be a friend, if people like him actually have friends. So, with all this, how can I be prepared to bring him down, if that's what it takes? That's what you were going to ask, wasn't it?"

"Yes." Patrese held up his hands. "Yes, it was."

"Listen, Franco. Two things you should know. First, my job is more important to me than any personal ties. The law comes first. Has to. Second, this is New Orleans. It's a corrupt place, everyone knows that. It's a great place, don't get me wrong, but here even plumb lines fall crooked. But there's a flip side to that. Just because you accept someone's hospitality doesn't mean you're blind to his faults. So if Varden's guilty, let's put him inside. Simple as that."

If the foyer of police headquarters had been typically public-sector utilitarian, that of Varden Industries wouldn't have disgraced a five-star hotel. Patrese sat on a sofa that was almost ludicrously deep and comfortable, and wondered idly how much all the art on the walls had cost.

Selma flicked through a corporate brochure. Men hard of hat and determined of face laying pipelines, rig workers cheerily adjusting drill bits, painters touching up a classroom in Baghdad, white men bringing light, might, and the American way to the natives' darkness. Numbers picked out from the text in bold: employees worldwide, countries of operation, charitable donations.

Selma put her tongue against the back of her teeth, hissed, and batted the back of her hand against the brochure. "They should stock these things in Barnes and Noble. Fiction section."

"What did Thorndike mean?"

"About what?"

"About you being very keen on no one being above the law."

"I worked Internal Affairs before I moved to Homicide. Busted a lot of cops who were on the take. Thorndike tried to protect some of them, said they were good cops. I said no cop who was on the take was a good cop. Don't matter what else they do or don't do. A cop can't be honest, he can't be a cop. End of."

"And Thorndike resents you for this?"

"Probably."

"You don't sound like you care very much."

"I don't. I don't give a shit, and I don't take any shit. I'm not in the shit business."

A young woman approached, heels clacking as she walked across the marble floor. One of Cindy's colleagues, Patrese thought; perhaps even her replacement already. Varden wouldn't have gotten to where he was by wasting time on sentiment.

The young woman took them up in the express elevator without speaking.

Varden Tower was the tallest building in New Orleans. Unsurprisingly, Varden's office was on the top floor; more precisely, it *was* the top floor. A decent-sized antechamber for his support staff, and for him, something the size of a ballroom, with views across the city to three sides: the Mississippi one way, Lake Pontchartrain the other, and a patchwork of roofs and roads in between.

Varden came around from the far side of his desk. Patrese was struck by how unimposing he was; lost in the vastness of his office rather than having the charisma to fill it. You wouldn't have given him a second glance on the street; a man in his sixties, average height, well turned out without being especially so, and with a look of perpetually mild surprise, as though he found the world and its people harder to read than a balance sheet.

"Agent Patrese. Detective Fawcett. Good of you to come." If Varden had been wearing a hat, Patrese thought, he'd have tipped it.

"I'm the lead on this case, sir," Selma said. Polite but firm.

"Are you?" Equally courteous, but without the slightest hint of apology. Older white men clearly didn't say sorry to young black women in Louisiana, Patrese thought, even in this day and age.

There were low chairs around a coffee table next to one of the windows. As Patrese sat down, he glanced out at the Mississippi, stretching lazy wide as barges and ferries churned it gray and brown.

"Do I need a lawyer?" Varden said.

"We're just here to ask you some questions about Cindy, sir," replied Selma.

"Do you always bring the Bureau with you on homicide cases?"

"We do when the victim worked closely with a man like yourself."

Varden's eyes flashed. "What does that mean, young lady?"

"It means you're an important citizen, sir, and we want to assure you that the New Orleans law enforcement community is doing everything it can—doing everything *we* can—to bring Miss Rojciewicz's killer to justice."

Spoken like a true pro, Patrese thought.

"In that case, Detective, fire away."

"How long had Miss Rojciewicz worked for you?"

"Four years, just about."

"And how would you describe her as an employee?"

"First class. As are all my staff. I don't employ anybody who's anything other. Not for very long, at any rate."

"Her father is a friend of yours, is that right?"

"That's right. I've—I'd—known Cindy for a long while, so I knew she'd be up to the responsibilities I entrusted her with."

"And what were those responsibilities?"

"She ran my life."

"What do you mean by that?"

"I mean exactly what I said. My meetings, organized. Any documents I needed, ready. Transport, in place. Bills, paid."

"Bills? Work bills, or home bills?"

"Both."

"She looked after your personal arrangements as well as your professional ones?"

"To me, there's no difference. My life is my work; my work is my life. Let me tell you something, Detective. Cindy's job, it's not one most people could do. You know why? Because she sacrificed her life to the dictates of mine. I went somewhere, she came, too. I needed something at three in the morning, she got it for me. I changed my plans at a moment's notice, she had to do so as well."

"Did she ever complain?"

"Never. Why should she? How many people her age have stayed in the places she has, met the people she has?"

"You say you involved her in every part of your life. Was the reverse true?"

"How do you mean?"

"How much did you know about her life?"

"As much as anyone knows about their staff. Things you find out over time."

"Did she ever talk to you about her social life?"

"Sometimes. Especially if my demands had dragged her away from a party."

"Love life?"

"Excuse me?"

"Did she ever talk to you about her love life? Boyfriends?"

"Good heavens, no."

"Did you ever sleep with her?"

Varden wasn't offended, Patrese saw; if anything, he was flattered. "I refer you to the answer I gave to your previous question, Detective. Good heavens, no."

"She was very attractive."

"She was indeed."

"And you weren't tempted? Rich, powerful man; young, beautiful secretary. It would hardly have been the first time."

"You asked me, I told you."

"Are you upset? That she's been killed?"

"What an imbecilic question. Of course I'm upset. I liked her very much."

"When did you last see her?"

"Tuesday evening, about eight o'clock. We'd been out of town that day . . ."

"Whereabouts?"

"Denton, Texas."

"Business?"

"I've found little reason to visit Denton for recreation, put it that way."

"And you last saw her where?"

"The airport."

"Louis Armstrong?"

"That's correct. We landed back there around seven forty-five. What with deplaning and so on, it was around eight before we went our separate ways. Yes: We'd left at eight that morning, and I remember thinking we'd been gone for twelve hours on the dot."

"What did you think when she didn't turn up for work yesterday?"

"I didn't *think* anything. I *knew* she was sick. She'd called to tell me."

"What time was this?"

"Just after eight, I think."

"Were you angry?"

"No. Why should I have been?"

"You said you needed her on call around the clock. She's not there for a whole day, that could mess up your plans."

"I have other staff, Detective, who are also very good. We can do without anyone for a day. Even me."

"And now?"

"Now what?"

"Have you replaced her?"

"Her responsibilities are being covered by her colleagues. I haven't yet considered a permanent replacement, no."

"Did you monitor her communications?"

"Excuse me?"

"Record phone calls, keep copies of e-mails, that kind of thing."

"All phone calls into and out of this building are recorded as a matter of course. All e-mails written on Varden computers are company property."

"Did you ever find anything that led you to question her loyalty?"

"Never."

"She must have been privy to some sensitive information."

"Much more than 'some,' I can assure you."

"Did she ever report approaches from other organizations? Attempts at corporate espionage? Bribery? Corruption? Anything like that?"

"Again, never."

"I find that hard to believe."

"Why so?"

"This is New Orleans, after all." Selma looked at Patrese, and then back to Varden. "How many computers did Cindy use?"

"Two. A desktop and a laptop."

"Are they both here?"

"As far as I know."

"She didn't have her laptop with her on Tuesday? When you went to Denton?"

"Yes, she did."

"Then surely she'd have taken it home with her?"

Varden shook his head. "She gave it to me at the airport."

"Why so?"

"I never let her take it home. Security. It always came with me."

Selma shrugged; it made sense. "We'd like to impound those computers."

"You have a warrant?"

"Not yet. But we can get one."

"Then you get one, and you come back, and you can have it. But not till then."

"I thought you said you had nothing to hide."

"About her murder, I don't. But as you yourself pointed out, Cindy was privy to commercially sensitive information. Much of that is bound to be on her computer."

"And you're going to delete that information before we get a warrant?"

"I built this company up from nothing, young lady. I am the reason it is what it is today. Nothing is going to jeopardize that. You understand?"

Varden Tower to police HQ was straight up Poydras, about twenty blocks. Patrese drove while Selma called the pathologist. She crooked the cell phone between her right ear and shoulder, and scribbled notes on a pad.

The Superdome slid by on their left, squat and bulbous. Patrese remembered a drunk cornering him in a bar a few months back, not long after he'd arrived in New Orleans, and telling him in all seriousness that the Superdome was a flying saucer, landed right in the middle of the city, and all the expressways and overpasses that coiled around it were hiding power lines and sewage pipes for the aliens living inside.

Funny thing was, that guy hadn't even been the craziest person there that night.

Selma ended the call and turned to Patrese. "Okay. Autopsy, prelim results. Far as they can tell, Cindy died from a combination of neurotoxins and blood loss. Either would have killed her on its own. Together, no chance."

"Neurotoxins. As in snakebite?"

"Perhaps. They can't be certain until they've done some more tests. But it seems pretty clear, what with the puncture marks on her right calf. And get this. You wonder why she didn't fight back? Because the venom had paralyzed her, that's why. Neurotoxic venom blocks nerve impulses to muscles, including the ones in the diaphragm we use for breathing. Can't breathe properly, can't move, can't speak, swallow—"

"—and all the while conscious that someone's cutting your leg off."

Selma nodded. Didn't say anything; didn't have to. Patrese winced.

"It was a rattlesnake, right?" he said.

"Right. A Yucatán rattlesnake, apparently. Latin name, *Crotalus simus tzabcan*. There are about thirty different species, but this one's one of the more deadly."

"Probably why he chose it."

"Exactly. Guys at the incident room are finding us a herpetologist to go see."

"Herpetologist?"

"Reptile expert."

"You learn something every day."

"You grow up around here, Franco, you get to know your snakes pretty fast."

"Yeah, and some of them even have scales."

Selma laughed, and for a moment all her attitude and spikiness disappeared. "Ain't that the truth."

Her cell phone rang. She answered, wrote a few more lines on her pad, checked a couple of details with whoever was on the other end, and hung up.

"Want to take a trip to the bayou?" she asked.

Murder investigation or not, Patrese felt the tension leach from his body with every mile they put between themselves and the city.

Clogged urban streets thick with traffic and tension gave way to highways smeared with garages and hypermarkets in the primary colors of corporate America; highways melted into back roads dappled under arboreal canopies. Patrese lowered his window and inhaled heavy marsh tang.

Selma peered at the upcoming street sign.

"Bayou Barataria. This is it. Make a right here," she said. "Then it's two miles after that. We're looking for a purple-and-yellow sign on a metal gate. Wyatt Herps."

Patrese laughed. "Great name. Wonder how long that took to think up?"

The sign was exactly two miles farther on, above a NO TRESPASSING warning in red and white. Patrese got out of the car, opened the gate—hot to the touch in the rising sunshine—and they set off down an unpaved road.

They hadn't gone more than a few hundred yards when a shot rang out.

Selma had her service revolver drawn almost before Patrese had hit the brakes. They were in an unmarked car; nothing to identify them as law enforcement.

"There a roof light anywhere in here?" he asked.

She rummaged in the glove compartment and under her seat. "Not that I can find."

"NOPD efficiency for you."

"Button it. Keep going. Slowly."

He inched forward. Selma lowered her window and rested her gun hand on the sill.

Around the next corner, a red-faced woman in a checked shirt stood in the middle of the road. The unblinking twin black eyes of her rifle stared at Patrese and Selma.

"Get the hell off my property!" she shouted.

Patrese stopped the car. Selma held up her badge with her free hand.

"NOPD, ma'am."

"Can't you people just leave me alone? I done tellin' those other fools everything. I ain't done nothin' wrong. I got nothing to say to y'all. Now, *get*."

Selma looked at Patrese, puzzled. He shrugged. Selma looked back at the woman.

"Ma'am, I'm afraid I don't understand. What other, er, people?"

"Fools from Wildlife and Fisheries."

"And what did they want?"

"Y'all don't know?"

"Not at all."

The woman squinted, decided Selma was on the level, and continued: "Comin' here askin' if I been stealing people's pets."

"Why would you have done that?"

"To feed to my snakes. As if!"

"What did you tell them?"

"That they didn't have probable cause."

Blame Grisham, Patrese thought. Everyone reckoned they were Perry Mason now.

"Ma'am, we're here because a young woman's been murdered in the city. We were told you're the foremost snake expert in the area, and we need your help."

The rifle came down. "Why didn't you say?" She indicated a low building behind her. "Park on round the side, under the cypresses. I'll see you in there."

"In there" was an office that looked about as organized as the last days of the Roman Empire. Invoices spilled out of colanders and cardboard boxes; in-trays were buried like earthquake victims under mountains of brochures.

The woman wiped her brow and offered her hand to Patrese, who took it without wincing. "Kat South," she said. "Sorry about just now."

"Forget about it. I'm Agent Patrese of the FBI; this is Detective Fawcett, NOPD."

Selma explained about Cindy's murder. She left out Cindy's personal information—name, job, address, and so on—but included as much detail from the crime scene as she could. She and Patrese had discussed this on the way down. Usual practice is to keep certain details of homicide scenes secret, in order to weed out the inevitable bunch of lunatics who call up claiming to have done it, but Patrese and Selma had agreed that in this instance they had to share as much as possible. To someone who knew about snakes, the smallest detail might be significant.

"Shoot," Kat said when Selma had finished. "That's *terrible*. Poor girl. Well, any way I can, I'll help, of course. What would you like to know?"

"Is there any particular significance to the Yucatán rattlesnake?"

"Not that I know of."

"Are they, for example, the most poisonous rattlesnake?"

Kat shook her head. "No. They're venomous, sure, but they ain't top of the charts. Tiger, neotropical, Mojave, twin-spotted, western, diamondback—eastern and western—timber, pygmy, red diamond, rock—they're all more venomous than the Yucatán."

"Are they easy to get hold of?"

"Yes indeedy. If you go to Yucatán."

Patrese laughed. "You deal with many yourself?"

"A few. Not too many. But if people want to buy 'em, sure."

"You sell any recently?"

"In the past year? A handful. Dozen, maybe."

"Can we see the customer list?"

"No problem. I'll dig it out." She gestured to the chaos on her desk. "It may take quite a while, though. I can't be doing with all this computer stuff."

"And these dozen—they come from the Yucatán itself?"

"Not anymore. The first few, obviously, but ever since, I've bred them here."

"Can we see?"

"Sure."

She led them from the office into a large outbuilding. It was about the size of Varden's office, but without the view, the furniture, or the art. Perspex cases marched in neat lines away from them.

"Here are my babies," Kat said; jaunty, but with a tinge of sadness that Patrese clocked immediately. Many a true word, he thought. "Yucatáns are at the far end, past the boas and pythons."

They started off down the rows of cases, each with its own lighting and foliage. Patrese couldn't help but think of those weird Tokyo capsule hotels he'd seen on TV, or of prisoners lounging in their cells, apathetic almost to the point of coma.

"Must be pretty safety-conscious," Selma said.

"Sure am. Cases are all secured, tops latched on. The holes you see let the air in but are too small to crawl through."

"What do they eat?"

"In the wild, things like mice, rats, small rabbits. Here, I give them frozen rodents, pre-killed. Saves a lot of thrashing around."

"Probably better for the rodents, too."

"I guess. I got one of them big industrial freezers, and it's full to burstin'. Darn things eat better than I do. Here." She tapped lightly against the front of a case. "This is one of the Yucatáns here."

Patrese and Selma peered closer, both aware that the only previous example they'd seen had been covered in Cindy's blood. The rattlesnake, rough-scaled in muted blue and gray, peered back.

"I'll be honest," Kat said. "They ain't the prettiest. I mean, to me, all snakes are beautiful, but some more than others."

"Are there any other breeders in the area?"

"For Yucatáns? Not that I know of. That's not to say that . . ." She stopped abruptly.

"Not to say that what?"

Kat winced. "Listen, I don't want to get no one in trouble, but it ain't a secret that Louisiana laws are pretty lax when it comes to my line of business. A lot of states are a whole heap tougher. So if you were, let's say, not so qualified, this is the kind of place you'd wanna come."

"You mean there could be breeders operating without official sanction?"

"Exactly. And unless you can get FedEx or whoever to tell you who they deliver to, you ain't never gonna find them. Not me, though. I'm fully registered."

"I'm sure you are."

"Listen, it's hot as hell, ain't it? Y'all want a lemonade or something?"

"Please," Patrese and Selma said in unison.

"There's a terrace out there," Kat said, indicating a door. "Y'all make yourselves at home. I'll be right back."

The terrace was on the edge of the bayou itself. Patrese and Selma each took a seat, and for a moment were content merely to be still. The water sloshed mud and silt gently against the bank beneath them. A pair of butterflies flashed rainbow colors as they whirled around a black willow. Out on the marshes, herons stood like soldiers, looking toward the point where the archipelago petered out into the Gulf of Mexico.

Selma gave a little, sudden shiver. "You feel it?" she asked, and the tone of her voice meant Patrese knew exactly what she was talking about, because he'd been thinking it, too. There was a darkness out here in the bayou, a presence beyond man or animal. It was little wonder that swamp monsters featured so heavily in local folklore.

"Yup."

"What do you think? About Kat?"

"Overall? She's on the level."

"Why so?"

"Too eccentric not to be."

Selma smiled. "One way of looking at it. Let's wait and see what her customer lists come up with. And if Wildlife and Fisheries do have a case, that might mean leverage for us, if we ever need it."

"Of course."

Kat came back with a jug of lemonade and three glasses.

"Heck of a place you got here," Patrese said as she poured.

"Thank you. My own little bit of paradise. No neighbors, no cell-phone reception. Sometimes it seems like I'm the only one who wants to keep it this way, what with everyone trying to build on top or drill beneath. Fools. We're supposed to be the most intelligent of animals, but sometimes I think we're the dumbest, you know? That's why I love snakes."

"Ms. South, no disrespect," Selma said, "but Genesis, chapter three, says that the serpent was slier than all the animals of the field. It was the snake who tempted Adam and Eve in the Garden. It was the snake who spoke to them with forked tongue. The snake is not a creature to be loved. It's a creature to be feared, and despised."

Kat smiled. Patrese figured she must have heard all this before.

"You can't see it, can you, Detective?"

"Can't see what?" asked Selma.

"You see only the scales, the venom, the danger. You don't see kaleidoscopes of color. You don't see the elegance of their movements. You don't see the purity of their design. No limbs, no ears, no eyelids. Evolution pared to the bone. May I ask: Do you have children?"

"What's that got to do with it?"

"Young children aren't afraid of snakes. They're perfectly happy to handle them."

"Only 'cause they don't know better."

"No, only 'cause they don't know *worse*. It's as they get older that they start to mistrust snakes, and you know why? Because they're encouraged to. By adults. When those children become adults, they pass it on to their children. And so it goes on. The snakes aren't the problem. *We're* the problem."

Roger Rojciewicz's house, all immaculate crown molded ceilings and travertine floors, was out in Metairie, one of the western suburbs in his congressional district. As its Lake Drive address suggested, it overlooked Lake Pontchartrain, though the view clearly meant nothing to him today. One look at Rojciewicz, and Patrese knew that he couldn't have had anything to do with the murder of his daughter. There was a special tier of anguish for parents who'd lost their children, and Patrese had seen that soul-numbing grief many times—too many times—in his Homicide days. Anyone who could fake it deserved an Oscar. In fact, the only person Patrese knew to have successfully faked it, at least for a while, really did have an Oscar.

Rojciewicz accepted their condolences with vague distraction, and answered their questions in a monotone. He'd last seen Cindy at Varden's party on Monday. On Tuesday he'd taken an early flight to Dallas on some congressional subcommittee business. Yesterday he'd taken the six-thirty evening flight back to D.C., arriving past ten at night. By the time he'd gotten the call about Cindy, it had been too late to get back to New Orleans, so he'd had to fly first thing this morning.

That was the congressman's whereabouts accounted for, Patrese thought.

"I appreciate the efforts you're making," Rojciewicz said. "Any help you need, you let me know. Just find the, the—*monster* who did this, you hear?"

It was past lunchtime by the time Patrese and Selma got back to police headquarters, and the heat was virtually a physical entity; wet, suffocating, like an airline towel.

There were about fifteen officers working the case. Selma called them together and asked for a situation report.

Cindy's severed leg had been found stuffed in her hall closet, which Patrese thought was interesting. He'd have expected the killer to take the leg with him as some sort of warped trophy. That he hadn't suggested that the rationale for removing Cindy's leg would be found either in the very act of cutting it, the arrangement of her body without it, or possibly both.

Forensics was still analyzing the usual mishmash of fingerprint, hair, and fiber evidence from Cindy's apartment. Whether any of it meant anything, or led to anything, only time would tell. The ax head and the mirror were also being examined. If they could find the manufacturers of one or both, they could find how many units had been sold in the immediate area, and from which outlets.

The murder's chief characteristics—severed leg, rattlesnake, mirror, ax head—had been entered into the Bureau's VICAP national database, which searched for correlations in any other homicides across the nation. No matches had been found.

Three judges had been asked to issue a search warrant for Cindy's workplace computers. All of them had said no. If you ever wanted to know Varden's power, that was it, right there.

Cindy had more than 150 numbers programmed into her cell phone. The cops were working through them, finding out if anyone knew anything. Some of her friends had heard the news; others were understandably shocked when they were told. Nothing suspicious so far, except for a text that had come in a couple of hours ago.

U want more stuff for weekend? Same as other night?

Someone who didn't yet know she was dead, obviously. Patrese read it twice. *Stuff, other night*: It could surely only mean exactly what he thought it did.

The sender was identified as "L."

"Has anyone called this person?" Patrese asked.

"I did," said one of the uniforms.

"And?"

"No answer."

"You called from a phone in this room?"

"This one right here." The uniform nodded to the handset on his desk.

Which meant it would have come up on L's phone as an unknown number. If L was Cindy's dealer—if he'd been the black man visiting on Tuesday night, the *other night,* dropping off the cocaine Patrese had found in her bedroom drawer—he probably wouldn't have answered a number he didn't know.

The first twenty-four, maximum forty-eight, hours are crucial in solving a murder. If there are no solid leads by then, the chances of finding the killer plummet. Even at the more generous limit, they were already a third of the way through, with nothing concrete to show for it.

They had to do something, Patrese thought. Change the game.

Patrese typed a reply to L's message.

"What the heck are you doing?" Selma said.

He pressed Send, then showed her.

    OK. Come 2nite. About 8?

"Outside," she said, eyes flashing. *"Now."*

Patrese heard a snicker from one of the cops as Selma led him out into the corridor.

The door had barely shut behind them before she was into him.

"Are you out of your mind? That's entrapment."

"It's initiative."

"This is *my* case." Her words came out fast and staccato through gritted teeth. She was as angry as she'd been the previous evening at Cindy's apartment. "You are here on *my* sufferance. Don't think for a second that because I tolerate that, and because in general I find your input useful, that you can take liberties and pull a stunt like that. *Especially* not in front of my men. You do not play to the gallery, you do not break the rules. This is *just* the sort of thing that gives the NOPD a bad name. And it's *just* the sort of thing that gets cases thrown out of court, as the Bureau well knows."

Cindy's cell phone shivered in Patrese's hand.

    8 gd see u there.

She held out her hand, unsmiling. He passed her the phone.

"Entrapment," she repeated.

"It's her dealer. Bet you anything." She opened her mouth, but he cut her off. "Yeah, yeah, I know you don't. Figure of speech. But think about it. Dealers are criminals. Dealers have records. Dealers cooperate with the cops when they don't want their asses slammed back in jail."

"It's still entrapment."

"It's a lead. You see any others around here?"

Selma took charge of the press inquiries. She didn't mention Patrese or the FBI, for fear that this would alert the media that there was more to the story than met the eye. In fact, she said as little as possible.

Yes, Congressman Rojciewicz's daughter had been killed in her apartment.

No, they didn't yet know who the killer was.

Yes, they were keeping an open mind and following up all leads.

No, she didn't have any details about the crime scene she wanted to share.

Yes, all Miss Rojciewicz's family, friends, and colleagues were being very helpful.

No, the police hadn't asked for help from outside agencies. (This was technically true—the Bureau had offered, the NOPD hadn't asked—and as far as Selma was concerned, when it came to the media, "technically true" was quite true enough.)

Yes, Selma was confident of an arrest soon.

No, she wasn't going to change her methods or tread carefully because Marie Laveau had been acquitted. That was one case, done and dusted. This was another.

Yes, she thought the crime rate in New Orleans was way too high. It was the murder capital of America, and she was doing all she could to help change this. Unfortunately, the nature of her work meant she was always dealing with crimes already committed.

No, she had nothing more to say. Thank you, and good afternoon.

Patrese and Selma were installed in Cindy's condo by half past seven, having removed all police-tape lines and made everything else look as normal as possible—which wasn't very normal, given that there was a bloodstain the size of Lake Pontchartrain in the living room.

But if things went according to plan, L—whoever he or she was—wouldn't even get that far before Patrese and Selma were asking some not-so-delicate questions.

Selma was jumpy. "I don't like this," she kept saying. "Should never have let you talk me into it."

"Will you give it a rest? We're here now."

"Yes, we are, aren't we? And no, we shouldn't be."

"You ever done surveillance, Selma?"

"'Course. Every cop has."

"Then tell me this: How the hell did you persuade *anyone* to go on stakeouts with you, if this is how jumpy you get?"

"My stakeouts weren't illegal."

"Anything's illegal if the other side's lawyer is good enough."

"This is different. A second-year law student could have this struck down."

Patrese was about to answer when the intercom system trilled.

Showtime.

He pressed the entry buzzer without speaking, and opened the apartment door.

Footsteps on the stairs, taking them two at a time.

Patrese stood behind the door, out of sight, ready to close it the moment L was inside. Selma was on the other side of the living room, with Patrese between her and the door. She had her revolver drawn, but down by her side.

Footsteps on the landing now, right outside.

Selma's face suddenly fell, her eyes closing above an agonized grimace.

Patrese didn't understand; didn't have *time* to understand, as the man was in the room now, black, six feet and 180 pounds, just as the neighbor had described him, and he looked as confused as Patrese felt.

"Yo. What the fuck, man?"

Patrese kicked the door shut, spun the man around, slammed him up against the wall, and began to go through his pockets. Possession with intent to sell would certainly provide him with an incentive to answer their questions.

The man wasn't struggling. He was staring at Selma.

"Selma?" he said.

"Luther." Her voice was soft, almost blank.

"You *know* him?" Patrese asked.

Luther laughed. "*Know* me? Hell, man—she used to be *married* to me."

Luther's appearance seemed to have shocked Selma into silence. It was several minutes before she could form a coherent sentence, and in that time Patrese had frisked Luther, found three wraps of cocaine, cuffed him, sat him at Cindy's kitchen table, and started to grill him. Figuratively, not literally.

The wraps were laid out on the table like a three-card trick, to remind Luther what was at stake if he didn't, wouldn't, couldn't play ball.

"Before we get down to why you're here—as in right here, right now—tell me how you got *here*," Patrese said. "More generally. One minute, you and Selma are married; the next, you're running coke to white kids in Faubourg? How does that work?"

"I fought for my country, man. I don't have nothin' to be ashamed of."

"Excuse me?"

"I was in the army. Fifteen years. Intelligence, 519th Battalion. Went to Panama a couple of months after basic training, then Iraq, Afghanistan, Iraq again. I was a good soldier. I *was*."

"And?"

"And then I got fucked."

"How?"

"Abu Ghraib."

Patrese nodded. American soldiers' abuse of Iraqi prisoners at Abu Ghraib jail in Baghdad had been all over the news, on and off, for more than a year now.

Luther went on. "Three months in the can, demotion to private, bad conduct discharge. All I was doing was—"

Don't tell me, Patrese thought; obeying orders.

"—obeying orders. Just like I was supposed to. But heads had to roll when it all came out, that's the way it is, and those heads weren't ever gonna be the big shots in D.C., were they? No, sir. They were gonna be the little guys on the ground. It was a crapshoot, and I lost."

"So you became a dealer?"

"Soldiering's all I ever wanted to do, you understand? No unit's ever gonna have me again now, not with that on my record. But a man's gotta earn his keep. And I got skills. So . . ." He gestured to the wraps.

"You could have been a mall cop."

Luther snorted. "I don't think so."

Patrese gestured to Selma. "And you guys were married for . . . ?"

"Seven years. Like the itch. Came down here from Bragg summer of '97, to see my cousin. Met Selma at church. That was it, man. Love at first sight."

Selma nodded; for her, too, clearly. "Got married that fall," she said.

"Whirlwind romance," Patrese said.

"When you know, man, you know," Luther replied.

"And you moved down here, Luther?"

"No. Had to stay at Bragg. Came down as often as I could, and Selma came to see me, but, you know, I had my job, she had hers, and ain't neither one of us wanted to give that up. They were good jobs. *Righteous* jobs."

"Must have been hard, though."

"Sure. Why the heck you think we split? Cops and soldiers got two of the highest divorce rates in the country, ain't they?"

"We could have survived without Abu Ghraib," Selma said.

"Abu Ghraib had nothing to—"

"If you hadn't done those things . . ."

"I *didn't* have a choice."

"What things?" Patrese asked.

"I can't . . ." Selma shook her head. "Look it up on the Web, Franco."

"I didn't have a choice, man," Luther repeated.

Patrese got the impression this conversation had been played out many times before; sometimes with a marriage counselor, perhaps, sometimes without. Maybe Selma would give Patrese her side of the story sometime.

He changed the subject.

"You came here around ten o'clock on Tuesday night, that's correct?"

"That's correct."

"And you brought cocaine for Cindy then?"

"Did I?"

"Remember the text you sent?"

Luther shrugged. "Maybe I did."

"And how did she seem to you then?"

"Fine."

"Fine?"

"Yeah, fine. A little tired, maybe. Said she'd had a long day."

"Stressed about anything?"

"Not that she told me about."

"How long did you stay for?"

"A few minutes. We chatted a bit, then I had to shoot."

"More deliveries?"

"I had to shoot, man. Where and why ain't your concern."

"Don't get lippy with me, Luther. You're in enough trouble as it is."

"Maybe."

Patrese let it go. "You talk a lot with Cindy? In general?"

"Man, we were . . . I supplied a service to her. We weren't buddies."

"You ever fuck her?" Patrese was watching Luther closely for his reaction, but even so he sensed rather than saw Selma wince.

Luther didn't miss a beat. "Never."

"You ever want to?"

"Oh, here we go. Black men violating white women. Man, your fear's forty years out of date. Ain't you never seen *Shaft*?"

Selma took personal charge of processing the paperwork for Luther's arrest, having belatedly roused herself to appreciate that she couldn't afford to be accused of letting her ex-husband off lightly. Luther would spend the night in a police cell, and would be transferred on remand to Orleans Parish Prison tomorrow. Drugs for sure, possibly murder as well; though if he had killed Cindy, he'd have known Patrese's text was a fake, so why would he have turned up? Unless he'd tried to double-bluff them by pretending not to have known.

Either way, the only question seemed to be how long he'd be going down for.

Luther hadn't mentioned entrapment. Maybe his lawyer would.

Maybe Patrese could make the texts disappear before then; he had Luther's cell phone as well as Cindy's now, so he could delete the evidence at both ends.

Luther didn't have any previous—not in civilian life, at least. Abu Ghraib, of course, was a different matter entirely. So, while Selma was filling out the usual mountain of forms, Patrese did as she'd suggested, and searched online for exactly what Luther had done in Iraq.

It wasn't hard to find.

Luther Marcq had been one of the intelligence officers assigned to interrogation duties, and with one particular detainee, Salman Faraj, he'd gone too far. He'd handcuffed Faraj to a radiator with his underwear over his face; he'd jumped on his leg (already wounded by gunfire); and he'd beaten him with a flashlight.

Speaking in his own defense, Luther had said he'd known that what he was doing was wrong, but that his superiors had put him under intense pressure to get results, reminding him over and over again that they were at war and that he was to use any means necessary.

He'd been convicted of dereliction of duty, battery, and making a false official statement to army investigators. Jail, demotion, discharge, as Luther had already said.

Patrese knew soldiers operated for months on end under conditions unimaginable to civilians in their comfortable suburban homes, but even so. Selma's disgust wasn't hard to understand.

He found her in her office, staring into space.

"I'm sorry," he said.

"I never, *ever* thought he'd do something like that." Patrese didn't know whether she meant the drugs, the torture, or both. "He's a good man. *Was* a good man. We married for life. I really believed that. God had brought us together. But I just couldn't go on with someone who could do those things. My minister told me to hate the sin while loving the sinner, but it was too late. Luther . . . he just wasn't the same man anymore." She dabbed at her eyes. "You never really know someone, do you?"

Patrese was about to agree when the door burst open. Thorndike, looking furious.

"Luther Marcq. What the fuck?"

"Excuse me?" Selma said.

"What the fuck are you doing arresting him?"

"Three wraps of cocaine, for a start."

"Right. And how did he know to meet you at Cindy's apartment?"

Selma looked accusingly at Patrese: *Told you so.*

"Let's not even start on *your* personal connection with him," Thorndike continued, looking straight at Selma. "In fact, I'm reassigning you."

"You're *what*?"

"You can't work on this case. Not if your ex-husband's a suspect. You see how this would look if it ever came to court? I tell you to tread carefully, and what do you do? Go running around like it's the Klondike out there. You forgotten who Cindy's daddy is? Her boss? That means we take no chances. Not one."

"Luther's a drug dealer. Pure chance that Cindy was one of his clients."

"Pure chance? Ain't no such thing. Not in law enforcement. And certainly not in law school."

"Then let the lawyers prove that."

Thorndike shook his head. "I let him go."

"You did *what*?" said Patrese and Selma in perfect tandem.

"A half hour ago. Let him walk free, no charge."

"But he's—"

"He's nothing. He was a lawsuit waiting to happen, if I hadn't done what I did. Franco, I'll assign a new lead detective in the morning."

"This case is mine," Selma said. "You know that."

"You prove Luther had nothing to do with Cindy's murder, you can have it back."

"How can I? You just let him go."

"Don't mean he's not still a suspect."

It was past eleven by the time Patrese got home, home being, for the moment at least, a two-bedroom bungalow hard up against the London Avenue Canal in the mixed-race, largely middle-class suburb of Gentilly.

He'd inherited it from another Bureau guy who'd been transferred to Sacramento. When the lease was up in the fall he'd probably move somewhere nearer the Quarter—where else would a single guy want to be, not just in New Orleans but very possibly the entire world?—but it was fine until then.

He'd been on the go for sixteen hours, nonstop. It was all he could do to make it to his bedroom without falling over.

As he brushed his teeth, he thought of what Selma had said about Luther; about the trust she'd put in him, about the standards she set for those she loved, and about the terrible impact when it all failed.

She liked to come across as a hardass, but she wasn't really, not deep down. She'd been brave enough to let Luther get in close, properly close.

Patrese knew it was more than *he'd* ever done with anyone.

Patrese slept fitfully, and gave up even trying shortly after dawn.

He made himself a coffee—proper stuff, from a French press, nothing instant—and cradled the mug with both hands as he sat on his stoop.

This was the only time of day when the city was cool and quiet. The night owls had staggered home to bed; the day shifters were yet to start in earnest. The dew sat heavy on the grass in Patrese's front yard.

New Orleans, just for a moment, felt as though it were on pause. He savored it.

He drove through early-morning streets, the traffic still light; across the London Avenue Canal and Bayou St. John, two of the five fingers that the lake stretched deep into the heart of the city. Water was everywhere, topography's definitive marker.

His cell phone rang while he was waiting at a stoplight in City Park.

"Patrese."

"Franco, it's Rafer." Rafer Lippincott was one of the tech guys in the Bureau office.

"Hey, Rafer. What's up?"

"You know those parameters we put into VICAP yesterday? Snake, ax, all that."

"Yeah."

"We got a hit."

"The system takes that long? It came back yesterday with nothing."

"The system's real time. We got a hit 'cause someone else—a local cop, by the look of it—just entered exactly the same key words."

"This cop—where is he?"

"Natchez. Natchez, Mississippi."

On a good day, with light traffic, Natchez was three hours from New Orleans. Today was a good day. Patrese was there just before ten.

The victim, Dennis Richards, had been staying at the Best Western on Grand Soleil Boulevard, a few yards from the Mississippi River. One of the local detectives took Patrese aside and briefed him.

Dennis had been found at about four A.M. by an early-morning street-cleaning crew, though the pathologist reckoned he'd already been dead a couple of hours by then. His body had been sighted a block or so away, around the back of the hotel, half hidden under trees near the junction of October and Bluff streets. He looked to have been in his mid-fifties, skinny with long, matted dreadlocks, and he was black.

Patrese raised his eyebrows. Different sex, different race: very unusual. Serial killers usually stuck to one gender, and rarely crossed racial lines.

Check this, the detective said: The address on Dennis's hotel registration card was a New Orleans one. Ursulines Street; did Patrese know it?

Patrese did indeed. Ursulines was in the Tremé neighborhood, heart and soul of the city's music scene. But he wasn't thinking about that, nor that this whole thing was clearly shot through with New Orleans, one way or the other. Patrese was thinking that a murder in Louisiana and one in Mississippi made it an interstate case, and interstate cases belonged to the FBI. This was his baby now.

He turned his attention back to the detective. What had Dennis been doing in Natchez?

They were still trying to find that out, but maybe the room was a clue.

The room? Dennis had been found on the street.

The detective led Patrese inside.

Dennis had certainly done a good job of disguising the Best Western corporate blandness. Dark red drapes hung from the walls, heavy and still in the warm air. Against the far wall stood a table laid with a white tablecloth.

Patrese let his gaze travel slowly over the table, registering each object in turn. A pile of stones. Two candles: one white, the other black, both held in miniature metal skulls. Midway between the candles, a glass of water. A candle snuffer. An incense burner. A pestle and mortar, next to a small pyramid of crushed herbs. A switchblade. A pair of scales. Two sheets of parchment. Four nails, each about five inches long.

Despite the heat, Patrese shivered. He didn't know for sure, but he could take a pretty good guess as to what this was—especially when a man from New Orleans was involved.

A voodoo altar.

There was a video camera on a chair in the corner. Not a tourist one, either: a proper TV camera with shoulder stock, attached microphone, and integrated Betacam tape. The kind of kit that news crews and documentary makers use.

One of the Natchez crime-scene officers hooked it up to the TV in the hotel room and began to play the tape.

It started with Dennis himself standing on a street in the French Quarter, talking to the camera.

"I'm a self-taught voodoo priest, a *houngan*. Everybody know me as Rooster, 'cause they say that during a ceremony one time, I put a live rooster in a trance, bit its head off, drank its blood using the neck as a straw, ripped the breast open, and ate it raw. As for whether that's true, I ain't sayin'. Don't seem to have done my rep no harm, though." He cackled as the camera panned back, revealing the shopfront behind him: Rooster's Voodoo Emporium.

Patrese recognized it. There were several places like that in the Quarter, all dolls, potions, charms, and paraphernalia. They claimed to be serious voodoo places, but most of their customers were tourists.

As if on cue, the footage cut to Rooster leading a conga line of out-of-towners through the streets. He was wearing a black top hat over his dreadlocks, carrying a long staff crowned with a plastic human hand and a monkey skull, and busy spinning improbable yarns about curses and spells. The camera panned over the faces of his audience. They were loving it.

A couple of seconds of screen snowstorm, and then Rooster was back, this time bare-chested and in a field somewhere. He ate some glass, lit a firestick, and swallowed the flames. Looked at the camera again. "I'm a seeker. I want to find things. Voodoo explained things to me better than anything else I ever come across. I like the ecstasy in voodoo, the acceptance of your true being, whoever you are. I'm gay. In voodoo, no problem. Voodoo takes your sexuality as just part of the way God made you. Ain't too many other religions do that, hey?"

Twilight. Fires blazing by the water's edge. The steady, hypnotic pulse of drums. A crowd; two, three hundred, perhaps, standing in concentric circles. In the middle were two people wearing robes. One was Rooster. The other was wearing a mask, but from her physique and gait, she was clearly a woman.

There was a box on the ground in front of them, about the size of a coffin. The masked woman, the priestess, raised her hands to heaven and began to chant, always staring at the box.

A slow, rhythmic shuffling in the crowd as the music began to seep into them.

The priestess bent down and lifted the lid from the box. She was saying one word over and over again, and it was a moment or two before Patrese caught it.

Zombie.

No way, Patrese thought. Zombies were the stuff of cheap horror flicks. They didn't exist in real life, surely? Even in New Orleans.

The box was the size of a coffin. Human sacrifice.

The priestess was chanting again, and now the crowd was taking it up.

Eh, eh, they sang. *Bomba hen hen.*

Shuffling around in their circles, they began to dance. Jerky, spasmodic; an arm flung out here, a leg kicked there.

Eh, eh. Bomba hen hen.

Rooster was leading the chant, Patrese saw. The priestess seemed almost to be in a trance; her head was rolling on her shoulders as though her neck was broken.

The crowd joined hands, spreading the current like electricity. The chant rose and fell in crashing waves as their dance became increasingly frenzied. Sweat flying in the firelight; glistening bodies strobed against leaping flames.

Rooster was a dervish in the middle. Infected.

Eh, eh. Bomba hen hen.

The priestess reached down into the box. With a yell audible even above the chanting and the drums, she pulled out what was inside and thrust it skyward.

A snake.

She wrapped it around herself. It looked too big to be a rattler—more like a python or boa—but Patrese couldn't be certain. He thought of what Kat South had said about adults teaching children to fear snakes.

The priestess suddenly ripped off her mask and looked straight at the camera. Patrese recognized her instantly: How could he not have? She'd been all over the news for the past couple of weeks.

It was Marie Laveau.

The footage cut back to Rooster right here, in this very hotel room.

"The voodoo I do is good voodoo." He laughed. "Try sayin' that after you had a few daiquiris. Most voodoo folks do good, whatever people think. But, like any place, there's always some bad apples around, too. And I been hearin' things on the vine, you know? That's why I come here to Natchez. I'm lookin' for a man named Toomey Tegge, who was last heard of as being 'round here, though some folks also say he's in New Orleans. Anyhows, I live in New Orleans, and I ain't seen him there yet. Tegge's a doctor, far as I can tell, but somewhere along the line he musta crossed over, 'cause I heard he got all mixed up with some bad men."

Rooster's face had turned serious, Patrese saw. No more showboating.

"Even today in Africa," Rooster continued, "there are people who put on animal skins and think they possessed by whichever animal they wearing. Leopardmen, owlmen, pythonmen, serpentmen, elephantmen, crocodilemen, wolfmen, lionmen. You name it, they out there, and they do some bad shit. The darkest, nastiest side of voodoo. Here in the South, I believe there are folks like that, too. They call themselves the Red Sect, *Secte Rouge,* and they're a cult.

"A human sacrifice cult."

Natchez was antebellum mansions and tree-dappled streets. A nice place to live, Patrese thought. Perhaps not such a great place to die, but then again, nowhere was.

Police headquarters was a short hop across town from the Best Western. The local cops gave Patrese a room and brought him everything they had on Rooster's murder. For obvious reasons—resources and expertise—smaller towns like Natchez tended to be a lot more cooperative with the Bureau than big-city police departments did.

The crime-scene photos showed beyond doubt that it was the same killer. Leg, rattlesnake, ax, mirror—they were all there, just as they'd been with Cindy. He'd had the photos from Cindy's scene e-mailed over and printed off, and there was no doubt. Same killer.

Witness reports weren't as helpful, principally because there weren't any. No one had seen or heard a thing. The door of Rooster's hotel room hadn't been forced, which suggested that Rooster had known the killer, or at the very least had felt sufficiently comfortable to open the door to him. Yes, the killer could have ambushed Rooster outside, at the spot where he'd been killed, but why would Rooster have been out there in the first place, at that time of night? Some sort of voodoo ritual? There wasn't anything else to do around there, not on a small-town back street past midnight. There was a casino across the way from the hotel, but the route from one to the other didn't go anywhere near the spot where Rooster's body had been found.

The autopsy was being carried out. They'd e-mail the results to Patrese the moment it was done, they said, if he wanted to go back to New Orleans. Did he want a few Natchez detectives on loan for a couple of days? If so, that could be arranged.

I bet it could, Patrese thought. A couple of days helping out with the investigation, a couple more partying their butts off in the Quarter. If I was a Natchez 'tec, I'd be halfway down the interstate already.

He called Phelps and told him what he'd found; the body, the voodoo.

"Heck, Franco," Phelps said. "What the hell is this?"

"It's our case now, for starters."

"Yes. Yes, it is. I'm behind you all the way on this one."

"Then can you ask Thorndike to reinstate Selma?"

"Why do you want to do that?"

"Because she's a good cop, a good detective, and Thorndike has it in for her."

"But Luther's still a suspect, right?"

"I haven't talked to him today. If you mean, could he have gotten from New Orleans to Natchez last night after being released, and killed Rooster in the time frame the cops here are working around, then yes, he could. He may have an alibi."

"Then shouldn't we wait till we confirm that? Conflict of interest, her and him?"

"There's only a conflict of interest if she's *leading* the investigation, and can sit on things or twist things to take the focus away from him."

"Or pin things on him that aren't there."

"True. But she's not leading the investigation anymore. I am. If Luther's involved, then she knows him well, she can be of help. If he's not, no problem."

"Thorndike won't like it."

"That seems a very good reason to do it."

Phelps laughed. "How to win friends and influence people, huh?"

"You got it. I'll be back in a few hours."

"Gotcha. Good work, Franco."

Patrese hung up. A young uniform poked his head around the door.

"Agent Patrese, there's someone in the lobby who wants to see you."

"Who's that?"

"Says her name's Marie Laveau."

Plenty of people in his position, Patrese figured, would have refused to see Marie. It never occurred to him to do so. Whatever she wanted, whatever she had to offer, she'd come all the way from New Orleans for it. That alone meant something.

The riot of colors on Marie's kaftan would have seared the retinas of a blind man, and she flashed teeth and eyes at Patrese as though he were the only man in the world.

"Agent Patrese," she said, sitting down opposite him without being asked. "You know who I am, of course."

"Of course."

"This is a terrible thing. Anything I can do to help, just say. I ain't no fan of the Bureau, but I'm even less of a fan of people who kill my friends."

"News travels fast."

"Don't insult me. I didn't get where I am now by not having my finger on the pulse. News does travel. Faster than you'll ever know."

This at least was true. In Patrese's experience police departments leaked like sieves; police chatter was picked up on scanners every second of the day. Someone like Marie probably knew what cops were doing before they did.

"Anything I can do to help," she repeated.

Am I being played? How much should I tell her? Risk nothing, gain nothing.

He took the plunge. "We found a tape in Rooster's room. Footage of you and him at a ceremony. And then him talking about a human sacrifice cult. The *Secte Rouge*."

"The *Secte Rouge* don't exist."

"You sure?"

"It's a myth. Rooster was obsessed with it. Making a damn documentary about it. I told him not to waste his time."

"On the tape, you're chanting something about a zombie."

Marie laughed; a touch condescendingly, Patrese couldn't help but feel. "*Li grand zombi*. It's the name of the snake."

Patrese again wondered whether to stick or twist, and again figured that the only way was forward.

"Rooster was murdered in a way that appears . . . ritualistic. And he wasn't the first. A young lady was killed two days before in just the same way. I'd like to show you some pictures of their bodies, and you tell me if you think . . . if you think that what the killer's done to them is voodoo. Or even *could be* voodoo."

Marie looked at him, unblinking. Exactly like a snake, in fact.

Patrese bit down on the temptation to fill the silence.

A beat, perhaps two; then she nodded, as if he'd passed some sort of test.

"Okay," she said.

Patrese handed over a thick brown envelope. "They're pretty shocking."

"I'm a big girl, Agent Patrese. I'm sure I've seen worse."

Maybe she had. She didn't flinch or wince as she went through the photos; not once. Examined them properly, too; didn't flick through like many people did. Went all the way through them twice, in fact, before putting them back down on the table and looking at Patrese again.

"You asked if they could be voodoo," she said.

"Yes."

"Then yes, they could."

The snake is very important in voodoo, Marie said. Voodoo gods are called *loa* . . .

Patrese didn't stop her, but he was thinking furiously. Loa. The last word Cindy had said to him at Varden's house had been "Noah." At least that's what he'd *thought* she'd said; it had been a little indistinct, what with her being drunk and slurry.

But what if it hadn't been "Noah"? What if it had been "loa"?

Loa, and sacrificing people?

. . . voodoo gods are called loa, and the father of them all is Damballah, the primordial serpent deity of new life and fertility who created the world. When the first man and woman came into the world blind, it was Damballah who, as the snake, gave them sight. Another snake loa is Simbi, the water snake. Loa of rainfall and fresh water, he oversees the making of charms, and speckled roosters are sacrificed to him.

In voodoo, snakes are not seen as symbols of evil as in the story of Adam and Eve; rather, they are a symbol of man, and women often dance with snakes to represent the spiritual balance between the genders, as Marie had been doing in the ceremony on Rooster's footage.

The snake also represents fusion and transformation; as the snake sheds its skin, so man can leave his corporeal self and transcend into light and knowledge. From the snake flows wisdom and power, making an oracle of those who channel its spirit. That, too, was what Marie had been doing; a snake dance to celebrate her link to the ancient knowledge.

The snake transmits that which is known intuitively. It is the beginning and the end, alpha and omega. It stretches itself out as a bridge across the various levels of consciousness, allowing man to travel freely to the realm of his ancestors, and to the astral plane.

This travel is also the role of the mirror, one of the symbols of the loa Legba. Beyond the mirror in voodoo is the place between what has been, what is, and what will come. Two magicians can use a mirror like a telephone, transmitting information to each other.

Marie began to sing. *Salue' Legba, Ai-zan vie, vie, vie Legba, Creoles sonde miroi Legba, Legba vie' vie', Creoles sonde miroi Ati Bon Legba.*

She translated for Patrese: Salute Legba, Ai-zan, old one, old one, old Legba, Creoles sound Legba's mirror, Legba old one old one, Creoles sound Ati Bon Legba's mirror.

The ax head is a symbol of the loa Chango. In voodoo myth, Chango hurls bolts of lightning at those chosen to be his followers, leaving behind imprints of a stone ax blade on the Earth's crust. Altars to Chango often contain a carved figure of a woman holding a gift to the god with a double-bladed ax sticking up from her head. The ax symbolizes that this devotee is possessed by Chango, and the woman's expression is always calm and cool, expressing the qualities she has gained through her faith.

That Rooster's body had been found near a crossroads was also significant. In voodoo, the crossroads is where the earth and spirit world meet. Virtually all voodoo acts begin with the acknowledgment of the crossroads. A murderer can evade capture if he goes to a crossroads and takes nine steps backward down the road opposite to that which he intends to travel along. The law will take the wrong road from the murderer, and their investigations will lead in directions other than his.

There are four main reasons voodoo practitioners offer sacrifices: to pacify or appease loa; to prevent disaster or misfortune; to purify an individual; or to offer a substitute for what the loa really desires.

But the sacrificial objects are always inanimate. New Orleans voodooistes don't even sacrifice animals anymore, whatever Rooster liked to have claimed about the source of his nickname, and they certainly don't sacrifice humans.

The killer wasn't a proper voodooiste, in other words, which meant he wasn't anyone in Marie's congregation. If he was working to a version of voodoo, it was a very warped and misguided one. Voodoo was a positive religion. It wasn't one that encouraged serial killers.

"Until now," Patrese said.

Now that the Bureau was in charge, the case incident room was moved from New Orleans police headquarters to the Bureau building on Leon C. Simon, up near the lake. By the time Patrese got back there, it was mid-afternoon. Phelps, Thorndike, and Selma were waiting for him. He told them what Marie had said.

"You trust a single word that woman says, you're dumber than a bag of wet mice," Selma said.

As a way of showing her thanks to him for getting her back on the case, Patrese thought, it was unconventional, to say the least.

"It all sounded sensible enough to me."

"Don't matter what the specifics are. She's mendacious and manipulative. She lies as easily as she breathes."

"She was cooperative. More so than I'd have been if I were her."

"Exactly. *Exactly.* Why would she be like that, except to yank our chain? Make us think she's being helpful, when in fact she's doing just the opposite?"

"And why would she do *that*?"

"To keep us from a truth she knows. Maybe just 'cause it amuses her."

"You think this theory, this . . . *voodoo* is plausible?" Thorndike said.

Patrese heard the skepticism in Thorndike's voice, and he couldn't blame him. In the Bureau building's utilitarian flatness, voodoo seemed to come not so much from another culture as another planet entirely.

"Yes. Yes, I do."

"Then let's go back to the start," Phelps said. "Cindy said something to you about sacrificing people."

"That's right."

"What words did she use? What *exactly* did she say?"

Patrese thought for a moment, careful to get his recall precise. Even a trained agent found it easy to confuse what he'd heard with what he *thought* he'd heard, or what he'd *wanted* to hear.

"She said there was—*is*—something terrible going on. She said she needed to tell someone about it. That someone was me, because I wasn't tainted."

"'Tainted'?"

"Everyone here knows everyone, she said. Tell one of them, you tell everyone. But I didn't know anyone, not properly. Which was why she chose me. She said that thing about sacrificing people— those were her exact words, 'sacrifice . . . sacrificing people'—and then something that sounded like 'Noah,' but which I guess could have been 'loa.'"

"You're sure about all that?"

"Positive."

"No indication as to who 'everyone' might be?"

"No. But I assume—and I know you should never assume, because of what it makes—but still, I *assume* she meant the kind of people who were at the party. You know: movers and shakers."

Phelps gestured at himself and Thorndike. "Including people like us?"

Patrese shrugged. "I've asked myself that, and I'm still not sure. On one hand, she said 'everyone.' But if she wanted to tell me, she must have known I'd have told you. So maybe not."

"Fair point."

"And you thought it was something to do with Varden?"

"It was at his house. She said she had documents, evidence, that kind of thing. How would she have got those unless it was something to do with Varden?"

"And now?"

"Now we have to consider the alternative. What if it *wasn't* Varden Cindy wanted to tell me about? What if it was something else entirely, and what it is, how she knew about it, has nothing whatsoever to do with Varden? What if it's just coincidence she worked there?"

"You want to give up on the Varden angle?"

"Not at all. We've hardly started looking into him. We're still working on getting warrants for her computers."

"By the time we get hold of them, they'll have been wiped cleaner than Fatty Arbuckle's plate," Selma said.

"There are ways of retrieving deleted files," Phelps said.

"And there are ways of deleting them so they're never found again. Who do you think has got the better tech guys, us or them?"

Frenzy in the incident room: a Chinese parliament of men barking down phones, tapping information into computers, stonewalling reporters, swilling coffee, and shouting at one another.

Sound and fury, and nothing. A perverse mixture of adrenaline and frustration: adrenaline that they had so much information to chase up, frustration that none of it was yet translating into solid, useful leads.

They needed a connection between the two victims. There had to *be* one, or else how would the killer have chosen them? Some killers went for a certain type of person: short blondes, for example. If so, the pattern was clear even when the victims otherwise had nothing in common.

But that wasn't the case here. Cindy had been a white woman, Rooster a black man. The connection would therefore be more subtle. Marie had spoken of balancing the genders. Did that go for races, too?

There was a large whiteboard on the main wall, and Patrese had written a list of everything they needed to check.

Did Cindy and Rooster have any friends in common?

Did any of the customers at the voodoo emporium where Rooster worked have anything to do with Cindy?

Were Cindy and Rooster on the same company mailing lists?

Did they hang out at the same bars or nightclubs?

Had they dealt with the same Realtors?

Did they get their cars serviced at the same place?

Did they use the same utilities companies?

Workmen? Electricians? Plumbers? Builders?

And drug dealers, of course. Forensics may still have been analyzing all the evidence they'd found at Rooster's house on Ursulines, but they didn't need a microscope to tell them that the small plastic bag they'd found in one of his kitchen cupboards contained half an ounce of Acapulco Gold.

And if they were looking for dealers, where better to start than with Luther Marcq?

Thorndike might have released him, but he hadn't banned Patrese and Selma from getting in touch with him again. Patrese suggested they pay Luther a visit later. Selma didn't volunteer what she felt about this, and Patrese didn't ask.

The snake, mirror, and ax head found at Rooster's house were being compared to those from Cindy's apartment, which were themselves still in the process of being matched to manufacturers, mailing lists, customs records, and so on.

When would they get a hit? Hours, days, weeks . . . take your pick. And even if they did get a manufacturer's name, and a production code, that guaranteed nothing. Anything mass-produced would be sold in such volume as to make tracing the killer that way near on impossible.

The media hadn't yet made the connection, and long might it stay that way. A white woman had been killed in Louisiana, a black man in Mississippi. Even though that man was from New Orleans, the connection was still far from obvious. In fact, ideally, the very things that were making this case such a bitch were the ones that would keep the press at bay for a while yet.

And sadly, murders in New Orleans were so commonplace that most of the time they were hardly news at all.

Patrese was pondering all this when Thorndike called.

"You and Selma, get your butts over to the courthouse. We got a judge who's going to give you a warrant for Varden."

The courthouse was right across the street from both police head-quarters and Orleans Parish Prison; a geographical arrangement that was either admirably practical or depressingly cynical, depending on which way you looked at it.

Judge Katash, who the previous week had been as astonished as everyone else when the jury had found Marie Laveau not guilty, had now considered Selma's application for a warrant to impound Cindy's computers.

Katash knew that three other judges had already turned down this application, and he was sure that they'd had good reason to do so—"reason" in this instance meaning "patronage," of course, though he wasn't vulgar enough to say so out loud—but things had changed since then. Specifically, there'd been another murder. Cindy's death was therefore no longer an isolated tragedy; it was, Katash had to assume, connected to the "something terrible" that she'd told Patrese about, and that had also clearly been responsible for taking Rooster's life.

Under the circumstances, Katash understood that law enforcement needed all the information they could get, and therefore he had no hesitation in issuing the warrant, to cover not just Cindy's computers but all her other work effects as well.

Selma clutched it as though it were the winning ticket in the state lottery.

"Let's see how high and mighty Mr. Varden is *now*," she said.

Badges and warrant held high like talismans, they went into Varden's office without waiting to be admitted, leaving sentinel security guards and scrambling secretaries in their wake.

Varden was on the phone. "Remember what Joe Zee said," he was saying, and that was all Patrese caught before Varden turned toward them in astonishment.

"I presume this is urgent," Varden said, "or else you would have had the courtesy to knock first, no?"

Patrese handed him the warrant. "You said we could come back when we had a warrant. Well, we do. So we have."

"I'll call you back," Varden said into the phone. He replaced the receiver and scanned the text of the warrant. "Yes. That all seems in order. Cindy's computers are outside, in the anteroom. I had them boxed up, to save you the trouble."

"And her personal items? The warrant covers them, too."

"They're there as well. Like I told you before, I have the highest regard for the law enforcement community. It's my duty, and my pleasure, to give you all the assistance I can."

Patrese almost smiled. Varden had had plenty of time to wipe the disks and weed out anything incriminating from Cindy's possessions. His elaborate courtesy was the magnanimity of the victor. Patrese and Selma knew that, and he knew they knew, but still he dared them to call him out on it. The old boy had some style, Patrese thought, but two could play that game.

"And we appreciate your civic-mindedness, sir," Patrese said. "It's an honor to protect and serve such illustrious citizens as yourself."

Varden acknowledged the comeback with a nod. He was enjoying this.

"Do let me know if you find anything germane to your inquiries," he said. "You need any help, call on me, day or night. And I wish you the happiest of weekends."

Patrese's cell phone rang when they were still in the elevator on the way down.

It was one of the detectives on loan from Natchez, and they'd found something. That guy Rooster had mentioned in his tape, the doctor gone bad, Toomey Tegge—well, they'd got some stuff on him. He'd had a medical license from the state of Mississippi, but it had been revoked a few months back. Not because of anything he'd done in Mississippi; because of something he'd done in Iraq.

Iraq?

Tegge had been a reservist. He'd been called up, done his tour. Cut a long story short, he'd ended up at Abu Ghraib. After the whole prisoner abuse thing had come out, he'd been court-martialed. Failure to provide the expected standards of care to the prisoners. Collusion with the soldiers responsible for the abuse. Covering up the crimes while under direct investigation.

Tegge had received a dishonorable discharge. He'd come back to Natchez, but then skipped town after losing his practice. No one had seen him since.

Patrese ended the call and turned to Selma.

"Let's go see Luther."

It was less than three miles, as the crow flies, from Varden's office to Luther's house, but it might as well have been three thousand. Somewhere between the two places, First World seemed to slip into Third.

They were on Lizardi, in the Lower Ninth. Marie Laveau's turf. Luther's place was a shotgun house well past its best, if indeed it had ever had one. The old Chevy on bricks in the front yard seemed to have fused itself with the undergrowth.

Patrese and Selma got out of the car. "No point locking the doors,"

Patrese said. "If someone wants to break in, they'll break in. Locking the doors is only going to piss them off."

"You being serious?"

"Sort of."

Patrese rang the bell. A shuffling from inside, and Luther appeared at the door. He was wearing a purple-and-yellow Louisiana State jersey and khaki shorts that looked as if they could do with a more frequent washing-machine interface than was currently the case.

"I thought y'all would come back," he said, looking neither particularly surprised nor particularly pleased to see them again. "What y'all want?"

"We want to talk to you."

"Then talk."

Three young men were sitting on the bonnet of an orange Camaro a couple of doors down, watching them. That Patrese and Selma were law enforcement was obvious even to a moron.

"Y'all in trouble again, Luther?" shouted one of the youths.

"Either that or I just won a free cruise," Luther shouted back.

The young men laughed. Luther turned back to Selma and Patrese. "Maybe you better come inside."

They followed him in, Luther checking himself in the mirror as he walked past. Patrese didn't know why Luther bothered; he wasn't exactly giving Denzel Washington a run for his money right now.

The place stank of beer, pizza, sweat, and feet, in no particular order. All the girls who'd ever complained about Patrese's bachelor habits, he should have brought them here. Luther made Patrese look practically Swiss.

Selma wrinkled her nose. "Luther, what the heck happened to you?"

"We ain't married no more. So don't you start naggin' me, you hear? Ask me what you wanna ask me, then leave me the hell alone."

"You ever know a guy called Rooster?" Patrese asked.

"Never heard of him."

"You didn't even think about it."

"You know someone, or you don't. I don't need to think about it."

"He was killed last night, maybe early hours of this morning. Killed the same way as Cindy Rojciewicz."

"What you want me to say? I didn't kill Cindy. I didn't even know she was dead, else I wouldn't have been enough of a dumbass to come over when you texted me. Now this Rooster guy's dead, too. I didn't kill him, either. We got pretty much the highest murder rate in the nation, or ain't you noticed?"

"He wasn't killed here. He was killed in Natchez."

The tiniest, briefest alarm behind Luther's eyes as he shrugged again. "What the hell's this gotta do with me?"

"Rooster was in Natchez because he was looking for Toomey Tegge."

No more shrugging. No more nonchalance.

"I ain't seen Toomey for a long while," Luther said eventually.

"Not since Abu Ghraib?"

"Not since Abu Ghraib."

"What did he do there?"

"He got hung out to dry, same as me."

"That doesn't answer my question."

"He did his best."

"He ever abuse anyone?"

"Shit no, man. He tried to help. That guy Faraj, the one I . . . you know . . . he got gangrene from his wounds. Toomey saved his life."

"How did he do that?"

"Took his leg off."

Patrese and Selma looked at each other. Patrese looked back at Luther.

"As in amputation?"

"That's right. Saved his life."

"Luther, we really need to talk to Toomey Tegge."

"Like I said, I ain't seen him since Abu Ghraib."

"You're certain of this?"

"Shit, man. We don't have reunions every fuckin' summer. It wasn't high school. It's not some place we're real fond of, you know?"

"And you didn't go to Natchez last night?"

"No, man. I came back here. The fuck would I be doing in Natchez?"

"Anyone able to confirm you were here?"

"I was alone. If I knew I'd need an alibi, I'd have found one."

No way to prove it either way right now, Patrese thought. See what Forensics came up with. Move on.

"Do you know Marie Laveau?"

"Sort of question is that?"

"Pretty simple one. You know her? Yes or no?"

Luther gestured toward the window. "It's the Lower Ninth. *Everyone* knows her."

"You run drugs for her?"

"I've no idea."

"What do you mean, you've no idea?"

"You think someone like Marie hands the stash out herself, like she's paying wages on a Friday? Get real. She lives in her big old house on the waterfront, she has control of hundreds of people. She don't get her own hands dirty."

"You ever meet her?"

He shrugged. "Coupla times."

"But you don't know her well?"

"No."

"What do people think of her around here?"

"Honestly?"

"Honestly."

"They love her. Fuckin' *love* her, man."

"*How?* Do they know what she does?"

"Yes they do, and let me tell you something: The Lower Ninth don't have much, but what it *does* have is down to her. Schools, day-care centers, libraries, street parties, you name it—it's her that funds it."

"Sure. From drug money."

"You think folks around here care 'bout that? Shit, they'd take money from bin Laden if it went to good use. Where else the money gonna come from? City Hall? Uh-uh. Not around here. No big shots come here to see how public funds being spent, so no public funds get spent here. Voodoo economics, 101. Marie Laveau puts her hand in her pocket and her money where her mouth is. There was a mayor of the Lower Ninth, she'd win by a damn street."

"Voodoo."

"What?"

"You said 'voodoo.' Economics. You ever been to Marie's voodoo ceremonies?"

Luther snorted. "Please. I don't have no truck with all that mumbo jumbo."

"You come across any voodoo stuff at all?"

"Tourist shops in the Quarter."

"Apart from that?"

"No."

Selma looked at Patrese. He shook his head: *No more questions.*

Luther walked them to the door. He checked himself in the mirror again on the way, and this time Patrese saw it for what he thought it really was: not vanity, but endless checking of a reflection amidst the swirling vortices of a vanishing identity.

"Ask you something?" Luther said to Patrese as they stepped onto the porch.

"Sure."

"You ballin' her?"

Selma's hand came up so fast that Patrese heard the smack first, right on the fleshy part of Luther's cheek. Luther pressed his palm against it.

"That's assaulting a witness," he said to Selma.

"No. It's an asshole reminding me why we're not married anymore."

Patrese's neighbor came over around breakfast time.

"Hey, Franco. Not disturbing, am I?"

"Not at all, pal. Come on in. Coffee?"

"Sure."

Cameron Wetzel was a doctor at Charity, New Orleans's largest hospital. He was mid-thirties, a couple of years older than Patrese, and had recently gained a measure of TV fame: TLC's documentary series *Code Blue* had been filming in Charity, and Wetzel had been one of the doctors they'd followed.

"You still getting fan mail?" Patrese laughed.

"You wouldn't believe."

"Panties?"

"Oh, yeah."

"Really?"

"Why? You missing a few pairs? Yeah, really. Not just panties, either. Letters, nude photos, marriage proposals. Even a Web site. www.codebluehotdoc.com."

"I set that up myself."

Wetzel laughed. "There are some kooks out there, man."

"Amen to that."

"Listen, Franco. You been getting water in your backyard?"

"Not that I know. But I've hardly been here this week. Let's take a look."

They went through the kitchen door and into the backyard.

"There you go," Wetzel said, pointing.

There was a pool of water smack in the middle of the yard: roughly a circle, seven or eight feet in diameter. Patrese went over and put his bare foot in the puddle. Six inches deep, give or take.

"I got the same thing," Wetzel said. "Little bigger than that, in fact. Weird, huh?"

"Are the aliens coming? Maybe these are, like, ET helipads. I'll call Spielberg."

"I'll call the water board."

"Spielberg'll get here quicker. Those guys at the water board think *mañana*'s a term of urgency."

Patrese's cell phone buzzed in his pocket, vibrating like a baby rattlesnake. He pulled it out and answered.

"Franco? It's Rafer. Been working on those computers you brought over yesterday."

"And?"

"Zilch."

"Totally clean?"

"Totally. Sterile. Those guys have got some serious tech, you know? I can't be sure, but the electronic footprints look like something the military uses."

Hardly a surprise, Patrese thought. Varden Industries had been working alongside the army for years: billion-dollar no-bid reconstruction contracts in Iraq, levee-building with the U.S. Army Corps of Engineers right here in New Orleans.

Wetzel waved and mouthed a good-bye. Patrese did likewise.

"Varden really expects us to believe Cindy kept no information whatsoever on either of her machines?" Patrese asked.

"They'll just say the hard drive crashed and they lost everything."

"Can you prove otherwise?"

"Probably, but I'd have to get *very* technical. It would take a while."

And probably not be worth it, anyway, Patrese thought. If Varden's tech guys weren't better than the Bureau's, his lawyers sure would be.

"Well, see what you can get, but don't bust your balls over it. We've probably got bigger fish to be frying."

"Got it."

Patrese knew Lippincott was one of the few guys working in the Bureau office today. Weekends were weekends, especially in New Orleans, and investigations followed the same pattern as everyone else's working week. Things like tracing mirrors and axes, getting customer lists, and so on—the people who could supply such information only worked Mondays through Fridays themselves.

It stuck in Patrese's craw—he wanted to get on with things—but he could go chasing his tail around the office and achieve nothing, or he could relax, get some rest, and be in better shape to deal with the breaks when they came around. Selma, for example, had told him after visiting Luther last night that she was a Seventh-Day Adventist, so she never worked Saturdays no matter what.

The man from the water board—Chad, name helpfully sewn on to the chest pocket of his shirt—arrived after lunch. Patrese took it all back about their inefficiency, and watched Chad poke around the water in his yard. Chad siphoned off a couple of quarts and ran it through various machines in the back of his truck.

"Any ideas?" Patrese asked as Chad inspected the readouts.

"Well, it's not potable, so it can't be from a leaking main. And the salinity levels are consistent with those of the lake . . ."

"Pontchartrain's saltwater?"

"Sure is. It's technically an estuary of the Gulf. So I reckon you got yourself a seepage pool from the canal." Chad gestured toward the levee, which ran a few yards behind Patrese's back fence, beyond which was the London Avenue Canal. From where they were standing, Patrese could just about see the superstructure of a barge that seemed to be permanently moored there.

"Seepage pool? Is that serious?"

"Nah. Not really."

"It sounds pretty serious."

"Happens all the time. Probably a tiny crack in the wall, or water finding its way through the earth surrounds. If it was serious, you'd have a darn sight more than what you got in your yard. You'd be living on the second floor. Anyhows, it's summer. You oughta be happy to get a bit of water for free. What can I say? This is a damp city. Live with it."

Patrese had lived here—this house, this city—long enough to know the usual medley of night sounds: the canal water's gentle lapping against its walls, the hiss of traffic on Mirabeau, the Doppler effect as passing drunks sang and shouted. Even in his sleep, Patrese knew what he should and shouldn't be hearing.

And he knew that he definitely shouldn't be hearing the floorboard creak that had woken him.

Hearthammer; wide awake in an instant.

Patrese rolled on to his side, reaching for the olive drab Glock 22 on his bedside table and checking the luminous digits on his clock radio: 3:28.

He held himself still for a moment, concentrating only on what he could hear. He thought he could make out quick, shallow breathing, and then realized it was his own.

The loose floorboard, the one that had creaked, was in the kitchen.

Sweat prickled Patrese's spine, fear and anticipation swirling together.

He swung his legs over the side of the bed and stood up. Two quick, silent steps to the bedroom door, and then low into a crouch.

Another creak. Living room this time.

Between the living room and Patrese's bedroom was about ten feet of corridor. Patrese weighed his options. Stealth or rush? Stick or twist?

The bedroom door was sufficiently ajar for him to slip through. He sidled into the corridor, back flat against the wall.

The intruder's shadow was moving slowly across the living-room floor.

Toward Patrese.

Patrese raised the Glock, sighting down the barrel in the gloom, and flicked the safety catch off.

The noise of the catch wasn't much, but it was enough. The intruder's own gun spat flame twice, the reports shockingly loud in the night stillness, and Patrese was firing back through sheer reflex, quicker than thought—certainly quicker than the realization that the warm wetness and dull pain in his right bicep meant he'd been hit.

His right hand was numb. He switched the Glock to his left, trying to see beyond the dancing orange starbursts in his vision, retinal imprints of the muzzle flashes.

The intruder turned tail, sprinting back out of the house like a scalded cat. Gritting his teeth against the gathering pain in his arm, Patrese gave chase.

A motorbike engine rasped into life outside. Patrese burst through the screen door, knowing he was too late. The bike was already fifty yards away, fishtailing slightly as it headed up alongside the canal wall toward the lake.

No rear plate, Patrese saw. Not that it made much difference; he'd have needed eagle eyes to read numbers on a moving target at that distance in the dark.

No point in giving chase, either. By the time he'd gotten his car keys and persuaded his aging Trans-Am to start, the bike would be halfway to Baton Rouge.

Next door, Wetzel came tearing out of his house.

"Franco? You okay? Man, you need me to take a look at that arm of yours."

Wetzel hadn't had time to call the cops, Patrese realized. He must have just heard the shots and come right on out in the middle of the night, with no heed for his own safety. Stand-up guy.

Patrese winced as Wetzel checked his arm over, humming to himself.

"Lot of blood here, man," he said at last, "but just a flesh wound. Passed straight through the fleshy part of your arm. Missed your muscles by, oh, about six feet."

Patrese laughed. Charity Hospital's doctors were, through grim necessity, the very best in America at dealing with gunshot wounds. Army doctors regularly did some of their battlefield training there.

"Probably find the bullet somewhere in your plasterwork," Wetzel added.

"Cameron, can I borrow your phone?"

"Sure. You lost yours?"

"Not at all. But my house is now a crime scene. I can't go back inside till the CSI boys have been round."

"At this time of night? The neighbors are going to *love* you."

It was dawn by the time the crime-scene techs had been and gone, and Wetzel was wrong: Their neighbors didn't much care, since half of them seemed to have been out partying at the time Patrese had been attacked. What else were they going to be doing on a summer Saturday night in New Orleans?

Patrese could, perhaps should, have been partying, too, but instead he'd gotten an early night; officially because he thought there might be some advancement in the Cindy/Rooster case at any moment, and unofficially because he still wasn't sure how well he was fitting in here in New Orleans.

That Southerners were different was an old cliché, but, like most clichés, it was so because it was true. Patrese had wanted a break from Pittsburgh, but now that he was gone, he was beginning to remember all the things he loved about it. On a July night in New Orleans, with the thermometer never getting below eighty, he felt himself hankering for those Pittsburgh February days when the air's so cold it feels like it'll tear the skin from your face, for the rough grumpiness of people trudging around in six layers and still shivering. New Orleans loved people, and people loved New Orleans, but a city that was special to everyone was special to no one. Pittsburgh would always be Patrese's; New Orleans never would.

He'd called Selma to tell her what had happened, and she'd come around, just in time to see the crime-scene techs find the bullet that had passed through his arm, and another that must have just missed him. Both of them embedded in the corridor wall, and both of them 40-caliber rimless Smith & Wesson.

"As used by the NOPD," Selma had said.

"And the FBI," Patrese had replied.

And half the criminals in New Orleans, too, they knew. If law enforcement rated a piece of ordnance, it was never long before the bad guys followed suit.

Patrese hadn't gotten enough of a look at the intruder to give any kind of worthwhile description; not even race or gender. As the motorbike had hightailed away, he'd seen that the intruder had been wearing a baseball cap. That apart, zilch.

In fact, the intruder had only taken one thing.

A shoe.

One of Patrese's loafers, to be precise. The pair had been by the back door, and now only the left one was still there.

And if what the intruder had taken was strange, it wasn't half as weird as what he or she had left behind.

On the living-room floor, a scattering of shrink-wrapped dry-ice pellets, and next to the front steps, an egg with Patrese's name written on it nine times and a small burlap bag containing salt, pepper, a rabbit foot, some ashes, and half a razor blade.

The dry ice, Patrese could make no sense of. The egg and the burlap bag, on the other hand, looked like voodoo; someone putting a spell on him, or at least trying to freak him out by making him think he was cursed, which he reckoned was pretty much the same thing. Did a curse work if the victim refused to believe in it?

Was that what the break-in had been about? To frighten Patrese, warn him off the case? Perhaps the intruder had fired deliberately off target, to hurt rather than kill. Hell of a good shot, if that was the case, since it had been dark; but very possible.

Patrese's arm was throbbing. He took two more painkillers, checked the dressing Wetzel had put on the wound, and went back to bed for an uneasy few hours.

Patrese felt a little bit more human come the evening, which was just as well. He had a ceremony to attend, and in all the commotion of the past few days, he'd almost clean forgotten about it. Tony Wattana, whose father, Panupong, was the Mr. Big of Khao Lak, had gotten in touch with Patrese after reading about him in the *Times-Picayune* a couple of months back, and said that he would like to present Patrese with an award on behalf of the Asian/Pacific American Society for all his help in Khao Lak after the tsunami. They'd settled on today, at dusk, in Audubon Park near the zoo.

At this time of the evening, the temperature a couple of degrees below the sledgehammer of mid-afternoon, the park was full; strolling couples, fathers playfully wrestling with young sons on the grass, even the odd jogger. Patrese found the delegation near the tennis courts: twenty or so Thai-Americans, the men in slacks and short sleeves, the women in brightly colored dresses, and all very glad to meet him, not least Tony, whose face seemed set to permanent smile.

There was someone else there, too, someone Patrese hadn't expected: Junior Varden, governor of Louisiana and St. John Varden's son, with a couple of state troopers standing a little way off.

"Agent Patrese." Junior clasped Patrese's hand in both of his. "I don't think we've met, but I've heard so much about you, especially these past few days. So good of you to come at such a busy time."

"It's my pleasure."

Junior turned to Tony. "Shall we begin?"

"Whenever you're ready, Governor." He indicated a photographer. "You don't mind, Agent Patrese? Just for our Web site."

"Not at all," Patrese said.

"It gives me great pleasure," Junior began, "to be here today. The Asian/Pacific American Society does a lot of good work in New Orleans and the whole of Louisiana, and I like to help them out whenever I can. Agent Patrese, what you did for the people of Khao Lak was selfless and noble. You represented the best of America, the spirit of endeavor and help on which this nation was built. I am proud to call you a countryman, and I bestow upon you this medal of thanks, which comes on behalf not just of the Asian/Pacific American Society, but of all the people of Thailand."

Tony handed Junior the medal. Junior slipped it over Patrese's head. Patrese adjusted it around his neck. Everyone clapped. The photographer clicked away.

"You have time to go down to the river?" Tony said.

"Sure."

Each member of the delegation had made Patrese a *krathong,* a basket made from banana leaves folded to resemble a lotus flower. Each *krathong* was full of flowers, incense sticks, and candles.

"We release them onto the river in your honor," Tony said. "In Thailand we make the *krathong* to symbolize the annual renewal of life and hope, and as an offering to the river gods, who know the value and importance of water in the lives of the Thai people. You helped us when the water destroyed rather than nurtured. Thank you."

A low wall separated the edge of the parkland from the Mississippi. One by one, the Thai men and women leaned over the wall and gently dropped their *krathong* into the water. The candles glittered and bobbed in the darkness, an armada of tiny beacons carried helplessly along and away by the great river, and Patrese was surprised to find tears starting to prick behind his eyes as he watched them go.

Eight A.M., full incident room; start of the week sitrep.

Toxicology reports for Cindy Rojciewicz and Rooster Richards were in. Neurotoxic poisoning consistent with the bite of a rattlesnake was now confirmed in both cases. More tests than usual had been necessary; such toxins were found primarily in the bloodstream, much of which had ebbed from the bodies following the removal of the victims' left legs.

There was therefore little doubt that the killer had subdued his victims the way Patrese and Selma had initially thought; snakebite had led to paralysis, and paralysis had meant he could do whatever he wanted.

Both bodies had now been released for burial. Cindy's family had requested a family-only funeral. Rooster's funeral was tomorrow, and his friends were planning quite the opposite: a street party send-off he'd have been proud of.

Both the mirrors and the ax heads had been traced back to their manufacturers. The mirrors were made by a Chinese firm, Shouguang Yujing, based in Shansong province. They were part of a range sold in Walmart. Uniforms were checking the records of all Walmarts in the immediate area, starting with the Supercenter on Tchoupitoulas Street down by the river.

The ax heads came from Barco Tools in Reading, Pennsylvania, and were part of the firm's most basic standard ax; head weight 1.25 oz, UPC number 036848082939. Barco had sent along a list of retailers in Louisiana, and were collating their online purchase records, too. The manager of a hardware store on North Rampart claimed to have sold a dozen such ax heads in one go a few months back, though he couldn't remember much about the purchaser other than that he was black and paid in cash.

Forensic analysis of hairs, fibers, and other trace evidence was still ongoing.

Extensive inquiries into various aspects of both victims' lives had failed to yield anything worthwhile. Cindy's and Rooster's last twenty-four hours had been reconstructed, their friends and colleagues had been interviewed, their finances examined. Nothing in any of those had raised a red flag.

They seemed to have had nothing in common with each other, apart from the most basic fact of living in New Orleans. Every likely point of cross-reference, such as mutual friends or interests, had turned up blank.

If anyone knew where Toomey Tegge was, they weren't telling. His details were being circulated among all the city's hospitals and medical centers in case he'd tried to find work there, either under his own name or a pseudonym. New Orleans health-care providers weren't so flush with staff that they could afford to turn away qualified doctors, especially ones who might not mention their loss of license.

Oh—and the guy who lived downstairs from Cindy's apartment had called in. He thought he'd heard someone in her apartment yesterday, and wondered when the hell the cops were going to stop tramping through his building.

The police tape was no longer on the door of Cindy's apartment, which Patrese knew was normal. Once Forensics had finished, there was no longer any need to seal the place off, and indeed several reasons not to, among them the landlord's desire to clean the place up and rent it out again as quickly as possible. Murder or not, real estate was real estate. If every property in New Orleans that had played host to a crime remained unused, the city would have been a ghost town in a matter of days.

What was very far from normal was the state of the apartment inside.

It looked as though a tornado had passed through. Pretty much every piece of furniture was upturned; drawers had been emptied all over the floor, their contents strewn in ragged lines like fox-ripped garbage sacks; the cut backs of cushions and paintings lolled floppy dog's tongue open.

Someone had been searching for something, that much was clear. But knowing who that someone was, and whether they'd found what they'd been looking for, was another matter entirely.

I t wasn't like any funeral Patrese had ever been to.

No church, no long faces, no hymnal dirges, no one wearing black. In voodoo, white is the color of death, and so it was that hundreds of people in clothes the color of angels high-stepped all the way from Louis Armstrong Square, right across the street from Rooster's extravagantly decorated shotgun house on Ursulines, all canary yellow walls and lipstick-red shutters, to St. Louis Cemetery Number Three, a thin sliver squashed between a racecourse on one side and Bayou St. John on the other. A brass band led the way, and if the songs they played—"A Closer Walk with Thee," "This Little Light of Mine," "Will the Circle Be Unbroken"—were familiarly funereal, the band infused them with such heat and richness that the long trails of people behind them never stopped dancing, not for a moment.

It was, Patrese realized, a celebration of life itself; a reminder that when someone died, it wasn't yet your time, and you could continue the dance with their memories as strong as their physical presence had been. He remembered having seen a jazzman on TV once, explaining it all. "For the short time you join the stream," the jazzman had said, "enjoy yourself and shake your damn ass."

Marie was at the head of the procession, a python writhing in lazy, sinuous folds around her neck and hips, and once passersby had gotten over the shock of seeing a woman with a snake on the streets—hell, once they'd gotten over the shock of the whole damn procession, period—they, too, stepped off the sidewalk and joined in for a few hundred yards, perhaps wondering whether this was some Mardi Gras rehearsal or piece of street theater. But no, Patrese knew, it was the real thing: a sweaty strut in honor of a man who'd known that, in New Orleans at least, being just a little eccentric wasn't enough.

"He was a beautiful brother, man," one of the revelers said to

Patrese. "You wanna know a story 'bout Rooster? Back in the day, I had a bar on Carrolton, 'bout to go under. Bank was gonna foreclose, couldn't get me no more credit, nothing. Then someone said, 'Why don't you ask Rooster to bless the place?' I thought it was stupid, but what the hell, huh? Didn't have nothin' else left to try. So I gave Rooster our last bottle of gin, he made the sign of the cross on all four walls and in the middle of the room . . . and next day, a bunch of students walked in, and when they came back next time they brought their buddies, and those buddies brought their buddies, and in a week flat we had all the students from Loyola and Tulane. All 'cause of Rooster. Walked with the spirits all his life, you know."

"That's what I heard," Patrese replied.

"He's walking with us right now. He ain't gone nowhere."

"Just to the other side."

"Not even there, man. Voodoo people, their souls keep on livin' right here."

"They do?"

"Sure they do. Priests use them in magic. Rooster, he used everyone's souls."

Before Patrese could ask anything else, the man took a swig of gin, poured a splash on Rooster's casket, and whirled to another part of the line.

Marie had explained to Patrese before the start of the procession how she'd arranged Rooster's body to help catch the murderer. An egg in both hands, ropes around his wrists, lying face downward with a red candle at each corner of the casket. In two days, she'd said, *two days,* the murderer's gonna be down on his knees, begging and praying for mercy.

If that turned out to be the case, Patrese had replied, he'd personally recommend Marie for Thorndike's job, and she'd laughed.

Now drivers were out of their cars, clapping and cheering. No one seemed even the slightest bit pissed to have had their journeys delayed. Pull this kind of stunt back in Pittsburgh, Patrese thought, and you'd have a riot on your hands.

He and Selma walked alongside the parade, hovering between

being part of it and being outside. They'd come not just because Marie had promised them an audience, but because funerals—like gravesides and murder scenes—were places to which killers were often drawn. Patrese's eyes were never still; roaming, scanning, assessing, trying to see if anyone was behaving suspiciously. Difficult to tell, when everyone was singing and drinking.

They were almost at the gates of the cemetery when Patrese saw him.

Luther Marcq.

Luther was inside the cemetery, a few yards from the main gate. But he'd told Patrese and Selma that he didn't know Rooster; had never heard of him, in fact.

Luther could have been visiting another grave, Patrese thought. Perhaps it was just coincidence that he was here at the exact moment when Rooster's long panoply came barreling through.

Cops didn't believe in circumstance. Nor did FBI agents.

Patrese looked across to Selma, intending to alert her, but she simply nodded; she'd already spotted Luther herself.

They followed the parade—Patrese couldn't think of them as mourners, even though he knew that's what they technically were—into the cemetery.

"City of the dead!" Marie shouted.

It *did* look like a city streetscape, Patrese thought; crypts, tombs, and mausoleums arranged in rows and piled head high and above, skyscrapers in miniature. Not for New Orleans a hidden death, tucked away the requisite six feet under; here, life's transience is always on display. A high water table, and the fact that half the city is below sea level, means that graves in New Orleans are all aboveground; otherwise the coffins rise to the surface and float away during floods. In the sauna that is the Louisiana climate, a tomb becomes an oven, a time-lapse cremation that boils a body down to bare bones in a year flat. Those bones are bagged and placed in the corner of the tomb, which is then ready for the next occupant.

Rooster's allotted space was down at the far end. Patrese watched as Luther fell in with the dancers, walking stiffly a few yards away from Marie. She said something to him, but Patrese was too far away to hear over the noise, let alone lip-read.

The sunlight fractured against bleached tombs and rusty iron fences. Votive candles melted onto crumbled stones.

The hearse carriage clattered to a halt. The door to Rooster's tomb lolled open. The brass band fell silent, and the hubbub began to subside.

Patrese looked around. Luther was suddenly nowhere to be seen.

A moment of silence, unnervingly loud after the constant din.

And a gunshot.

The shot came from the next row. Patrese was halfway there before most of Rooster's mourners had reacted; it took more than gunfire to interrupt a party in this city. Hell, some people thought a party wasn't a party *until* there was gunfire.

Luther was lying on the ground, alone. His hands were pressed against his right thigh, from where a steady, lava-like flow of blood was oozing between his fingers and onto the fabric of his trousers.

"Selma!" Patrese shouted. "Ambulance. *Now!*"

"On it," she said, pulling her radio out as she appeared from around the corner.

"What happened?" Patrese asked Luther.

"Got shot, man." Luther's face was slick with sweat. "What does it look like?"

"Who shot you?"

"I ain't saying."

"Which way did they go?"

Luther pointed down the main row of tombs, back toward the cemetery entrance. Patrese couldn't see anyone, but there were several smaller "streets" leading off the principal thoroughfare. The shooter could have ducked down one of those. He'd have had to be quick—Patrese reckoned the gap between hearing the shot and being by Luther's side was ten seconds, tops—but it was possible.

More people were arriving, screaming and gasping when they saw Luther.

"Stay with him," Patrese said to Selma. He pulled off his tie and thrust it into her hands. "Tourniquet. I'm gonna see if I can find the shooter."

He was gone before she could argue; into the warren of the dead, knowing he might be joining them unless he was careful.

Gun out, safety off, working out the angle of the sun and the shadows; he needed as much surprise as possible if the shooter was hiding out, waiting for him.

First side street.

Pause at the corner, a quick sighting down the tombs. *In Loving Memory. Never Forgotten.* Portraits as though in lockets.

No movement. No shots whipping through the air at him.

Patrese ran on to the next turning, wiping the sweat from his eyes with his sleeve.

Someone *was* down this one. From his angle at the corner, Patrese could see a shadow, about ten yards away.

He took three quick breaths.

Gun held front and center; right hand on the grip, left hand on the right.

Out into the open, shouting as loud as he could.

"Freeze! Hands where I can see 'em! Now!"

She was old and black, she was tending flowers by a grave, and she looked up at Patrese without fright. With puzzlement, yes, and then with a contempt that he knew came from a lifetime of seeing the police as the enemy, agents of an alien and oppressive ruling class rather than impartial upholders of law and order.

Where better to want the ground to swallow you up than a grave-yard, he thought.

"Sorry," he muttered, in the sotto voce of deep shame.

The old lady rolled her eyes and went back to her flowers.

Patrese went on to the next row, but the momentum had gone. If there was anyone hiding out, they must have made themselves scarce by now, because Patrese didn't find anyone. He searched thoroughly; by the time he made it to the cemetery gates, in fact, Luther's ambulance was turning in. Patrese hopped a ride the last couple of hundred yards, showing them where to go.

The paramedics were out of the vehicle and down at Luther's side with a speed that spoke of many years' practice. Quick, concise questions, a rapid examination of his leg, and then they were loading him onto the stretcher and into the back of the ambulance. Selma intercepted the driver as he climbed back into the cab.

"How's it looking?" she said.

He made a moue. "Not good. Might lose the darn thing altogether, we don't hurry."

Patrese thought fast. "I'll come with you," he told the driver.

"For what?" Selma said.

"There's some strange shit going on here. I want to find out what it is." He turned back to the driver. "Where we headed? Charity?"

"Yup. And we're going right this minute."

Patrese ran around the ambulance and climbed into the passenger seat. "See you there when you've finished with Forensics," he called out to Selma, but she'd already turned back to the spot where Luther had been lying, and was shouting at the gawkers to step the heck back, like *now*.

It was two hours before Wetzel emerged from the operating theater, and in that time Patrese had read the *Times-Picayune* three times and the notices on the hospital bulletin board four. Pretty much every handbill was a request for money, in one way or another: donations, fund-raisers, appeals. He indicated them to Selma when she arrived.

"It's well named, if nothing else," he said.

"What is?"

"This place. Charity."

She nodded. Charity was where New Orleans's poor and uninsured came, which meant it cost the city a huge amount every year, which in turn meant the city was forever trying to find ways of closing it down.

"Walk with me," Wetzel said. "I need to go get a drink."

Patrese and Selma fell in alongside. "What's the prognosis?" Selma asked.

"Good news is, we've saved his leg. He won't be walking for a while, and it'll be a few days before he's out of here, but he won't be looking like Long John Silver."

"Could he have been?"

"Hell, yeah. Ambulance hadn't been so quick, he hadn't come somewhere so used to dealing with gunshots . . . His femur's pretty messed up, he's lost a lot of blood. I've seen limbs taken off for less than that."

"Can we talk to him?" asked Patrese. He'd hoped to get some information out of Luther in the ambulance en route to Charity, but Luther had already been drifting in and out of consciousness. Besides, people wearing oxygen masks didn't tend to be the most sparkling of conversationalists.

"Not yet. He's still under general."

"How long till he comes around?"

"Another hour, maybe two. Even then, you'll have to be easy with him."

"He's—"

"I don't care what he is, Franco. Most folks I treat in here ain't exactly angels. But while they're here, their welfare's my responsibility, and I'm not going to do anything, or let anything happen, that jeopardizes that, you hear?"

Patrese and Selma nodded as one; Patrese in acceptance, Selma in appreciation. It wasn't so long ago that she'd been Luther's next of kin, after all.

They reached the cool-drink vending machine. Wetzel fished in his pocket for the requisite quarters.

At the main door of the ward, there was a sudden flurry of sound and color; Marie, trailing hospital staff like a comet's tail.

"I don't give a good goddamn what state he's in," she was saying. "I *will* see him, and I will see him *now*, you understand?" Seeing the triumvirate of doctor, detective and Bureau agent, she altered course without breaking stride. "Take me to Luther."

Patrese opened his mouth, but Selma was quicker. "What the heck's he got to do with you?"

Marie stared Selma down. "*Ex*-wife, aren't you?"

"That's right. More to the point, *current* detective. What's your interest in Luther?"

"Not the same as yours, I assure you."

"What's that mean?"

"I'd like to see him. Now, let me do so, or give me a good reason why I can't."

"He's still unconscious, that's why."

"Then I'll wait."

"When he comes around, we—and only we—will be talking to him."

"About what?"

"You, for a start."

"I'm flattered."

"Don't be. Luther told us he didn't know you. But there he was this afternoon, talking to you in the cemetery. You want to tell us what that was about?"

"No."

Even though Patrese was lead on this case, he held back now, letting Selma and Marie go at each other. People revealed things about themselves when they got angry.

"Luther was also Cindy Rojciewicz's dealer," Selma continued. "And Luther lives in the Lower Ninth, where not an ounce of narcotics goes through without your say-so."

"My say-so? If *you* say so."

"Don't mess us around. Luther's working for you, isn't he?"

"You wanna see a contract of employment?"

"We already know your connection with Rooster. Now you're linked to Cindy, too. And add the voodoo nature of the killings . . . We should haul you in right now."

Marie held her hands out in front of her. "Then cuff me. I got nothing to hide. But you better be damn sure you got probable cause. I just got off of one murder charge. I spend more time in custody for something else I didn't do, I'm gonna sue the ass off of the police." She turned to Patrese. "I'm doing all I can to help you, Agent, but I have my limits, you know."

"Don't think I don't know what you're doing," Selma snapped. "Agent Patrese and me, we're on the same side. You try and drive a wedge between us, you'll lose."

Marie gave her a smile of insolent sweetness. "Just trying to help, Detective. You want that help, or you want me to go tell the *Times-Picayune* that the cops passed up an opportunity to solve this thing?"

"Enough, both of you," Patrese said. He took Marie's elbow and steered her away from Selma and Wetzel, walking till they were out of earshot.

"I got attacked in my house on Saturday night," he said. She looked at him levelly; no murmured *Sorry to hear that.* "Chased him off, but he left some things. Dry-ice pellets, an egg with my name written on it nine times, and a small burlap bag with salt, pepper, a rabbit foot, some ashes, and half a razor blade."

Marie stopped walking so abruptly that Patrese was three paces farther on before he realized.

"They're curses," she said.

"I figured as much."

"Writing your name on the egg is designed to send you away. The contents of the bag are to make you do whatever that person wants. Basic hoodoo."

"Hoodoo?"

"Hoodoo."

"Not voodoo?"

"Absolutely not."

"What's the difference?"

"Voodoo's religion. Hoodoo's sorcery."

"You ever do hoodoo?"

"Never."

"You prepared to swear to that?"

She turned on him suddenly, eyes flashing. "You want to know what this is about, Franco? Then you have to trust me. Trust not just that I'm trying to help you, but trust the way I do it. Mirrors are portals, you understand? Snakes are bridges. You want to come with me through the portal, across the bridge, you have to leave your white-boy mentality behind. This is ancient stuff here. This ain't about forensics or taped confessions. This is primal. You want to find it, you *really* want to find it, then I'll help you. But you have to *believe*."

From somewhere within the depths of her kaftan, she produced a business card, empty apart from a cell phone number, and handed it to him. "Your choice," she said.

That Luther had lied to them about knowing Marie didn't in itself give Patrese and Selma sufficient grounds for a search warrant. That Luther was in Charity, however, meant they could go to his house unhindered. They didn't tell Phelps or Thorndike, and Selma didn't raise any objections. Either she was used to his rule-breaking, Patrese thought, or else she simply didn't care any longer. Maybe both.

They went after dark, in Patrese's Trans-Am, to make their identity less obvious. Patrese circled the block twice before he was satisfied that neither the three youths with the Camaro, nor indeed anyone else, were around. Patrese wasn't worried about being caught—house searches in the Lower Ninth were less a constitutional violation than a rite of passage—but he didn't want news of their visit leaking out once Luther was back home.

Selma had a lock-picking kit; official police issue. It took her twelve seconds to have the back door open.

Summer heat and closed windows meant the place stank even worse than before. It was all Patrese could do not to gag when he walked in. He'd been to murder scenes that smelled better than Luther's house.

They went through the place quickly and efficiently, careful to leave no trace of their presence. They took nothing but fibers from carpets, sofas, and bedding, bagged and sealed for Forensics to test against those found at Cindy's apartment and Rooster's shotgun house. Cross-transfers of fibers often occur in cases in which there is person-to-person contact.

They checked drawers and cupboards, replacing everything exactly as they'd found it. Selma felt a catch in her throat a couple of times, when she found things that dredged up silted memories of her marriage to Luther—a vacation snapshot, a hotel receipt—but neither she nor Patrese uncovered anything they could see as being immediately germane to their investigation.

There was a laptop in Luther's bedroom. They turned it on and searched through the desktop files, but nothing seemed out of the ordinary. Most of the files concerned Luther's discharge from the military following Abu Ghraib: documents detailing points in his defense, letters to congressmen and senators, a heartfelt essay about what being a soldier meant to him. The remainder was standard personal correspondence. Nothing about Cindy, Rooster, or drug dealing.

If Luther's Internet history offered anything more helpful, they couldn't tell. Internet Explorer asked them for a password, and they didn't dare hazard a guess at even the most obvious candidates for fear that the system would log their attempts. Next time Luther logged on, he might be alerted that he only had a number of tries left; or worse, be locked out altogether. Either way, he'd know someone had been there.

They were inside exactly half an hour. No one on the streets when they came out the back door; no one watching the Trans-Am pull away, at least not that they could see.

On the way back into town, Patrese got a call from Rafer Lippincott, the tech guy. Lippincott had, he said, just installed a surveillance camera above the front door of Patrese's house: digital recording, motion sensor, remote operation.

"Remote operation?" Patrese asked.

"Sure. Wherever you are, you can go online and control it."

"Hell, Rafer. I'm not ungrateful, but don't you think that's a bit excessive?"

Lippincott chuckled. "You never know. One day it might just save your life."

Patrese had turned Marie's card over and over in his fingers so often that he now knew the number by heart.

He was delaying the call for no reason other than pride, he realized; to make it look, even—*especially*—to himself, as if it had been a genuine dilemma rather than a done deal from the start. Deep down, he'd always known what he was going to do.

He figured Marie had known, too.

Your choice, she'd said; but it wasn't a choice, not really.

He punched the number into his cell.

She answered on the second ring.

"Congo Square," she said. "Ten o'clock tonight. Just you."

And gone.

"You're insane," Selma said.

"I don't agree," Patrese replied.

"I'm with Franco." Phelps flipped a quarter across the backs of his fingers. "What have we got to lose?"

"She's wasting our time."

"Maybe she is. But what if she's not?"

"Why the heck should she—*she*—be helping us?"

"That, I don't know. But the fact we can't see a reason doesn't mean there isn't one." Phelps turned to Thorndike. "What do you reckon, Ken?"

"Let's do it. But Franco, you need backup."

"She said I was to come alone."

"And you will. But we'll have audio and video on you the whole time."

"Video? At night?"

Thorndike and Phelps exchanged the shrug of the perennially under-resourced. The bean counters at the Bureau had deemed night-vision equipment too expensive; the NOPD had saved themselves the trouble of a budget committee refusal by not even putting in for it in the first place.

"Fair point," Phelps said. "Audio, for sure. And good old H.E., Mark I."

"H.E.?"

"Human eyeball."

"How many?"

"Many as we've got." Phelps paused. "You're *sure* you want to do this, Franco?"

"Absolutely."

"There's always an element of—"

"I said, I'm sure." Firm; just the right side of polite.

"Then you're a fool," Selma snapped. "What's wrong with you? All of you? All *men*? Can't you *see*? She clicks her fingers, and you follow her around like you're darn baby ducks or something. It's like she has some sort of, I dunno, some sort of *spell* over you or something. You know about her? Men leave their families for her. They never have a chance. She talks to the devil, I'm telling you."

They put a wire on Patrese; a 300mW transmitter nestled against a pad of cotton wool in the small of his back, held there by several feet of surgical plaster and duct tape. It was a dollar to a dime that wherever Patrese was going, it wouldn't have aircon, which meant he'd be sweating buckets in the night heat. Sweat could dissolve the adhesive on tape or short-circuit a transmitter; hence the precautions.

The transmitter's effective range was one hundred yards, line-of-sight. Selma would have the receiver, and would be in radio contact with all backup officers. Since Patrese couldn't wear an earpiece without it being obvious, communication would be strictly one-way. They'd be able to hear Patrese, but not vice versa. They couldn't give him instructions, feedback, or warnings. Every decision he'd make would be his alone.

The officers would refer to Patrese for simplicity's sake as *Half-*

back, his college football position. And they needed an emergency code word; one that meant *Come get me the hell out of here NOW*, and that would be both commonplace enough not to arouse suspicion and rare enough for Patrese not to say it inadvertently.

He settled on it almost instantly; *Steelers,* as in Pittsburgh Steelers, his hometown football team. It was a reminder, not that he needed one, that he was now a long way from home in pretty much every way.

Congo Square was an open space within Louis Armstrong Park, right across the street from Rooster's house. In the colonial era, slaves had gathered here—"back of town"—on Sundays, their day off. Their owners had hoped that allowing them the Sabbath free would encourage them to go to church and become closer to God; instead they were just as likely to hold markets and dances. Now, almost a century and a half after emancipation, Congo Square played host to music festivals, brass band parades, drum circles, and the odd demonstration march, in the kind of ratio you'd expect from a city that would party rather than protest any day of the week.

At ten to ten on a hot summer night, the square's benches were empty, and the leaves of its trees dotted sodium light shadows on overlapping circles of inlaid stone. Patrese wiped his forehead with his sleeve. The sweat was not just from the heat, he knew. His breathing came slightly short, and he had to damp down the tight churning in his stomach. Nervous, excited, apprehensive.

White.

Between them, the FBI and NOPD had found nine men to watch Patrese, under Selma's command. They were all in the darkness somewhere, though Patrese had no idea where. He could neither hear nor see them, which he supposed was the point.

He didn't know how many other pairs of eyes were trained on him. He wasn't really sure he wanted to find out, either.

Who was he waiting for? Marie herself? Or a minion, come to escort him into the great lady's presence?

In the distance, the clock on St. Louis Cathedral struck ten, the chimes sidling their way to him between traffic hum and the shouts of drunken revelers.

Patrese was suddenly aware of a man next to him, though he had neither seen nor heard him arrive, and he was sure the man hadn't been there a moment before. He was a head shorter than Patrese, his shirt as white as his skin was black. He jerked his head in the general direction of the river, and set off without a word.

"Where are we going?" Patrese said, as much for the watchers as himself.

The man did not reply; simply checked over his shoulder to make sure Patrese was following. Around him, Patrese fancied he could hear rustling bushes and footsteps on sidewalk as the watchers scrambled to keep them in sight. The man was double timing; Patrese almost had to run to catch up to him.

They came out of the park's riverside entrance and turned right on North Rampart.

Patrese looked around as subtly as he could, trying to spot the spotters. If they were doing their job, they'd be front, back, and to each side, forming an invisible and elastic box around Patrese and his silent companion. The watchers would swap places as they moved, but the shape would remain largely the same, and Patrese would always be in view.

Selma was fifty yards behind, just coming out of the park. "Halfback heading uptown on Rampart," she said into the radio. "Repeat, uptown on Rampart."

Rampart was the dividing line, Patrese knew. The hardware store that had sold a dozen ax heads to a black man who paid in cash was located on Rampart. Riverside of Rampart was safe, light, clean, the French Quarter. The NOPD even ran a border patrol, cop cars that cruised up and down Rampart to keep the tourists and businessmen in the Quarter, spending their money and as out of harm's way as New Orleans could manage. Lakeside was dark, seedy, dangerous, where the only people out after dark were up to no good.

Wherever they were going, he doubted it was riverside.

Two side streets, then right on St. Louis, left on Basin, and suddenly the silent man was darting through a gate on the right. Patrese followed.

"Where's he going?" Selma asked the radio net.

A hiss of static before one of the watchers responded.

"That's St. Louis Cemetery. Cemetery Number One."

Faces in between the tombs, watching Patrese with a curiosity he felt—*hoped*—stayed the right side of hostility. They must know he was here on Marie's invitation, and therefore presumably under her protection. While that lasted, he'd be safe.

But if Marie turned against him . . . well, there were at least a hundred people here, and the cemetery was walled on all sides. By the time backup made it through the throng, it might all be too late.

Best to keep the crowd sweet, he thought.

The cemetery wasn't supposed to be open this time of night, but Patrese already knew that Marie had a way around problems far greater than municipal access hours. He wondered briefly how everyone had known to meet here. In the old days, there'd been some sort of voodoo grapevine—the blacks had spoken in Creole, which the whites couldn't understand, and in that way had sent messages around the city like pulses of hidden electricity in an underworld hidden from sight and comprehension.

Probably used text messages now; but the underworld bit looked to still hold true.

He knew why Marie had brought him here. Cemetery Number One held some of the best-known tombs in the city: a playboy who went broke, a chess champion who went mad, a woman who fought for sixty-five years to secure her father's estate. But there was one that was more famous than all the others put together: that of the original Marie Laveau.

New Orleanians like to boast that the grave is the second-most visited in all America, behind Elvis but ahead of JFK. A singer, a voodoo queen, and a president, in that order: It said something about America, though whether it was good or bad, Patrese still wasn't sure. Visitors leave gifts for the spirit of Marie or mark X's on the side of the tomb, requesting that she grant them their wishes. The power of hope over reason, Patrese thought; also known as faith.

The current Marie, whether reincarnation, descendant, or simply namesake, was waiting by the tomb. She was in the same ceremonial robes she'd worn in Rooster's video. She nodded at Patrese but did not address him directly. Around her were arranged life-size dummies of warriors in slave chains, clad in shapeless red and black uniforms. They had human skulls for heads, mirrors for eyes.

Outside, Selma stood at the intersection of St. Louis and Basin, near enough to see the cemetery gate, but too far—she hoped—to arouse suspicion from any lookout.

"The cemetery has four corners," she said into her mike. "I want a man on each corner, high enough to see in. Cover all the angles, make sure one of you always has eyeball on Halfback. Don't let yourself be seen. Any side or rear entrances, I want them covered, too. *Move*."

If that woman's having a voodoo ceremony in a Christian cemetery, Selma said to herself, *I will rain down holy hell on her.*

Marie raised her arms and waited for silence.

"We are here to give thanks to the loa."

She was not speaking loudly, but her voice carried a long way in a night that seemed suddenly stiller than before. They were just half a block from a main road, Patrese thought; where had all the noise gone?

"The loa are everywhere around us—in the rocks, the soil, mountains, trees, rivers. Air ain't just a mix of gases; it's where the loa live. We can't see them, but they're always there. They run the universe. You know how tiring that is? They sure is exhausted. We gotta give them some rejuvenation. We gotta give them a gift."

She held up something black in her right hand. It took a moment before Patrese realized what it was.

A cat, with its hind legs tied together.

The animal jerked its body this way and that, trying to escape Marie's grasp. Its claws scratched parabolas of thin air. Marie continued:

"This animal gonna revitalize the loa. Then they come and mount us. They take over our bodies for a while. When they come, we're gone. Don't matter where we go. No honor greater than this, you know? Our bodies are just vessels. We lend them to the gods so they can be with us, speak with us, answer our questions, give us strength. It's an exchange. We give life to the gods. In return, they help us."

Patrese felt a nudge in his ribs. The man who had brought him here from the park was holding out a small cup of chipped china. Patrese took it and sniffed at the liquid inside. Some sort of tea. He thought he could detect a hint of jalapeño in the odor. Too dark to see what color it was.

"But to make this exchange," Marie continued, "you gotta believe. You gotta *believe*, for the magic to work. If you don't believe, and you wanna work conjure, you gotta keep mesmerizin' yourself until you do; gotta get to the trance, let your unconscious take over."

Patrese looked around. Other people were drinking from cups, too. Still he hesitated.

Marie was looking at him. *Leave your white-boy mentality behind,* she'd said.

He didn't know what was in the cup. He wouldn't drink anything he didn't know.

But wasn't that the point? Trust? Faith. *Leave your white-boy mentality behind.*

He'd come so far, he figured there wasn't much point in stopping now. If anything bad happened, he had backup.

He drank. Marie nodded.

"Religion and magic aren't separate from life," Marie finished. "They *are* life."

Everyone sat down. Patrese followed suit.

Marie held the cat up again.

Savage and swift, she pressed the animal close to her face, bit clean through its throat, and began to skin it with her teeth.

"Jesus *Christ.*" One of the watchers, already in position on his corner.

"What?" Selma snapped. "What's happening?"

"Freaky bitch just tore a cat's head off, pretty much."

They could charge Marie with cruelty to animals, Selma thought, and instantly recognized the flaw. The only recordings they were making tonight were audio, not visual, and everyone in that cemetery would swear blind that nothing had happened. She'd gotten away with it before, after all, in the lakeside restaurant on Boxing Day. Even if Marie *did* admit it, she'd probably get some smart-ass lawyer to prove it was freedom of religion or something.

In the cemetery, Patrese held himself stock-still. Was this what Marie had wanted to show him? Maybe Selma was right about Marie yanking their chain; or worse. He remembered something from an FBI course on serial killers; a construct known as the homicidal triad. Cruelty to animals, bed-wetting, fire-starting. Pretty much every serial killer ever caught exhibited at least one of these traits, usually as early as childhood.

The crowd began to chant.

Eh, eh. Bomba hen hen.

Canga bafie te.

Danga moune de te.

Canga do ki li.

Canga li.

Marie smeared the cat's blood over her face and looked toward the heavens. She yelled something unintelligible and, with the blood, daubed a cross on the side of the original Marie Laveau's tomb. Then she peeled the last piece of skin from the cat, and laid both corpse and skin down on the floor by her feet. More blood sprinkled on the ground, making a circle around the grisly offering.

Marie began to high-step her way around the outside of this circle. All the way around one way, and all the way back the other. "We make three turns each way," she said. "To the Orient, to get power and grace for this magic. To the Occident, to signify his return with the same power and grace."

Next to Patrese, an old man was gabbling in a language Patrese didn't recognize. Patrese turned toward him but could see no old man; just a handful of young women. The gabbling continued. He looked around for the old man.

It took him a long, long moment to realize.

There was no old man. It was the young woman nearest him who was talking in this voice.

Patrese stared at her. She didn't notice, let alone respond. He stared for half a minute, more, until he was sure beyond doubt that the voice was indeed coming from the woman, that it wasn't some kind of recording or ventriloquism.

She didn't just have an old man's voice, either. Her shoulders were hunched, her hands trembled slightly, and there was a rheumy wateriness in her eyes when she finally turned to look at—*through*—Patrese.

If it was an act, he thought, she was another one who should get a damn Oscar.

"Possession is healthy," Marie said, as though reading his mind. "It ain't evil. If you can't understand what they're saying, don't worry. The spirits understand. That's what matters."

Voodoo. Possession. The man who'd killed Cindy and Rooster, had he been possessed? Or *thought* he'd been possessed?

Patrese nodded. The young woman/old man kept talking, a non-stop monotone. The longer Patrese listened, the weirder it seemed. He had to go somewhere else.

He looked around for Marie. She was why he'd come here, after all. Someone possessed and gibbering wasn't going to help him, not when it came to finding out why Cindy and Rooster had been killed.

No sign of Marie. He had to go look for her.

He got up and almost fell over. There was something wrong with his balance.

When he looked down, the ground seemed very far away. *Very.* His arms seemed to be about a foot and a half longer than usual, and his eyes felt as though they were at the back of his skull; he was sure he was seeing in much wider angles than usual.

He had to lean his body a long way forward to keep upright, and felt like he was picking his way blindfold through a boulder field. He took a step forward, pressing down hard to ensure that he was still anchored to the ground. *So light I might fly away.* Another pace.

"Halfback is walking through the cemetery." The watchers were all in place now.

"He's looking a little weird to me."

"Roger that."

"Weird, how?" Selma said.

"Like he's drunk, or stoned."

Is this what Marie meant about being possessed if a young woman can turn into an old man why can't something like this happen to me?

Patrese was aware of each thought almost before it had occurred to him. They piled on top of each other at breakneck speed, each one swimming into his consciousness so he could grab it before the words were clear, and then immediately discard it as the next one in line appeared. Thoughts running, jumping, tumbling over themselves.

This is distraction interference static a blind taking me away from why I'm here

"Hey, Franco. What's happening?"

"Mark. Hey."

It was Mark Beradino, his old Homicide partner. They weren't in the cemetery anymore; they were back in Pittsburgh, walking across the Andy Warhol Bridge with the swirling gray eddies of the Allegheny beneath them.

"You got tickets for the game on Sunday, Franco?"

"Sure have. But I can't take you. I'm going with Holden Caulfield."

Beradino laughed. "Man, Holden Caulfield's a guy from a book. He doesn't exist."

Patrese laughed back. "Nor do you."

And like that, Beradino was gone—*snap!*—and Patrese was back in the cemetery.

His mouth was dry, drier than he could ever remember it being. It was an effort just to prize his lips apart. When he tried to talk, his tongue wouldn't respond; just sat there, filling his mouth like a big, fat, desiccated slug. He tried to swallow, but it felt as though he were forcing razor blades down his throat.

"You see that?" Patrese managed to croak. "Beradino was here."

"Who?" Selma replied, before realizing Patrese couldn't hear her. "Hey. Any of you guys know who Beradino is?"

No joy from the radio net.

"Keep an eye on him," Selma continued. "Something's not right."

"You want us to go get him?"

"No, not yet. But like I said, keep an eye. Tell me what's going on."

Patrese had made Beradino disappear just by thinking it, so now he tried it the other way. He thought about his sister Bianca, and here she was, in her hospital scrubs. When he wanted her to disappear, she vanished. Here was Phelps, again materialized through the power of thought alone. Phelps melted into St. John Varden; Varden lay flat on the ground and then stood up as his son; Junior dissolved into pixels that made George Bush.

This was exhilarating. If he could change his thoughts, he could manipulate every facet of reality. What power! What control!

Kind of power a serial killer has life and death snakes mirrors axes legs

Every time a new person appeared, Patrese felt a mild jolt, as though he was riding a slow, oscillating wave constantly shifting from one reality to another. He tried to stop, but now the people were coming of their own accord. His father. Cher. Kat South, the crazy snake woman down on the bayou. They aged in seconds in front of him, died, decayed, dissolved into bones.

Not fun anymore beginning to get scary look at the spirits whirling around me like electrons around an atom Marie is the life force it's her no she's tricky she's evil she dissipates into a million energy particles and reassembles somewhere else that's how she moves so fast that's how she can be in two places at once look at her change now a seven-foot totem pole staring at me a large silent vortex forming in the middle of the cemetery starting to swallow the tombs like they're painted on a big sheet of cloth and the vortex is pulling it down the moonlight a shower of cool warmth time starts to slow down slower and slower and now it's stopped altogether everything suspended on pause the whole world come to a stop I'm dead this is hell no demons no hellfire no brimstone just dark hopelessness the never-ending void not at all how I'd imagined it but worse than I ever thought it could be the most profound reality I've ever experienced punishment for wasting the gift of life my family and friends at my funeral this is what'll happen

Time began to move again, fast-forwarding to catch up with it-self, and suddenly Patrese was back in the cemetery with everything as it had been before, the chanting so loud he wanted to clap his hands to his ears, and he didn't know how long he'd be here this time, so he fought his way through the salt-cracker dryness of his mouth to say it as loud and clear as he could.

"Steelers! Steelers!"

They came in fast and slick, one man under each of Patrese's armpits, half carrying and half dragging him, while the others cleared a path through the worshippers, most of whom barely seemed to notice them, let alone make any kind of challenge.

Selma could feel the heat radiating off Patrese's skin from three feet away. Under the nearest streetlight, she examined his face. His pupils were so wide that there was barely any iris visible around them.

"Sheesh, Franco. What have you taken?"

"Look," Patrese said. "The Japanese blood islands."

"The *what*? We need to get you to a hospital. Fast."

We're driving down this dark road that seems to be covered in oil it feels like we're floating above the road and sliding from side to side a large sign flashing CHARITY *in all colors of the rainbow I'm in a room where the corners are flashing bright red and every time they flash it hurts I cover my eyes but nothing stops the light bright like laser beams here's Wetzel what's he saying sounds like he's talking backward some secret language so I won't know what he's planned for me*

Outside one of Charity's several emergency rooms, Selma explained to Wetzel, as quickly and concisely as she could, what had happened to Patrese.

now she makes sense "This is the new inquisition" she says "I am here to inquire and cause pain. Now lay down and die"

Wetzel turned to a nurse. "Gastric lavage. Get me some activated charcoal."

"Gastric lavage?" Selma said.

"Stomach pump."

Wetzel tells me he's a wizard and has a magic potion to cure me he hands me a cup of black liquid and tells me to drink it this isn't a potion it's death the nurses are all monsters I leap up and hit them fast movements sending shock of electricity through my body they knock me down again

Two of the watchers had come with Selma. They leaped on Patrese and pinned him to the bed. Wriggling, punching, kicking, biting, he wrestled himself free again.

"Security!" Wetzel yelled. "We need security!"

more monsters running whooping fangs blood tossing me around like a rag doll

The two watchers and Selma, along with two nurses and two security guards, swarmed over Patrese.

"Wrists and ankles!" shouted Wetzel. "Pin him at the wrists and ankles, one of you on each. One on his waist, one on his neck, last one holding his right forearm. I want to put a line in him, sedate him. Nurse, give me an IV, Valium."

Selma took Patrese's forearm. Darn, she thought, but he was strong; he was being held down by seven people, all of them trained in restraint techniques, and still he was thrashing around like an angry shark.

Wetzel, cool as you like, tapped the inside of Patrese's right arm, in the crook of his elbow, found a vein, and slid the needle in.

"Keep holding him. It'll take a few minutes before the sleepy stuff kicks in."

Patrese's spasms became less violent and more infrequent. The people restraining him first tentatively relaxed their grip a touch, and then eventually released it altogether. Wetzel ran a tube into Patrese's mouth, checked that it had gone down into his stomach rather than one of his lungs, inserted a funnel into the visible end, and began to pour a black tarlike ooze in.

"That's the charcoal?" Selma asked.

"Sure is. And y'all better stand back, unless you got a change of clothes handy. First rule of gastric lavage: What goes down must come up."

It was twilight outside when Patrese was next aware of Selma being in the room. He squinted at the clock on the wall, and his eyes hurt so much it was several moments before he could decipher the minute and second hands.

Half past eight.

Slowly, laboriously, Patrese did the math in his head; a simple calculation that felt like crawling through treacle.

"I've been here a whole day?" His throat still burned when he spoke.

"Sure have."

Snatches of memory floated in his head, twisting and re-forming like spots of oil. His clothes rearranging themselves into people. Insects emerging from the shadows. A monkey in an observation room. The devil in a scientist's white coat. An open-plan office with booths marching away to the horizon. TV programs showing on the ceiling panels.

They weren't like dreams that you remember as dreams. These were things Patrese was sure had really happened, even though he knew they couldn't have.

"What the hell happened?"

"Datura."

"What?"

"You took datura. You drink anything, smoke anything in the cemetery?"

"Drank a cup of tea."

"That, then. Datura's freaky stuff."

"Thanks." Patrese's tone was as dry as his mouth. "I already got that."

Selma laughed. "I guess. Wetzel said datura's bad even if you're used to it. Disastrous if you're not. He told me a rhyme they teach at med school. 'Blind as a bat, mad as a hatter, red as a beet, hot as hell, dry as a bone, the bowel and bladder lose their tone, the heart runs alone.'"

"Damn right."

She put her hand on his. "Okay, here's the deal. We called for backup, went in, and arrested the whole lot of them. Public order charges. Checked alibis for Cindy and Rooster's murders. Still got a couple in custody, just 'cause they can't tell us for sure where they were those nights, but they ain't the ones; these guys can hardly remember their own names. Everyone else, we had to let go."

"You checked the men against Tegge's details?"

"Of course. If he was there last night, he's sure got a good plastic surgeon. How soon do you reckon before you get out of here?"

"I could go now."

"Seriously?"

"Seriously. I feel a bit shaky, that's it. Why?"

He knew what she was going to say even as she opened her mouth, and this time it was nothing to do with drug-induced thoughts arriving ahead of themselves.

"Because we've got another one."

Within Orleans Parish, the coroner's office is responsible for determining the cause and manner of all suspicious, sudden, or unexpected deaths. By accident or design, their office was right across the way from police headquarters, which meant it was also hard up against the courthouse and the jail. If the city authorities moved Charity Hospital a bit nearer, Patrese thought, they'd have the entire life cycle of the city's many hardened criminals all contained within the space of a block or two; birth, arrest, sentencing, imprisonment, death.

The walls of the morgue were painted bilious green and sweated death beneath the tangling odors of chemicals and rotting humans. Patrese forced himself to concentrate. Here, in the body farm, he had the distinct impression of straddling two worlds; one foot in the land of the dead, the other still with the living.

She lay on the slab. A rubber body block under her back pushed her chest up and forward so her arms and neck hung down; all the better for cutting her open. No dignity in death; not here, at any rate. Not most places.

Selma had briefed Patrese on the way over. She was—had been— Emily Stark.

Color: black.

Age: eighteen.

Occupation: working girl, streetwalker, prostitute, or whore, depending on how euphemistic you were feeling.

Place of occupation: Bourbon Street—where else?

Place of residence: a skanky apartment in a high-rise in Melph, a public-housing project notorious even by New Orleans standards.

Place of death: an alleyway off Bourbon Street, the French Quarter's most notorious thoroughfare. And yes, her body had been left at a crossroads. Not a big crossroads, but a crossroads, a corner, nonetheless. Half hidden. Not hidden enough.

Estimated time of death: twelve hours before. It had taken ten of those hours for the stench of a body decomposing in steam-room conditions to register over the top of all the Quarter's other olfactory nightmares.

"I hope you don't think I've tried to undercut you on this one," Selma said. "But the call came in, and you were still in the hospital, so . . ."

"I don't think anything at all. I'd have done just the same."

Selma nodded her thanks.

The pathologist had eyeglasses and a comb-over. Patrese thought they'd met before but couldn't recall his name.

"From my initial examination," the pathologist said, "it appears the immediate cause of death was consistent with that of the previous victims; that is, exsanguination, primarily through the severed femoral artery."

"Tell us something we don't know," Selma muttered.

He gave a thin smile. "I'll do exactly that, Detective." He pointed to the stump where Emily's left leg had been. "This is not a new stump."

"Excuse me?"

"Your killer didn't remove the leg. It was already missing."

It was still early for Bourbon Street, so they went first to Melph instead, and they went to Melph mob-handed; it was the kind of place where a visit necessitated at least two police cruisers, preferably more. Pockets of young men melted away into the shadows at the first glimpse of flashing blues and reds; an open-air drug market that could rearrange itself in seconds flat.

The threat of violence crackled as they got out of the cruisers. Eyes, bodies, stances, all radiating hostility. Patrese had worked his share of gang homicides back in Pittsburgh, but this place felt in a different league. It was almost as if Melph needed not police but soldiers, patrolling back-to-back as they did on the streets of Baghdad or Fallujah.

The centerpiece of Melph was a twelve-story high-rise, the tallest building in all the projects. Emily had lived on the ninth floor. There was an elevator, of course; it stank of urine and worse, of course; and it was out of order, of course.

Sweat sprang in great blooming drops on Patrese's forehead as he climbed. A prostrate junkie here, a couple hurling insults at each other there.

"Hard to blame them," Patrese said.

"Huh?"

"I'd turn to drugs, or shout and scream, if I lived here."

"I did."

"You did what?"

"Live here."

"You did?"

"Till I was fifteen. Grew up here. And I didn't do any of that stuff. Never got into any mess, never talked to my mom and pop any type of way. Went to church on a Saturday, every Saturday. I was brought up right. Plenty of people here, even here, doing their best to bring their kids up right." She paused. "But yeah, Franco. I see why people do that kind of stuff. Takes someone strong to survive in the kinda place where a beef's never squashed till someone dies."

The place was tiny; less an apartment than a small studio, with bedroom, living room, and kitchen all in one, and a bathroom partitioned off to the side. It didn't look like it had been cleaned since the turn of the century, and very possibly longer.

Evidence of Emily's disability was all around. A pair of crutches sagged against the far wall; a prosthetic leg lay across some dirty plates.

"Why would you," Patrese mused, "if you're the housing authority, take a kid with only one leg and put her on the ninth floor of a place with no elevator?"

Selma gave him a look that he took to mean *You still have plenty to learn about this place.* "*Because* you're the housing authority," she said.

There was one shelf in the whole place, and on it was nothing but three pink books.

"Diaries," Selma said, reaching for them.

"How do you know?"

"I'm a woman. These are diaries." She took them down, flicked through them, and nodded. "Like I said." She handed him one and took two for herself. "We gotta read these, cover to cover. Girls write down *everything* that happens to them."

Patrese opened the diary, squinted, stared, shook his head, and handed it back.

"I'm sorry."

"What's up?"

"I can't read it."

"You don't even know what's in it."

"No. I can't *read*. Can't make out the letters. Jeez, Selma, what's happened to me?"

She came up close and stared in his eyes.

"Your pupils are still as big as saucers. Must be the aftereffects. It'll wear off." She gestured to the diaries. "Let's go back to the station. I'll read, you listen. Then we'll go to Bourbon after midnight, when it's really getting going, and see what her, er, *colleagues* have to say."

Emily's handwriting was girly through and through; hearts over the letter *i*, stars in place of the letter *a*, and never just one exclamation point when five would do.

Nothing girly about some of the things she wrote of. Nothing girly at all.

> **Sunday, August 1.** *Six months now since I done lost my leg and getting used to it I guess!? Folks say I should sue the s-o-b who ran me down but no lawyer gonna take my case on. I gots no money and even if I did there ain't no witnesses, I didn't get the plate, guy was probably drunk or trippin' and ain't got no dead prez of his own even if I found him. Katisha from around the block said attorneys do things for free if they think they gonna win but I don't see how in this case.*

> **Tuesday, December 7.** *Man there are some freaks out there most guys don't seem to mind whether I gots one leg or two some of them aks for someone else when they see my stump but this one guy tonight was actually getting off on it!!! He kept lickin' and caressin' it. Gross!!!!! I told him to cut it out but he said he didn't mean no harm by it. He only got one leg himself, came in on crutches, kept his pants on throughout as he says there's sores and stuff on his stump where it got infected I really thought I was gonna barf right there!!!!*

> **Friday, January 28.** *Freaky dude on crutches came back tonight said I could call him Stump Lover I said I ain't gonna call him no such thing but he said he payin' for me so I call him what the hell he likes and I thought shit if that's what gets him off then I'll do it else he might start beatin' up on me or somethin' anyhows he starts tellin' me about this film he watched the other night on cable boxing somebody about some fucked up dude some*

OTHER fucked up dude I should say!!!! who wants to cut off some girl's arms and legs so she falls in love with him and how this was all wrong 'cos people like him they don't wanna control nobody they admire folks like me 'cos me like him we able to overcome so much he called me his sexy supercrip made me wanna barf again oh yeah this time he brought me flowers like I his damn girlfriend!!

Monday, February 14. Stump Lover—he ain't given me any other name, real or not, so it's either that or Freaky Dude, dear diary!!!! back again tonight and all the other girls on my case laughin' and sayin' he's my boyfriend as it's like Valentine's Day it was real funny I have to keep tellin' myself he's harmless enough just a lonely guy who wants company and gets off on being with another amputee. Anyhows, check this. He aks me if I think he's freaky. Yeah, say I, a little, gotta be honest!!!! Then he launches into this big ol' speech 'bout how people's attitudes toward sex changes over time, and he keeps goin' on 'bout the Chinese, how for like a thousand years Chinese mothers broke bones in their daughters' feet and wrapped them in bandages to make the feet grow all twisted and disfigured and shit, and how to us this looks gross, but for the longest time Chinese men found them real erotic, you know? Then he gives me these things, and now I'm gettin' weirded out, but I figure best to keep 'em, just in case, you know? Like evidence or somethin'.

"Evidence?" Patrese said. "What, like in case he turned nasty?"

"I guess."

Emily had pressed some pieces of paper between the pages of her diary. Selma took them out and unfolded them.

The first was an advertisement from the London *Times* of 1906; a marriage proposal for "a young lady of about 19 or 20, pretty, fond of dress, a devotee of tight-lacing and high heels, and with only one leg, the other having been amputated, preferably at the thigh. Write, enclosing a photo and giving particulars of amputation."

The second was a page from *Penthouse*—no date, but from the seventies if the hairstyles were anything to go by—headed "Monopede Mania," and containing two letters from people claiming to have fetishes about amputees.

Selma shook her head. "Some people," she said. "Some people."

She flicked through the rest of the diary, skim-reading. He appeared twice in March, once in April, twice again in May, three times in June. All of them more of the same, or so it seemed. He'd never got violent on her—not that she'd written about, at any rate—but from the tone of her entries, she'd never quite gotten used to his fetish.

Patrese clapped his hands. "Let's go find him. Stump Lover."

As far as the wider world was concerned, New Orleans *was* the French Quarter, and the French Quarter *was* Bourbon Street, a place where sinning was as natural and primary as breathing, where they'd taken all the "not"s out of the Ten Commandments.

Close to midnight, America's premier party thoroughfare throbbed and pulsed with everything that had made it infamous. Life-size posters of airbrushed temptresses crooked beckoning fingers for subterranean fleshpots: *Barely Legal, Teen Girls, Temptations*. Drag queens with big hands stood in doorways and cackled at the shadowmen and their constant sotto voce patter for every drug you'd ever heard of and several you hadn't. Music swelled and ebbed, thumping dance bass lines giving way to jazz trumpets. Nervy, predatory hustlers cruised the crowds, looking for their next mark, for the idiots who'd left their brains back at the hotel with their inhibitions. Bourbon Street was pretty much an open-air frat party; beer sloshing in plastic cups and already fermenting in the heat as it spilled into the storm drains, men hollering drunken mating calls at women who lifted their tops with unsteady hands.

Dorkadents, Patrese thought; dweebs who'd never, ever dare do this stuff at home.

Strip clubs were many times more visible than bordellos, but it wasn't hard to find the working girls. They were the ones chatting with the cops, cozy as you like.

Patrese and Selma approached the nearest huddle; two cops sitting on the hood of their cruiser, three ladies whose skirts looked more like belts.

"Hey!" one of the hookers called out. "Yo! Ebony and ivory! Y'all can change before coming out, you know. This is party street, man. It ain't the office."

The hookers and one of the cops dissolved into peals of laughter, high-fiving one another. The other cop, recognizing Selma, frantically tried to get the others to shut up.

Selma had her badge out ten strides away, and was glaring at the lippy hooker.

"You know what's good for you, young lady, you'll zip it, like *now*."

The laughter stopped as abruptly as it had started.

"I tried to tell you, Crystal," muttered Sensible Cop.

"It's Scripture Selma," Crystal said, bold again. "Always tellin' us where we goin' wrong and tryin' to get us into rehab. Tell me, darlin', you a cop or a social worker?"

Selma pulled two photos out of her pocket, and handed one—a head shot of Emily that they'd found in the apartment—to Crystal.

"Y'all recognize her?"

Crystal glanced at it and shook her head.

"Take another look," Selma said.

Crystal did, though it was hardly more perfunctory than the first, and then passed the snapshot on to the other two. They shook their heads.

"Never seen her," Crystal said. "None of us."

No surprise, Patrese thought. Hookers might have been comfortable with the patrol cops they knew, but their default position was that everyone else with a badge was out to bust their chops until otherwise proven.

"There's a reason we're called Homicide," Selma sighed, taking the first photo back and giving Crystal the second, "and this is it."

The second photo was also a head shot of Emily; in this case, her face adorned with an ax head, a shattered mirror, and what looked like enough blood to fill Lake Pontchartrain. Crystal pressed a hand to her chest and dry-retched.

"That Destiny?" she asked.

"Her name is Emily."

"Round here, she's called Destiny. Y'all think Crystal's my real name?"

As often as not, Patrese knew, strippers and prostitutes didn't use their real names; a mixture of wanting something sexier for their clients, protecting their own identities, and putting some clean air between themselves and what they were doing in order to pay the bills. He knew, too, that, in the hierarchy of somewhere like Bourbon Street, strippers ranked way higher than hookers. Strippers could take home a grand a night—of which the IRS never saw a cent, of course—and had bouncers to make sure no customers laid so much as a finger on them. Strippers turned to prostitution when they were no longer pulling the customers into the clubs. It never worked the other way around.

"She ever have a client who was missing a leg? An amputee?"

"Yeah, I think so. We used to laugh about it."

"You ever see this guy?"

"Coupla times."

"Can you describe him?"

"He was, er . . . he was a black guy."

"That's it?"

"I didn't get a real good look. And when some dude got only one leg, and you laughin' 'bout it, that's all you really notice, you know?"

"How old?"

"Hard to say. He weren't a real old guy—he didn't have white hair—but he wasn't dressed like a B-boy, neither."

"You see how tall he was?"

"He was on crutches. Hard to say."

"*Try.*"

Crystal shrugged. "Average height."

"Build?"

"Average."

"Eyeglasses? Distinguishing features? Beard? Mustache? Scars? Tattoos?"

Crystal shrugged again. "Sorry."

Patrese sighed to himself. They might as well have interviewed Ray Charles. He tried to console himself with the thought that even if a Superdome's worth of people had seen Stump Lover, they might have been more confused. Eyewitness testimony was notoriously unreliable; for as many people as saw the same incident, you'd get that many different accounts of what happened. In this case, all he could say with any certainty was that Stump Lover was black, old enough to vote, too young to retire, taller than Mickey Rooney, shorter than Kareem Abdul-Jabbar, fatter than Keith Richards, and skinnier than late-era Elvis.

Neither of the other two hookers, or the cops, could add anything useful.

"She have a pimp?"

"No, man. Self-employed. Her own boss. Livin' the American Dream, you know." Crystal's laugh couldn't quite cover the bitterness beneath. "I'm surprised you're botherin', to be honest," she added.

"Bothering?"

"Dead hooker. Never known cops give two fucks 'bout one before."

"Yeah, well, this is different."

Patrese saw the regret on Selma's face the moment the words had left her mouth; not because they'd come out wrong, he reckoned, but because they'd come out right. This *was* different. It was part of something bigger, and that made it more important than it would otherwise have been. Was that correct, morally? Maybe not. Was that the way the world was? Absolutely.

Bourbon Street's red-light district runs for eight blocks down-river from Canal Street, the vast avenue of so-called neutral ground that separates the French Quarter from the Central Business District. Patrese and Selma walked the entire eight blocks, asking every hooker they could find about Emily—Destiny, rather—and her amputee client. No one could add anything useful to what Crystal had told them. Yes, a couple of people had seen him, and yes, he was black, and only had one leg, but apart from that . . .

It wasn't as if hookers were the most reliable of witnesses, Patrese thought. They were probably drunk or high pretty much all the time; the only way to get through being pawed by the kind of men most women would cross the street to avoid.

Patrese and Selma stopped at the corner of St. Ann, the "velvet line" where the gay bars start in earnest and where Bourbon's red-light district becomes the pink-light one. In the sultry night air, rainbow flags hung limp above signs advertising Southern Decadence: 100,000 GAYS. LABOR DAY WEEKEND. WE'LL BE THERE. WILL YOU?

"That was a lot of effort for not very much," Selma said.

"You could say that." He paused for a moment. "Feel like a drink?"

"Not here. Anywhere but here."

"What's wrong with here? There must be more bars per square foot than anywhere else in America."

"Come on, Franco." Selma waved her arm in a huge arc, to encompass the totality of everything around them. "If Dante was alive, he'd put in another circle of hell just for this place. Everything that's wrong with this country, with this world, is right here on Bourbon. Men cheating on their wives. Men exploiting girls—yes, girls, no matter what the law says. Drug pushers wrecking lives. Gays leading lives of filth and spreading disease. All of it against the word of the Bible."

"Why do you stay, then? Why not go and be a cop someplace else?"

She looked at him as though it were the dumbest question ever. "Because this is my home, Franco. I love it. I love it for its energy, its *joie de vivre.*"

"And where does that *joie de vivre* come from? From accepting that we ain't perfect. None of us. That the darkness is never far away. You can't have one without the other. Jeez, Selma. It's a city, not a strip mall."

"I get that, Franco. I've forgotten more about this place than you'll ever know. Nothing personal, but it's true." Her voice was rising now, and Patrese was conscious that people were skirting a little bit wider around them. *Couple having an argument. Stay back.* "You saw those cops with the hookers, the first ones we spoke with? Those guys could give you reviews, recommendations, and price lists for pretty much every bordello in town. They're *cops,* for crying out loud. What's that about? They took an oath to protect and serve, not to get freebies from working girls in exchange for not doing their jobs. You remember what the man in the film said?"

"What man? What film?"

"All the animals come out at night—whores, skunk pussies, buggers, queens, fairies, dopers, junkies, sick, venal."

Patrese was enough of a film buff to recognize the reference. Hell, so he should have. The guy who'd said it was Italian, after all.

He finished the quote for her. "Someday a real rain will come and wash all this scum off the streets."

She looked surprised, pleased. "You're darn right it will. You're darn right."

That Emily had already been an amputee might change everything, they agreed. Until now, they'd assumed that the amputation was only one part of the killer's pathology; that it was all of a piece with the rattlesnake, the ax head, and the mirror.

But what if the amputation itself was the driver?

What if the killer was someone who got off not just on the *act* of amputation, but also on the *state* of it? *Stump Lover.* It was the kind of half-cute, half-sick nickname that the media loved to bestow on serial killers.

Perhaps these murders didn't have anything to do with voodoo at all. They'd found a good deal of circumstantial evidence, yes, but nothing that would stand up in court. Datura poisoning, skinned cats, home invaders with gris-gris, mirrors as portals, snake loa— they all looked suspicious, individually as well as collectively, but they didn't prove a thing.

They'd also suspected Luther of killing Cindy and Rooster, with or without voodoo. But he couldn't possibly have killed Emily Stark;

he was still in the hospital, recovering from being shot in the leg. Another reason for considering this new line of inquiry.

They didn't know who Stump Lover was; Emily's diary hadn't given them a name, let alone a description. He was a black man, and he was missing a leg; that was the sum of their knowledge. And of course there was nothing to say he had anything to do with the murders.

But right now, they didn't have much else.

It was past ten when Patrese woke, and even then he could hardly muster the energy to haul himself out of bed. The whole datura episode, followed by the discovery of Emily's body, had left him somewhere beyond exhausted. He felt as though he could sleep for a week. At least it was no longer as if the world was coming at him through a thin layer of gauze, though when he padded into the kitchen and glanced at the pile of mail on the table, he could still barely make out the words.

His distance vision was pretty much intact, however. He saw Wetzel in his yard next door, and took a cup of coffee over for him.

"Hey," Wetzel said. "I was about to come by, see how you are after the other night."

The other night. It had been just thirty-six hours since Patrese had turned up at Congo Square and gone to the voodoo ceremony. It felt like a lifetime ago; maybe several.

"I'm okay. Better for a good sleep. Listen, Cameron"—the last thing Patrese wanted was for Wetzel to start examining him—"can I pick your brains about something?"

"Sure."

"It's confidential. Police stuff. So I'd appreciate it if . . ."

Wetzel mimed a zipping motion. "Hey, I'm a doctor. Confidentiality is my middle name. Cameron Confidentiality Wetzel. You can call me CC."

Patrese laughed, and told Wetzel about Stump Lover.

"Hmm," Wetzel said when Patrese had finished. "Yeah, there should be records of pretty much every amputee in the country, but finding those records, that's gonna be a lot of legwork."

"Legwork's *my* middle name."

"Legwork and Confidentiality. We should set up a PI agency. Anyhows. It's gonna be a lot of legwork, as there's no central amputee database, far as I know. Not a state one; not federal, neither. So you have to check hospitals, personal physicians, prosthetic clinics, maybe even prosthetic manufacturers."

"She said the guy was missing a leg, not wearing a prosthetic."

"People with prosthetics don't always wear them. Sometimes they get sore, especially in the summer when it's hot and sweat makes the artificial limb slippy. And if your guy wanted sympathy and stump action, he'd have probably gone down the whole crutches route rather than make himself look able-bodied."

"Good point. What about the VA? For war wounded?"

"Absolutely."

"How many people do you think we're looking at here?"

Wetzel made a moue. "How long is a piece of string?"

"Give me a ballpark figure."

"Okay. No one knows for sure how many amputees there are in the whole country, but best guess is around a million and a half. That's one for every two hundred people."

"Leg amputees, or all amputees?"

"All amputees. Leg, arm, hand, foot. Okay. The population of New Orleans—we're assuming he's a local, right?—is around four hundred and fifty thousand, which means that the national average extrapolated across that would mean about two thousand two hundred and fifty amputees, any limb, men and women. But"—Wetzel held up a finger—"it's reasonable to assume New Orleans has more."

"How so?"

"Because of *why* people get limbs amputated. Cancer and trauma amputations are actually decreasing, and congenital defects are running pretty much unchanged. The fastest-growing sector is dysvascular. Complications to the circulation or blood vessels; call for the knife. Four-fifths of new amputations are dysvascular, and almost all of these, percentage high nineties, are legs rather than arms."

"Complications to circulation. That include diabetes?"

"You got it. Diabetes accounts for far and away the majority of dysvascular amputations. And which sector of the population is most prone to diabetes?"

"African-American."

"Which city's population is two-thirds African-American?"

Patrese smiled. "Right here."

"And which hospital is the prime carer for the city's African-Americans?"

"Charity."

"Damn right. So what do we do, faced with a growing diabetes problem? Close our specialist ward, of course. We, Charity, had a specialist diabetic ward, and it shut its doors last year. Every time I think the administrators couldn't get more boneheaded, they prove me wrong. Listen, I'm not saying the answer to your problem's definitely there, in Charity, but it's a good place to start. And it'll save you guys some time and effort, so y'all can get on with other things. I'm back on shift at two. But I'll go in right now and dig around, see what I can find."

"I'll make sure the city buys you the largest daiquiri ever made."

"My pleasure, man."

"And that ballpark figure?"

"Oh, yeah. Okay. Let's do a little head math. Assume a local average higher than the national, adjust for pre-retirement-age African-American men, take out upper-limb cases . . . Hell, Franco, you've still got to be looking at north of a thousand people."

The case sitrep meeting was called for one o'clock. Patrese told the room what Wetzel was doing, and divided the other searches up among fifteen uniforms—five to check through the city's other hospitals, four to do the same with registered physicians, three to get manufacturers' mailing lists, two to get names from the VA, and one to New Orleans New Limbs, the only prosthetic provider in the city certified by the American Board for Certification in Orthotics and Prosthetics. It was already Friday lunchtime, so they probably wouldn't get much in the way of solid leads until after the weekend, but they could at least make a start.

Ballistics had been all over the area in the cemetery where Luther had been shot. They'd found nothing; they hadn't even been able to agree among themselves about the angle and distance from which he'd been shot. Uniforms had questioned most of those there that day at Rooster's funeral, and if any of them had seen anything, they certainly weren't saying. Nor was Luther.

Fuck him, Patrese thought. Luther didn't want to help them nail whoever had shot him, that was Luther's problem.

Selma said she'd had a thought.

"Anyone noticed the victims' progression?" she asked.

General blankness. Progression? What progression?

"Okay," Selma continued. "Put it this way. If I was to ask you whether the next victim will be male or female, what would you say?" There was a chorus of "male"; the victims so far had gone woman, man, woman. "And if I was to ask you what letter that man's Christian name will start with, what would you say?"

This one took them longer to get. They were so used to thinking of the middle victim as Rooster that many of them had forgotten his real name: Dennis.

Cindy. Dennis. Emily.

"Alphabet?" Patrese said. "You really think so?"

"C-D-E. What are the odds of that falling naturally?"

"I guess. But what are we going to do? Warn every man whose name begins with F to watch his ass? Every Freddie, Felix, Franklin, Felipe?"

"Every Franco?"

There was a sudden churning in Patrese's gut.

"Oh, no," he said. "He comes after me, he's gonna wish he hadn't."

"We can give you protection."

Patrese patted his Smith & Wesson. "I got all the protection I need."

"Franco, someone broke into your house the other night and tried to kill you."

"That might have been nothing to do with this."

"Don't be dumb. You're a potential target."

"So are hundreds of other people. There's nothing in the pattern to indicate this guy's targeting law enforcement. None of the other victims have had anything to do with the Bureau or the police department. I'm not being babysat by two good officers who've got better things to do with their time."

"I'm just saying . . ."

"And I'm not listening."

There was an uncomfortable silence, as though the uniforms in the room were being forced to listen to a domestic dispute and didn't quite know where to look. Selma raised her hands in surrender. "Okay. Question is, do we tell the public?"

"And panic a lot of good people? No way. If you say, 'Men whose name begins with F, watch out,' then you have to do it for women with G, men with H, all the way through the alphabet, A to—"

"Oh, my goodness." The implication occurred to them both at the same time. "You don't think . . . ?"

"I can't see how, but yes, you gotta ask—what if Cindy wasn't the first?"

They put three uniforms onto the missing-persons detail.

As with amputees, there was no single, central database to make their task easier. Instead they had to try several avenues. The police had their own list, but many folks never reported missing persons to the police, either because they felt nothing good would come of it or because the reason those persons were missing was that they were on the run from the law in the first place. So, too, with the Bureau, which in any case tended to concentrate on people whom they felt would cross state lines.

Then there were milk carton manufacturers, neighborhood fliers, and Internet forums, the last of these flashing screen litanies of heartbreakingly estranged families, amoral hucksters offering nonexistent investigative services at thousands of dollars a pop, and the odd imbecile wanting to know the best place to watch Mardi Gras.

The uniforms were told to start with the most recent cases and work back. Three people dead inside ten days suggested that if there were more victims yet to be found, they'd have been killed pretty recently.

Patrese didn't say so, as he didn't want to undermine the uniforms' confidence, but now that he'd thought about it some more, he couldn't for the life of him see how there could be anyone undiscovered. Cindy had been killed in her own apartment, Rooster and Emily had been left on the street. It was inconceivable that someone could lie dead in a residential area, in a Southern summer, without being noticed. The stench alone would surely have been enough to strip paint from walls.

He hoped he was right.

The deputy mayor came to see them. His name was Erskine Infuhr—Patrese vaguely remembered him from Varden's Fourth of July party—and the tan and weather marks on his face suggested he spent more time outdoors than in smoke-filled back rooms.

"I'm not here for the good of my health," Infuhr said. "I'm here because New Orleans is heavily, heavily dependent on the tourist trade. Far as the public's concerned, voodoo's a harmless sideshow for the tourists—right up to the moment the media start yelling about human sacrifices, gris-gris, all that. There's thousands of folks out there—hoteliers, restaurateurs, bar owners—who'd go bust in a week without our visitors. And while everyone knows this city's got a terrible crime problem, everyone also knows that if you stay out of certain areas, you'll be okay.

"But what's happening here is blurring those boundaries. Cindy lived in Faubourg, Rooster in Tremé. These aren't tourist hotspots, except with the younger crowd who don't spook easy anyway, but they're not far from places that *are*. But the Quarter, Bourbon Street, that's a whole different matter. Everyone knows public finances ain't the greatest. New Orleans needs every buck it can get. The tourist trade vanishes, and this city's going under."

Patrese took the press conference this time. He'd done plenty back in Pittsburgh, and he was used to them; hell, he even kind of liked them. The way he looked at it, you could treat the media as a pain in the ass and piss them off, or you could accept that they were here to stay, and try to get them to help you. The press would turn on a dime when things were going badly; no sense in letting that happen a minute sooner than it had to.

So he took every question thrown at him for an hour. Didn't mention the snakes, the ax heads, the mirrors, of course: Those were the kind of details law enforcement kept secret to screen out the wackos. He said at least three times how well the Bureau was managing to work with the police departments of New Orleans and Natchez, and twice appealed to the public to call in with any information they had, no matter how small or unimportant they thought it was.

An hour of talking loud and saying nothing; but it had to be done.

He came back into the incident room just in time to hear a cell phone's ringtone; more precisely, a tinny polyphonic version of "Lose My Breath."

That was Emily's cell phone. They'd kept it switched on and plugged in ever since Forensics had finished with it, just in case. A similar tactic with Cindy's phone had led them to Luther, after all, though a fat lot of good that had done so far. Maybe this time would bring them more joy.

The phone was supposed to be on Patrese's desk, but it was nowhere to be seen. "Where is it?" Patrese shouted. "Where is it? Hush, people! *Quiet!*"

There. Under a pile of papers. He pulled it out and tossed it to Selma; she could pretend to be Emily if need be.

"Hello?"

"Could I speak with Emily Stark, please?"

"That's correct." Not an outright lie, which should keep the lawyers happy.

"Ms. Stark, this is Milan Medical Center. We're calling about your appointment."

"What about it?"

"Well, you didn't keep it, and we were wondering why, and whether you'd like to reschedule. As you know, the state-mandated twenty-four-hour consideration period is now over, and—"

State-mandated twenty-four-hour consideration period. What sort of medical procedure required such a safeguard?

"This is about the termination, right?"

"That's right."

Selma hung up, picked up one of the landlines, and dialed the coroner's office. Three transfers and two bursts of tinned hold Muzak later, she was put through to the duty pathologist.

Yes, he'd just finished Emily Stark's autopsy. No, he hadn't done it earlier; there was a backlog. Yes, he'd been about to have the report typed up and sent over. No, he hadn't felt the need to phone through preliminary findings. Yes, Emily had been pregnant; eight or nine weeks, by the look of it.

"Let's go," Selma said to Patrese.

Finding the Milan Medical Center wasn't the problem. Getting into it was.

Protesters thronged the sidewalk five or six deep. Patrese guessed about a hundred people in all, jabbing placards angrily at the sky or in the faces of passersby. STOP ABORTION. NO CHRISTIAN SHOULD VOTE FOR DEAD BABIES. IT'S A CHILD, NOT A CHOICE. Three women were dressed as angels, white dresses stained from the waist down with what was meant to be blood.

The police had formed a cordon around the front of the medical center itself. A dozen or so officers shifted uneasily from foot to foot, eyes flickering as they looked for trouble.

A large black man, sweating profusely in the heat, was shouting into a microphone.

"When God destroyed his *own* city of Jerusalem, and his *own* temple, and his *own* people, the Scripture says: 'Surely at the commandment of the Lord came this upon Judah, to remove them out of his sight, for the sins of Manasseh'—you know who Manasseh was? He was a wicked man, a king who sacrificed children, and what is abortion if not *exactly that?*—'for the sins of Manasseh according to all that he did; and also for the innocent blood that he shed: for he filled Jerusalem with innocent blood which the Lord would not pardon.' Oh, New Orleans, repent of your innocent blood shed before God sends his divine judgment on you!"

The man turned to stare at Patrese.

"Are you a deathscort, young man?"

"Excuse me?"

"A deathscort. Come to walk your whore inside so you can help kill her baby."

"You get out of my face before I hurt you."

Patrese held his badge up. The uniforms cordoning off the clinic moved swiftly into position, clearing a corridor for him and Selma through the crowd. It wasn't quite as elegant as Moses and the Red Sea, but it did the job.

The Milan Medical Center's reception room was painted in soft colors, and Kenny G was playing through the wall-mounted speakers at the annoyingly precise level where Patrese could neither ignore it nor hear it without straining. All designed to soothe, no doubt, and make the experience as painless as possible.

Patrese saw the elephant in the room immediately, though it was an absence rather than a presence. Pretty much every medical establishment he'd ever been in had laid out toys for children or tacked up posters of laughing, loving families.

Not this one. This was no place for children, in every way.

There were four women—three black, one white—waiting in reception, all of them fixated on their respective magazines as though the text within was the most engrossing narrative ever committed to paper. No nervous chitchat or smiles of mutual support. This wasn't a doctor's waiting room, where your ailment could be one of a thousand, or even imaginary. Here, everyone knew the reason for everyone else's visit, and none of them wanted to be here.

"Help you?" the receptionist said.

Selma held her badge low in front of her, so that only the receptionist could see it.

"We'd like to talk to the manager," she said.

"She's very busy today."

"So are we."

The receptionist considered this for a moment, then said: "If you take a seat over there, I'll—"

"We're not taking a seat anywhere. You're gonna buzz us through. *Now.*"

The manager was several years past forty and had a birthmark on her right cheek that looked as though she'd spilled claret there. Blinking uncertainly behind tortoiseshell eyeglasses, she introduced herself as Geraldine Lefevre.

"Help you?" she asked, using almost exactly the same half-obsequious, half-insolent tone the receptionist had. Maybe it was company policy, Patrese thought.

"Emily Stark was due for an appointment here," Selma said. "She missed it because she'd been murdered."

"How terrible."

"You don't sound surprised."

"Surprise, Detective, is something I gave up on long ago."

"We're trying to find out who killed her."

"How is it you think I can help?"

"Who assessed her when she was here? What was her state of mind? Did she mention anything, er, untoward? Anything suspicious? Had she come to you before?"

"I'm afraid I can't divulge that kind of information. Patient confidentiality."

"Your patient is *dead.*"

"You have a warrant?"

Patrese sighed to himself. Another Grisham reader.

"We were hoping you'd be cooperative without the need for one," Selma said.

"Detective, places like this clinic don't exist without the strictest confidentiality. I can't talk to you unless you have a warrant. Please understand."

"Ms. Lefevre, could you come here for a second?" Patrese asked.

She looked puzzled. "Excuse me?"

"Come here for a second, if you would."

He was standing by the window. She went over to him, a touch uncertainly.

Patrese gestured out of the window, down to the protesters in the street below. The double glazing muffled most of their chanting, but it didn't—couldn't—obscure the rage twisting their faces.

"You know what the crime rate in this city is?" Patrese said.

"What's that got to do with anything?"

"There are a dozen places those officers could be right now. A lot of people who need their help just as much as you do, if not more. You've got locks here, you got security alarms. You'll be okay if we relocate those officers, won't you?"

"Are you being serious?"

"Of course."

"Have you listened to those people? Listened to what they're saying? The *hate*?"

"Whatever they say, they've got every right. First Amendment."

Patrese felt rather than saw Selma smirk.

"Those kind of people kill doctors, you know," Geraldine said.

"And those people outside—they've made specific threats against you?"

"Me personally? No."

"Anyone else in this clinic?"

"Not that I know of."

"Then there's nothing to stop us from relocating the officers."

"And if one of my staff gets hurt? Or worse?"

"That would be *terrible*." Two could play at the insolent-obsequious game.

"Are you threatening me?"

"Not at all. I'm giving you a choice. We can all do the right thing here."

Geraldine sighed, and Patrese knew they'd got her.

She went over to a filing cabinet, rummaged in a drawer, pulled out a folder labeled with a typewritten "Emily Stark," and handed it to Patrese without a word.

The appointment Emily had missed yesterday wasn't for her first termination. It would have been her fourth, all of them in the past eighteen months.

"That poor girl," Geraldine said.

"You knew her well?"

"I don't know any of my clients well. They're clients, not friends. But someone comes here more than once, you get to know a little bit about them. I first met with Emily when she came in for her second procedure, last year, and then I'd try and see her at every appointment she made."

"You took a personal interest in her?"

"She needed help. I thought . . . I thought I could do my bit."

Patrese indicated the point in the file where Geraldine had noted Emily's most recent consultation, three days ago; the one that must have been preparation for the procedure that had never happened. "You see her for this one? Just the other day?"

"Surely."

"How was she?"

"How do you mean?"

"Was she agitated? Fearful?"

Geraldine shook her head. "She was as she always was. Quiet. Polite."

"So why did you think she needed help? In general?"

"People don't come here unless they need help, most of them."

"Was she nervous about the termination?"

"I think she was pretty used to them by then, you know."

"Four abortions; must have been almost routine."

"The mechanics, maybe. What she felt deep inside was a different matter entirely."

"She didn't mention anyone who'd been threatening her?"

"No."

"A man without a leg? An amputee? Called himself Stump Lover?"

"I'd have remembered *that*."

"You know what Emily did for a living?"

"Of course."

"Then you know people like her come across a lot of dangerous folks."

"And *you* know they don't often talk about it. Especially not in places like this. This isn't the hairdressers, where women tell you all their secrets."

"Did it bother you?"

"Her line of work?"

"Yes."

"Not at all. We see a lot of working girls, for obvious reasons."

"They give you good business, you mean," Selma said.

Patrese shot her a warning glance—he'd feared Selma wouldn't be able to restrain herself—but Geraldine was already batting the question back.

"We provide a service, Detective."

"A service for which you charge plenty of money."

"We make a living, as we're entitled to. It's perfectly legal, and it's perfectly necessary. Always has been, always will be. You ask me, better a place like this—clean, caring, trained staff—than some backstreet huckster."

"You don't have any ethical problems with what you do?"

"None whatsoever."

"You don't think it's against the word of God?"

"I don't see what my religious beliefs have to do with anything."

"Just answer the question, please."

"This whole *city's* against the word of God. Listen, Detective, the people who come here, they don't plan their pregnancies. They're not happily married, painting the nursery, and organizing baby show-ers. The procedures we perform . . . those kids are not wanted. And there's nothing worse in the world than a kid who's not wanted. Those kids, if the mothers didn't come here, they wouldn't be loved, cared for, nurtured. They'd be beaten, neglected, abused. You think Emily could have looked after a kid? She *was* a kid. She hadn't come to us, she'd have had three, four on the way, hungry mouths to feed. She could barely look after herself. Let's be honest, kids who grow up in those conditions—and it's not just Emily, it's thousands like her—don't stand a chance, most of 'em. They're not gonna be Nobel Prize winners. They're gonna be crack dealers, pimps, pushers, whores.

They're gonna be in and out of jail. They're gonna kill people, they're gonna get killed."

"So you think you're doing society a favor?"

"I do what I'm asked to do."

"You think you're doing society a favor? Yes or no? One word."

"One word? Yes."

"Well, I got one word for you. Eugenics."

"Eugenics?"

"You know, like the Nazis. Kill the inferior race."

Geraldine Lefevre looked genuinely bemused, Patrese thought: Inferior race?

"What proportion of your, er, *clients* are African-American?"

"I have no idea."

"Ballpark figure."

"I . . ."

"More than half?"

"Oh, yes."

"Three-quarters? Four-fifths?"

"Something like that, at a guess. But what do you expect? This is a black city. Two-thirds African-American, no? So *of course* most of our clients are black. It would be strange if they weren't."

"Two-thirds ain't four-fifths."

"Most unplanned pregnancies happen lower down the socioeconomic scale. That end of the scale, in this city, is overwhelmingly African-American."

"They're black. According to you, their kids are gonna be criminals. You see how this looks to someone like me, don't you?"

"Their kids are going to be criminals because of the way they'll get brought up. In Kentucky, it's a white trailer park. In Arizona, it's a down-at-heel Indian reservation. In Miami, it's a Cuban ghetto. And in New Orleans, it's black housing projects. Race has nothing to do with it."

"This is New Orleans. Race *always* has something to do with it. Look at it this way: You get a lot of your clients murdered?"

"A few. The ones I know about. See them on the news, read the *Times-Picayune*."

"And how many of them are black?"

"Most of them. But like I said—"

"*Most* of them?"

"That's right."

"When you last have a white girl murdered, then?"

Geraldine looked suddenly, strangely defiant. "Last week."

Patrese looked at Selma, wide-eyed, and then back to Geraldine.

"Cindy Rojciewicz," he said, hardly making it a question.

They stayed at the clinic the rest of the afternoon; going through records, interviewing staff, looking for dates, times, connections, motives.

Cindy had come in three months before, when she'd been ten weeks into her pregnancy. It had been her first time at the clinic. She hadn't been asked for the name of the father—it was clinic policy not to—and she certainly hadn't volunteered it. She'd come in alone and left alone. And she'd done it on a Saturday, presumably because Varden had kept her too busy for time off during the week. Saturdays were by far abortion clinics' busiest days, Geraldine explained.

Cindy had been unusual by virtue of being white, which they'd already established put her in a minority of clients. That apart, there'd been nothing memorable or untoward about her appointment. She hadn't seemed overly distressed or agitated, even though it had been her first time. Drunk? Not that anyone had noticed.

Patrese and Selma spoke to every member of the staff they could find, not just those who'd come into contact with either Cindy or Emily, and found nothing useful. No one had come across either woman outside of the clinic, either socially or otherwise. Every member of the staff was thoroughly trustworthy, Geraldine said; she'd had them all vetted by an investigations company before hiring them, to check that what they'd said on their résumés was true and that they had no criminal records.

By now convinced of the case's importance, she also showed them how to search the clinic's database, so they could try to find—well, who knew? More links between the two women, obviously, though

what form those links would take, they had no idea. Geraldine batted the most obvious candidate straight out the park. No, she assured
them, there was no way anyone outside the clinic could have ac-
cessed the database; they had a tech guy come to check the firewalls
every month.

They searched and searched, and found nothing. Neither woman
had suffered complications. The procedures had been performed by
different doctors. They'd come in on different days and at different
times.

When Patrese and Selma had run out of possible links between
Cindy and Emily, they turned their attention to Rooster. Could he
have had a connection to this place? Not as a client's boyfriend or
as father of one of the unborn, obviously; he'd been gay. There was
only one Richards in the database, and according to the records,
Diane Richards's ethnic group was Caucasian, and she lived out in
Slidell, the other side of Lake Pontchartrain, so she was extremely
unlikely to be any relation of Rooster's. A couple of clients lived on
Ursulines, the same street Rooster had, but the house numbers put
them at least six blocks away; hardly neighbors, and even if they had
been, what would it have proved? Rooster had lived in a primarily
black area, and most of the clients here were black, as Selma had so
angrily pointed out.

Since uniforms were already on the case of missing persons
whose Christian names began with A and B, in case they'd missed a
victim or two, Patrese suggested looking through the database here
for the same thing. Yes, there'd be hundreds, but a team of uniforms
working through the list could eliminate most of them with just a
quick phone call to check whether they were alive and well. Besides,
they'd have a handy way of cross-referencing to any missing-persons
report; which is to say, it would be a red flag if a name appeared on
both lists.

They *did* find hundreds: 639, to be precise. Patrese printed
their details out, and gave Geraldine his word that they'd be
shredded seven ways to Sunday the moment they were no longer
needed.

And if they were searching backward, he added, they should also search forward.

"Forward?" Selma said.

"Either this alphabet thing is a coincidence, which we'll only know when there's another victim—"

"*If* there's another victim."

"—or there's something to it, so there's no point just looking at what might already have happened. We've got to look ahead: F, G, H, and so on."

"We already agreed we couldn't warn everyone in advance. Sheesh, Franco. This ain't *Minority Report*. We can't stop crimes before they happen."

"We can try. Let's start with F."

"No, start with G. Woman, man, woman, remember; he alternates."

"So far. But maybe *that's* coincidence. We didn't just look for A here, did we? We looked for B, too, even though, according to you, B should be a man."

He clicked the cursor back into the search box and typed *F*.

"G," she said. "Start with G."

But he'd already hit Return, and the names were scrolling down the screen.

The default sort setting on the database was surname/forename, not vice versa. On both previous searches, A and B, Patrese had had to manually switch the setting so Christian names came up first, and he was just about to do the same here when one of the names on screen caught his eye.

Fawcett, Selma.

Clinic workers and protesters alike had gone by the time Patrese and Selma left.

They stood on the sidewalk for a moment, letting their bodies adjust to the hot-towel heat after the clinic's aircon coolness. Patrese waited for Selma to break the silence. She owed him that much, and they both knew it.

"This is best done over a daiquiri," she said, wobbly smile under glistening eyes.

They found a bar around the corner, half full of people for whom Friday evening looked to be indistinguishable from pretty much any other time or day of the week. Patrese ordered two daiquiris. What he really wanted was a beer, but he figured this whole conversation was going to be difficult for Selma. The more he could show empathy, even in something as basic as their choice of liquor, the better.

She took three long draws at the drink, more glugs than sips, and a deep breath.

"It was a long time ago," she said at last.

"How long?"

"You let me tell this my own way? You'll get to know everythin' you need."

"Sure. Sorry."

"You remember the other night—last night, sheesh, it was *last night*, feels more than that—last night, when we were at Emily's place and you said, 'Imagine growin' up here,' and I said, 'I did'? That's Melph. Pretty much as shitty as public housin' gets, anywhere in the country you care to think of. It's no better now than it was then. I grew up in a two-bed apartment, and there were eight of us—six kids, my mom, and first my dad and then my stepdad. Cramped, no privacy, too much noise, unbearably hot in the summer, everyone gettin' antsy with each other, a lot of hittin' and slappin'. By Melph standards, in other words, absolutely routine.

"I was the youngest of six, and the only girl. Conditions like that, you know where this is goin', and you got a pretty good idea of where it's comin' from, too. Not my brothers, no sir. Other families, yeah, but my brothers never laid a finger on me. My stepdaddy, he was a different matter. Started when I was fourteen or so."

"You have no idea how familiar this sounds."

She opened her mouth to continue, then cocked her head, raised her eyebrows, and nodded; in satisfaction, Patrese thought, not at the fact he'd suffered, too, but that she'd chosen the right person to talk with. He got the impression she'd been waiting a very long time to get all this off her chest.

"First a bit of kissin', then some fumblin', then it started gettin' heavy. Usual progression, though of course at the time I didn't know 'usual' or not, I didn't have no one or nothin' to compare it with. He said my momma wasn't interested in him no more, nor he her, because I was much more beautiful than she was, I was gonna grow up so pretty she'd be jealous of me, and all the boys my own age didn't know one end of their you-know-whats from the other, but he was a man of the world, he'd teach me 'bout love and all that."

She looked up and away from Patrese, not with the effort of recall—he sensed she remembered it all too well—but almost as though to keep the memory at arm's length.

"I hated it, but I was too scared to ask him to stop. Not that he would have anyway, of course. And then it was like he read my mind, 'cause he said, 'Next time you go to church, don't you go prayin' to God and sayin' you've sinned, 'cause you ain't done no such thing. God is glad you have a man who loves you.'

"This went on for a couple of years, on and off. And then I missed my period.

"I must have known what it was, deep down, 'cause I was always regular like clockwork, but I hunted around for all these other reasons. All moonshine, of course. Finally, I went to a pharmacy in town—miles away from home, so no one would see me—and bought one of those kits, and it told me, clear as day.

"I told him. He said it was my choice, but you ask him, we should terminate. Think what it would do to Momma, to the family. This was our little secret, and if there was a little baby in a few months' time, it wouldn't be no secret no more, would it? 'Think of everyone else,' he kept sayin'. One day, we'd have a baby together, but not now, not when I was still so young, not when Momma needed him and me so bad in our different ways. 'Your choice,' he kept sayin'; but it weren't, not really.

"The day I went to the clinic, I knew I was makin' a terrible mistake. If there'd been one of them sidewalk counselors you see now outside some places, some kind and gentle lady askin' if she could have a minute of my time, just to make sure I really knew what I was doin', then maybe things would have been different. Folks like that, they know kindness is a thousand times more powerful than rage. But there weren't no one like that, so I went in alone, knowin' I was makin' this big ol' mistake. I tried to tell myself I wasn't. Life would go on as before, I thought. They were kind, they listened, they gave me all the other options. They saw hundreds of girls like me, they said, and all of them, for every single one of them, this was the best choice, else there'd be another kid out there in foster care or somethin', and every time I saw a kid 'bout the right age, I'd be wonderin' if that was my baby.

"I saw that. It made sense, you know? What they were doin' here, it was all legal. Would it be legal if it weren't right? Would it be legal if it weren't safe?

"'But in the end, your choice,' they said. Just like he had.

"It was over in minutes. So short and easy, for somethin' so momentous. My baby, sucked up like ashes at a cocktail party. I'd killed a baby. I'd killed a baby. I'd destroyed a life. More than that; I'd destroyed a part of myself. There was no word for what I was now. When you get married, you become a wife. When you give birth, you become a mother. But when you've been to the clinic, somethin' just as seismic and life-changin' as gettin' married or becomin' a mom, you're . . . like I said, there's no word. You're an *other*. Your life's never goin' to be the same again, and you have nothin' to show for it. Not a baby, not a ring. Everythin' you have, and you have a lot, is all locked up inside; festerin', corrodin'. I hated myself. When I tried to tell him how I felt, he didn't want to know. 'You made the right choice,' he said. 'Don't worry if you feel a bit weird for a while; it's just your hormones. You made the right choice.'

"But I didn't choose. I was pressured, badgered, almost blackmailed into it. And I vowed there and then that I'd never submit again; not to any man, not to anythin' of what people expected of me. I'd take the world on my own terms or not at all.

"Then I got an infection. Pelvic inflammatory disease, they

said. Very common after such, er, such *procedures*; especially when you've got the clap, which I had, 'cause he'd given it to me, hadn't he? Infection led to tubal adhesions. By the time the doctors got around to seein' me, let alone diagnosin' what was wrong and treatin' the darn thing, it was too late. They didn't tell me at the time, but they must have known what I didn't find out till years later, with Luther.

"I was sterile. That was it; my one and only shot at bein' a mom, flushed down the plughole. No second chance.

"I couldn't do it after the infection; it was so painful, such agony, that even he understood, and that was the end of it with us. My momma kicked him out a few months later—I don't know if she ever suspected about us, but I think by then she knew what kind of man he was—and I never saw him again.

"And now came the atonement. I went to church every day, tried to make sense of what had happened, and say sorry for not havin' let God guide me before. God had tried to tell me, when I'd known this was wrong. He'd tried to tell me not to go through with the procedure, but I hadn't listened to him. I thought I was wrong, but it was him speakin', not me. I went to church, and I joined the police, to do some good. Growin' up in Melph, I'd never seen no lady police officer, *ever*. I wanted to show people you could grow up like I had and still do somethin' with your life, rather than waste it away.

"And that's what I saw today, you know? Those women in that clinic, waitin' for their appointments; I don't know what you saw in their faces, Franco, but I'll tell you what I saw: despair. That's what I saw. Clenched teeth, fixed eyes, lookin' only to the future. They daren't look at the present, 'cause they know the present will forever be their past. When Geraldine said this time around would have been Emily's fourth, I almost cried there and then. You know how many people go back again and again? They regret the first abortion, so they get pregnant again, a replacement pregnancy, then they get the same pressures as before, so they go to the clinic, then they feel bad again, and on it goes. I know it may not have been as simple as that with Emily, but still. That thing happens, Franco, and places like that don't care; they're set up like slaughterin' cattle, production lines. They make money, they're happy. End of.

"And we *help* them, Franco. I know you got embarrassed back there when I started goin' on about the whole race thing, but it's true. You don't understand, Franco, not really, and I don't expect you to. You ain't black. You have to be black to understand, *properly*. She ain't black, either, Geraldine, so maybe I shouldn't blame her, or people like her, and you know why?

"We don't *need* other people to kill us. We're doin' it all by ourselves. For every three black babies born, two are aborted. And like this: A third of all abortions in this country are to black women. When we devalue our kids like that, when we tell them they're worth killin', what happens? Every minute of the day, a black kid quits school somewhere in this country. Every ninety seconds, a black kid's born into poverty. Every ten minutes, a black kid's arrested for violent crime. Every four hours, a black kid's murdered.

"If we accept that a mother can kill even her own child, how can we tell people not to kill one another? God created each of us to fulfill a divine purpose, Franco. You think he looks at us now and thinks he did a stand-up job?"

Patrese called for two more daiquiris before replying. He felt he'd found out more about Selma in the past ten minutes than he had in the rest of the ten days he'd known her. Telling, how one incident could shape someone's personality so drastically. Telling, but not unusual. He'd gone through something similar himself, after all.

When the second round of daiquiris came, he told her about what Father Gregory Kohler had done to him back in Pittsburgh, when Patrese had still been in school. He told her of the shame, the guilt, the anger, the confusion. He'd waited till his parents had died—it would have killed them to find out—and he'd told Kohler that he was going to bring him down.

Then Kohler had been killed. Not by Patrese, but by the killer he'd been investigating. Nothing to do with Patrese, in the end, but looking at Kohler's charred body on a cathedral floor, Patrese had felt . . . well, many things, but above all, cheated. *Cheated*. He'd wanted Kohler to face not only justice, but a very public reckoning. He'd wanted Kohler destroyed.

Yes, what Kohler had done had been years before; a decade and a half, more or less. So what? Rage didn't diminish with time, not when the crime was that heinous; as Selma herself had said just now, it festered and corroded.

What had been done to them now bound them together; a mutual understanding of pain and violation. They'd reacted to their respective traumas in very different ways, of course. Selma had found her faith; Patrese had lost his. Selma had shied away from sex; Patrese had buried himself in it. Two paths more divergent could hardly be imagined, but they'd looped around and ended up at the same place—a career in law enforcement, a way of righting the wrongs done them.

"I knew you were the right guy to talk to about this," she said.

"Apart from one thing."

"What's that? God?"

"Exactly. I envy you your faith, Selma, I really do. I envy the way it gives you solace, structure. But it's not for me; not yours, not anyone's. I don't believe. I *can't*. You understand?"

"Of course I understand. Different strokes for different folks, you know." She drained the dregs of her daiquiri. "You hungry?"

They went down to near the river; the F & M Patio Bar on Tchoupitoulas. It was a favorite with the student crowd from Tulane and Loyola up the road, but being students, they wouldn't get here till much later, so the place was only just gearing up for the evening when Patrese and Selma arrived.

They sat in a courtyard heavy with faux-tropical foliage under strings of colored lights, and ordered up hamburgers, cheese fries, chicken fingers, and a bottle of Californian merlot.

This wasn't a date, Selma emphasized. Just two colleagues unwinding after a hard week and getting to know each other a bit.

Of course, Patrese said. And before they started, here was a suggestion: No talking about the case. Anything and everything apart from that, but not the case.

Agreed.

He told her about Pittsburgh, and what it had that New Orleans didn't: winters so cold they hurt, and a football team that actually won things. When he said he loved Pittsburgh in a way he couldn't explain, Selma laughed and said heck yeah, she got *that,* that was the way she felt about New Orleans, too. Some of the worst schools in the nation, highest murder rate around, a police department that could be scarier than the criminals, corruption so advanced it was practically an art form, weather like wearing a steaming towel around your head, and everywhere you looked not just all seven deadly sins but some that hadn't even been named yet—all this, and *still* she loved it. Hated it, much of the time, but loved it, too; loved it more.

They discussed cases they'd been on; the fist-pumping thrill of nailing a crook who really deserved it, the teeth-grinding frustration when a case fell apart at the last minute and months of work went down the can. They talked politics; Iraq, neocons, idiots in the White House. Not much love for the Republicans either in Pittsburgh or New Orleans, for sure. There hadn't been a Republican mayor of Pittsburgh since the thirties, nor one of New Orleans since the seventies. The 1870s.

Another bottle of merlot, and Patrese's head was buzzing. He looked at his watch when Selma went to the john, and did a double take at the time: way past eleven. He'd thought it was around nine, at the latest. He was having more fun on this non-date than he'd had on plenty of real dates.

When Selma came back, she asked if he wanted to play eight-ball. There was a table inside, but they'd better get on it quick; the place was beginning to fill up now. He followed her through to the front bar; all rowdy jocks and cheap furniture. All they needed to complete the *Road House* look was Swayze himself.

Selma set the balls up and made the break.

"Stripes," she called as the twelve ball disappeared down one of the end pockets.

"Nice shot."

She grinned, teeth flashing white in the dim light. "You ain't seen nothin' yet."

Patrese saw a light sheen of sweat high on her chest, and realized she must have unbuttoned her blouse a notch while she was in the john.

Balls nine, thirteen, and fourteen disappeared in short order, the last of them from an angle tighter than a flea's butt over a rain barrel.

"Where did you learn to play like this?" he laughed.

"Look and learn," she said, bending over in front of him to line up her next shot.

"With pleasure."

She looked back over her shoulder at him. For a moment, he thought he'd gone too far, but then she laughed and rolled her eyes in a *Boys will be boys* kind of way.

He'd never seen her like this. Okay, he hadn't known her that long, and until now it had been pretty much exclusively in a work environment, but still. Off duty, Friday night, and she was a different person: getting drunk, shooting some pool, and flirting a little. None of them mortal sins, sure, but this was the woman who bristled like a porcupine when she walked down Bourbon Street.

Maybe it was because they'd crossed a line earlier, Patrese thought. You couldn't just pour your heart out like she had to him and then act as if nothing had happened. You trust someone enough to share that kind of thing with them, you trust them enough to have a little fun with them, too.

Selma clattered two more balls into their respective pockets, the muscles in her calves rising and tightening as she leaned forward to take the shots. Patrese noted, amused, that he wasn't the only guy there checking her out.

She sank the last of the stripes and, barely pausing, sent the eight-ball fizzing into the middle pocket. Patrese applauded. She gave a little bow and a tinkling laugh, and said something he couldn't hear over the music. He gestured to his ear; *speak up.*

She pressed her mouth up against his cheek. He could feel the warm alcohol sweetness of her breath.

"Glad you ain't one of those guys who can't stand a lady beatin' them."

"I have two sisters. I'm used to it."

"Come on. Let's dance."

She half led, half pulled Patrese upstairs, where there was a small hardwood floor beneath a glittering disco ball. A dozen or so people were already there, caught frozen-strobed in an infinity of strange contortions. As Patrese and Selma stepped onto the floor, "Ride on Time" segued into "Gonna Make You Sweat." Early-nineties night.

Selma danced with a frenzy. Not so much a line being crossed, Patrese thought, as a dam bursting. She pulled him close and grabbed hard at him; she pushed him away and high-stepped to the other side of the dance floor, her hair flying in great backlit arcs. The other dancers whooped and cheered.

And Patrese kept up with her. He was no mean dancer himself—he had balance, poise, quickness, all the things that had made him such a good halfback—and he was drunk enough to lose himself, too; in the music, in the laughter, in her.

Kissing her on the dance floor would be way too sophomoric, he thought.

He did it, anyway.

P atrese was the first to wake. For a second, he thought he'd escaped the night's drinking unscathed; then his momentary smugness was dashed against the sheer, unyielding rockface of an emperor-sized hangover.

He moved slowly, so as neither to aggravate his nauseous headache nor wake Selma. Sleep smoothed and softened her features into a vulnerability she'd never consciously have allowed herself. Patrese watched her chest rise and fall for a few moments until he began to feel like a voyeur.

He got out of bed, spreading his feet wide on the floor for balance, and padded slowly into the kitchen. Headache pills, water, coffee. Morning-after survival kit.

Looking out of the front window, he saw that his car wasn't there. Stolen? No; he remembered he'd left it down at the F & M. Both he and Selma had been way too drunk to drive, and getting a DUI was one of the quickest ways to derail a career at the Bureau.

He vaguely remembered clambering into a cab with a black-and-white logo on the door, and the driver joking with them that this had once been a police cruiser, except now the rides weren't free and could sometimes be two-way. Patrese had thought this was the funniest thing he'd ever heard.

And then he and Selma had been here, alone in his house, and the trail of discarded clothes across the floor suggested they hadn't even made it to the bed first time around.

Patrese brewed a French press of coffee and took two mugs back into the bedroom. Situations like this could be awkward— more than once, he'd pretended to go to work just to get a girl out of the house, and walked around the block before scooting back inside—but he figured he knew Selma well enough by now to be adult about it.

And in any case, he didn't want her out of the house. If he was really honest, he quite wanted her to stick around for a while. They could get some breakfast, go back to bed, make out some more; and then at work on Monday morning, he'd have that delicious thrill of seeing her dressed for business and tip-to-toe professional, all the while knowing that a few hours before they'd been naked and raw together.

He set the coffee down on her side of the bed. She stirred, opened one eye, shut it again, and then opened both wide in unmistakable alarm.

"Oh no," she said. "Oh *no*. Tell me we didn't."

"I hope it wasn't *that* bad." Make a joke of it; defense mechanism.

She sat up, looking around her. "I've gotta go. Can you call me a cab?"

"Selma, *please*."

"No. You *please*. We should never have done this."

"Can't we even talk about it?"

She climbed out of bed, hunched over to hide her nakedness. "I've sinned, Franco."

"Oh, for God's—"

"*Don't*. There's nothing to talk about. Call me a cab. Please, Franco. Just do it."

They sat in silence for twenty minutes before the cab came, twenty of the longest minutes Patrese had ever experienced. Selma hardly looked at him, let alone spoke to him, and when the cab arrived she was out the door and into the backseat at a speed that would have impressed Carl Lewis.

He knew Selma's shame and remorse were aimed largely inward, at herself rather than at him. It wasn't as if he'd forced himself on her, or even talked her into it. She'd made as much of the running as he had, perhaps more. And now that he knew about her past, he had some idea why she was reacting this way.

But it still hurt. More than that, it *niggled*. If she'd just have talked about it, they could have thrashed it out one way or the other, but now it remained an itch he couldn't scratch, and he hated leaving things undone.

When Selma had gone, Patrese walked over to Wetzel's place.

Wetzel looked him up and down, and laughed. "Big night? *Another* big night, I should say."

"Someone once told me daiquiris don't give you a hangover."

"And?"

"They were talking out of their ass."

"Hell, Franco. Datura one night, daiquiri the next. You're a regular party animal. Have pity on an overworked doctor and take me out drinking with you next time, heh? Cops partying harder than medics. Only in New Orleans."

Wetzel was just heading off to Charity, so he gave Patrese a lift back to F & M; not exactly on his way, but he was early, and traffic was light. At a stop sign, Wetzel rummaged through the files on his backseat and passed one to Patrese.

"What's this?"

"What you asked for. List of all the amputees on our books."

Patrese flicked through; twenty-five pages or so of typed names. "How many did you find?"

"In all? More than a thousand."

"*A thousand?* Just from one hospital?"

"That's everyone on our books; men and women, black and white, arms and legs. I haven't had time to sort them out yet. Sorry. Hey, you can do it easy enough. You see those little grids next to each name? Sex, age, race, contact details, nature of amputation. A is above, B below, E elbow, K knee, L left, R right. So, er, LBE means left arm below elbow, for example. RAK is right leg above the knee. AKs are the ones you want, right?"

"I think so. Thanks, man. Appreciate it."

"Pleasure. Just remember you owe me a large daiquiri."

"And you remember you'll be drinking it on your own."

"Don't tell me. You're never gonna drink again?"

"Damn right."

"Until the next time."

Patrese laughed. "Damn right."

Patrese picked up his car—probably still way over the limit, he thought, but no one was going to stop him on a Saturday morning—and drove to FBI HQ. There was only a skeleton staff on duty, of course; it was the weekend. Patrese handed the list to one of the NOPD uniforms.

"These are all the amputees registered with Charity. We got lists back from any of those other places?"

"Not yet, sir. Not as far as I know."

"Then let's start with this."

The uniform looked through the typewritten pages. "You want me to do all this?"

Patrese thought for a moment. He could sit at home getting himself in a pickle about Selma, or he could do something useful and take his mind off her.

He took the list and split it in two. "Not all of it. You do half, I'll do half."

Patrese worked the phones till sundown, by which time his hangover had pretty much evaporated. They'd narrowed down Wetzel's list to 572 possibles—that was, African-American men with above-the-knee amputations—and gotten hold of more than half of them. The majority clearly had nothing to do with the murders, but Patrese had noted 47 to follow up on; those without discernible alibis, or who had just sounded shifty.

Five times he'd picked up the phone to talk to Selma, and five times he'd put it back again before the connection was made. He'd had any number of valid reasons to call her—the state of the investigation, possible leads, and so on—but he'd only have really been calling for one reason, and she'd have known it as well as he would.

When he got back home, he saw that someone had dropped something on his front walk—a potato chip packet, to judge from the way it glinted in the streetlight. Damn, he hated litterbugs. What was it with people, that they'd just toss something like this over his fence? Was it really so hard to take it home and put it in the trash?

He bent down to pick it up, and froze.

Not a potato chip packet.

A photograph, a Polaroid, half buried in the dirt, with a nail through the middle of it, a couple of bloodied feathers stuck to the edge, and a slice of red pepper alongside.

The photograph was of a man's face.

The photograph was of Patrese.

He slept only fitfully.

Left-brain logic said he shouldn't worry about the photograph. If it was another piece of voodoo, and it sure looked like it, he should pay it no mind. Curses and spells didn't exist, so they couldn't work. It was just someone trying to scare him, and they could only do that if he let them.

Right-brain instinct said that someone was doing a pretty damn good job.

The camera that Rafer Lippincott had installed was no good; which is to say, it was perfectly good, but the mysterious photograph-leaver had been better. The camera had caught not just his approach—Patrese was sure it was a man, just by his build and the way he carried himself—but also his leaving the photograph on the path, heaping dirt up onto it to keep it in place, as though it were some sort of graveside tribute.

But he'd been wearing a wide-brimmed hat (nothing inherently suspicious about that, in this relentless heat) and had kept his head tilted forward, never allowing the camera a glimpse of his face. Long pants, long-sleeved shirt, and what looked like thin gloves, too, presumably to guard against fingerprints, so Patrese couldn't even tell what color he was.

Wetzel had been on shift at Charity at the time. None of Patrese's other neighbors had seen or heard a thing; if anyone had been outside in the heat, they'd been in their back gardens, not out front.

And in the small hours, when every noise had seemed a harbinger of spirits from the otherworld and the outline of Patrese's clothes on a chair had reassembled itself into the form of a monster, he writhed in a cocoon of his own sweat and tried to stop his brain from twisting his stomach into a knot too tight to ever undo.

Darkness eventually faded into dawn, and Patrese gratefully got up and set off for work. On his way out, he noticed a small pile of scattered twigs on the sidewalk outside his house. Another hex, or simply the randomness of where the twigs had fallen? He wasn't sure he trusted himself to know the difference anymore.

The daily sitrep meeting.

Hundreds of phone calls meant hundreds of memos. Hundreds of memos meant paper trails forming endless labyrinths of information, most of it—all of it?—useless. If there was a golden nugget in there, a key to this whole case, it was well hidden.

All police missing persons records had been checked, with no match found. Each missing person whose Christian name started with A or B had either been gone for some time or had last been seen many miles from New Orleans, often in other states. The milk-carton manufacturers had provided their own list. Where these names hadn't overlapped with police records, they, too, had been checked out. Internet forums were still being searched, so far without joy. Overall, a big fat *nada*.

If there weren't any unfound victims out there, Patrese thought, why the hell had the murderer started with C? Unless, of course, the name progression was purely happenstance. But C, D, and E seemed a hell of a coincidence.

The search through the amputee lists had been more urgent—this was to find Stump Lover, whom they knew existed, rather than as yet hypothetical victims—but no more fruitful. Hospitals, physicians, prosthetic manufacturers, and the VA had all been helpful, even though many of the names they provided were duplicated on others' lists. A few more suspects had been added to the forty-seven Patrese had deemed worthy of further investigation, and if need be they'd run an ID parade for some of the Bourbon Street hookers to see if they recognized anyone, but again, so far, another *nada*.

The meeting broke up after an hour. For the rest of the afternoon, Selma didn't say a single word to Patrese that she didn't have to.

A lmost a fortnight after the first murder, and—finally!—good news from Forensics. They'd discovered a provisional match between fibers found at Rooster's house and those that Patrese and Selma had taken from the carpet in Luther's living room.

Heavy emphasis on the word *provisional*, along with what Patrese felt was Forensics' perpetually defensive undercurrent: *Hey, this ain't CSI. Real analysis of real things in the real world takes time, and even then we can't always be certain. It's not done and dusted by the closing credits. Cut us some slack.*

The "provisional" caveat had nothing to do with any lack of thoroughness. The technicians had used four types of microscope—compound, comparison, phase-contrast, and electron—plus a spectrometer, a spectrophotometer, and several other machines that Patrese had never even heard of. State-of-the-art stuff. They'd compared the fibers' shape, size, general appearance, dye content, and chemical composition, and found none of them wanting.

The problem was more fundamental. Fibers, unlike fingerprints or DNA, are not unique. Two fibers can be similar in every way, and yet no one can say with total certainty that they've come from the same place. There's not even a central fiber database to provide a probability of origin.

Most fibers have solid round cross sections, which are simplest and cheapest to manufacture. The ones in this instance were trilobal, Y-shaped, which are often used in carpets; not only are trilobal fibers more rigid and resilient, but they also scatter light, which helps hide dirt. That narrowed down the possibility of the fibers coming from the same source, as did the choice of color: light brown.

A half-decent defense lawyer would have the evidence thrown out in seconds, of course; there are many light brown carpets in apartments, houses, and businesses. But they weren't in court yet. They were building a case, and they needed all the links they could get.

Thorndike and Phelps came in to discuss the next move.

The possible fiber link was in itself enough to have Luther questioned again. There were two problems with that, however. First, they'd arrested him once already. If they brought him in again and still didn't charge him, they'd leave themselves open to accusations of racial harassment, always a sensitive issue in New Orleans. Second, and crucial to the issue of charging him or not, he simply couldn't have killed Emily Stark. He'd been in the hospital at the time, with an armed guard outside his door.

"Maybe he had an accomplice?" Patrese said. "Someone who's been to his house?"

"If he has, that's not the kind of thing he's just going to tell us the moment we start grilling him," said Phelps.

"That's no reason not to ask him."

"Sure. But maybe we can be more subtle about it. Remember, we might be able to kill two birds with one stone here. Luther's working for Marie Laveau, isn't he? I'm sure Ken agrees we want to bring *her* down."

"Damn right," said Thorndike.

"And she was right there when he got shot in the cemetery. He still won't say who shot him, which makes me think maybe it's a drugs beef, and either he's too scared of whoever did it to say, or he's plotting revenge. Either way, she'll be involved. So why don't we run something covert on him? This fiber link is evidence enough for a warrant. Go in there, tap his phone, hide bugs, put spyware on his computer. That way, we find out what's really going on."

"How long's that gonna take?" Thorndike said. "Might be weeks. *Months.* We have that long? How many more people we gonna find dead by then?"

"I don't see the downside," Patrese said. "Say he has an accomplice, which explains how Emily was killed while he was still in Charity. We record what goes on in his place, the accomplice comes there, we find out who it is, what they're saying."

"Then we have to do it absolutely on the QT," Phelps said. "The moment he has any idea we're listening, it's useless. Worse than useless, in fact, as he can start giving us disinformation. Ken?"

Thorndike tutted. "I still say bring him in. Ask him direct. Put the pressure on."

"What do you think, Selma?" Patrese asked.

"I'm with Ken."

No surprise. Departmental loyalty aside, full surveillance would provide endless details of Luther's life. Selma would hardly want to sift through those.

Deadlock, then; the Bureau wanting surveillance, the NOPD, interrogation.

No prizes for guessing who won.

The rising sun logo of Entergy, the electricity company, is so commonplace in New Orleans as to be effectively invisible. Perfect disguise, then, for Patrese and Rafer Lippincott, the Bureau tech guy.

They arrived outside Luther's house just after breakfast, their silver van suitably beat up behind the logos. To conceal their faces as much as possible, they wore hard hats and wraparound sunglasses. Though Luther knew Patrese, it was unlikely that he'd see beyond the workmen's getup—overalls, candy-striped plastic fencing, tools, and radio tuned permanently to WRNO. Context is a large part of recognition, and Luther wouldn't be expecting to see Patrese working on his street. It was a risk worth taking.

Patrese and Lippincott set out their stuff and began "work" on the nearest junction box. Lippincott was the one elected to go up the pole, since he had enough tech knowledge to stand a half-decent chance of not electrocuting himself. Patrese stayed on the ground, never too far from the van.

It was a couple of hours before Luther emerged. He was on crutches, and negotiated the few steps down from his porch to the sidewalk with care. Patrese silently begged him not to fall; if Luther went tumbling, Patrese would have to do the decent-citizen thing and go help him, which would blow his cover.

Luther didn't fall. Nor did he give the "Entergy" boys a first glance, let alone a second. He simply set off in the other direction like a slightly ungainly quadruped, crutches and body swinging in strict rotation.

Patrese watched him go, counted three minutes from the moment he was out of sight, and then whistled up to Lippincott.

A quick check both ways to make sure no one was looking, and then around the back of Luther's house, out with the lock-picking kit, and in through the rear door.

Lippincott had four transmitters. Three were disguised as electric plugs, and one as a phone splitter. They all also worked perfectly as plugs and splitter, respectively.

Lippincott removed the splitter in Luther's living room and replaced it with his own. That left the kitchen and both bedrooms; the bathroom was too small and had no appliance outlets, so he couldn't install a bug there without it being obvious.

He chose the kettle in the kitchen, a bedside lamp in one bedroom, and a stereo in the other. Patrese took photos of them *in situ* on his cell phone, and Lippincott set to work. With each item, he unscrewed the existing plug, removed the wires, inserted them into the replacement transmitter plug, and screwed it all tight again. Patrese put the items back exactly as they'd found them, checking against the cell-phone photos to make sure.

Lippincott fired up Luther's laptop.

"How long will this take?" Patrese asked.

"Ten minutes, maybe fifteen."

Patrese glanced out of the window. The street was still empty.

Lippincott inserted a disk into the laptop's drive.

"Remind me what this is doing again," Patrese said.

"Everything, basically. The program I'm installing will record every keystroke he makes, including all log-ins, user names, passwords. Every e-mail he sends and receives, every Web site he visits, everything he writes in documents or on the clipboard, all there."

"And we can see this happening in real time?"

"If he's online, yes. If not, the program sends us a complete log every twenty-four hours, or whenever he next goes online."

"And there's no way he can tell this is running?"

"No. The software is set up to work in kernel mode."

"What?"

"Kernel mode. Central systems. Most important parts of a computer's processing power. The place where the CPU assumes all software is to be trusted."

"I don't really understand."

Lippincott chuckled. "I do."

He tapped away at the laptop.

There was a pile of Luther's papers next to him, and Patrese began to rifle through them, more to keep himself occupied than in expectation of finding something. And it wasn't the papers that caught his eye, but what was beneath them.

The packaging for a cell phone.

Pay-as-you-go, by the look of it; number one choice for criminals nationwide, since pay-as-you-go phones don't need personal registration. Of the phone itself, there was no sign, but the phone number was helpfully printed on the outside of the box. Patrese eased it into Lippincott's sight line.

"That any good to you?"

Lippincott glanced down. "Oh yes." He took a pen and small pad from his pocket, wrote down the phone number, twisted the box around till he found another number, wrote this one down, too—it was longer than the first, Patrese saw—and then turned his attention back to the screen.

"Three minutes, and we're out of here."

Patrese went back to the window and looked out.

"Three minutes?"

"Yup."

"Can you make it any faster?"

"Not really. Why?"

"'Cause Luther's coming back."

Patrese did a quick calculation. Luther was a couple of hundred yards away, but with crutches, the heat, and a grocery bag hanging from one wrist, he was moving slowly. It was that, and only that, that would give them a chance.

He stepped quickly back to the laptop.

Installing. 82 percent complete.

"Is there any way of making it go quicker?" he asked Lippincott.

"No."

"What if you just end it now? Won't most of it be installed?"

"No. The whole thing has to be done, or else it won't work at all."

Patrese went back to the window. Luther was closer now.

What to do? If they could find a way to stall him . . . but how? Anything that involved Patrese talking to Luther was out; Luther would recognize him then, Entergy uniform or not.

Patrese could send Lippincott out there while he, Patrese, finished the installation—how hard could it be, to click on a dialogue box a couple of times?—but there was no way either of them could get out, even around the back way, and onto the sidewalk without Luther seeing them emerge from his house.

If Luther found them, the whole covert surveillance operation would be off; their best, perhaps only, chance gone.

Installing. 90 percent complete.

No one else on the street. No nice old grandma to exchange pleasantries with Luther, ask him how his leg was, Jeez ain't it hot, gets worse every summer, all that. No one to delay Luther even that minute or so that might make all the difference.

Luther was twenty yards away. Lippincott had to wait for the installation to finish, pop the disk out, close the laptop, and they had to get out the back door and lock it again . . . there wasn't time, there simply wasn't time.

Patrese's hands were clammy. He wiped his palms against the legs of his overalls.

There. In his pocket. Keys to the van.

The fob had a panic button, he remembered. When you pressed it, the van alarm went off.

Installing. 97 percent complete.

Luther was by the front gate now, as near to the van as he'd ever be.

Patrese stood flush to the wall, next to the window so Luther couldn't see him, and pressed the panic button.

The alarm *whoop-whoop*ed, loud and sudden enough to make Luther start a little.

He looked around the side of the van. The alarm stopped.

Luther shrugged, and made as if to start heading toward his front door.

Patrese set the alarm off again, hardly daring to look.

Luther, puzzled, swung himself around to the back of the van, where the rear doors were open, and peered inside.

Installation complete.

"Got it," Lippincott said, popping the drive open and powering down the laptop.

"Let's go," Patrese said.

Lippincott grabbed his stuff, did a two-second check to make sure he hadn't left anything, and bolted for the back door, Patrese hard on his heels. They were closing the door behind them when they heard Luther come in the front. Patrese took the lock pick from his pocket and, clamping it tight between slippery fingers, locked the door again.

Sweat sprung from Lippincott's forehead in great, monsoon-sized drops.

"Just the heat," he said, wiping the sweat away with the back of his hand.

"Just the heat," Patrese agreed.

Back at the office, Lippincott checked that the transmitters and computer spyware he'd placed in Luther's house were all working, and then took from his pocket the numbers he'd copied from the cellphone packaging.

"Franco, you want to see this?" he asked.

"See what?"

"Watch and learn, my man. Watch and learn."

Patrese saw the Nextel logo appear on the screen.

"We enter the phone number here," Lippincott said, half to himself, "and the handset's unique serial number here, a-a-a-a-nd . . . *Voilà!*"

"What?"

"Luther's cell phone is now a roving bug."

"It's *what*?"

"Every cell phone has a microphone inside. Every handset is basically a miniature computer. All I've done is combine the two—

change a bit of software around—and remotely activate that microphone."

"So we can listen in on Luther's cell-phone calls?"

"More than that. Wherever that cell phone is, we can hear all conversations in the immediate vicinity."

"Whether he's on the phone or not?"

"Franco, listen to me. His cell phone is now a transmitter, just like the bugs we planted. Don't matter whether he's making a call. Don't even matter whether the handset's switched on or not."

"You're not serious?"

"I'm perfectly serious. The only way he can disable it is to take the battery out."

"How many people do you know who take the battery out of their phones?"

"Exactly."

"Rafer, man, you're a genius. But listen: Is this legal?"

"You want legal, Franco, or you want to get results?"

Results. Patrese could barely remember what they felt like.

It wasn't through lack of effort that they'd come up short. The task force working on this case, Bureau and NOPD personnel alike, had been pounding away like dervishes at any and every lead they could find.

They'd interviewed everyone on the various amputee lists, and brought the most likely suspects in for an ID parade with a couple of the Bourbon Street hookers behind the one-way glass. No joy.

They'd gone through every Internet missing-persons forum out there, to add to all the official lists. No joy.

They'd checked religious radicals and those previously convicted of hate crimes—specifically, attacks on gays, prostitutes, and abortion clinics. No joy.

They'd constantly monitored the surveillance transmitters in Luther's house, and the most exciting thing they'd found was that he liked to watch *Judge Judy.*

Patrese went home at four, having been at the station since dawn. His mind was whirling around and around in fruitless circles, like a dog chasing its tail. He needed to go for a run and exhaust himself into some kind of tranquillity.

Only lunatics went running mid-afternoon in a Louisiana summer. Suited Patrese just fine. Maybe he'd come across the killer on the way.

He changed into his running gear and began to warm up. Even the simple act of stretching was an instant comfort; it reminded him of being in the locker room before big football games, priming his body.

He followed his old routine, in front of a mirror as always to ensure correct posture. Start at the feet and work up: ankles twisted first one way, then the other; calves extended by leaning against the wall and pressing heels flat against the ground; sitting on the floor with legs straight out in front of him and reaching forward to work the hamstrings; back on his feet now for the quad stretch, grabbing his right foot with his right hand and pulling it up toward his butt as he balanced on his left foot . . .

. . . and stop.

Patrese held the position, staring at himself in the mirror.

And he knew. He *knew*.

Patrese had read Emily's diary so often he could quote whole chunks of it verbatim.

The first time she'd met Stump Lover, she'd written:

> *He only got one leg himself, came in on crutches, kept his pants on throughout as he says there's sores and stuff on his stump where it got infected I really thought I was gonna barf right there!!!!*

And, since Patrese knew what the diary said, he also knew what it *didn't* say: that, in any of Stump Lover's subsequent visits to Emily, he'd ever taken off his pants and showed her his stump, even though he'd seemed obsessed with hers.

What if Stump Lover wasn't an amputee at all? That would explain why he hadn't shown up on any of their lists. What if he'd tucked his leg up inside his pants, presumably tying his ankle to his thigh? Then he'd have looked just like Patrese had while doing his quad stretch; like a man whose leg stopped at the knee.

An able-bodied man with an amputee fixation so strong that he was prepared to go through the considerable discomfort of strapping his leg up for hours at a time. Why? For sympathy from Emily? To pretend to be an amputee himself? Both?

Patrese heard Wetzel's car draw up outside, and went out to meet him.

"Hey, Franco." Wetzel registered Patrese's shorts and sneakers. "You're a braver man than I am, in this heat."

"Actually, I might skip the run. I just had an idea."

"I know what *your* ideas are like."

"You ever come across folks pretending to be amputees when they're not?"

"This for your case?"

"Yup."

Wetzel thought for a sec. "Sort of."

"How do you mean, sort of?"

"People pretending to be amputees, not as such, though nothing would surprise me anymore. But there was a guy I heard about the other day. Came into Charity wanting his arm cut off."

"What was wrong with him?"

"Nothing."

"*Nothing?*"

"That was the weird part. His arm was perfectly healthy."

"So why'd he want it cut off?"

"Said it felt strange and he'd only feel complete without it."

"Complete *without* it? That doesn't make sense."

"Does if you're a wacko."

"What did they say to him?"

"What do you think? Referred him to a psychiatrist."

"You remember which one?"

"I can find out. Is it urgent?"

"Do I ever ask you anything that isn't?"

Algiers Point is a quiet, handsome neighborhood; quiet due to its position across the Mississippi from New Orleans proper, and handsome enough with all its nineteenth-century houses to be deemed a National Historic District.

Irene Kolker lived in one of these houses, on the corner of Pelican and Bermuda; all high ceilings, polished wood floors, crown molding, and a rear screened porch. She ran her psychiatric practice from two of the downstairs rooms, where the decor, neutral and calm, was a good deal quieter and more relaxed than the minds of those who came to see her there.

She was good, which meant she was busy, which in turn meant she could give Patrese and Selma no more than twenty minutes between appointments. That was fair enough, Patrese thought. No shrink worth her salt was going to be twiddling her thumbs these days, not with modern America's cornucopia of conditions, neuroses, and phobias.

Selma had agreed to let Patrese do the talking. Perhaps it was her continuing embarrassment at the fact that they'd slept together, or her frustration—felt no less keenly than his—that they'd so far gotten nowhere, or the fact that they now had her ex-husband under surveillance, or a mixture of all of this. Whatever it was, she seemed rather to have ceded control of the investigation to him in the past few days. Not that he minded. The bigger and more intractable this case got, the more he wanted to solve it.

Irene Kolker was in her mid-fifties, at a guess. Her hair was streaked with gray, a pair of reading glasses hung on a chain from her neck, and she spoke in a slow, deliberate voice that seemed almost a parody of gentle reasonableness.

"You understand," she said, "that I can't discuss specific individuals. Doctor-patient confidentiality. Not without a warrant. I deal with some severely damaged people, and their details stay in here." She tapped the side of her head.

"I get that," Patrese said. "And I hope *you* get this: We're looking for a killer."

Irene shrugged. "My caveat aside, I'll help you any way I can."

The manager of the abortion clinic had made the same noises about confidentiality, but it hadn't lasted long. Without a baying crowd outside and a clear link to two of the victims, however, Irene Kolker wasn't going to cede so easily.

Patrese knew which battles to fight, and which ones to leave. He briefly explained the background—the murders, Emily's diary, the mysterious "Stump Lover," and now the possibility that Stump Lover might not be disabled at all.

"You've come to the right person, at least," Irene said. "I don't wish to sound immodest, but I've got more experience of this than—well, than any other practitioner this side of Mason–Dixon, at the very least."

"Which is why Charity referred the would-be amputee back to you?"

"That's right. But the term *wannabe* is used more often than *would-be*."

"Wannabe?"

"Let's back up a bit. In the realm of amputation fetishism, there are three main types of people: devotees, pretenders, and wannabes." She ticked them off on her fingers. "Devotees—stump lovers, in the vernacular—have an erotic fascination with amputees. Pretenders make like they're missing one or more limbs; they ride around in wheelchairs, bind their limbs to their bodies, use crutches, that kind of thing. And the wannabes . . . well, they wannabe amputees, that's clear enough."

"And these three categories; they fixed, or fluid?"

"Very fluid. You can be more than one; sometimes you can be all three at once. Or you can start off as one and gradually—I hate to use the word *progress* in this context, but you know what I mean—gradually progress to another."

"So the man we're looking for—*if* he's the one who visited Emily, and *if* he's fully abled, and *if* the amputation aspect of the killings is somehow important—he could be all three? A devotee, a pretender, *and* a wannabe?"

"Easily."

Patrese pulled Emily's diary from his pocket and passed it to Irene. "The passages on the pages marked are the ones that mention, er, Stump Lover. Could you read them, and tell me whether they're consistent with what you'd expect from a devotee?"

Irene put her reading glasses on, studied the text in question, and looked up.

"Absolutely. Even down to the little details."

"Such as?"

"Such as devotees tend to prefer leg amputations to arm amputations, single amputations to double ones, amputations that leave a stump to those that don't."

"Why? Why in general? What attracts them about amputees?"

"That's a good question. It depends on the devotee, largely. Some of them get off on the way they think amputation makes the woman look weak and vulnerable. For others, it's just the opposite; they get off on the amputee living a relatively normal life despite her disability. The sexy crip, they call it."

"So presumably there's some amputee pornography about?"

"Oh yes. Especially on the Internet, of course. There are lots of user groups, bulletin boards, file-sharing forums. More secretive than other forms of pornography—most of these sites require user names, passwords, maybe subscriptions or exchange of photos to prove your bona fides—but essentially, it works the same way."

"Amputation aside, is there anything unusual about these women?"

"No. Devotees' idea of attractiveness—the obvious aside—is pretty mainstream."

"And pretenders? Would it be logical, feasible, for Stump Lover to be a pretender? Visit Emily in character, as it were?"

"Oh yes. That's the thing about pretending: It's best in public. Experience people's reactions, see who's sympathetic, who's hostile, who's confused. You can also work out practical issues, such as the difficulties of getting around without a limb."

"Surely that segues into being a wannabe?"

"Of course. And this is the stage that is most serious, as it's a full-blown disorder rather than simply sexual deviance or role-playing. We call it Body Integrity Identity Disorder—BIID, for short."

"Identity disorder? As in gender identity disorder?"

"Yes. And that's a good comparison. Both groups need extensive surgery to realign their external image with their internal one. Both groups feel trapped in a body that somehow doesn't fit. In the case of BIID, sufferers feel in a strange way incomplete—maybe *over*complete—with a normal body. They believe amputating a limb—and it's usually *a* limb, not more than one—will make them feel complete. Not just any old limb, either. They're very specific about which body part is responsible for these feelings. And the sight of an amputee, a real amputee, makes them very jealous."

"What can they do about it?"

She spread her hands wide. "I tell you, Agent Patrese, you ask all the right questions. What can they do about it? This is where it gets *real* tricky. The short answer to your question is real short. Nothing. There's nothing they can do about it."

"Nothing?"

"Nothing short of surgery. You see, these people, they're normal."

"They want to cut a perfectly healthy limb off!"

"I know, I know. But aside from that, they're normal. Pretty much everyone I've seen with this condition—"

"How many is that?"

"I can't say."

"Ballpark figure?"

"It's in the hundreds."

"The *hundreds*?"

"That's right. And of those hundreds, all but a handful have been perfectly lucid, rational, intelligent people. No matter how many therapy sessions we have, no matter what techniques I try, the answer's always the same. The only thing that'll make the condition, the disorder, go away is amputation itself."

"Drugs? Antipsychotic drugs?"

She shook her head. "These people aren't psychotic."

"So where does the disorder come from? What causes it?"

"If we knew that, we'd know how to treat it. The most widely accepted theory at present is that it's a neurological failing of the brain's inner body-mapping function, located in the right parietal lobe. In this theory, the brain mapping doesn't incorporate the affected limb in its understanding of the body's physical form. But as to *why* this should be the case, or even if it's true, no one knows. You get people who say the disorder comes because the sufferers saw an amputee when they were infants and always had the image imprinted on their psyches. Or it's people who don't feel loved and reckon cutting a limb off will change all that. Or it's karma for being a torturer in a past life . . ."

"Are you serious?"

"Perfectly. I've had patients tell me they used to cut legs unevenly in China so the victims would topple over, or they were Romans bleeding out major arteries, or Mayans draining blood before the main killing rituals."

"I thought you said they weren't psychotic?"

"Believing in reincarnation is not psychotic, Agent Patrese. You can't say they're wrong. No one can. The thing is, on this issue, we can't yet fix the mind. Maybe we never will. Or maybe it's just around the corner. Maybe in twenty years' time, people will look back and say, 'Good heavens, we actually even bothered to debate this,' or maybe they'll say, 'What were we doing, cutting people's legs off when another solution was right there?'"

"Cutting people's legs off?"

"Yes."

"You—you think surgery is *right*?"

"In certain cases, yes."

"You're shitting me."

"I'm doing nothing of the sort."

"Where the hell would you get the surgeons to do it, for a start?"

"There are plenty."

"Plenty of backstreet hucksters, you mean."

Patrese glanced at Selma, and knew she was thinking the same as him: *Tegge.*

"Plenty of reputable surgeons, too," Irene said.

"So why don't they do it?"

"Because society's not ready for it yet, which means the surgeons would face personal vilification, professional sanctions, maybe even legal action."

"What about the Hippocratic Oath? Do no harm, and all that?"

"You assume health pertains only to the body? What about the spirit? What if you can't heal the soul without harming the body? If you have malignant cancer in your leg, surgeons will amputate without a second thought. They'll harm the body for the greater good. So why not here, where the anxiety of living with this disorder is greater than removing the offending limb? Keeping the limb is to do harm and violate the oath. Removing it is to alleviate suffering and misery."

"I don't see it."

"Of course you don't. Nor should you. It took years, *decades,* for people who felt they'd been born the wrong sex to get their plight recognized by doctors and psychiatrists, let alone governments. Now transgender individuals are protected by antidiscrimination laws. You can see the same kind of progress with abortion. It's not so long ago, not really, that abortionists were backstreet outlaws—just like the kind of guys who'll take on elective amputations nowadays."

"And the similarities don't end there," Selma said. "You cut off a perfectly healthy limb, you kill a perfectly healthy baby in the womb—where's the difference? How far will we go before we turn back to God, the only one who can heal such illness?"

"Listen, I'm not going to start debating abortion here. But what

I *will* say is this: The pro-choice movement uses the slogan 'My Body, My Choice.' You ask me, there are other areas that can be applied to."

Patrese saw the sense in what Irene was saying. Besides, hadn't surgeons made the human body fair game, especially in America? Pay enough money to the right person, and he'd suck fat from your thighs, tuck your tummy, reshape your nose, enlarge your breasts or your penis, redesign your labia, even fork your tongue like a snake or implant silicone horns in your forehead.

And when you described yourself as incomplete, or said you wanted to become yourself, wasn't that exactly what you'd find in every self-help book Barnes & Noble had ever stocked? That was the language in which people talked and thought; that was the way they sold sneakers and educated their children. Nothing was anything without a "self-" prefix.

"So if therapy's useless, drugs don't work, and surgeons won't do it, what's the answer?" he asked.

"Simple. Do it yourself, or go somewhere like Mexico or the Philippines and get someone unlicensed to do it."

"What's the difference?"

"About ten grand."

"People really do it themselves?"

"Sure."

"How?"

"Sometimes they won't actually sever the limb, but'll do enough damage to force surgeons to make an emergency amputation rather than an elective one. Shoot themselves in the leg, for example. But just as often, they'll pluck up courage and go the whole way. Sit across a railway track and let the train run them over. Or pack the leg in dry ice till it's frozen solid, and then take a hacksaw to it."

Patrese was vaguely conscious that he was staring stupidly at Irene, but he couldn't process what she'd just said and look halfway intelligent at the same time.

Pack the leg in dry ice.

The man who'd attacked him in his house had dropped pellets of dry ice.

Judge Amos Katash had granted them a search warrant once before, to impound Cindy Rojciewicz's computers. He wasn't so accommodating the second time around.

Yes, he said, he appreciated the urgency of the request; and no, he didn't doubt for a second that the various pieces of evidence all pointed in the direction Patrese and Selma thought they did.

But—Patrese could see the "but" coming a mile off—Katash simply couldn't agree to Irene Kolker, a respected medical professional of more than twenty years' standing, being forced to open up *all* her files. If Patrese and Selma knew the name of the man they were looking for, then fine. A specific request for a specific individual, Katash would grant. But a blanket order, no way. There would be hundreds, perhaps thousands, of people in Irene's database. They would not appreciate their records being opened to law enforcement, nor should they.

Katash quoted the law to them. In Louisiana, patient confidentiality was routinely waived only in cases of child abuse or HIV infection. Neither criterion applied in this instance. They could demand that Irene ask all her patients whether they consented to their records being handed over to law enforcement, but that would take days, perhaps weeks, and in any case, no patient would be obliged to give their consent. If the killer *was* on Irene's books, he would hardly accede to the request, which meant his records would remain confidential and the cops would be none the wiser.

They argued for forty-five minutes. Whatever Patrese tried, Katash was unmoved. Every other judge in the city would tell them the same thing, he said. What they needed to do was go away, find a name, and come back.

But they wouldn't know the name without access to the database, Patrese replied. Catch-22.

Sorry, Katash said; not his problem.

On the sidewalk outside, Patrese took several deep breaths to stop himself from screaming in frustration.

"Don't worry about it," Selma said. "You did good in there."

He gave her a weak, quizzical smile. "Huh?"

"I said, you did good in there."

"I heard what you said. It's just—"

"The first nice thing I've said to you all week?"

"You got it."

She puffed her cheeks out. "Listen, I've been meaning to talk to you about that."

"You already did."

"I did?"

"You said you *didn't* want to talk about it."

"Franco, I've been a jerk. Don't you be a jerk, too." She paused, and for once he didn't hurry into the gap. "What we did last week . . . I've never done anything like that before. *Ever.* If I've reacted badly, that's why. 'Cause it's all new to me. It's nothing to do with you. It wasn't your fault, you didn't force me into it, I don't blame you. You're a lovely guy. I like workin' with you, I like hangin' out with you, all that."

"But?"

"Heck, Franco. You wanna know somethin'? You're the third guy I've ever slept with. The third. Just the third. And that includes my stepdaddy, which weren't exactly a case of consentin' adults. Just you and Luther. So it's not a situation I'm used to, and then havin' to see you every day . . . I didn't know how to deal with it, so I just *didn't* deal with it. And now I'm trying to."

"I don't know what to say."

"Then don't say anythin'. Just listen to what I'm sayin', and if you can forgive me, I'd appreciate that. I'd like to start again."

"Start again?"

"Back to where we were this time last week. *Before* the daiquiris."

Disappointment shivered across Patrese's face, and he wasn't quite quick enough to catch it. Selma batted a hand against her chest. "Heck, Franco . . . I thought you wouldn't care."

"I told you I cared."

"But not about *that*. You must have been with a whole heap of women."

That was true enough. Any number he gave—half the real total, a quarter, even a tenth—would seem unimaginably high to her.

He was still thinking how best to answer this when his cell phone rang.

"Patrese."

"Franco, Tony Wattana here."

"Hey, Tony. What's up?"

"I . . . I need help. It's my dad. He's been arrested."

"In Thailand?"

"Yeah."

"What for?"

"They're saying he stole money. From the reconstruction fund."

Millions of dollars had been sent to Thailand after the tsunami, Patrese knew.

"And did he?"

"Did he what?"

"Steal money?"

"He says it was a misunderstanding."

Patrese was about to ask how much money the misunderstanding involved, and then thought better of it. Money was money. Either Panupong Wattana had stolen or he hadn't.

"What do you want me to do?" Patrese asked.

"I don't know. You're with the FBI, you have contacts. Talk to people, I guess."

"Tony, this is something for the authorities in Thailand, not me."

"The authorities in Thailand are politically motivated."

The lines between politics and business were blurred wherever Patrese looked. The lines between politics, business, and crime, too, perhaps.

"Tony, I'm going to ask you a question, and I want you to answer honestly, okay?"

"Sure."

"Did your father steal that money?"

Patrese wasn't listening for the answer. He was listening for the pause before Tony answered, and it was right there, just as Patrese had expected.

"No," Tony said. "He didn't. I'm sure he didn't."

"Tony?"

"Yes?"

"Tell your dad he can go to hell."

P atrese had barely opened his *Times-Picayune* when the head-line shrieked at him.

SNAKE WOMAN LOSES EMINENT DOMAIN BATTLE

Beneath were pictures of Kat South, the bayou herpetologist Patrese and Selma had interviewed after Cindy's death, and of St. John Varden Sr.

Patrese skimmed the text. Kat South was selling her land for oil development. Well, *selling* was perhaps the wrong word, as it implied a level of consent that the story made clear was totally lacking. The Louisiana state government had invoked eminent domain, claiming the land was needed for the public good; in this instance, oil extraction and transportation. Kat South had been given no choice in the matter.

That the Louisiana state government was run by the man whose father stood to take over this land was, of course, pure coincidence. Patrese thought of Panupong Wattana. What Wattana had done wasn't right, but it wasn't unique, either.

Patrese didn't read the horoscopes, but if he did, he reckoned his would say that there was a trip to the bayou in his very near future.

Last time Patrese had visited Wyatt Herps, he and Selma had been greeted halfway down the road by Kat South herself, waving a double-barreled shotgun in their general direction. This time, the first firearm Patrese saw was at the gate, and it belonged to a large man in wraparound shades and a black Varden polo shirt.

"Private property," he said.

Patrese showed his badge. "I'm here to see Mr. Varden."

"Which one?"

"They're both here?"

"Yes, sir."

"Then whichever one I come across first."

Wraparound Shades examined the badge, unclipped a walkie-talkie from his belt, and spoke into it. "Two for Mr. Varden, coming through."

He opened the gate. Patrese gave his best shit-eating grin and received in reply a nod three-quarters of the way to surly.

Junior was in front of the main building, talking with Kat South. Even from fifty yards away, you could tell the conversation was not a cordial one. Kat was jabbing her finger at Junior; Junior had his arms folded across his chest and was shaking his head.

Patrese pulled up and got out of the car. Kat and Junior stopped in mid-sentence and looked at them.

"Am I glad to see you." It was Kat who spoke first. "Officer, what these men are doing is *totally* against the law, and I want them to—"

"I have the court order here," Junior said. "It states *specifically* that—"

"Hey!" Patrese held up his hands. "Governor, can I talk to you a minute?"

Junior shrugged. "Sure."

They began to walk. When they were out of Kat's earshot, Patrese said, "You know we came to see Ms. South here a couple of weeks back?"

"No. I didn't know that."

"It was in connection with Cindy Rojciewicz's murder." Patrese waited for a reaction, got none, went on. "We wanted her advice on snakes. Slightly coincidental that you're now taking over her land, isn't it?"

"I'm not taking over a thing. My father's been seeking an eminent domain ruling over this land for several years. I'd suggest his interest predates yours by quite a long way, Agent Patrese."

Touché, Patrese thought.

"What were you and Ms. South arguing about when we arrived?"

"The terms of the court ruling."

"Specifically?"

"She claims my father has no right to start putting security measures in place while she's still here."

"And?"

"And it's not true. Here—read the ruling for yourself." Junior handed Patrese a wad of paper bound with treasury tags. "There's a summary on the first page. She has forty days to vacate the property—September the first—and my father's not disputing that. But in the meantime, he's allowed to begin those measures, as I said."

"What kind of measures?"

"Security systems. They won't be activated till she leaves, of course."

"Why not just wait till she's gone? You said yourself your father's been trying to get this land for several years. What's another month?"

"He's just doing what he's entitled to."

Patrese remembered a piece *The New York Times* had run earlier in the year. It had described Junior as a "theocon" and quoted him as comparing the U.S. soldiers in Iraq to Jeremiah rebuilding the Temple in Israel: "a sword in one hand, a trowel in the other."

"You're a Christian man, aren't you?" Patrese asked.

"That's right. I donate money to a lot of Christian organizations. I believe in encouraging as many people as possible to live a Christian life."

"Then shouldn't you also consider what's *right*, rather than just what's allowed?"

"This *is* right. It's the history of man, to tame nature. Does the Mississippi River run naturally? No, it's shaped by levees and locks, it's been pushed where engineers need it to go. Heck, would New Orleans even *exist* without engineering? Without its own levees and canal walls? We are the dominant species. We must use such things or lose them. Now, if you'll excuse me, I have things to do."

He walked away. Patrese saw that Kat had started to cry. He went over to her.

"Come back this evening, if you like," Kat said, trying to sniff away the tears. "There's a frog chorus. Loud as all hell, raucous, discordant. Most beautiful thing you'll ever hear. Enjoy it while you can, 'cause it won't be here in a few months' time, not once those asswipes put up their damn rigs and pipelines. They give me a fair price, and say what's under here's gonna keep automobiles runnin' for another twenty years, like that's all that matters. Know what I reckon? This is the tipping point, right now. This is where our intelligence runs ahead of our survival instinct. This is where civilization turns on itself. There's a link between us and the planet, you know. You cut that link, you can never mend it. That's all I ever wanted to do, keep that link intact. Do my little bit to ensure that. Breaks my heart, man. Breaks my fuckin' heart."

"You can fight it, can't you?" Patrese said. "Appeal, or something?"

Kat South wiped her nose with the back of her hand. "Come on. Who's gonna have the better lawyers? Best I can do is just blockade myself in when the time comes." She smiled, as though the idea had only just occurred to her, and she seemed to stand a little straighter. "I guess. You know, I always vowed I'd leave this place feet first. I'll tell Varden sure, he can have it. Over my dead body."

On the way back into town, swooping high above the Mississippi on the twin cantilevers of the Crescent City Connection, Patrese's phone rang.

"Franco?" It was Rafer Lippincott. "Got something you might wanna see."

One minute later, Patrese was in the back room.

The electronic surveillance on Luther Marcq had finally given them something. He was online, logged into an Internet chat room under the handle ABUGHRAIB.

His first posting, ten minutes before, was what had alerted Lippincott.

ABUGHRAIB hey guys just checkin u all still on for tonight

No clue as to what "tonight" might entail. The chat room was entitled "+vdeWy," running off the "ubuntu" channel, and none of

Luther's fellow correspondents were using anything approaching their real names, either.

> AGENT64 can u post details again where and when thanks
> VAN1SH1NGPO1NT this aint no open forum is it?
> ABUGHRAIB no man password only

"This is live?" Patrese said, never taking his eyes from the computer screen.

"Real time," said Lippincott. "Like we're in his house, looking over his shoulder."

> VAN1SH1NGPO1NT u the admin abughraib u vouch 4 everyone?
> ABUGHRAIB damn right everyone here paid dues all cool

"Can we find out the identities of these other guys?" Patrese asked.

Lippincott shook his head. "Not from here. Not even from Luther's own computer. You'd need to hack into the chat room's ISP and check the cookies."

> AGENT64 so where is it?!
> ABUGHRAIB top floor 424 pirates alley get there b4 10pm
> TIEGOESTOTHERUNNER u got it

"Pirates Alley—number 424," Patrese shouted. "Someone check the records and tell me who owns that building."

"Notarial Archives," Lippincott added. "They do land records in Orleans Parish."

> BLACKWIZARD & remember to bring $100 yeah?
> ABUGHRAIB yeah $100 or no entry
> AGENT64 that's a lot
> ABUGHRAIB I know but about 30 people say they're coming which makes $3K and that's what it costs u ask me that's pretty good odds

MIERDACABRON what about masks?

BLACKWIZARD yeah im wearing one for sure nothing personal but no one on here knows my real ID and I want 2 keep it that way

ABUGHRAIB yeah masks of course and remember password on the door

MIERDACABRON what kinda masks?

ABUGHRAIB anything you like

"Got it," said one of the uniforms: "Four twenty-four Pirates Alley is divided into three apartments, all owned by—what a surprise—Marie Laveau."

MIERDACABRON gotta make sure no outsiders get in

WARRRGAMES specially no cops

TIEGOESTOTHERUNNER what's the password

VAN1SH1NGPO1NT gotta be prepared for blood

ABUGHRAIB name of this gathering

TIEGOESTOTHERUNNER ??

ABUGHRAIB secte rouge, dumbass.

Patrese jumped back, as though the computer itself had stung him.

Secte Rouge—Red Sect—was the voodoo cult Rooster Richards had been investigating before his murder.

The human sacrifice voodoo cult.

They had one shot at getting this right, and only hours to arrange everything. If they screwed up even a touch, they'd lose their chance; certainly this time, maybe forever.

They needed three things: enough evidence to justify arresting everyone who turned up in Pirates Alley; enough manpower to effect those arrests; and enough time to ensure that the victim, whoever that might be, got out safe and well.

To get the evidence, they needed someone in there, right in the room itself. Other people might have sent an underling in and chosen to direct operations by remote. Not Patrese. He wanted to be the man in the arena, the man marred by dust and sweat and blood. And if he hadn't exactly covered himself with glory the last time he'd tried to get information at a voodoo ceremony, well, that was one more reason to get it right this time. Besides, everyone there would be wearing masks.

They wired him up as before. Same 300mW transmitter, effective over a hundred yards. Lippincott couldn't say for sure that it would work perfectly inside a building—much depended on the thickness of the walls—but it was the best they had, so they had to go with it. Also as before, Patrese would be able to talk to the listeners but not vice versa, since there was no way they could conceal an earpiece, even with a mask; and they'd use *Steelers* as a code word to bring in armed officers, either when Patrese felt he had enough evidence for arrest, or if someone's life was in danger.

Selma had arrived, which was something in itself, given her flat-out opposition to working Saturdays. Twenty members of the NOPD SWAT team were stood to, some of them having to be pulled off regular duties. SWAT would be the first men in after Patrese gave the signal, with another twenty regular officers securing the area outside and assisting with arrests if need be. That meant a lot of officers, which the department could ill afford, especially on a Saturday night. Patrese didn't give a hoot. If this came off, the rest of the city could be in flames by the morning for all he cared.

Finding a mask for him wasn't a problem. There were several in the building's lost-property department, most of them left over from one party or another. Patrese chose a jester's one with hair in the Mardi Gras tricolor of gold, green, and purple, for no other reason than it was a full face mask. He'd probably sweat like a fiend behind it, but the fewer chances he took on being recognized, the better.

Standing in front of a mirror, adjusting the mask so he could see properly through the eyeholes, Patrese was unnerved to see this jester's blankly grinning visage staring back at him, unchanging. But then that was sort of the point, he guessed. Wearing a mask wasn't just a way of keeping your identity secret from other people. It was also a way of dissociating yourself from what you were doing, if the face you presented to the world was that of someone else entirely; someone who wasn't even real.

A useful disconnect to have when you were party to human sacrifice.

Like many places in New Orleans, and especially in the French Quarter, Pirates Alley is shrouded in folklore. Legend has it that pirates used to congregate there, though skeptical souls point out that this is unlikely, given that at the time there was a cathedral at one end and a dungeon at the other, neither of which tended to appeal to the piratical fraternity.

Whatever the truth, modern-day Pirates Alley is a place whose mood changes not just with the season but with the time of day. On a sunny morning with tourists in their endless Brownian motion around the Quarter, it was full of warm, welcoming laughter. To Patrese, tonight, it felt coldly menacing, even though the evening could hardly have been hotter this side of Venus.

More pertinently, as far as the police were concerned, Pirates Alley is easy to seal off. It runs for barely a block between Chartres and Royal, with a single pedestrian intersection at about halfway. Put men at either end and at the crossroads, and no one could get in or out.

Luther had told people to be there before ten. Uniformed police wouldn't move into position until after then; they didn't want to stop people going to the *Secte Rouge,* merely to catch them there. The SWAT boys were a block away, hidden inside two marked vans. Once everyone was inside 424, one vanload would take up position on the ground outside the building, and the other would scale the roof.

Patrese approached the building at 9:40, having checked for the umpteenth time that there were as few clues to his real identity as possible. The mask covered his face and much of his hair, and he wasn't wearing anything Luther might associate with him, even subliminally. His usual watch was at home; he was wearing casual clothes, where Luther had only ever knowingly seen him in office dress; hell, he he'd even changed deodorants for the occasion.

Standing on the sidewalk, Patrese took three quick breaths, just as he had before the start of every football game he'd ever played, quickening mind and body alike.

"Ready for anything," he said, half to himself and half to those listening. "Ready for anything . . ." *Even a trip into the bowels of hell.* And the thought was only half fanciful.

He pressed the buzzer marked *Top.*

There was a crackle of static. "Yes?"

Patrese spoke through his hand to distort his voice. *"Secte rouge."*

"How much money you brought?"

"Hundred."

The intercom buzzed. Patrese pushed the door open, and heard it swing shut behind him when he was halfway up the first flight of stairs. The scores of backup officers suddenly felt very far away. To all intents and purposes, he was on his own now.

He was sweating by the time he reached the top floor, and it wasn't just the heat. He pushed his bottom lip out and blew upward, trying to cool his face.

The apartment door was open, and led on to a small hallway half blocked by a desk at which Luther sat. He, too, was masked—an ersatz African tribal headpiece—but what the mask hid, the crutches leaning against the wall behind him gave away.

Patrese placed five twenty-dollar bills on the desk, fanning them out like a croupier. Luther took them, counted them, dropped them in a small square tin, handed Patrese a cloakroom ticket numbered 022, and nodded toward the living room.

"Rest of the folks are through there. We got some liquor, some food. Make yourself at home. And don't lose that ticket, you hear?"

Patrese nodded and went through. There were about twenty or twenty-five people there; hardly surprising, he thought, given that he was number 22. Most were men, and all were masked. A handful of half-face opera phantoms, a smattering of butterflies, and of course some pirates; he also saw eagle feathers, tigers, devils, clowns with and without wigs, zebras, elephants, a geisha, a Pulcinella, and even a welder's mask.

There were a few pockets of conversation, but most people stood or sat in silence. It wasn't much of a party. Not yet, at any rate. There was a buffet table against one wall, and a large plasma TV screen on another. Patrese didn't take any food or drink, not after what had happened in the cemetery with the datura tea. He looked around the room for Marie—she was tall and carried herself so distinctly that he felt sure a mask alone couldn't disguise that—but he couldn't see anyone who might be her.

He sat on an untaken chair and looked around the room, trying to keep calm.

After a while, he heard the bells of St. Louis Cathedral chime ten, and almost instantly Luther came in on his crutches, took a wineglass, and tapped it with a fork. The room, already pretty quiet, fell silent almost immediately.

"Hey, y'all," Luther said. "Thanks for comin'. Hope y'all are excited about what's gonna happen next. We all know why we're here, and why we have to keep this secret. So, without further ado, here's what's gonna happen. Everything's set up in the main bedroom, just next door. We got— Could the doctor and his assistant step forward, please?"

The man in the welder's mask and the geisha peeled themselves off the far wall and walked over to Luther.

"Thank you, Doctor. Miss. Rest assured, Doc here is well qualified, he's done plenty of these things, and he has all the necessary equipment. I haven't taken any chances on this one."

And Patrese knew, just knew, that the man in the welder's mask was Toomey Tegge. Tegge had been with Luther in Abu Ghraib. Rooster had been looking for Tegge in Natchez. Tegge was part of the Red Sect. Luther had told Patrese he hadn't seen Tegge since Iraq. Luther had lied.

Luther held up a glass jar full of the cloakroom-ticket counterfoils. "Y'all got your tickets to hand? I'm gonna ask the doc to pick out one of these pieces of paper here. You got the matching number, you're in business."

Patrese's head was whirling. How did this work, this macabre raffle? Your number came up; then what? You got to choose who was sacrificed? Or you went yourself? If you went yourself, who the hell would go voluntarily, especially having paid a hundred bucks for it?

He remembered reading a short story once about a woman who won her town's annual lottery and got stoned to death by all the other townspeople, not because they were jealous, but because that was the "prize." The lottery was an annual sacrifice.

Maybe Patrese wasn't the only one in this room who'd read that story.

When to call in the cavalry? He had to choose his moment. If he went too early, they might not have enough evidence to prosecute, but if he went too late, they might not get there in time to save whoever the unlucky victim was. His heart said better to go too early than too late, but there were plenty on the police force who'd have it the other way around. Not that they'd ever say so publicly, of course. One more corpse in return for a conviction—it was a fair swap in police math.

"Okay," Luther said. "Here we go. Doc, if you'll do the honors."

What if it's me? What if 022 comes up? What the fuck do I do then? Try to find out what the hell's expected, or go straight for backup and save my narrow ass?

The doctor in the welder's mask—Tegge—put his hand into the jar, stirred the counterfoils with his fingers, pulled one out from near the bottom, and handed it to Luther. Luther unfolded it and held it high so everyone could see.

"Number seventeen!" he shouted. "Number seventeen!"

It took all Patrese's self-control not to give a slump-exhale of relief.

One of the men in a half-face phantom mask leaped to his feet. "Seventeen! That's me! Check it!" He thrust his ticket in Luther's hand and embraced the doctor. "Man! I been waiting for this all my damn life."

The others whooped and clapped, seemingly more thrilled that Seventeen was happy than that they'd all effectively chucked a hundred bucks down the drain. Patrese went along with the applause so as not to stand out, though a part of him wanted to laugh at how surreal this entire thing was becoming.

"Man, the doc will take you out back and get you ready," Luther said, raising his voice to be heard above the hubbub. "Now, it's a small area back there, and there ain't too much room, specially with all the equipment and stuff, so I'm gonna pick out five more tickets, and those five can go to the bedroom and watch it happen live. All y'all others, we got ourselves a video feed, and you can watch it right here." He turned back to Seventeen, who was grinning all over what Patrese could see of his face. "Hey, brother. Where you cuttin'?"

"The classic, man, the classic. LAK. Left leg, above the knee."

Thoughts tumbled helter-skelter in Patrese's head.

This *Secte Rouge* was nothing to do with voodoo, or human sacrifice. It was for amputation wannabes, pure and simple. No reputable surgeon would touch them, and they clearly didn't have the money to go abroad and get it done there. Hence this lottery; and, Patrese guessed, the comfort of seeing fellow sufferers in the flesh rather than just through an Internet forum.

Luther had never revealed who'd shot him in the cemetery at Rooster's funeral. Irene Kolker had said that wannabes would sometimes shoot themselves in the limb they want removed in order to force surgeons into an emergency amputation. It was a dollar to a dime, Patrese thought, that the two were connected, that Luther had shot himself—and, by extension, that he'd been the one who'd attacked Patrese in his home and had dropped the dry-ice pellets when he'd fled.

Luther began to pull out the next five tickets. The doctor was explaining to the room what he was going to do, keen to impress on them that he wasn't some butchering huckster. The geisha woman was a trained anesthetist, he said, and would give Seventeen a local in his left leg. Then he, the doctor, would clean the skin with antiseptic solution, before making the necessary cuts; through the skin, through the muscle tissue, and finally through the bone. He'd ligate the blood vessels, pad and reshape the tissue around the bone to make a good stump, and sew the nerve endings in to prevent them from regenerating into a neuroma. After it was all over, he'd stay to administer antibiotics, painkillers, and compression bandages.

Irene had made the case for allowing people with BIID to have their limbs amputated; harm the body to salve the soul. Put that way, Patrese thought, didn't it make some kind of sense? Look how happy Seventeen was at the prospect of having his leg cut off. Irene's words floated in Patrese's head. *These are perfectly lucid, rational, intelligent people. The only thing that'll make the condition, the disorder, go away is amputation itself.*

This wasn't a death cult. No one was here against their will.

But it was still illegal, whatever the rights and wrongs of it, and Luther was still the prime suspect for the murders. Besides, the police listeners would have heard every word. Even if Patrese did want to let this slide, he couldn't do so, not without risking a serious reprimand at the very least, and probably much worse.

"Steelers," he said. "Steelers."

Luther froze midway through pulling a ticket from the jar.

"What did you say, man?"

Patrese could hear the blood pounding in his head.

Where the hell is the SWAT team? They're supposed to be right outside.

Luther began to limp toward Patrese. "Man, what *the fuck* did you say?"

Every mask turned toward Patrese; motionless, faceless, and merciless, too, no doubt, once they found out who he really was.

"Steelers," Patrese repeated, louder this time. "*Steelers!*"

Luther lunged at Patrese, grabbing for his mask. Patrese threw an instinctive punch, but his knuckles caught the sharp edge of Luther's own tribal facepiece, and then Luther had Patrese's mask off.

"Cop! Cop!"

They all rushed Patrese; hitting, clawing, stamping, kicking. He went to the ground and curled into a ball, hands around his head, and gritted his teeth against the jagged sharps of pain; a kick to his kidneys, a stamp on his ribs.

This is it; this is how it ends, right here right now, organs ruptured and drowning in my own blood while the serve-and-protect boys pick their asses outside.

Then the world exploded.

The whole thing was over after ninety seconds and a dozen stun grenades. By the time Patrese's sight and hearing had returned to something approaching normal, the men in black had plasticuffed everyone else there and were herding them into police vans.

At the station, while Luther stewed in a cell and the uniforms processed the others, Patrese had himself checked out by a doctor. He'd been lucky, and got away with nothing more than heavy bruising. If the SWAT team had come in a few seconds later, he'd have been looking at broken bones; a few minutes later, and it would have been severe internal bleeding, possibly fatal. As it was, it was nothing that some Extra Strength Tylenol couldn't handle.

Word came up from the cells that Tegge had admitted his identity. Patrese went down to see him.

"You're in a whole heap of trouble," Patrese said.

"I been knowing that."

"So, tell me this: How did it work? You and Luther. You in it together?"

"In what together?"

"Don't fuck with me, man."

"I'm not . . . I don't know what you're talking about."

He didn't; Patrese could see that clear as day. Tegge really didn't know what he was talking about.

"You mind telling me where you were the sixth, eighth, and fourteenth?"

"This month?"

"This month."

"On vacation."

"Whereabouts?"

"England. Got some relatives over there. Got back yesterday morning. Check my passport."

"I'll do just that," Patrese said, knowing already it would be no good. No one would be dumb enough to lie about something that could be checked so easily, not when they were facing jail time over the amputation lottery. Tegge might be many things, but he sure wasn't an idiot.

Patrese went back upstairs and found Selma. She looked as though she'd been the one who'd taken a beating: Her face drawn with pain, her voice barely a whisper. It wasn't every day that you found out something like this about your ex-husband.

"You know," she said, "finding out Luther was dealing drugs was bad enough, but at least it's kind of—well, not normal, but *understandable,* no? I mean, drugs are terrible, but you don't have to be deranged to take them. But *this* . . . you think it's bad when you hear it in abstract, you know, from the shrink, but when it's someone you know, someone you were *married* to, and all this time you had no idea . . ."

"You really didn't know?"

" 'Course I didn't know, Franco. Don't be a darn fool. I wouldn't have countenanced something like that, not for a second. You learned nothing about me all this time? But listen—"

"Don't even think about telling me to go easy on him."

"He's not a well man."

"I don't give a damn whether he's well or not. I give a damn whether he's guilty."

Patrese ordered Luther to be taken from his cell to an interview room, where Patrese could watch him on the closed-circuit. Luther sat down, stood up, fiddled with his crutches. Nervous.

Good, Patrese thought.

He went in.

"How the hell you get yourself there?" Luther barked.

"This is a cop shop, Luther, and you're under arrest. Convention is, *I* ask the questions, *you* give the answers. You got that?"

"You been spying on me, man?"

Patrese drove his knee hard into Luther's thigh, pretty much directly on the gunshot wound. Luther yelped and collapsed back into the chair, clutching his leg.

Patrese pressed his face close. "I said, I ask the questions. You're in a whole heap of trouble, Luther. If I were you, I'd be dialing down the attitude and going big on cooperation, you know?"

Luther began to massage his thigh. "That's a dead leg, man. I can't even feel it."

"Want me to do it again? Maybe you can save on the dry ice."

Luther stopped rubbing and stared at Patrese.

"I don't know what you're talking about, man."

"Don't be an asshole, Luther. You know *exactly* what I mean. Dry ice to freeze the limb before you hack it off. Dry ice like you dropped in my house the night you attacked me." Luther's eyes widened slightly, and Patrese knew he had him. He went on. "We know you visited a one-legged hooker on Bourbon called Destiny—real name, Emily Stark—and called yourself Stump Lover. We know you've been seeking psychiatric help from Dr. Irene Kolker. And we know who shot you at Rooster's funeral—*you*. You shot you. You shot yourself."

Luther put his hands up. "How you know all that?"

"You admit to it?"

"You know it already, so yeah, I admit to it. But how d'you know?"

" 'Cause you just told me."

"What? You tricked my ass?"

"No. I just saved myself the trouble of showing your photo to the girls down on Bourbon and getting a warrant for whatever files Dr. Kolker has on you. I didn't know for sure, but who else could it be, after tonight?"

"I didn't do those killings, man."

"Come on. Why else did you attack me, if not to try and get me out of the picture?"

"Yeah, sure, but not because I was the murderer."

"Why, then?"

" 'Cause you were pokin' around, and I was worried that you'd find things out. Like this. Like what happened tonight. There's things you don't know."

"Like what?"

"I can't tell you."

"Like voodoo stuff?"

"Excuse me?"

"You left voodoo hexes."

"To frighten you, man. Nothing else."

"You practice voodoo?"

"No, man."

"Then how d'you know how to make a hex?"

"How do you think? I asked Marie."

"Luther, all this makes you look as guilty as O.J. Not to mention that you lied to me about Tegge. I have to assume you're the killer."

"I'm not, man. I swear to God. Everything else you just said, yeah, but not those killings. You know I can't have killed Destiny, for a start."

It always came back to that, Patrese thought. The one major, insurmountable flaw in the theory of Luther's guilt. He'd been in the hospital when Emily Stark had died.

"Then you had an accomplice. One of the guys who was there tonight."

"I'd never met any of those guys before tonight."

"None of them?"

"Not one. Apart from Tegge, you know."

"You could still have arranged it online."

"I guess. But I didn't. Why would I have killed any of them?"

"I told you, Luther. I ask the questions."

"Then ask me. Ask me why I'd have killed them."

"As part of this amputation fetish you have."

"Huh?"

"To pluck up courage to do it to yourself."

"Like some kind of, I don't know, dress rehearsal?"

"If you like."

"That don't make sense."

"Why not?"

"It just don't."

"You have to do better than that, Luther."

"Then tell me how."

"No. *You* tell *me*. Tell me where this comes from."

"The amputation disorder?"

"Yes."

Luther rubbed his hands over his face and through his hair; taking his time, marshaling his thoughts.

"It started when I was about four," he said at last. "I was walking down the street with my mom, and I saw this guy missing a leg. It was one of those moments of clarity you get; I knew, I absolutely knew, I wanted to be like him."

"Why?"

"Dunno. I just knew. It kept going through my head, all the time. When I went to bed, into the dream world, that's what took me there. I got talking to the man now and then, whenever I saw him. Turned out he lived down the road from us. Young guy. Stepped on a mine in Vietnam. Told me stories about the army. Amazing stories."

"Made you want to join up?"

"Damn right. He gave me a GI Joe, too." Luther paused. "I used to tear its leg off."

"Serious?"

"As cancer, man. Pulled the leg off, put it back on, pulled it off again. That was what I did. I know what you're thinking, man: This is how serial killers start, no? But I was never cruel to animals, never wet the bed, never started fires . . ."

"Just dismembered action figures?"

"Yup."

"And while you were serving, you were still thinking about cutting your leg off?"

"Damn right, again. Ironic, ain't it? Did fifteen years in uniform, musta seen a hundred guys lose limbs. And me, the one guy who really wanted to? Not a scratch! Not a fuckin' scratch! Doing the Thunder Run into Baghdad, out on patrol in the Afghan mountains, mines everywhere . . . I coulda tap-danced through them, man. Someone up there just didn't want me to get hurt."

"You ever tell anyone?"

"Not a soul."

"You ever tempted to tell anyone?"

"Of course."

"Who?"

"Army buddies. And Selma."

"Why didn't you?"

"I knew what they'd say. They'd tell me I was batshit crazy."

"So you hid it?"

"I was in the army, man. We hid a lot of things."

A thought fizzed in Patrese's synapses. "That guy you beat up on in Abu Ghraib? The one whose leg Tegge chopped? You were there when he cut it off, weren't you?"

"Yeah." Faint.

"How did you feel?"

"Like it was my turn next."

"So why haven't you done it yet?"

Luther snorted. "It ain't as easy as that, you know. Plucking up the courage to go through with it; it's not, oh, wake up, have a cup of coffee, slice your leg off."

"You were in the army. You must have done brave things pretty much every day."

"Maybe. But only when you have no choice, when the adrenaline's flowing. The ragheads are trying to turn you into a colander, it ain't hard to be brave. You sitting at home with nothing but dry ice and your own demons, it's a whole different ballgame."

"Sure. But let me ask you this: You want to be in the army, you want to be an amputee—how can you have both? You cut your leg off, you can't be a soldier. Not a frontline soldier, anyhows."

"True. But you can do other things. And you an amputee, you doing what normal folks take for granted, that makes you something special."

Ah, Patrese thought; now we're getting somewhere. "*Something special.*"

"You ever been to a military hospital?" Luther continued. "It's like you never left the army. The amputees, they're all bantering and dishing it out. You know, designing T-shirts that say 'Dude, where's my leg?' or 'I went to Iraq, lost my leg, and all I got was this lousy T-shirt.' When you leave the army, you can't carry it around with you every day, you can't wear your uniform no more. But you're missing a limb, everyone can see that. Then you run a marathon, climb a mountain, I don't know. And that's something folks admire. People respond to spirit and determination."

"That's it? You want people to think you're special?"

"Don't we all? Yeah. I do. That ain't the main reason, but it's part of it."

"Sounds miserable."

"You think? Only if you let it. Imagine sitting on a roller coaster and yelling, 'Don't get on this ride, it'll rip your leg off!' Or telling kids who ask about it, 'I didn't eat my greens, and look what happened!' You could get away with murder. Who's gonna yell at an amputee?"

"That's an interesting choice of words, Luther."

"What is?"

" 'Get away with murder.' "

"Oh, man, I didn't mean it like that. I meant—you know . . ."

"No, Luther. I don't know. I don't know at all."

Patrese was back at police headquarters just after breakfast. When Selma turned up ten minutes later, he told her as quickly and concisely as he could what Luther had, and hadn't, said the previous night.

"And?" Selma said when Patrese had finished.

"And what?"

"You think he did it?"

"Everything in me wants to say yes, apart from one thing."

"Emily."

"Exactly. We get past that, we've got him." He saw her face fall, and instinctively put a hand on her shoulder. "Hey, I don't say it with any relish."

She nodded.

"You want to go see him? See if a night in the cells has, I don't know, persuaded him?"

"If you're up to it."

"I'm okay. Had some sleep, feel better."

They walked down long corridors to the cells.

"You're limping," Selma said.

"Stiffening up after last night. I'll be okay."

"You taken anything for it?"

"Anything? *Everything.* My medicine cabinet looks like Elvis just moved in."

At the door of Luther's cell, Selma turned to Patrese.

"You got *lucky* last night, Franco. That's twice now. Next time, get someone else to do it."

"But I'm the—"

"But nothing."

She unlocked the door to Luther's cell and walked in.

It was empty.

"What the fuck?" Patrese said. "Where the hell's he gone?"

Selma looked down the corridor. At the far end was the duty sergeant's booth.

"Hey!" she yelled. "Where's the guy who was in this cell? Luther Marcq?"

The duty sergeant looked up from his newspaper. "Made bail about an hour ago."

"Bail? Who the heck authorized his release?"

The duty sergeant gave a thin smile, the kind of smile you give when someone bawling you out is about to be reminded of their own place in the pecking order.

"Thorndike."

"*Thorndike?*"

"He was the one who released Luther last time, wasn't he?" Patrese said. "When we first arrested him after Cindy's death."

"Yeah, he was."

Patrese and Selma looked at each other.

"There's some strange shit going on here," Patrese said.

"Only one way to get to the bottom of it."

Patrese and Selma took the stairs to Thorndike's office two at a time, and went in without knocking. He was on the phone, but seemed neither surprised nor offended at their entrance. He waved them into chairs and held up a finger; *Won't be a minute.*

"Yeah, okay," Thorndike said into the receiver. "They just came in, matter of fact. Yeah, I will."

Patrese looked around the room. Departmental bulletins on the bulletin board, and on the desk a vacation property brochure, all golden beaches and lush palm trees.

Thorndike replaced the receiver and looked at them.

"This is a Bureau investigation," Patrese said. "You have no right—"

Thorndike gestured toward the phone. "That was Wyndham Phelps. I was telling him what I'm about to tell you."

"Why'd you let him go?"

"Luther Marcq is an undercover cop."

•   •   •

The NOPD had been trying to get someone inside Marie's organization for years. They'd even succeeded on a couple of occasions, but both had ended in disaster; one agent had been blown and forced to skip the country, the other had gone native and become a dealer for real.

Marie, like any gangland kingpin, was as paranoid as she was well connected. Now she knew the names and details of every cop with undercover training within a hundred miles of New Orleans. What Thorndike had needed was someone totally new; someone with the necessary skills, but none of the baggage.

In Luther Marcq, he'd found that man.

Years in the army had made Luther an intelligence-gatherer of the highest quality. Life out of uniform had left him craving something that could approximate the excitement of life in a combat zone. Growing up in New Orleans had given him firsthand knowledge of the city's shitty housing projects where the dealers congregated. And dishonorable discharge had given him a plausible public excuse for hating not just the army but every form of institution.

Luther could hardly have been a more perfect fit if he'd tried.

He'd been inside Marie's gang for nine months now, but only in the past three or four, had he gotten really close to her; taking instructions, running errands, organizing shipments. That was the way of these things; nothing happened without trust, and trust took time, especially when Marie knew the Bureau had been on to her.

The trust had to work both ways, too. Marie had to believe Luther was who he said he was, an embittered veteran cast out on the heap, and Thorndike had to trust Luther to know how best to get results.

That was why Thorndike hadn't warned Luther about the surveillance. Not hadn't, exactly; hadn't been able to. Their agreement was that Luther would get in contact when he had something to report. It was strictly one-way. Thorndike had no means of getting in touch with Luther, since the security of Luther's incoming communications could never be guaranteed. Luther could find a safe time and place to contact Thorndike, but not vice versa. All it took was one phone call answered by the wrong person, one text message or e-mail that Marie got to first, and that was it, months of investigation down the drain, and Luther's life on the line.

And that was also why Thorndike hadn't told Patrese and Selma about Luther's real role until now. Compartmentalization, need to know, call it what you wanted—Thorndike had kept it a secret until he could do so no longer, no matter the sleepless nights it had caused him. Truth be told, he'd almost been relieved to find Luther in the cells last night, and finally be able to talk to him face-to-face.

They needed Luther back in Marie's inner circle; that was the bottom line. In the meantime, so as not to give Marie any cause to believe Luther was getting special treatment, they could prepare charges against Luther for what had happened the previous evening—you could take your pick on what those charges would be, though you could start with running an unauthorized lottery and abetting unlicensed medical practitioners—but Marie had paid Luther's bail (while claiming ignorance of what Luther had been using the apartment in Pirates Alley for), and they could keep Luther out there for months, maybe years, while those charges worked their way through the system.

Patrese thought of the first time he and Selma had been to Luther's house, and the way in which Luther had checked himself in every mirror. At the time, Patrese had thought of it as some kind of misplaced vanity. Now he wondered whether it had been something deeper—the fear of disappearing, perhaps, a constant need to check one's very existence when every face you showed the world hid another one beneath. Undercover cop, drug dealer, soldier, amputation wannabe—hell, Patrese would have been ten miles to crazy with only half those identities.

He glanced across. Selma was doing a passable impression of a guppy fish; eyes glazed, mouth open. Patrese could hardly blame her. Every time she discovered something unknown and unwelcome about her ex-husband, there seemed to be something even worse around the corner, pulling rug after rug out from under her feet.

The wonder was not whether Luther was cracking up, Patrese thought. The wonder was that Luther was as together as he was.

"You think he's reliable?" Patrese asked Thorndike.

"Luther? Yes."

"Why?"

"He's a loyal guy. Loyal to institutions. First the army, now us."

"You'd bet on that?"

"He's given us some excellent information. I know him to be a good man."

"None of us know him," Selma said sadly. "None of us know him at all."

Monday-morning traffic, heavy and leaden in the steambath heat. The cars ahead shimmered in the haze of a thousand exhausts.

Patrese's cell phone rang. One way or another, it seemed to do little else these days. He picked up.

"Patrese."

"I gotta talk to someone, man. I gotta talk to *you*."

"Luther? What's up? What's wrong?"

"Not on the phone, man. You know the Greyhound bus station?"

"Sure." It was right across the street from the Amtrak railroad station, pretty much in the lee of the Superdome.

"Meet me there tonight, yeah? Nine o'clock."

"Luther, listen—"

"Nine o'clock, man. You gotta be there. Just you. No one else. Promise me."

"Tell me what—"

"Promise me."

Patrese spent half the day thrashing it out with Selma, Thorndike, and Phelps.

Thorndike and Phelps, the two bigwigs, initially insisted on the works—snipers, full radio coverage, and enough officers to lock down the bus station in ten seconds flat.

Patrese refused. Luther had asked for him and him alone, which meant Luther would check for backup, and he'd sure as hell check Patrese for a wire after what had happened in Pirates Alley less than forty-eight hours before. If Luther saw either of those, he'd be out of there so fast he'd leave skid marks, crutches or not.

Thorndike disagreed, pointing out that they'd already lost most of their existing sources of information on Luther. Ever since his arrest in Pirates Alley, Luther had refused to continue undercover work until all listening devices and computer spyware had been removed from his house. Lippincott had been around there a few hours before to do just that. So if Luther had something to say now, Thorndike sure as hell wanted a way of recording him.

Again, Patrese refused. He'd given Luther his word, which he liked to think still counted for something. And Patrese knew he had the whip hand here: If he didn't show, Luther almost certainly wouldn't either, and then they'd have lost everything.

What if it's a trap? asked Selma.

If it's a trap, Patrese replied, Luther would have to be a moron of intergalactic proportions to have arranged it for the central bus terminal of a major city.

Phelps had a suggestion. He, too, was unhappy about Patrese going in alone, but equally he understood Patrese's concerns about having backup and wearing a wire. So how about a compromise? What if he, Phelps, came along, too? Luther had never met Phelps, so there was no danger of him being recognized. Phelps would dress as an ordinary Joe, and stay within twenty or thirty yards of Patrese, close enough to help out instantly if needed (they'd both be armed, of course), but sufficiently far away not to attract attention to himself.

One person, watching Patrese's back. It was only sensible. And right now it was a request. Phelps didn't want to have to make it an order.

Reluctantly, Patrese agreed.

Patrese and Phelps were there twenty minutes early, though they arrived separately and didn't so much as look at each other, let alone exchange any words. Dressed in an old pair of chinos and an even older polo shirt frayed at the collar, Phelps had messed his normally immaculate hair into a state of artful dishevelment; all in all, he looked exactly like the kind of guy who'd be hanging around long-distance bus terminals at night in the first place.

And "hanging around" was the operative phrase. Transport terminals are ideal for clandestine watchers, as they can do nothing for hours without looking suspicious. Pretty much everyone in a bus terminal, a train station, or an airport is waiting, either to leave or to pick up someone coming in. Everyone is reading, or playing with their cell phone, or trailing headphones, or just staring into space. In such places, the only people who attract attention are the perpetually busy.

Patrese had a copy of the *Times-Picayune*. He sat on a bench near a bus whose destination sign read TAMPA and turned to the paper's sports section, glancing around every minute or so to see whether he could spot Luther. Phelps was two bays farther along, looking as though he were heading for Atlanta.

"Hey, man. You're early."

Luther's eyes were wide and his voice quavery. Definitely nervous, Patrese thought; possibly high, too.

Patrese smiled. "So are you."

"Let's take a walk."

Patrese folded his paper and stood up.

"You come alone, man?" Luther said.

"Sure."

Luther looked around the bus station. "Sure you're sure?"

"Sure I'm sure."

"I don't believe you."

"I don't give a shit what you believe. You asked me, I told you. I came alone."

"See, I scoped this place out 'fore I came over to you, and I reckon you got at least five guys here." Luther gestured to the pair of uniformed officers standing by the main doors of the terminal. "Not them, of course. They always here." Patrese shrugged, apparently uninterested. "Don't you wanna know who the five I clocked are?"

"No, 'cause whoever they are, you're wrong."

"There, there, there, there, and there." Luther indicated a man picking up trash, a canoodling couple, a woman by a cool-drinks vending machine . . . and Phelps.

Lucky guess? Or survival instinct fighting its way through Luther's nerves?

Patrese kept his expression rock-solid neutral. "I told you. I came alone."

How to let Phelps know Luther was on to him? They hadn't agreed on any kind of hand signal. Stupid. Have to trust in Phelps's professionalism.

"Lemme frisk you for a wire."

Patrese stood up. "Sure."

"Let's pretend we're old buddies. Give me a hug. That way, no one'll see I'm frisking you. Maybe they'll think we're fags, huh? Plenty of *them* around here."

Close up, Luther smelled like he hadn't washed for days. Patrese's hug was not so much a full-on embrace as a light clasp of the shoulders, trying to keep as much distance between the two of them as possible. Luther worked his hands over Patrese's shirt, front and back, with expert precision.

"Okay," he said, evidently satisfied that Patrese was clean. "Let's go."

"Go where?"

"Out of here."

"I thought you wanted to talk to me."

"I do. But not here."

"What's wrong with here? I don't see anything wrong with here."

"I do."

Luther turned and headed for the exit, swinging his body through the axis of his crutches with each step. Patrese followed, though not before risking a glance at Phelps, who gave him the slightest of nods. Patrese put one hand behind his back and fluttered it, hoping that Phelps would get the message: *Keep your distance.*

Patrese hurried to catch up with Luther. "Where are we going?"

"Amtrak."

"Why Amtrak?"

"Public place, man. Wanna keep in full view, don't wanna be cornered."

The Amtrak station was right across the street from the Greyhound one; they were separated by nothing more than a strip of tarmac, a patch of grass, and a Technicolor modern art sculpture. Luther slalomed through a batch of taxis.

"*Luther*. What do you want to tell me?"

"When we're inside."

Luther stopped suddenly. Pivoting on his crutches, he swiveled through a full turn.

"What are you doing?" Patrese asked.

"Checking for tails, man. Whaddya think? You figure I was born yesterday?"

Hardly daring to breathe, Patrese followed Luther's gaze.

Phelps was nowhere to be seen. He must have understood Patrese's gesture.

"You're paranoid," Patrese said.

"I'm alive, too. Just 'cause you're paranoid don't mean they're not after you."

"Jesus, Luther. Who are 'they'? The fuck is all this about? You want me to help you, man, you've got to start giving me some answers."

They passed under a Stars and Stripes hanging limply in the still evening air, and in through the main entrance to the Amtrak station. Away to the left, an air-conditioning unit sounded as though it were on its last legs.

Luther pointed to a mural high on the far wall, all Cubist lines and color slabs, dotted with men in frock coats pointing, shooting, achieving.

"See that?" Luther said.

"Sure."

"History of Louisiana, four parts. Exploration, colonization, conflict, modern age."

"So?"

"They'll need a fifth."

"I don't understand."

" 'Course you don't. Nor did I, for a long time. It's . . . heck, Franco, I hope you're the right person to be telling this to."

Jesus, Luther, will you just spit it out, Patrese thought; but he'd already pushed far enough, and to try any harder was to risk Luther clamming up altogether. If Patrese had learned one thing in Homicide, it was that people take their time about confessions. They don't just dive right in; they hem and haw, take a few tentative stabs, work around it from a few angles, and only get there in their own sweet time.

"I hope so, too. I'm sure I am."

"You're not part of them. That's why I chose you."

Patrese felt a clutching in his gut. "What do you mean, 'not part of them'?"

"You're not from here. You're an outsider. You're not . . ." And Patrese knew which word Luther was going to use next, because it was exactly what Cindy had said to him at the start of all this: "You're not *tainted*."

Fluorescent light pooling on the stone floor, and Patrese with a sense of teetering on the cusp of something monumental, like a scientist a finger snap away from eureka. Around them, people lounged on benches or in molded plastic chairs: the transient, the itinerant, carting backpacks from one place to another in blissful oblivion.

"That's what Cindy told me," Patrese said.

Luther nodded, unsurprised. "Cindy knew, too. She told me."

"Told you what?"

"You probably think I'm crazy, but I swear to God . . ." Luther looked over Patrese's shoulder, and his eyes widened. "Who's that? Who the fuck is he?"

Patrese followed Luther's stare, back toward the main entrance, knowing what he'd see; that Phelps had just walked in.

"Who's who, Luther?"

"That guy. The guy from the bus station."

"Which one?"

Luther nodded slightly toward Phelps. "The one I told you was a cop."

"Luther, I've never seen him before in my life."

"Then how come he's here?"

"Waiting for a train?"

"Where's his bag, then?"

"Maybe he's not going far. Maybe he's picking someone up."

"He was in the bus station. Now he's here. That ain't normal."

"Luther, you trust me enough to tell me whatever it is you want to tell me, then trust me that I don't know that guy." Lying came easy in a good cause.

"Maybe you don't, man. But that don't mean he ain't a cop. Maybe they're playing you, too, you know. You think they tell you everything?"

"Luther, listen—"

"You got your badge with you, man?"

"My Bureau badge? Sure."

"Good."

Luther set off toward the nearest gate: A, marked Amtrak Crescent: New Orleans–Atlanta–New York.

"Where are we going?"

"Onto the platform. Show them your badge. If that guy follows us in here, I'll know he's a cop."

What if I admitted it now? Just said yes, his name is Wyndham Phelps, he's head of the FBI field office, and he's here to watch my back, but he's the only one? Would that make things better or worse? Worse, no doubt, as it would prove I'd lied, and every last bit of trust Luther has placed in me would be gone.

"Or you'll know he's got a ticket for the next train, bag or not. Listen, Luther, you're worrying about him, I'll go sort him out. Stay here for a second, yeah?"

Before Luther could answer, Patrese had set off across the concourse toward Phelps. Phelps was too much of a pro to look surprised; he stood his ground, like any innocent person would do, and turned to face Patrese only when Patrese spoke to him.

"You followin' us, man?" Patrese said, loud enough for Luther to hear.

"Excuse me?"

"I said, you followin' us?"

"I've no idea what you're talking about." Phelps had his tone just right, surprise giving way to mild alarm; when someone approaches you after dark in an Amtrak station, they're as likely as not to be a little nuts.

"If you *are* followin' us, man, you better back off, you know what I'm sayin'?" Patrese waved his finger in Phelps's face, but stopped short of making physical contact. If he prodded Phelps, for example, and Phelps still didn't react, Luther might become suspicious. This was New Orleans; folks got shot for less.

Patrese went back to Luther. "Come on, man," he said, no longer letting Luther control what they did. "You wanna go, let's go."

He pulled out his badge and headed for Gate A. Behind him, he could hear Luther's crutches scuffling for purchase on the ground.

"You got a ticket, sir?" said the guard at Gate A.

Patrese flashed his badge. "FBI." He gestured toward Luther. "He's with me."

"Yes, sir." The guard swung open the gate and stepped back.

Patrese and Luther began to walk along the platform. The train squatted alongside, a giant silver centipede churning with people who sat, slept, chatted, stowed luggage.

"Okay, Luther," Patrese said. "I don't know who that guy was any more than you, but I got rid of him. Now you tell me what the hell's going on."

"Down there." Luther was sweating with the effort of keeping up with Patrese.

"Down where?"

"Beyond the train. There's no one there. I'll tell you there."

Ambush? Patrese had pooh-poohed the idea earlier, but now, heading to a deserted part of the station way after sunset, he wasn't so sure. He felt his waistband at the rear, checking that his gun was close at hand.

They walked the length of the train in silence.

There was a gate where the platform ended, and on it a sign, white letters on a red background: NO UNAUTHORIZED PERSONNEL. It was closed but not locked. Luther opened it and went through.

"What the fuck is this, Luther?"

"Just follow, man."

Patrese took his gun out.

"What the fuck is *that*, Franco?"

"What do you think? All I know, you could be leading me into a setup."

Luther laughed. "Franco, Franco, the only person gonna get hurt around here is me."

They began to walk down the middle of the rails. A train came past on the adjacent track, all white headlights and screeching brakes. Patrese kept his eyes averted, the better to maintain what night vision he had.

Every ten paces, he'd spin around and peer into the darkness for a gun barrel trained on him or a bunch of heavies materializing from the gloom, knowing even as he did so there was nothing he could do about it.

No sign of Phelps. *Could do with some backup now. Shouldn't have been so convincing in warning him off.*

A quarter of a mile from the end of the platform, give or take, Luther finally stopped.

"That's far enough," he said, and sat down on one of the rails.

"You can't sit there," Patrese said.

"I'm tired. Just for a sec." He sighed. "So. You know why I brought you here?"

"This had better be worth it."

Again the laugh. "Worth it? I should say, man."

"Then tell me."

"Put your gun away, Franco."

Sodium lights hazing through the darkness; the clanking of machinery instead of human voices. Far from help. "No. I'll keep my gun right where it is."

"Then what's to stop you shooting me once I've told you?"

"I thought you trusted me."

"*You* clearly don't trust *me*."

"Hey!" A third voice from the darkness.

Phelps.

Luther had his own gun out and pointing toward Phelps in a

flash. Phelps, coming into view, stopped dead. He held his arms up, gun in his right hand.

Patrese drew a bead on Luther. "Drop it, Luther."

"The fuck is this, Franco? You said you didn't know this guy."

"*Drop it.*"

"I ain't sayin' shit in front of him."

On the track by Luther's feet, the faint, fractured edge of a beam of light.

"Train's coming, Luther. Get off the track, and we can talk about this."

"I ain't goin' nowhere." Slowly, never lowering his gun arm, Luther shifted position until only his left thigh was resting on the rail. His left leg was stretched across the sleepers; his backside and right leg were outside the line of the track.

Patrese suddenly realized. The train would slice Luther's leg clean off.

Just as Luther had always wanted.

The beam from the train's headlight worked its way up Luther's trunk.

"Luther." Patrese had to raise his voice to be heard above the train. "I'm not going to let you do this."

"You don't have a choice." Luther's gun was still trained on Phelps.

"I'm gonna count to three. You're not away from the track by then, I'm gonna shoot you myself."

"Then you'll never find out what you want."

"One."

The beam dazzling now; fifty-odd tons of passenger train bearing down on them, and even just out of the station and going slow, it would never stop in time.

"Two."

Phelps wasn't taking his eyes off Luther, not for a second.

"Three!"

Luther twisted his torso suddenly to face Patrese, his gun coming around with it, and Phelps fired, three times, very fast, Luther's body jerking in puffs of blood.

Patrese ran forward, grabbed Luther under the shoulders, and hauled him off the track. Luther was a dead weight, hanging without resistance in Patrese's arms.

The train was almost on them, pushing the wind in swirling eddies. Phelps made as though to try to get across to Patrese and Luther, but thought better of it, and he was hidden from sight as the train rumbled past.

Luther grabbed at Patrese's neck. Instinctively, Patrese twisted away, but Luther grabbed again, and this time Patrese understood.

Luther wanted to talk to him.

Patrese pressed his ear hard against Luther's mouth, the only way he'd hear a thing above the noise of the train.

"Noah," Luther said.

"Noah?"

"Noah." Luther's breathing sounded like a tide on pebbles. "Protect Noah."

Interlude

Unencumbered by questions of legality or the need for warrants, Patrese and his men tore Luther's house apart, and found there all they needed.

Under the floorboards of Luther's bedroom, files on each of the three victims. Names, addresses, photos, daily habits, favorite spots to hang out, friends, colleagues, associates—you name it, it was in there. Couldn't fault Luther for lack of thoroughness; any private detective would have charged thousands for this kind of information. Luther must have been watching, collating, *stalking* the three for months.

And running through Patrese's head, a single refrain: *Luther couldn't have killed Emily Stark, as he'd still been in the hospital at the time of her murder.*

Taped to the underside of one of Luther's kitchen drawers was a typewritten sheet.

Genesis refers to a city in a well-watered circular area. Sound familiar?

A city where the inhabitants give themselves over to fornication and going after strange flesh. Still sound familiar?

Well, guess what. This ain't New Orleans we're talking about. This is Sodom and Gomorrah, and remember what happened there?

God said he would destroy the cities, because their cry was great, and their sin was very grievous. Abraham pleaded with God. If he, Abraham, could find 50 righteous people in Sodom and Gomorrah, would God spare the cities?

Yes, God said.

So Abraham went out, but he couldn't find 50 righteous people.

He went back to God. What about 45? What if he could find 45 righteous people?

And again God said yes; and again, when Abraham couldn't find 45 and asked for 40, then 30, then 20, then even 10.

But Abraham could find only one righteous person living in Sodom and Gomorrah; his own nephew, Lot.

So the angels told Lot and his family to leave, and the Lord God Almighty rained upon Sodom and upon Gomorrah fire and brimstone from out of heaven.

We've known for decades that New Orleans is a place where immorality is flaunted. It's a place where Christian values are laughed at. It's a place where God is mocked.

It's time that New Orleans, symbol of America, everyone's favorite second city, is seen for what it is: a putrid, toxic, stinking cesspool.

A putrid, toxic, stinking cesspool of fag-semen-rancid fecal matter, of murdering child butchers, of harlots who offer themselves to men like the Whore of Babylon.

Patrese almost jumped back from the paper.
He rubbed his eyes and read it again.

A putrid, toxic, stinking cesspool of fag-semen-rancid fecal matter, of murdering child butchers, of harlots who offer themselves to men like the Whore of Babylon.

Rooster Richards had been homosexual. Cindy Rojciewicz and Emily Stark had both had abortions. Emily Stark had been a prostitute.

Was that why they had been chosen? Because of their sins? If so, why had they been killed in such a voodoo manner? Voodoo accepted sins, didn't it? Then again, voodoo borrowed from Christianity, setting Catholic saints alongside pagan gods. One belief system didn't automatically invalidate all the others.

Patrese had always been the kind of person who wanted to know *why*. Most law enforcement work deals with *what, when, how,* and, most important, *who. Why* was a bonus. If the other four were in place, that was usually enough; and so it seemed here. Luther had been the prime suspect for the murders, and Luther was now dead. *Ergo,* the murderer had been brought to justice, and eternal justice at that, helped on his way by the bravery of two FBI agents who'd apprehended him at considerable personal risk.

Except, of course, Luther couldn't have killed Emily Stark, as he'd still been in the hospital at the time of her murder.

Patrese insisted that the case of Emily Stark be kept open. Phelps agreed, but told Patrese not to waste too much time on it. Perhaps the pathologist had gotten his timing wrong, and Emily was killed when Luther was still on the street. Perhaps Luther had an accomplice, but if so, that person was going to be doubly hard to find now that Luther was dead. Or perhaps Emily's death was a copycat. Yes, they'd kept the details of the murders as secret as possible, but think of all the people who knew—Bureau agents, cops, staff at the coroner's office, and anyone any of those people had told—and the total ran into the hundreds. Luther was dead. No more bad publicity for the city. No more tourists being scared and canceling their trips. Let it be.

Every day for a week after Luther's death, the *Times-Picayune* ran ever more detailed exposés of Luther's troubled existence: his experiences at Abu Ghraib; the trauma of divorce; his amputation fetish; the contradictions and stresses of life as an undercover cop; his absorption into Marie's world of voodoo. By the time the paper had dissected Luther's life and laid out its entrails like fish on a slab, it no longer seemed surprising that Luther should have become a killer; it seemed inevitable.

That the articles' author was a golfing buddy of Thorndike's was, of course, complete coincidence.

The Bureau and NOPD held a joint inquiry—strictly internal, strictly closed access—into Luther's death. Phelps testified that he'd shot Luther only after Luther had turned toward Patrese. There was no way, Phelps added, that he'd ever have risked a fellow agent's life in such circumstances. Shooting Luther hadn't just been the right thing to do; it had been the *only* thing to do.

Besides, it wasn't as if Phelps had cut Luther off mid-confession, depriving law enforcement of potentially valuable information. Luther had told Patrese nothing useful; pretty much his only specifics had been in his very last words, which were so cryptic as to be meaningless, even if Cindy had said much the same thing.

Protect Noah.

They contacted every man named Noah in the city, using the most recent census (four years old), the phone directory, and Social Security records. Not one had had any contact with either Luther or any of the three victims. Every one of them but two said they had no need for protection: Of those who demurred, one was in dispute with his neighbor over a boundary fence, and the other believed that George Bush and Queen Elizabeth II were twelve-foot shapeshifting alien lizards.

Patrese left his number with them all; call anytime, he said. He didn't add what he'd already worked out, that if the progression of victims was both alphabetical and gender alternate, N would fall on a man's name; so why not Noah?

But what if Noah wasn't an actual, living person? What if Luther had been referring to someone else? The Biblical Noah, for instance?

Noah had survived the Flood, of course; and Patrese had been in New Orleans long enough to know that flood was never far from the city's mind. Most of New Orleans was below sea level, which meant that every drop of water had to be physically pumped out. In most riverine cities, the river was low ground. In New Orleans, the banks of the Mississippi were the highest points around. There was nowhere for water to drain to. The levees and canal walls were all that kept the city dry.

In the Bible, Noah was most notable for two things. First, he had taken two of every animal on earth into his ark. Second, Noah's son Ham had seen his father naked and drunk. As punishment, Noah had cursed Ham's own son, Canaan, and somehow through the ages, this episode had gotten tied up with the belief that Canaan had gone to Africa, that Noah's curse had included some kind of skin-blackening order, and that therefore slavery in antebellum America had been a veritable celebration of the word of God.

That was the Bible for you, Patrese thought. It meant precisely what you wanted it to mean, and you could skew it any which way you liked. Myths didn't need facts, they needed supporters, and in this case there were plenty around, even now.

Patrese found an online article entitled "Slavery and the Curse of Ham." In the comments section below, someone brave enough to give their location (New Orleans, LA) but not their real name (daviddukewasright) had written:

> Africans are cursed. They are savage and criminal, and have dark minds to this very day. They have never been blessed with even the ability to create the mosquito net to prevent malaria, and they routinely rape and mutilate their own women and, in Europe, white women. Blacks are evil. Without the help and guidance of blessed Caucasian people, the only people who have been manipulated into helping them through their crooked tongues, they would have nothing and not a single one would be free of their anarchistic societies.

Patrese wondered what the author would have made of Selma, a black woman born into nothing who'd worked her way up helped by little more than her own intelligence and determination.

Selma had taken a leave of absence following Luther's death. That he had been her *ex*-husband, rather than her current one, clearly hadn't diminished her feelings for him too much. For the time being, she was in no fit state to do her job. Go, said Thorndike; take as much time as you need.

She'd ended up paying Luther's funeral expenses out of her own pocket. Marie had wanted nothing to do with it, unsurprisingly, having found out exactly who Luther had really been. Thorndike's decision to hang Luther's life out to dry in the *Times-Picayune* meant the department couldn't in all consistency give Luther an official send-off, which in turn meant that Selma asked—no, *told*—Thorndike not to bother coming to the service. Not Thorndike, not Phelps, not Patrese; not even anyone from the army high brass, after what had happened at Abu Ghraib. Just Selma, and a few of Luther's soldier buddies, and some other flotsam and jetsam. A dozen people there, at best. Not much of a turnout for someone's life.

Patrese wanted to see Selma, not just to check on how she was doing, but also because he felt—perhaps selfishly—that he needed some sort of atonement for his role in Luther's death, and only she could give him that. She didn't pick up the phone when he called, call back when he left messages, or reply to e-mails.

After a few days, he stopped trying.

Phelps assigned him to other cases; white-collar crime, mainly. Patrese went through the motions of investigating, of being part of a driven, cutting-edge Bureau team, but as July slid into August, he still couldn't get out of his head the thought—rather, the certainty—that the rattlesnake murders hadn't yet run their course.

Part Two

August

S tevie Wonder had sung about it being hotter than July. In New Orleans, hotter than July meant only one thing. August.

Patrese hadn't thought the thermometer could go much higher, at least not anywhere designed for human habitation. His skin was permanently sheened in sweat, which bubbled through his pores like escaping lava. The heat was around him, inside him.

Thick Northern blood, Phelps had said; totally unsuited to a Southern summer. In contrast, the workmen out by the canal wall had been there since midweek, and they seemed supremely unbothered by the weather.

They'd uprooted two huge oak trees and were now pile-driving large concrete slabs in their place. Routine management, they explained. The roots of the trees provided pathways for water to work its way through the soil, which could in turn weaken the foundations of the canal wall itself. Hence the concrete slabs, to stabilize the sodden soil and therefore help secure the canal wall.

Patrese was on his way out the back door to see whether the workmen were okay or wanted any water, lemonade, whatever, when his cell phone rang. He answered, but couldn't hear whoever was on the other end over the noise of the pile drivers.

"Hold on!" he shouted into the phone. He ducked back inside the house and closed the rear door. "Hello?"

"Franco?"

His breath caught slightly in his throat, but he tried to make his voice as cool and casual as possible. "Hey, Selma. How you doing?"

"I just got something in the mail."

"What?"

"Too hard to explain on the phone. I'll come show you. Where are you?"

"I'm at home."

"Be there in half an hour."

She was on time, to the minute. Patrese made her a glass of lemonade—it was too hot for coffee—and waited for her to start.

"A lawyer called me yesterday. Said he was dealing with Luther's will, and could I come see him, as Luther had left everything to me. So I did."

"And?"

"And everything turns out to be rather interesting. Fifty-grand-in-the-past-month interesting, for a start."

"I don't get it."

"Two separate payments, twenty-five thousand dollars each, into Luther's account. First one dated July eighth, the second July eleventh."

"Just after the murders of Cindy and Rooster."

"And allowing for the banks being closed on the weekend."

"Where did the money come from?"

"An account in Mérida. Mexico."

"Mexico? What the hell's Mexico got to do with any of this?"

"I've no idea."

"And no name on the account?"

"'Course not."

There were ways around that, Patrese knew, but the legal ways took a lot of time, and the illegal ones a lot of money.

"But no payment after Emily's murder?" Patrese asked.

"No. And that's not all." She took a large padded envelope out of her bag and passed it to Patrese.

"What's this?"

"Open it and see."

He did so. Documents; a couple of hundred pages all in, by the look of it. Pamphlets, printouts, brochures, and some stray sheets of paper.

First out of the envelope, a handwritten note from Luther to Selma.

Darling, Cindy gave me this. Said she was scared of what it meant. They don't know I have it. By the time you read this, it'll be too late for me. I'm sorry. I really am.

Patrese looked at Selma. She nodded back toward the envelope: *Keep going.*

He spread the documents out, first over his kitchen table and then all across his floor, the better to organize them and try to deduce a pattern from on high. It was no use. The contents of his wastepaper basket made more sense.

In no particular order, they had:

- A record of three payments made by Varden Industries to Erskine Infuhr (September 1989, January 1990, May 1990, $80,000 each time)
- A piece of paper with the names of three women—Holly Oakdale, Shannon Bell, and Teresa Crawford
- A glossy Realtor's brochure for a development of vacation homes in Paradise Valley, Arizona
- An American Airlines schedule for flights between New Orleans and Dallas–Fort Worth
- A long and excruciatingly tedious engineering appraisal of a Varden pipeline project in the Gulf of Mexico
- A shorter but completely incomprehensible collection of data, page after page of figures in columns without any indication as to what they might represent
- Intermittent records of Varden imports and exports through the Port of New Orleans
- A copy of the 2000 New Orleans urban census

Nothing about voodoo, or snakes, or amputations, or mirrors, or ax heads, or Rooster, or Emily, or Marie Laveau, or anything that might help them in the slightest goddamn way at all.

•   •   •

They took the envelope in to Phelps and Thorndike, who also seemed at a loss as to what—if anything—it all meant.

Patrese detailed an agent to check out the three women, and another to get on to the Port of New Orleans and find out whatever he could about the Varden imports and exports in question.

Then Patrese and Selma went to see Infuhr at City Hall.

Patrese slid the sheet of paper detailing the payments across the table. Infuhr studied it for a few seconds. Patrese watched Infuhr's face for reaction. Seeing none, he looked out of the window, across roofscapes toward the Superdome.

"And?" Infuhr said.

"And we were wondering why Varden Industries had paid you close to a quarter of a million dollars back in 1989 and 1990."

"You make it sound somehow questionable. I can assure you, it's quite the opposite. Consultancy."

"Consultancy? For what?"

"I'm a qualified engineer. Before I came into politics, I had a real job. Twenty years in the Army Corps of Engineers. You know what I'm talking about?"

Patrese nodded. The Corps was the world's largest public engineering agency, with a résumé that included the Washington Monument, the Panama Canal, and the Bonneville Dam. If you saw a dam, a flood wall, or a dredger in the States, likely as not it belonged to the Corps.

"I was division commander, Mississippi Valley Division. Based out of Vicksburg, but spent a lot of time down here in New Orleans. We—the Corps—worked with Varden Industries to repair and maintain the city's flood defenses."

"Was that usual practice?"

"Absolutely. Like any government agency, the Corps outsources a lot of its work. Sometimes there are contractors better suited to do the job."

"And Varden was one of those?"

"Of course. Varden has got more experience than pretty much

any other company in the world. They were—*are*—the go-to guys for all kinds of construction. I project-managed the whole flood-defense refurbishment program, above and beyond my other responsibilities. I was basically second to Varden for a year or so. That's what the payments were for. All legal, all approved by the Corps, all declared to the IRS. By New Orleans standards, that practically makes me Gandhi."

Patrese laughed.

"You have any idea why Cindy should have this document?" Selma said.

Infuhr shook his head. "None whatsoever. That's, what, fifteen years old now? She'd still have been in high school then. She have anything else like this?"

Patrese hesitated for a moment.

If Infuhr was on the level, there'd be no harm showing him the rest of the envelope's contents; indeed, he might be able to give them some insight into what it all meant. But if he wasn't on the level . . .

. . . well, if he wasn't, it was too late already.

Patrese glanced at Selma. She nodded.

He handed Infuhr the rest of Cindy's documents. "Any of these mean anything?"

Infuhr skimmed through the pile; quick but efficient, Patrese saw.

"Not that I can see," Infuhr said.

The Varden shipments all seemed to be entirely routine transportations of industrial machinery. The Port of New Orleans confirmed that the consignments had all gone through the usual customs checks. Varden Industries had been using the port for decades, and there'd never been any problems on either side.

The Gulf of Mexico pipeline project had also been going on for decades, and again without any problems other than the usual maintenance ones.

There was one Holly Oakdale in the New Orleans area—Terpsichore Street, Lower Garden District, to be precise—and an officer had already interviewed her.

She had no connection with Varden or the three victims; had never heard of Teresa Crawford or Shannon Bell, the other two names on the list; and had absolutely no idea why she would have appeared in such a context.

There were no Teresa Crawfords or Shannon Bells in New Orleans.

S elma called early, and got straight to the point.

"We got another one," she said.

Patrese felt a strange mixture of vindication and trepidation.

"You mean what I think you mean?"

"Uh-huh."

"Must be serious, for you to be working Saturday. Who is he?" A man whose name started with an F; that was next in line.

"Not he. *She*. Luther's shrink. Irene Kolker."

The Algiers Point corner where Irene's house stood was usually sleepy almost to the point of catatonia. Not today. Patrese counted four police cruisers, an ambulance, two unmarked Bureau cars, and two football teams' worth of police officers, paramedics, and crime-scene technicians. Not to mention Phelps and Thorndike. After the fuckup, the ass-covering; a sequence of events as inexorable as night following day.

Patrese ducked under the crime-scene tape, flashed his badge, and went inside.

"In here," Selma shouted.

He followed the sound of her voice into the living room.

"How did you know I was here?" he said.

She nodded toward the mirror above the mantelpiece, but said nothing.

He could guess what she was thinking, or at least part of it. They'd killed Luther, and all for nothing. Here was the evidence; another murder. Luther couldn't have killed Emily Stark because he'd been in the hospital, and he couldn't have killed Irene Kolker because he'd been dead for three weeks. Was that enough?

In her shoes, Patrese thought, I'd sure as hell feel bitter, too. And I'd sure as hell break my Sabbath to get to the bottom of it.

She briefed him, fast and angry. Irene's body had been found this morning, though she'd been dead for several days; she'd taken the past week off, to do some home renovations and have a mini-break down at a resort near Mobile. The resort confirmed that she'd never shown up. The pathologist reckoned she could have been killed as far back as Monday. If Patrese thought the stench was bad now, he should have been here before all the doors were opened. The room was well sealed, which had kept the smell from leaking outside.

The main tropes of the scene were exactly the same as with the previous three victims: left leg removed and replaced with a rattle-snake, mirror smashed into her forehead with an ax head. Uniforms were doing house-to-house now, but as yet without joy.

Thorndike appeared in the doorway. "Let's take a walk."

They followed him and Phelps out of the house and down the street, till they were a good distance not just from Irene's place, but also from the crowd that had gathered outside the police cordon.

"We've got ourselves a situation here," Thorndike said.

"A *situation*?" Selma's voice dripped with sarcasm. "Why don't we call it what it is? A fuckup. We got ourselves a twenty-four-carat, emperor-sized, royal-flush fuckup. That's what we got."

"It's a copycat, clearly."

"Oh, for . . . goodness' sake." Selma might cuss, Patrese thought, but she'd never blaspheme. "It's not a copycat. We all know that. Luther was never the killer. We all know that, too. I don't know how he was involved in this whole thing, if he was at all, but he was *never* the killer, no matter how much it suited you to put out that he was."

Thorndike was firm. "A copycat is what we tell the media."

"What about the others?" Patrese said.

"What others?"

"F, G, H. He's gone straight from E to I."

"And we never found an A or a B either, did we? Because they don't exist." Thorndike was talking faster and louder now. "The letters thing, it's just a coincidence. And don't tell me there's no such thing. If you didn't believe it was a coincidence before, believe it now. Forget about the fucking alphabet progression. Just find whoever did this."

Patrese nodded. "And I know just where to start."

• • •

The filing cabinet in Irene's office had three drawers, each one of them neatly labeled: A–G, H–N, O–Z.

"That's where the name comes from," Patrese said, pointing at the bottom drawer.

"What name?" Selma replied.

"Oz. *The Wizard of Oz*. The guy who wrote it took the name from a filing cabinet."

"Heck, Franco. You know the strangest things."

Patrese opened the middle drawer. "We need to look through all these files, see if any names ring a bell, but first, I want to find Luther's records. I'm sorry, I know it's hard for you, but maybe he told Irene something that . . . I don't know. Something."

Selma shrugged, and batted her hand vaguely in the air: *Go ahead.* As far as she was concerned, Patrese reckoned, Luther's memory had been so thoroughly trampled underfoot over the past few weeks that another indignity made little difference.

Patrese flicked through the file tabs, reading out names at random. "Laraway, Lenihan, Lockyer, Luft, Luscombe, Maguire, Malone, Marriott . . . That's funny." He went back a few tabs, checked more slowly. "No. He's not here. No Marcq."

"He must be."

"I'm telling you, he's not."

"Try under L."

Patrese did so. "No. Not there, either."

After Luther's arrest the previous month, the NOPD had applied for a warrant to seize whatever records Irene Kolker had on Luther Marcq. By the time that warrant had been granted, however, Luther was already dead, so they'd never used it.

And now Luther's file was nowhere to be found.

They took out all the files, three drawers' worth, and divided them up. Patrese took the first half and Selma the second, split exactly where Luther's file should have been. They were looking for that very file, and for anything else, any*one* else, that might link to the previous murders.

They read for two hours, and found nothing. Nothing pertinent to the case, that was. Plenty about the neuroses of contemporary Americans. Some of the conditions these people had; it wasn't that Patrese had never heard of them, rather that he could hardly have imagined them existing in the first place.

Back to the question of Luther's file. There were three possibilities.

First, that Luther's file had never existed. Scratch that. Irene's office was meticulously organized, with everything just so, and her files were no exception to this. Luther had been a patient of hers. She'd have had a file on him, no question.

Second, that Irene had somehow lost or misplaced Luther's file. Scratch that, for the same reasons as above.

Or third, that someone had removed Luther's file.

Patrese offered Selma a lift back to headquarters, but she declined. She'd brought her own car, she said, and besides, she wanted some time alone.

He watched in the rearview mirror as she walked away, conscious that seeing someone who couldn't see you was always tinged with the slightest thrill of illicit power . . . and his mind made a sudden, muscular leap of realization.

Mirrors. Angles. Sight.

There was a ferry that plied back and forth across the Mississippi all day, from Algiers Point to downtown, but Patrese couldn't be bothered to wait for it, so he went the long way around, up and over the Crescent City Connection, and all the way through the French Quarter to Faubourg-Marigny.

To the apartment Cindy had lived in, to be precise.

He parked outside and rang the bell. The intercom crackled to life.

"Yeah?"

"I'm with the FBI. I need you to let me in."

"Yeah, *right*. That's funny. Who's there? George, that you, man?"

Patrese remembered that Cindy's living room had looked out

onto the street. "Go to the window and look down. I'll be holding my badge up."

"Listen, man, I'm—"

"*Do it.*"

"Okay. Just to shut you up."

Twenty seconds later, a man's head—mid-twenties, spiky hair—appeared thirty feet above Patrese. "Shit," he said when he saw the badge. "*Shit.* I'm coming."

He made it from window to intercom a good deal faster than he'd gone from intercom to window, and buzzed Patrese in.

"Am I in trouble?" he asked when Patrese made it to the apartment door. His face was as eager to please as a young spaniel's.

"Should you be?"

"No, sir. Not at all. No, sir."

Patrese stepped inside. "Then you got nothing to worry about."

"This about the girl who was killed here?" the man asked.

"You keep talking, I'm going to be here for a while. You shut up, I'll be in and out in minutes. Your choice."

The man nodded, and moved to shut the door.

"No," Patrese said. "Leave it open. I need it open."

He went over to the other side of the living room, trying to remember . . .

Here. Right here. This was the spot where Selma had been standing the night after Cindy's murder, when they'd ambushed Luther. Patrese had been behind the door, and Selma had been standing right here. Patrese remembered watching her face fall in anguish even before Luther had come through the door. He'd thought at the time that she must have seen him come across the landing.

But you couldn't see the landing from here.

The way the room was angled, the open door would hide someone coming through it until they were pretty much all the way in.

Which meant Selma's face had fallen before she could possibly have seen Luther.

Which meant she'd already known it was him.

•   •   •

The easiest thing to do would be to ask Selma. Easiest, and wrong. She'd give Patrese an explanation that sounded plausibly innocent, and in the time it would take him to establish whether that explanation was true or total bullshit, she'd have plenty of opportunity to get her defenses in order.

Patrese's big advantage in all this: She didn't know he knew. He wanted to keep it that way; expand it as much as possible, in fact, find out everything he could before confronting her. Fail to prepare, prepare to fail, and all that.

He went across the street, got himself a coffee, and tried to marshal his thoughts.

Selma had known it was Luther before he'd walked through the door. But Luther hadn't spoken before coming in—even when he'd rung the bell, Patrese had simply buzzed him up without speaking—and there was no way Selma could have seen him approach the building; she'd been on the other side of the room from the window.

So she'd known that Luther had been Cindy's dealer, and that wasn't the kind of thing you find out casually.

Which in turn meant they must have been in contact beforehand.

And if Selma had lied about it, so, too, had Luther. They'd both claimed not to have seen each other for some time. Why lie, unless it was to cover up something nefarious?

Luther had been their only decent suspect, and yet he couldn't have committed two of the four murders. Someone else must have killed Emily and Irene. But that didn't mean Luther hadn't killed Cindy and Rooster, the first two.

An accomplice? Someone taking over when Luther was indisposed? A tag team?

Was Selma covering for Luther? She clearly still held a torch for him—just look at the way she'd reacted after his death—and Patrese knew better than most how love could warp people's judgments. Mark Beradino, his Homicide partner back in Pittsburgh, had tried to cover for his own wife in a serial-killer case. Beradino had been as straight an arrow as they come, and profoundly Christian to boot, just like Selma. If it could happen to Beradino, it could happen to anyone.

Patrese could see why Selma would cover for Luther, but not for an accomplice . . .

. . . unless, of course, she herself was that accomplice.

Impossible. Absolutely impossible. Why the hell would Selma be killing people?

Because they were sinners.

Look at it from a Christian fundamentalist point of view; from Selma's point of view. Cindy had been a good-time girl; got drunk, took lovers. Rooster had been a gay voodoo priest. Emily had been a prostitute. Patrese remembered the vehemence with which Selma had called voodoo devil worship, the way she'd bristled while walking down Bourbon Street, the relish with which she'd predicted a rain would come and wash away all the scum.

From that point of view, these murders weren't even wrong. They were *righteous*.

Patrese had made the sinners' connection before, though never with a particular murderer in mind.

But what about Irene? How did she fit into this?

They were looking through her life now, piecing together the usual death-shattered fragments: friends, relationships, finances, and so on. Patrese had no idea what they'd find, but if he had to select a particularly egregious sinner from the hundreds of thousands of people who lived in New Orleans, a sensible, intelligent, sensitive psychiatrist wouldn't exactly be top of his list.

Unless, of course, Irene's murder was linked to the disappearance of Luther's file.

Perhaps Luther had said something, told Irene the truth about the murders. Perhaps Irene had been preparing to tell the police, for example, feeling that doctor-patient confidentiality didn't apply posthumously. How better to stop her than by killing her? And how better to muddy the waters still further than by making it look like she was part of the series?

Another question. If Selma *was* involved, why bring Luther into it at all?

Patrese knew the answer to that one. Couples who killed had a

ιology, with each party providing something the other
.. A traumatized, confused war veteran angry at the world,
ιgious police officer who dealt with unpunished sin every day.
One wanted to kill, but had nowhere to focus his rage; the other had
the focus, but was reluctant to carry out the deed. Individually, they
may never have acted on it. Together, they could unleash a *folie à
deux* of remorseless power, each murder further binding them together. They were divorced, sure, but what if they'd rekindled their
relationship, and then realized that the divorce was actually a perfect
cover? What if they'd gotten divorced purely to provide that cover?

Questions tumbled over one another like acrobats in Patrese's
head. If Luther had killed Cindy and Rooster—got the ball rolling,
as it were—had that given Selma the confidence to take over herself? Female serial killers were much rarer than male ones, and their
crimes were seen as a greater transgression from the norm. Where
men were brutish and aggressive, women were supposed to be caring, maternal, *pure*.

Luther had been pretty much their only suspect for the first two
murders. If Selma was involved, she must have been worried that
sooner or later they'd find enough evidence to charge him. How better to shift suspicion from Luther than to have committed a murder
that he simply could not have done? That would give Patrese and the
rest a conundrum they couldn't work out.

Selma would have had to steel herself, sure, but the first time was the
worst. Patrese had met serial killers, read about them, and they all said
pretty much the same thing. When you first kill, you kill two people:
the victim and yourself. Your old self is gone, and in its place is a new
persona. Second time around, with that new persona, is much easier.

Patrese looked at his watch. He'd been sitting here for an hour,
pondering it all. Had he nailed it, or was he way off base?

Only one way to find out.

Patrese went through the motions of conducting the daily sit-rep meeting—Sundays be damned, this was, if anything, even more urgent than it had been at the start of the killings—but his mind was elsewhere. As uniform after uniform spoke up, saying what they had (and, more often, hadn't) found out, Patrese thought about what he'd managed to unearth about Luther and Selma.

Selma's cell phone was on the Verizon network. Patrese had gotten Lippincott to gain access to the Verizon server—quite how, Patrese didn't want to know, but he suspected that it was about as illegal as clocking an old lady over the head and stealing her purse. Then Lippincott had, on Patrese's suggestion, wandered off to make himself a cup of coffee for ten minutes or so, while Patrese had scrolled through Selma's phone records, incoming and outgoing alike.

His suspicions had been correct. Selma and Luther *had* been in contact before that night at Cindy's apartment, and after it, too. Patrese counted twelve phone calls (eight from her to him, four from him to her) between April 10 and July 19—the last date, Patrese realized, being the day before he and Lippincott had gone into Luther's house to install the surveillance bugs.

Had Selma been trying to warn Luther about the surveillance? Possibly. That call was the shortest one listed: only three seconds, too short surely for her to have told him. Perhaps it had gone straight to voice mail. The longest call on the list was at 21:42 on June 30, a week before Cindy had been murdered. That night, they'd spoken for twenty-seven minutes. The other calls had lasted between three and seven minutes.

It could all still have been innocent, of course. After leaving the coffee shop yesterday, Patrese had made himself a promise: Make the theory fit the facts, not the facts fit the theory. So these calls between Luther and Selma in themselves proved nothing other than that two people had been in contact when they said they hadn't.

Patrese had also checked the NOPD shift logs.

Emily Stark had been killed around breakfast time on July 14. Selma had finished a shift about four hours before that (after leaving Patrese at the hospital following his datura ingestion, in fact) and hadn't been back into the station until late afternoon.

Irene could have been killed anytime from August 15 onward.

Nothing in either of those cases to rule Selma out of contention as the murderer. That she *could* have done it didn't mean she *had* done it, of course. But alongside the thrill of the hunt, Patrese felt a nagging sense of disappointment. He'd been hoping to find something to prove conclusively that Selma couldn't have killed Emily and Irene. Now, one way or the other, he'd have to confront her. He didn't want her to be guilty, nor did he want to make her justify her innocence when she'd been through so much.

All he had were phone calls and shift logs. Not enough. He needed more.

He needed to go to her apartment.

She lived on Cherokee Street. On the wall outside her condo block, someone had spray-painted *N-Town* in pink and green—Niggertown, the locals had called this place back in the sixties. The city authorities had introduced the name Black Pearl in the seventies; now Realtors preferred the even more politically correct Riverbend.

The condo block had a main door, locked, but no doorman. Patrese didn't need to buzz another apartment, or pick the lock, or shinny up the drainpipe like Spider-Man. All he had to do was unlock the door and walk in. How?

Because he'd taken Selma's keys from her purse, that was how.

He'd made up some bullshit excuse about needing to go for a meeting on one of the white-collar cases he was working for the Bureau. Sure, she'd said; I'll be here all day, see you back whenever. And off he'd gone. Chances were that Selma wouldn't even look in her bag till at least lunchtime, if she went to the cafeteria. Even if she noticed her keys were missing, she'd just assume she'd dropped them somewhere.

So now Patrese walked in the main door and up the stairs to her apartment.

If she had a burglar alarm, he was screwed, as he had no idea what the code would be, but he figured it unlikely. Any apartment on a cop's salary was unlikely to have too much worth stealing.

At the door to Selma's apartment, Patrese tried a couple of keys before he found the right one. He was just about to open the door when . . .

. . . *there*. A strand of hair running from door to frame. Easiest way to tell whether someone had been in without your knowledge; open the door, and the hair would fall to the floor.

Simple cop precautions? Or a deeper paranoia?

Patrese took a photo of the hair, close up, with his cell phone. He worked it free and laid it on top of the door frame. He'd replace it when he left.

A quick check to make sure there were no more hairs or other markers on the door, and in he went.

The apartment was small and compact: living room, kitchen, bedroom, bathroom. In the living room, three metal lamps sprang from a heavy base, long necks bending and bowing like willows. A mirror covered one of the walls, floor to ceiling, to make the place look bigger than it was.

Patrese thought of the mirrors found on the victims' foreheads.

He started in the bedroom. What Patrese knew of women—and he'd have been the first to admit that what he didn't know was about ten times greater than what he did—suggested that if Selma kept anything intimate or personal, she'd do so close to where she slept.

There was a crucifix above the bed. He was glad she hadn't brought him back here the night they'd slept together. Seeing that would have put him right off his stride.

He worked fast, unable to shake the feeling that he was trespassing. Not just legally—that was a given, he was breaking the law by being here—but morally, too. Sneaking around a woman's bedroom without her knowledge was violation, no two ways about it.

She had a double bed hard up against one wall, with a bedside table on the free side. Patrese flicked through the books piled there. *Divine Secrets of the Ya-Ya Sisterhood; Bible Stories; Wuthering Heights; Practical Homicide Investigation.*

Now, that was a combination you didn't see every day, he thought.

Nothing hidden between their pages.

In the table's solitary drawer, a circular from the New Orleans Adventist Academy. Selma was a Seventh-Day Adventist, he knew: This must be where she worshipped. The masthead was laid out in sloping graphics: NOAA.

New Orleans Adventist Academy. NOAA. Noah?

He went across to the closet. Her clothes were hanging in a neat row, all the hanger heads facing the same direction. Light colors down one end, darks the other, like a spectrum chart.

Patrese ran his hands over each item in turn, frisking. Nothing.

Shoes arranged on a rack at the bottom of the wardrobe. Nothing in any of the shoes, apart from shoe trees.

Selma's scent everywhere, flitting into his nostrils with silent reproach.

Her jewelry arranged neatly on the dressing table; bracelets, rings, necklaces, brooches, earrings, all in little clumps like high-school cliques in the dining hall. Nothing hiding among them.

There was a mirror attached to the table. Patrese peered around the back.

There.

A padded envelope, taped to the mirror's wooden back.

Patrese snapped another photo, and gently peeled the adhesive strips off the wood.

The envelope was half full. Handwritten letters.

Love letters.

They went back years, missives from Luther on forces paper, airmailed from all over the world, wherever he happened to have been serving at the time. Some were virtually novellas, reams and reams of writing without so much as a paragraph break; others, usually the ones scribbled just before going into combat, were shorter, terser, fiercely poignant in their brevity.

Patrese skimmed them, reading as fast as he could, partly to save time, partly because reading other people's love letters was spine-crushingly transgressive.

Selma had arranged them in chronological order, naturally, and he flicked through the pile toward the end to find the more recent ones.

Several from Luther to Selma begging her not to divorce him, and trying to explain what had happened at Abu Ghraib. That gave the lie to the admittedly slim possibility that they'd staged the divorce, Patrese thought. A couple from Selma back to Luther, saying how much she loved him but how she couldn't live with someone who'd done what he had.

How come she still had the ones she'd written? Had she not sent them, or had he given them back to her?

The last letter, her to him, was dated March 23. The first phone call they'd had had been almost three weeks after that.

No need to write once you were talking.

Had he persuaded her to join him? And as what? Lover? Killer? Both? Neither?

Patrese put the letters back in the envelope and looked around the room, wondering if there was any hiding place he'd missed.

Of course there was; the very spot where teenage boys hid girlie magazines and where teenage boys' moms found those magazines while changing the sheets.

Under the mattress.

There was enough room for Patrese to squeeze beneath the bed. He crawled in on his back, and looked up toward the lines of springs and the bulging folds of mattress.

There.

A manila file, exactly like the hundreds they'd found in Irene Kolker's office.

Luther Marcq's psychiatric file.

Patrese spent an hour reading the file. Irene had written meticulously detailed accounts of every session she'd had with Luther; what they'd discussed, how Luther had been feeling at the time, what physical symptoms he'd been displaying, and much else besides.

Irene had been treating Luther for his amputation fetish, and it was that which formed the vast majority of her notes. As far as Patrese could see, in more than a hundred pages, he hadn't once mentioned Marie Laveau, or the police department. Whatever stress he'd been under, however much he might have felt his identity disintegrating, he hadn't shared an ounce of it with a psychiatrist he clearly trusted otherwise.

Luther's last session with Irene, and the only one they'd had between his coming out of the hospital and his death, had been on July 21. Patrese had skimmed some of the other reports, but he read this one closely, not just because it was the last one, but also because he wondered what Luther would have had to say after doing something as drastic as shooting himself in the leg.

It was one sentence buried deep in the notes. Patrese almost missed it.

Irene had written: *Luther asked me if I was aware of the serial murders being committed in the city. I replied that I'd read about them and seen news reports, but hadn't taken much interest. He said there was a lot more to the murders than met the eye. I asked him what he meant. He was silent for perhaps a half minute, and then said, rather abruptly, "Project Noah."*

Noah. Protect Noah. That was what Luther had told Patrese as he'd died.

Except Patrese had misheard. The noise of the train, Luther's gasping for breath . . .

Not "protect," *Project.*

Project Noah.

Patrese dropped the papers on his lap and stared at the wall.

What the hell was Project Noah?

Patrese took Luther's file with him, but left everything else—down to the hair across the door frame—exactly as he'd found it.

Driving back to police headquarters, he turned over the options in his head.

He had enough, more than enough, with which to confront Selma. She'd be furious that he'd snuck around behind her back, and especially that he'd taken her keys and snooped around her apartment. That was a given.

If his suspicions were correct, he'd argue that the ends justified the means. But if she had an innocent explanation—and it was always possible, no matter how convincing the evidence seemed to him right now—she'd probably report him, and he'd be in a whole world of trouble.

What to do?

Cover his ass, that was what. Find someone he trusted, tell them what he'd done and what he'd found, and sound them out as to what they thought he should do next.

He trusted Wetzel, but Wetzel wasn't law enforcement. That left only two real possibilities: Phelps and Thorndike. And Thorndike would hardly be happy that a Bureau agent had been conducting illegal searches of a police officer's effects.

Phelps it was.

Selma was away from her desk. Checking that no one was looking, Patrese dropped the keys back in her purse and then returned to his own desk and phoned Phelps.

Phelps's cell phone went straight to voice mail. Patrese hung up and dialed Phelps's office number instead, though without much hope he'd be there on a Sunday.

"Special Agent-in-Charge's office."

"Hey, Sondra. Franco here. What are you doing in on a weekend?"

"Off sick earlier this week. Have lots to catch up on. You looking for Wyndham?"

"Sure am."

"He's not in till tomorrow morning."

"Can I have ten minutes with him?"

"If you're early. He's got a breakfast meeting here at seven."

"How about six forty-five?"

"That's fifteen minutes."

"My math was always terrible."

She laughed. "Six forty-five. You got it."

Patrese hung up.

Six forty-five tomorrow morning. Long time to wait. But nothing he could do till then.

Patrese was there right on time. Sondra, perpetually vigilant gatekeeper to the inner sanctum, was already at her desk.

"I got bad news for you, Franco," she said.

"I'm going to be forced to drink Bureau coffee for the rest of my life?"

She smiled. "Even worse. Wyndham's not here."

"Where is he?"

"Had to rush off."

That wasn't exactly answering the question, Patrese noted.

"When's he going to be back?"

"Not for a few days, he said."

"Where's he gone?"

"Er . . . some family bereavement, I think."

It might have been the way Sondra had held herself unnaturally stiff while saying that last sentence, or the way her voice had squeaked a little. Maybe it was both. Whatever it was, Patrese was sure Sondra was lying, and that in itself was unusual.

"That's too bad," he said. "Well, I guess I'll just have to see him when he gets back." Patrese coughed. "Excuse me. I . . ." More coughing, louder and violent this time.

"Are you all right?" Sondra said.

Patrese clamped his hand to his mouth. His cheeks puffed like bellows.

Sondra pushed her chair back. "I'll get you some water."

There was a watercooler at the other end of the corridor, twenty yards away. Sondra hurried off toward it.

The moment she was out of sight, Patrese stopped coughing and went over to her desk. He reckoned he had a minute, tops, before she was back.

Sondra kept Phelps's appointments in a large, leather-bound

diary. The IT department had set up all sorts of electronic calendars, but she was old school. She'd been writing appointments into diaries for decades and wasn't going to change now.

Patrese opened the diary on the tasseled spine marker, set at today's date.

N7846K dep MSY 0830 arr MID 0940.

Sondra used Post-its like they were going out of fashion. Patrese grabbed one, copied the details down, stuffed it in his pocket, and was back across the room when Sondra reappeared.

"Here you go," she said, handing him a plastic cup of water.

"Thanks." Patrese drank it down in a single gulp, which caused him to cough again, this time for real.

Sondra put her hand on his shoulder. "Easy, Franco."

He nodded through the coughs. "Went down the wrong way. Sorry. I'm fine."

She kept him there a few minutes, until his face had faded from crimson and he could get through a sentence without spluttering. He thanked her again, went back to his office, and logged on to his computer.

N7846K dep MSY 0830 arr MID 0940.

Clearly a flight; MSY was the airport code for New Orleans. Patrese didn't know what MID stood for. Midland, Texas?

He Googled "airport code MID."

Not Midland. Not Texas. Not even the United States. MID was Manuel Crescencio Rejón airport, located just south of the Yucatán capital Mérida.

The rattlesnakes on the bodies had come from the Yucatán. Luther's $50,000 had come from an account in Mérida.

And now Phelps was going there.

Patrese knew commercial flights are all listed in the same alphanumeric manner: a two-letter airline code followed by a four-figure flight number. N7846K didn't fit this template; therefore it wasn't a commercial flight.

Private plane, then; and that combination would almost certainly be its tail number.

Patrese Googled "tail number lookup." The first link to appear was to the Web site of the Federal Aviation Authority. He clicked on it, entered N7846K into the search box, and pressed Return.

The answer came back in a flash.

N7846K was registered to Varden Industries.

Patrese got breakfast from the staff cafeteria and pondered his options.

Phelps took off on a Varden private jet to the Yucatán at the drop of a hat and didn't want people to know about it. There were links between the killings and the Yucatán; there were links between the killings and the Vardens.

Now there was a link between the Vardens and the Yucatán.

Just as well he hadn't confided in Phelps, Patrese thought. And since he didn't want to involve Thorndike—especially without Phelps there to run interference for him—he'd have to have it out with Selma directly.

He finished breakfast and drove over to police headquarters. Selma was already in.

"Hey," she said. "What's up?"

She seemed breezy enough. Patrese couldn't tell whether she'd discovered that Luther's file was missing—how often would she check that it was still there?—and, if so, whether she suspected him of having taken it. If either was the case, she was doing a pretty good job of hiding it.

He shrugged. "Usual. Any progress on Irene?"

"You want the good news or the bad news?"

"Bad."

"Most people say 'good' first."

"I like to swim against the tide."

"I already got *that*." Patrese couldn't tell whether her tone was affectionate or catty. "Bad news is, we ain't got no progress worth the name."

"What's the good news?"

"Thorndike ain't here to bust our chops about it."

"No? Where is he?"

"Some sort of family bereavement. Ain't comin' back in till later in the week."

Jigsaw pieces tumbling, clicking, fitting into place. "Says who?"

"Says his secretary."

"You know her?"

"Sure."

"What's her name?"

"What the heck, Franco?"

"Just tell me her name."

"Erin. Erin Mandoli."

"You got a number for her?"

"Six-four-three-eight."

Patrese dialed.

"Deputy Chief's office, Erin speaking, how can I help?"

"Erin, it's Franco Patrese, FBI. I'm working on the—"

"I know who you are, Agent Patrese."

"Listen, I need a favor."

"Shoot."

"I need to get a package to my boss, Special Agent Phelps, and I know he's gone to Yucatán with Mr. Thorndike and the others, but I've lost the address. Sondra—Mr. Phelps's secretary—isn't answering, and I'd really appreciate it if you could—"

"Sure." Patrese breathed a silent sigh of relief; his chummy tone must have convinced Erin that he was in on the deception. "You want me to read it out? It's a little complex, and my Spanish ain't—"

"No. I'll come and get it."

"Okay."

Patrese put the phone down. Selma was staring at him.

"What the hell was that all about?" she asked.

"That's a question I could very well ask you."

In an empty meeting room, door firmly closed against the endless stream of people with questions and suggestions about the case, Patrese told Selma what he'd done and what he'd found: the sight lines in Cindy's living room, Selma's own phone logs and police shift rotas, and finally his going to her apartment yesterday.

He expected her to be furious.

She wasn't.

She was something worse: *disappointed.* He'd have preferred furious; she could have ranted and raved for a few minutes, and gotten it out of her system. Instead she made him feel as though he'd let her down.

Yes, she said, she and Luther had been in contact before Cindy's murder. They'd discussed getting back together, but they'd decided they couldn't. She hadn't been able to get over what he'd done at Abu Ghraib, nor that he was now dealing drugs, and he'd accepted that.

But he hadn't told her any of the things that the homicide investigations had later uncovered: that he was working undercover for Thorndike, that he would only be happy without his left leg. She'd found those out at the same time Patrese had, and her shock had been genuine.

Yes, of course she should have told Patrese at the start. It would have saved everyone a lot of time and trouble later; heck, it may even have saved Luther's life. But she hadn't, because she'd known how suspicious it would have looked, and once she'd decided not to come clean, there'd been no way she could have gone back on that without it looking even more dubious. The first lie was the foundation stone; after that, you had to keep building and building, piling untruth upon untruth.

That was why she'd taken the file from Irene's office; she'd done it impulsively, on scene, with Irene's body still in the room. The place had been crawling with crime-scene technicians, but they'd all been poring over bloodstains or fingerprints. None of them had seen her take it from the filing cabinet, and even if they had, they'd have just assumed it was a piece of evidence. She'd taken it because she'd feared that Luther might have told Irene something about them, and that Patrese would in turn read the file and find out . . . well, find out exactly what he'd been smart enough to do by other means.

So she'd grabbed the file without thinking, and stuffed it under her mattress when she'd gotten home. She hadn't even opened it, let alone read it. Nor had she noticed that it was gone from her apartment, or that Patrese had been in there. He was wasted in the Bureau, she said: With skills like that, he should apply for a job in Langley.

Patrese was silent for several minutes when Selma finished speaking. He wasn't doing it to make her uncomfortable, though he was aware it was having that effect. He was trying to work out whether she was telling the truth or not.

Yes, she'd lied to him before. That didn't mean she was lying to him now. Everyone lied sometimes. Most of them did it for good reasons, or at least for what they *thought* were good reasons. Besides, it wasn't as if he'd always been entirely straight with her. Taking her keys and searching her apartment, for one.

There *was* something going on in the Yucatán, that was for damn sure. If Selma was part of that, why was she still here, rather than down there with them? To keep Patrese away from the truth? But they'd have no reason to believe he was on to the truth in the first place. No one knew he'd found Luther's file, and Phelps hadn't known why Patrese had asked to see him.

All of which suggested that Selma had nothing to do with this.

Suggested; not proved.

Maybe she *was* in it up to her neck, and everything she'd just told him was a lie. Maybe she was double- or triple-crossing him. If so, he probably wouldn't find out till it was too late. But he had to make a decision, and making a decision meant taking a chance, whichever course he chose. You could only prove suspicions, he thought, because no answer other than a confirmation satisfies the suspicious person. You can never disprove a suspicion, unless you choose to trust.

"I think we should go to Mexico," he said at last.

The next flight out was late afternoon. New Orleans to Mérida may have been just over an hour in a private jet, but flying commercial— in this case, United via Houston; there were no direct connections— took more than four times as long. By the time Patrese and Selma had gotten through passport control in Mérida, it was past ten.

The address Erin had given them was only an hour's drive from Mérida, but neither Patrese nor Selma was up for a drive in the dark on unfamiliar roads. Besides, there was nothing to be gained from arriving there late at night. Better to get some sleep and set out half-way fresh in the morning.

They took a cab into town, past a sign saying WELCOME TO MÉRIDA, TWINNED WITH NEW ORLEANS, and tried the Holiday Inn first off. Unimaginative, sure—even under streetlights, Mérida looked like the kind of elegant place that would have its share of funky boutique hotels—but you knew where you were with a Holiday Inn. It wouldn't be the Ritz, but neither would it be a rat-infested cesspit run by a fat man in a sweaty string vest.

"Do you have any rooms available?" Patrese asked the receptionist.

"A double?"

"Two singles," Selma said with a quickness that made Patrese smile.

The receptionist tapped at her keyboard. "Sure. Two singles."

She took their passport and credit-card details, programmed the entry cards, indicated the elevators, and wished them a pleasant stay.

Their rooms were right next to each other. They wished each other good night and stepped inside their respective front doors with an almost comical synchronicity.

Patrese had a long bath, soapy water sliding away the sweat, and then opened a beer from the minibar and watched CNN.

Hot summer night, strange town. He wanted Selma to knock on his door. He reckoned she wouldn't.

He was right.

Avis car rental was right across the street from the Holiday Inn, so they went over there after breakfast and rented a Dodge Stratus; beige, the better to hide the dust.

Actually, Patrese thought, Mérida was much cleaner than he'd expected. White limestone walls gleamed in the morning sun; colonial buildings jostled each other in gentle pastels of turquoise and ochre. He half expected Crockett and Tubbs to appear.

In the car, they followed signs to Highway 281, suburbs giving way to countryside, and joined the procession heading toward the coast—families packed in station wagons, Bimbo bread delivery vans, donkeys and dogs sharing space in the flatbeds of ancient pickups. Every few minutes, they passed another makeshift roadside tribute, tinfoiled flowers withering in the heat around a picture of some impossibly bright-eyed youth.

Through small towns with Scrabble rack names—Hunucmá, Kinchil—and then back out on the open road. Trees and shrubs crowded close to the verge like expectant spectators at a rally, though there were plenty of gaps where trunks and branches lay flattened and broken.

It was easy to miss a turning, especially an unmarked one, in the foliage, and it was only a glimpse of a parked black SUV through the trees that allowed Patrese to slow down in time.

He made a right turn off the highway. There was a large gate ahead, with a guard hut to one side. Patrese slowed. Four men emerged from the hut, looking more like paramilitaries than security guards. They wore black uniforms and baseball caps, and they carried Heckler & Koch MP5 submachine guns. One of them came over to Patrese's window; the others stood in front of the car, fingers on their triggers.

Professionals, in other words.

Patrese lowered the window. "We've come to see Mr. Varden."

"Engine off." Patrese complied. The guard continued. "You are?"

"I'm Agent Franco Patrese, FBI. This is Detective Selma Fawcett, New Orleans Police Department." He showed his badge.

The guard could hardly have looked less impressed if he'd tried. "FBI mean *nothing* here."

"Our bosses are staying inside. Mr. Phelps, Mr. Thorndike. We need to see them."

"They know you here?"

"No."

The guard thought for a moment. Patrese looked at the logo on his baseball cap. It was a shield divided into three segments. At top left, a yellow shape on a black background. Top right, a yellow Z on a black background. At the bottom, another yellow shape—the outline of Mexico, Patrese realized—on a red background.

The guard held out his hand. "Passports."

Patrese handed them over. The guard gestured for him to open the door.

"We search car."

Patrese and Selma got out. The guard went back into the hut and picked up the phone. Two of his colleagues popped the car's trunk and hood open, and began to search the vehicle. The fourth stayed close to Patrese and Selma.

Patrese had the impression that this guard wasn't the only one watching them. He wondered how many cameras were mounted high in the leaves, how many more black-clad badasses were beyond the gate.

Selma stared straight ahead. Patrese felt his skin prickling beneath his shirt as the hot outside air chased away the chill of the aircon. He shifted position, slowly so as not to alarm the guard; no sudden movements.

The first guard came back out of the hut.

"SUV beyond gate. You follow."

"Passports?"

He shook his head. "We keep."

"No way."

The guard shrugged. "Then you no go in."

Patrese looked at Selma. She shrugged. He turned back to the guard. "You'll return them when we leave?"

"*Claro.*"

Patrese nodded. "Okay."

The gate swung open. The other guards stepped aside.

"Into the lions' den," Patrese muttered as he started the engine and engaged the gear.

A black SUV was waiting just inside the gate. It pulled out in front of them and set off down the road. In his rearview mirror, Patrese saw that another SUV had swung in behind. They were taking no chances, clearly.

The road was paved for roughly two hundred yards before becoming dirt. Whether it was flat and smooth during dry weather, Patrese had no idea, but this was the rainy season, and it was pitted and scarred. He had to work the Dodge hard to keep up with the SUV in front and avoid being rammed by the one behind.

"Heck, Franco," Selma snapped as a particularly large pothole had her smacking her head on the roof.

"Sorry." And lucky it's a rental car, too, he thought.

The road dived into deep, lush forest. Zebras and elands darted between sandalwood trees. Jaguars prowled, crocodiles snoozed. Frigate birds and snowy egrets rode the helices of warm air above a mangrove swamp.

"Good place to dispose of us," Selma said.

"Just what I was thinking."

"*Now* you tell me." She looked around. "What *is* this place?"

"If I didn't know better, I'd say it was Jurassic Park."

"We'd best find a lawyer quick, then."

"Huh?"

"Doesn't the lawyer get eaten first in *Jurassic Park*?"

He laughed. "Good point."

The road began to rise. Patrese looked at the car's odometer. They'd driven eight kilometers since passing through the gate; that was five miles.

The slope became steeper. Patrese shifted down one gear, then another. More fallen trees, these ones with torn roots visible.

And then they were at the top; an escarpment, with the green carpet of forest on one side and white-sand beaches sliding into the ocean on the other.

But it was neither of these that caught Patrese's eye. It was what was directly in front of him.

A riot of ziggurats and causeways, roof combs and statues, friezes and courtyards.

A Mayan palace.

Not a real Mayan palace, of course; an ersatz reconstruction, but clearly built with no expense spared. Patrese was hardly conscious of stopping the car, he was so mesmerized. It was part Xanadu, part Escher sketch, part alien installation.

Four men were waiting by the main gate: Varden, Junior, Phelps, and Thorndike.

Patrese and Selma got out of their car. The doors of the SUVs stayed shut. Clearly, the two of them were not deemed a threat. They went over to the four men.

"My staff is coming with cold towels and margaritas," Varden said.

Not the welcome Patrese had been expecting. He smiled. The old buzzard sure has a way of surprising you, he thought.

Behind their sunglasses, Phelps's and Thorndike's faces were unreadable.

"We'd prefer not," Selma said.

"Nonsense, young lady. It's hotter than hell, and you've come a long way. Cold towels and margaritas are the very least you need. Then a swim, perhaps?"

"We need to ask some questions."

Varden made a moue, as though Selma's directness was unspeakably vulgar.

"Not before *I* ask *you* some questions," Thorndike said.

"Such as how we knew you were here?"

"For starters."

"We're detectives. That's our job. To find out things other people don't want us to know." Patrese saw Varden smile; at least one person was enjoying this.

"Such as?"

"Such as why the deputy chief of the NOPD and the head of the FBI field office both take off at a moment's notice when there's a major investigation going on, and spin some moonshine to their staff about family bereavements."

Thorndike opened his mouth to answer, but Varden beat him to it.

"You'll have to forgive me, that was my idea. Selfish of me, I know, but that's what happens when you're as old and as rich as I am; you can get pretty much what you want, and you don't care what people think anymore."

"That doesn't answer my question."

"Every year, I invite people down here—friends, colleagues, business contacts, whoever. As I told you, I like to help law enforcement every way I can. You all do such a good job, in extremely difficult circumstances. This is one of the ways in which I say thank you, by inviting Mr. Phelps and Mr. Thorndike, among others, to come and recharge their batteries for a few days."

In plain English, Patrese thought, that translated as just a slightly more sophisticated form of bribery than hundred-dollar bills in a brown envelope.

"This couldn't wait? They had to drop everything and come running the moment you snap your fingers?"

Varden shrugged. "The actions of a child, I know. Unforgivable." A soft smile, which Patrese took to mean *I don't give a fuck, and you know I don't give a fuck, and I know you know I don't give a fuck, and I don't give a fuck about that either.*

Selma turned back to Thorndike, eyes blazing. "And when he says 'jump,' all you say is 'how high?' Is that it?"

"Don't use that tone with me."

"*Is that it?*"

"Mr. Varden is one of the city's most generous donors to police charities. It's in everyone's interests that we maintain good relations."

"Puh-*leaze*. Spare me the party line."

Varden leaned forward slightly to interject. "My dear, this is Louisiana. Well, not right here, of course, but you know what I mean. This is Louisiana, and in Louisiana we do things different from other places. That's not good or bad. It's just the way it is. Now, you said you had some questions, and they must be pretty important if you've come all the way here. So ask away."

Selma looked at Patrese.

"What's Project Noah?" Patrese said.

Varden laughed. "That's it? That's what you came to ask?"

"Yes. What's Project Noah?"

Varden swept both arms through the air, describing a huge arc.

"This, Agent Patrese. All this. *This* is the Noah Project."

Varden sat them down on a terrace, waited while white-clad staff handed out the cold towels and margaritas, and then explained.

He'd bought this land—twenty thousand acres, give or take—off the Mexican government, and had created an ecological biosphere; not just his sanctuary, he insisted, but one for the world, too. Ideally, he'd want two of every animal here, just as Noah had taken on the ark, but of course there were plenty of species unsuited to the climate. As with the fauna, so, too, with the flora. There were more than a thousand different types of plants and trees, and he wanted more.

He was getting older, he said, and the old, like the young, tended to worry most about the big things. Climate change, overpopulation, terrorism, resource shortages—the list went on and on, and no one did anything about it.

Take this piece of coast right here. In a few years' time, this biosphere would probably be the last remaining piece of rainforest. The poor farmers burned the vegetation on their property to raise cows; the rich chopped down the trees to build hotels. Only the super-rich like him could afford the luxury of constructing this, a universe unto itself. Every morning here, he felt clean, reborn, newly virginal.

Oh yes, he could see the hypocrisy. It was all very well to go on about saving the world when he, and people like him, had done so much to destroy it; all very well to preserve the delicate and complex ecosystem of the mangrove swamps here when his oil pipelines had stripped away half the wetlands between New Orleans and the sea. But man needed oil and buildings. How could you reconcile the two?

And if he was worried about the future, he sought answers in the past. Hence his obsession with the Mayans, a civilization in many ways more advanced than our own. This complex had taken three years and three thousand workers to build, not to mention historians from the National Autonomous University of Mexico to ensure that every last detail was historically correct; every hieroglyphic, every mural, every monument, including the one to Noah, whose legend was well known in Mayan culture. Varden had even designed his own elaborate tomb here.

But as for why Luther should have mentioned this place, or why it should have anything to do with the murders, Varden had no idea. Yes, Cindy had been here, of course, but none of the other victims— nor Luther—had had any connection with the project. Varden knew everyone who worked here, and he figured he'd sure as hell know if one of them had been stalking the streets of New Orleans slicing people up.

And if they thought there might be some sort of weird Mayan connection, forget it. Sure, the Mayans had been a bloodthirsty bunch—by modern standards, if not their own—but as far as Varden knew, and he knew a great deal, none of their rituals involved anything like what had been done to the victims in this case.

If Patrese and Selma wanted to look around, see what they could find, they were more than welcome. *Mi casa es su casa,* and all that. Varden had nothing to hide. And then, just to extend his appreciation of law enforcement personnel a little further, why didn't they stay? There were guest villas available, and they could hitch a ride back to New Orleans on the corporate jet on Thursday afternoon.

No pressure, he said. Do exactly what you want. But listen, if you need to justify it to the guys back in New Orleans working the case, it's an investigation. If you need to justify it to yourselves, it's a couple of days in paradise. And if you need to justify it to your bank managers or departmental bean counters, it's free.

Patrese and Selma took Varden at his word, and spent the next few hours interviewing everybody they could find: security men, waiters, chambermaids, cooks, zoologists, estate management staff, maintenance men, and so on. Most of them spoke passable English. None of them, clearly, had anything to do with the murders.

There was never a single moment when they decided to take Varden up on his offer; just the gradual realization that they'd never get the opportunity to stay somewhere like this again, that they'd never make it back to Mérida in time for the last flight back, and—most important—that the longer they stayed, the more chance they had of being on hand if someone let slip some detail that would give them the lead they were looking for.

There were twelve guest villas off to one side of the complex, arranged around a large central courtyard. Varden had earmarked one of them for Patrese and Selma. It had two bedrooms on either side of a large living room. The floors and walls were painted in white enamel—"makes spotting scorpions easier"—and the tables, chairs, sofas, and bed bases were all stone and built-in, splashed in cushions and spreads of deep, strong colors—crimson here, mustard and pink there. No air-conditioning, of course, not in the eco-paradise. Thick walls, high ceilings, and the sea breeze kept the interior cool.

At sunset, Patrese saw vultures hovering high above the mangrove swamp.

This—this whole place—is the ultimate male fantasy, he thought. Varden's just doing what other men never do, can't do, never allow themselves to do. He's like someone from another time; a king, an emperor, a sultan.

Dinner was outdoors, under an enormous *palapa* that Varden told them had been made from palm fronds collected around the estate and, as per local tradition, woven together on a full moon to ward off scorpions. And Varden was clearly taking his gratitude to the local great and good seriously. Phelps and Thorndike were not the only ones staying; also there were Roger Rojciewicz, Cindy's congressman father; Erskine Infuhr, the deputy mayor whom Patrese and Selma had interviewed about the payments on record in Cindy's files; Landon Dempsey, deputy sheriff of Orleans Parish, a man so enormously fat that his belt seemed little more than a stripe around the widest part of his gut; Marc Alper, the New Orleans assistant DA who'd prosecuted Marie Laveau; and a man named Marshall Waxman, who said he was an old buddy of Varden's from way back.

Patrese didn't have to know Selma as well as he did to be aware of what she was thinking: Aside from her, everyone was white, and everyone was male.

"Funny kind of getaway, ain't it?" Selma said as the waiters brought lobster.

"How so?" Varden asked.

"None of y'all bring your wives?"

Varden gave the kind of laugh with which an adult greets a child's gauche truthfulness. "Consensus was for a boys' weekend."

"Then I must be spoiling it for you."

"On the contrary, my dear. Without you, who knows how low the tone would be."

There was an awkward silence. Patrese knew they were interlopers, but the hell with it; they'd been asked, they were staying.

"So." Varden clapped his hands. "Anything you'd like to do tomorrow? A trip to Chichén Itzá, perhaps? You know Chichén Itzá? Pretty much the most famous Mayan archaeological site in the world. Amazing place. Be happy to take you."

"Sure," Selma said. "If it's not too much trouble."

"Quite the opposite. I could go every day for the rest of my life and never tire of it. And you, Agent Patrese? A bit of Mayan culture at its finest? Or perhaps something more energetic? You look like a sporty kind of guy. We've got windsurfing, kayaking, sailing, snorkeling, scuba, cave diving—"

"Cave diving?"

"You've been cave diving?"

"Every summer for a few years, when I was younger."

"Whereabouts did you go?" Junior asked.

"Florida, mainly. But also Mammoth Cave and Wookey Hole." Mammoth Cave was in Kentucky; Wookey Hole was in Somerset, England.

Junior looked impressed. "A man who knows what he's doing. But you ain't never dived in Yucatán?"

Patrese shook his head. "But everyone says . . ."

"And everyone is right. We'll go tomorrow, yes? There's a great cave system not far from here."

Patrese suddenly had a sense of danger. Cave diving was notoriously hazardous, people died doing it all the time. The basic problem was a simple one: There was no chance of a free ascent. The cave's ceiling and walls hemmed the diver in, and often the only way out was the way in. If you got in trouble, you couldn't just head for the surface. As such, cave diving played on all man's most basic fears—drowning, darkness, claustrophobia, asphyxiation—and called for complete self-reliance and independence of judgment. Even apparently trivial mistakes could be fatal.

"I'm not sure . . ."

Junior leaned over to him and spoke quietly, so no one else could hear. "All these other guys are either too old or too fat for it. Come on. You'd be doing me a favor. It's no fun diving alone."

Patrese thought for a moment.

Two possibilities. One, this was an elaborate plot to kill him, either down in the cave system or somewhere en route, and make it look like an accident. But surely if they wanted to get rid of him, or Selma, they could have done so a hundred different ways by now? Besides, Patrese himself had been the first to enthuse about cave diving; it wasn't as if Varden had pressed it on him. Which left the second possibility: This was a genuine offer. Junior was a state governor, for heaven's sake. Even in Louisiana, you had to trust politicians to get you to sunset alive.

"You'd be doing me a favor," Junior repeated.

Something in his tone intrigued Patrese. Did Junior know more than he was letting on? Was this his way of confessing something, or pointing Patrese in the right direction, without anyone else finding out? Even his father? *Especially* his father?

"Okay," Patrese said. "Let's do it."

They were out and on the road early, Junior driving one of the SUVs, Patrese in the passenger seat, all the equipment piled up in back.

After a few minutes, Junior slowed, pulled over, and stopped.

"We here?" Patrese said.

"Not yet. Just got something to do. 'Scuse me a sec." He stepped out of the SUV.

Patrese looked around. The road was a ribbon laid across endless scrubland. No cars in sight, not this early in the morning.

A perfect place to kill someone, in other words.

Junior looked left and right before walking across the road.

Was this an ambush? Was that the signal? Junior getting clear of the vehicle before a bunch of thugs emerged from the undergrowth and shot Patrese to bits?

Patrese looked across at the driver's seat. Junior had left the keys in the ignition, and the engine was still running. He'd hardly have done that if it *was* an ambush, would he?

Unless he'd thought that removing the keys would have aroused Patrese's suspicions in the first place, of course.

Patrese unclipped his seat belt. If they came for him, he'd dive into the driver's seat and hit the gas. He was safer inside the vehicle than out, that was for sure. Getting out of the SUV and making a run for it would be suicide. If the bullets didn't get him, a Yucatán's summer day without shade sure would.

On the other side of the road, Junior was squatting down, his back to Patrese. Beyond him, Patrese could see a stone cross. It was a couple of feet high, and flowers were piled up around the base in the colors of Mardi Gras—gold, green, and purple.

Junior stayed stock-still for a few moments and then leaned forward, touched the cross, got to his feet, crossed himself, came back to the SUV, got in, and pulled away without speaking.

Patrese felt absurdly foolish. *Get a grip*, he told himself.

"My mother," Junior said.

"I'm sorry. I didn't know."

"It was a long time ago. I was nine, almost ten. Car crash."

"You were on vacation?"

Junior shook his head. "She was Mexican. Rosalita. Big, prominent family." That explained Junior's darker skin, Patrese thought.

"My parents died the same way," Patrese said. "It's brutal, the shock."

"Yes."

"Mine was just last year. What it must have been like as a child . . . I can't imagine."

"No. You can't."

The road unrolled beneath their wheels for minutes before Junior next spoke.

"Every time I get in a plane or a helicopter, I think about it crashing. A car, never. Funny, no? People get killed in cars all the time. Your mother dies in a car crash. But it doesn't put you off driving, does it?"

"Maybe because it was a while between your mother dying and you driving?"

"I was driving at the age of eleven. Big estates. Private roads."

"Your dad teach you?"

Junior gave a snort-laugh. "You think he had the time? Anyway, he doesn't drive himself anymore."

"He's not that old."

"Nothing to do with age. He hasn't driven since that day."

"Since your mother was killed?"

"Uh-huh."

"Sheesh."

"Never anyone as good as her," Junior said, as though reading Patrese's thoughts.

An only child with a father who sublimated everything to the attainment of wealth and power. Those kinds of families had secrets buried like fossils in the strata of their histories, and they seldom dug too hard for them.

Patrese wondered how often Junior talked about this. Perhaps he never did. Perhaps that was why he buried himself in achievement: the army, politics.

Junior turned right off the main highway, bounced the SUV down a dirt road, and came to a stop around the back of a dilapidated shed.

"This it?" Patrese said.

Junior laughed. "Doesn't matter what it looks like up here."

"True."

Junior ran through safety procedures, fast and efficiently. He worked on the mnemonic The Good Divers Are Living, he said: T for training, G for guideline, D for depth, A for air, L for light.

Training: Patrese had enough experience for this dive, even if he hadn't been down for a while. Junior would take the lead. Patrese would soon be back in the groove. It was like riding a bike, Junior said; you never forgot how to do it.

Guideline: A thin nylon line ran from the entrance to the cave all the way down to where they were going. If for whatever reason Junior and Patrese became separated, all Patrese had to do was follow the line back to the surface.

Depth: Junior had done this dive often enough to know what gas mixture corresponded to the maximum depth they'd be going, and how long they needed to spend decompressing on their way back up.

Air: They were using the rule of thirds, no question. A third of your air to go in, a third to come out, a third for emergencies. When they'd used a third of their air, they'd turn back. It didn't matter how well the dive was going or how clear the water was. The moment you'd used a third, around you turned.

Lights: They each had three independent sources of light: one headlamp and two flashlights. The moment one failed, again, out they came, no questions.

Patrese felt reassured. A lot of cave divers skimped on safety procedures. A lot of cave divers also died. The connection wasn't coincidence. Someone who respected and insisted on rules was someone worth diving with. Cave diving was uniquely beautiful; geological formations you could find nowhere else on earth, visibility clearer than in any ocean water. But with the beauty came the danger, the dark side.

The tailgate of the SUV opened flat. They used it as a table for the equipment—wet suits, air tanks, regulators, knives, lights, all laid out and put on with care. Junior's wet suit was all white with black patches at knees and elbows; Patrese's was a more standard black one with flashes of crimson at the shoulders.

The entrance to the cave was a small pond, no more than thirty feet in diameter. Patrese could have walked past it a hundred times without realizing what lay beneath.

"You know what the Mayans call cave entrances?" Junior said, checking the straps on his mask. "*Cenotes.* Doors to the underworld."

Fully kitted out, he walked over to the pond, secured the mask over his face, snapped a pair of flippers on his feet, and slid into the water. He had two air tanks on his back and another in his hands.

Last chance for Patrese to bail out, but he knew the moment for that had already come and gone.

The sunshine was the color of melted honey as Patrese stepped into the shallows. The water was dark and chilly, and he saw bats nestling in the cracks of the rock above. He was about to enter a world as unknowable as the mountains of the moon.

In he went; submerged, baptized. For a moment, he felt as though he were passing through the throat of a whale and entering its stomach. Ahead of him, Junior pointed to the marker line studded with fluorescent plastic arrows that ran down one wall of the cave. In this drowned world, Coleridge's words looped in Patrese's head:

> *Where Alph, the sacred river, ran*
> *Through caverns measureless to man*
> *Down to a sunless sea.*

Patrese followed Junior into a tunnel, narrow enough to block out the sunlight from above. He reached up and flicked on his headlamp.

The beam slashed through the darkness, illuminating Junior's gliding form as though he were an aircraft caught in a wartime searchlight.

Ahead of Patrese, the water was clear. He checked behind him and could see virtually nothing. For a moment, claustrophobia rose in him like bile. Then he realized that the opacity was simply him stirring up all the silt in the tunnel. Out of practice, he was kicking too hard. Junior was flicking his legs at ankles and knees, rather than all the way from his hips. Patrese followed suit.

Walls and roof, pressing down hard on them; tight, peristaltic.

Patrese glanced at his watch. They'd already been down here a quarter of an hour. He could have sworn he'd submerged only about two minutes ago.

The tunnel forked, and the guideline with it. Junior headed right. Patrese followed.

Up to a bottleneck, so tight that Junior could only proceed by unhooking his tanks and passing them through ahead of him, the airlines snaking out from mouthpiece to valves like umbilical cords.

No way, thought Patrese. No way. He was too out of practice for this.

From the other side of the bottleneck, Junior peered back at Patrese as though he were looking through a window. He gestured with his hand: *Come.*

Patrese clenched his hands into fists to stop them trembling.

Nothing to it. Just unhook the tanks and pass them through. You're still connected to them. Easy as you like.

He took the tanks off his back. They floated ahead of him like torpedoes. Junior took hold of the first one and pulled it through the gap, nodding reassuringly.

Patrese handed him the second. Junior took it and pulled again, hard, catching Patrese off balance. With both his air tanks on the other side of the opening, Patrese half stumbled and was half dragged against the rock wall.

Junior pulled again. Patrese bit down frantically on his mouthpiece to stop it from coming free. Panic flooded his guts: *This is it this is it this is Junior killing me here and now.* Making himself as flat as possible, he slipped through the hole.

Junior stopped pulling. Patrese glared at him, eyes wide and angry behind his mask. Junior gestured to the tanks and held up his hands in apology; a simple misunderstanding, thought you were coming with them, got snagged, whatever.

Could have been, Patrese thought. Could have been something else. He didn't know, *couldn't* know the truth. Best just to get on with it.

Tanks hooked back on, they continued.

There was a natural alcove away to the right. Junior lay his spare tank down there gently, presumably as an extra safety measure, and continued into the darkness.

The tunnel suddenly opened out into a cavern so vast that it seemed suspended in infinity. Patrese's light petered out into nothing; no marker line, no cavern walls, just a lip of rock below him, and as he swam past and over it, he felt as though he were falling off a precipice, vertigo in zero gravity, a body falling and twisting as it escaped the normal laws of physics.

Disoriented, a snatch of long-lost training came back to him: *Check the bubbles.* Bubbles escaping from the scuba tanks will always go upward.

He found the bubbles, righted himself, and caught sight of Junior again.

Lit up by both their beams, the cavern's features came gradually into view. Ahead of them was a massive flowstone wall that cascaded from ledge to ledge like a frozen waterfall, each tier spiked with candles of stalagmites. Beneath, right at the edge of their lights' range, was a field of canyons and pinnacles, boulders poking from the sand like tombstones.

To Patrese, the monotone of his own breathing sounded like organ music.

Junior turned to him and gave the thumbs-up. Patrese returned the gesture, smiling as best he could around his mouthpiece.

They swam around the cavern for a few minutes before Junior made a circling motion with his hand: *Let's go on.* He headed into a tunnel on the far side of the cavern. Patrese followed, picking up the marker line again as he did so.

This tunnel was as narrow as the earlier one, and much siltier, too, to judge from the amount of dirt Junior was kicking up. Patrese could barely see him anymore; a flipper here, half an air tank there, no more. He swam faster to keep up, always conscious of the marker line, like the thread Theseus had laid in the Minotaur's labyrinth; if all else failed, his last, best hope.

He wanted to call out to Junior to slow down, but of course he couldn't. The silt and sand swirled hard up against his mask. Total brownout. A flash of white wet suit; Junior's leg. Patrese made a grab for it; it was the only way he could alert Junior.

He was still reaching for Junior's leg when the world exploded.

It was the shock as much as the pain that had Patrese gagging for breath; that sharp agony of a blow to the head that could arouse untold fury in the most placid of saints.

Instinctively, he brought his hands up, his left one to rub his skull at the point of impact, his right to ward off Junior if he attacked again. Patrese flailed his right arm around in the silt, trying to clear a patch of vision so he could see what was going on, but the silt rushed in anywhere he'd tried to clear.

No point listening for Junior; Patrese couldn't hear a thing above the sound of his own breathing, hoarse, ragged, and fast, burning down the contents of his air tank far faster than he wanted. He tried to rein back his galloping heart rate, knowing the vicious circle: The more he panicked, the faster he'd breathe; the faster he'd breathe, the less air he'd have; the less air he'd have, the more he'd panic, and so on. Some divers were found with air still in their tanks, having died of nothing more than their own panicked fear; they'd hyperventilated so badly that they'd overloaded their air tank's demand valve, which had shut itself off.

That's not going to happen here.

Arms and legs splayed to give him even a split second's warning if Junior came back, Patrese stayed very still until, finally, his breathing began to slow.

The silt hung thick as a curtain. Patrese knew he couldn't wait for it to disperse totally; it might be hours, and he didn't have enough air left in his tanks. He pressed the air gauge right up against his mask so he could read it.

Nearly down to two-thirds. Pretty much time to think about heading back.

He checked the direction of his bubbles, shifted position slightly . . . and cracked his head again.

He felt upward, and his hand brushed rock; part of the tunnel.

What if the first impact had simply been rock, too?

He'd been so on edge about Junior that he'd instantly presumed the first blow had been deliberate, Junior intentionally kicking up the silt before using it as cover for an attack. There were plenty of hard objects at hand—rocks and air tanks, for a start.

But in zero visibility, flailing around, Patrese could just have smacked accidentally against the tunnel wall, and his imagination had filled in the rest.

No way of knowing the truth; and not that it mattered right now either, as there was no sign of Junior. He could have swum blithely onward without realizing Patrese was no longer behind him, or he could be waiting somewhere in the pea soup to attack Patrese again.

Patrese felt around for the marker line, his fingers opening and closing on nothing but silt and water. In the silt-out, Junior could have been inches away and Patrese would never have known.

Don't panic. If you panic, you'll die. If you don't panic . . . you might still die. "Might" is a good deal better odds than "will."

Time to go. He had to make a decision and stick to it. It could be taking him back to the surface, it could be taking him farther in, but staying here was no longer an option.

Holding his arms ahead of him, he kicked out . . . and was suddenly yanked back, gripped hard around his right ankle.

Patrese kicked furiously down and out, trying to dislodge the grip on his ankle. He was held even tighter than before, and again he kicked, both feet this time, thrashing around as he tried to land some blow, any blow, on Junior.

Nothing. Nothing but water and silt, and something digging into his ankle. *Cutting* into it.

Patrese reached down and felt around.

A nylon line. The marker line.

He tried to untangle it, but it was too tight. Trying to kick it free just made it worse.

Patrese's hand brushed against the knife on his belt.

It would have been a dilemma, he thought, if there was any other option. But as before, to stay here was to die. It was either cut the line or cut his foot off—and even Luther wouldn't have been crazy enough to try *that* in these circumstances.

He unclipped the knife from his belt, very carefully—dropping it would be pretty much a death sentence—found a point on the line where he could just about work his finger underneath, and cut it there.

He unwrapped the line from around his ankle and pulled it to see in which direction it would go taut.

It didn't go taut. It went slack in his hands.

Patrese knew instantly what he'd done. The line must have been wrapped twice around his ankle, and he'd cut through two adjacent points rather than just one, meaning he'd cut the line in three rather than two—two long segments, the main parts of the marker line, still attached to the cave wall; and one short segment, attached at neither end, which he was holding in its entirety.

His light beam backscattered against the particles of silt, diffuse and useless.

Patrese checked his air gauge again. Below two-thirds now; he must still have been breathing too fast, or else one of the tanks had been knocked and sprung a small leak. No time to find out. Time to get going.

Got to move. Got to try something, anything. Got to concentrate on something other than impending death.

He reached out his right arm, moving it in ever-increasing circles until his fingers brushed something solid; a tunnel wall. Keeping his hand in permanent contact with the wall, he began to swim. Whether he was going farther in or coming back out, he had no idea.

The silt began to subside. Patches of clear water appeared in his light beam. If he'd gotten it right, he'd soon be coming back out of the tunnel and into the vast underground cavern, where he could pick up the marker line again.

The tunnel began to widen. There was a patch of light in the water ahead of him. Hard to tell distance underwater, but Patrese reckoned about a hundred yards.

Junior's head-beam?

Patrese stopped swimming and squinted. The light held still. It looked as though it was coming from *above* the water.

Light from above meant only one thing: the outside world.

Patrese waited a few more seconds, just in case the light source moved and proved to be Junior after all, and then he kicked out toward it for all he was worth.

The beam was coming through an opening just about big enough for Patrese to squeeze through. He didn't remember the tunnel from the cavern being this narrow, but maybe he hadn't been paying attention properly, or maybe he was coming back to it from another direction.

Patrese wriggled through the opening, pressing his chest flat against the rock to give his air tanks space to clear.

He felt the water drain away from around his mask and mouthpiece.

Not the cavern. Something different. A dry chamber. An air pocket.

He clambered onto a ledge, took off his mask and mouthpiece, and gulped down the natural air. The chamber stretched high, high above him; the height of a ten-story building, Patrese estimated, all the way up to the small hole letting light and air in, as though it were a window high in the dome of a cathedral.

There was no marker line anywhere Patrese could see. He knew caves were forever being discovered and mapped, so it was entirely possible that this one had yet to be marked. Entirely possible, in fact, that he was the first person ever to find it.

If so, that meant his chances of being found and rescued were almost zero. How could someone locate him if they didn't know that where he was even existed? This place might as well be the far side of the moon. There was no way he could climb the chamber walls, and even if he could, the air hole wasn't big enough for him to fit through. If he stayed, he'd have air to breathe and water to drink, but nothing to eat. Sooner or later, he'd just waste away.

No. If I'm going to die, I'm going to die trying.

He checked his air gauge. Just over a third remaining. The last third was for emergencies, Junior had said.

Well, if this doesn't count as an emergency, I'm not sure what does. Could have stayed with Selma. Should have gone to Chichén Itzá. Would have been safe. But everyone knows what could have, should have, would have are: last words of a fool.

Feeling every inch that fool, and then some, Patrese put his tanks, mask, and mouthpiece back on. For a moment, he was even tempted to cross himself, a long-held Catholic superstition dragged to the surface by seeing Junior do it earlier.

No. No crosses. I'm going to get out of this myself, or not at all.

He checked his breathing rate. Normal, more or less. The panic had subsided. The more desperate his situation became, the calmer he felt. Something to do with lack of options, probably. Fewer choices meant fewer worries.

He swam back the way he'd come; at least he *thought* it was the way he'd come. In the darkness, pretty much everyplace looked the same.

Ahead of him, the tunnel forked. No marker line in either branch. Which way?

Pick one and go with it.

He went right. The tunnel sloped upward. He followed it.

Another intersection. Still no marker line. He started to go right again, and then stopped. If he kept going right, mightn't he just end up where he'd started?

He tracked back and went left instead.

Around and above him, blank, uncaring rock.

His temples throbbed. Carbon dioxide buildup; he wasn't breathing enough, because he was trying to preserve his air for as long as possible.

Patrese felt his air tanks brushing the tunnel's ceiling. They were becoming lighter, pulling him upward. He checked the air gauge again. Less than a quarter; way less than a quarter, in fact. If he was a car, the refill light would be on by now. And the less air there was, the lower the pressure in the tank, so the more effort was needed to unseat the regulator's demand valves, so the harder it was to breathe . . .

Another vicious circle, spiraling in on itself until the inevitable.

This is it. My time has come. Too tired, too woozy to care. Just stay here and sleep, floating like a jellyfish. Maybe they'll never find me. Doesn't matter if they don't, not to me at any rate. I won't be around to care either way. Want to know who the killer is though hope Selma can find out hope they haven't killed Selma funny she'll never know she was pretty much the last thing I thought of tunnel opening out suspended in a green-saturated infinity again feeling like an orbiting spacecraft over the surface of a strange planet.

The realization fought its way through the fog in his brain.

This is the cavern. This is the cavern we came through.

The marker line, away to his left.

Too late not enough air to make it back might get to the surface in time but have to decompress at ten feet seven minutes Junior said seven minutes at ten feet or was it ten minutes at seven feet doesn't matter don't have seven minutes left on this tank let alone ten but if I don't decompress all the dissolved nitrogen will come boiling and fizzing out of me like a giant Alka-Seltzer like a bottle of fizzy pop shaken hard and then opened nitrogen disintegrating all the tissue in its path every nerve cell in the body simultaneously set to maximum pain a terrible way to die that's my choice quick searing agony or a slow asphyxiation.

He grabbed for the marker line anyway, following it into the tunnel.

A flash of red in his light beam.

The backup tank. The one Junior had left in the alcove.

No more air left in Patrese's tanks now. Running on vapors, in every way.

He held his breath on empty lungs and reached for the spare tank with the last ebbs of desperate strength. His arms moved in ghastly, mocking slow motion.

Lift the tank up come on fumble for the mouthpiece going black behind the eyes now change the mouthpiece over vision closing in like a camera shutter don't swallow any water when you bite on the new mouthpiece need air fading fading.

His lungs suddenly expanded and filled with the new air, the breath of life.

Patrese crawled out of the cave entrance half an hour later.

Junior was rummaging in the back of the SUV. He looked up.

"Franco!"

Surprise? Despair? Anger? Disbelief? Patrese couldn't tell. He rested his hand lightly on the knife in his belt. If Junior had meant to kill him in the cave and wanted to finish the job now, Patrese would be ready for him.

If Junior had a gun, of course, the point would be moot; but if Junior had a gun, surely he'd have disposed of Patrese long before now?

Junior hurried over to Patrese. "Here. Let me help you." He put his shoulder in Patrese's right armpit and lifted Patrese to his feet. "What the hell happened, man? I was just about to get some more tanks and come down to look for you."

"You hit me on the head."

"I did *what*?"

"After the cavern, in that little tunnel, in the silt-out—the silt-out *you* caused, by kicking too hard—you hit me on the head. Trying to kill me."

"Franco, what the heck are you talking about? Tell me what happened."

Patrese had dealt with a heap of liars in his time; it came with the territory, when you were in law enforcement. He reckoned himself pretty good at spotting them.

But now, when he stared at Junior, he couldn't for the life of him tell whether Junior was on the level or not.

"Got hit on the head," he repeated. "In the silt-out."

"You must have banged it against the rock."

Which was exactly what Patrese *had* done the second time around. That was the thing. For every event that could have been Junior trying to kill him, it could equally have been an accident, or some fevered product of Patrese's paranoid brain.

"Then I got tangled up in the marker line, so I had to cut it free—but then I lost it. Ended up in some weird air pocket, this huge chamber, a hundred feet high. Came back. Almost ran out of air when I found that cavern again, the one we swam through before the silt-out—and I got to that spare tank you left just in time."

"That's *why* I left it there. I lost you, looked for you, couldn't find you anywhere. I figured if you *did* need more air, you'd know where to find it. Listen, you've had a terrible time. Get in the car, we'll head home."

Patrese did just that. But he kept his hand on his knife all the way back.

Patrese slept late and hard. It was past nine by the time he woke, and the sunlight was splashing bright and sharp on the white floor.

He padded to the bathroom, brushed his teeth, and went out onto the terrace. Selma was looking out to sea. On the table in front of her was a fruit salad, which looked as though it had come from Eden itself.

"Hey," she said. "You okay?"

"Yeah."

"Must feel better for the sleep, no?"

Patrese poured himself some coffee. "For sure."

Talk at dinner the previous night had been all about Patrese's narrow escape. He'd been obliged to repeat his adventure in forensic detail. If he'd worried that he sounded hysterical or exaggerated, the shocked looks on everyone's faces soon put his mind at rest. Even to him, it sounded every bit as hairy as it had felt.

Of course, their shock might have been simply that he'd survived, but if that was the case, they'd *all* had to have been in on it, and Patrese couldn't believe that every one was a sufficiently good actor to make it convincing. Junior, perhaps. Six or seven others, no. This wasn't *Murder on the Orient Express*.

Patrese sipped at his coffee. "In all the excitement last night," he said, "I never got to ask you; how was Chichén Itzá?"

"Less eventful than cave diving, by the sound of it."

"But good?"

"Amazing. Mind-blowing. One of the seven modern wonders of the world, you know? Wish I'd brought my camera." She nodded toward her cell phone. "Took some pictures on that, but it's not the same as a proper camera. You should go sometime."

"If you go back, I'll come with you."

305

She smiled. "Deal."

They sat in silence for a while.

"You sure you're okay?" she said.

"Yeah, fine. Why?"

"You seem very quiet, that's all."

He knew what he wanted to say. *I was convinced I was going to die, and I thought of you.* Maybe this, a sunny morning in paradise, was the perfect time and place to say it. But what would she reply? If the situation was reversed, and she said that to him, what would *he* say?

"Just waking up," he said. "What time's the flight back?"

"After lunch, I think."

"After lunch? How nice. To have a private jet, and not worry about something as inconvenient as a schedule."

She laughed. "How the other half live, huh?"

"You got it."

"Any plans before then?"

"Thought I might just explore. We didn't really get to see the place on Tuesday, did we? Too busy interviewing all those folks. And since we're probably never going to be back here again . . . Wanna come with me?"

"Sure. I got time for a shower?"

"No hurry. I'll wait for you."

"Okay."

It was quite some place. Two identical ziggurats stood at either end of the complex: 114 steps up to the summit of each, from where the views across the reserve and out to sea were even more spectacular than down on ground level. On the east edge of the escarpment was an enormous ball court, four times as long as it was wide, flanked by gently sloping walls, and with a statue of a jaguar at each corner. Halfway down one of the long sides, a vertical ring like a basketball hoop turned on its side protruded from the top of the wall. Beneath it, about three feet off the ground, was a small bronze plaque stating that the ring was positioned so that twice a year, on the vernal and autumnal equinoxes, the sun shone directly through the ring as it set.

They headed toward the complex's main building, a long, low reconstruction of a Mayan palace.

It was like a labyrinth inside. Rooms led into one another and back through on themselves again; corridors wound up where they'd started or came to juddering dead ends; doors led on to courtyards with tinkling fountains.

"This what the cave system was like?" Selma said.

"Just about. More air here."

Ahead of them, a maid scuttled across a corridor. Patrese glanced inside as they passed the room she'd just left, and stopped dead.

Varden's study.

He grabbed Selma's arm and indicated. She nodded.

Patrese checked that the maid was nowhere in sight, and then stepped inside.

Mi casa es su casa, Varden had said. I've nothing to hide, he'd said.

Time to test those statements, Patrese thought.

You could have played table tennis on Varden's desk, it was so huge. A leather-bound blotter sat in the middle, with a desktop computer at the near right-hand corner and a forest of silver photo frames on the left-hand side. On the wall behind Varden's chair was a framed poster—an original theatrical release one-sheet, by the look of it—of *Snow White and the Seven Dwarfs,* the 1937 original, signed at the bottom: *Dear St. John, with all best wishes, Walt.*

Patrese nodded toward the poster. "In a survey, six out of seven dwarves said they weren't Happy."

Selma laughed. Patrese tried the desk drawers. All locked, unsurprisingly.

He looked at the photos. Varden and Junior on a golf course with George Bush *père* and *fils.* Varden in hard hat and high-vis jacket on an oil rig. A black-and-white Varden, much younger but still very recognizable, on his wedding day, laughing next to his bride.

That must be Rosalita; Junior's mother. The monochrome highlighted rather than diminished the jet black of her hair and the whiteness of her teeth. My, but she'd been beautiful, Patrese thought; eyes shaped like almonds, nose crinkling above her smile.

There were more pictures of Rosalita, these ones in color. Rosalita on a beach in a two-piece hip-rider swimsuit; late sixties, by the look of it. Rosalita in a restaurant with a small boy on her lap; Junior, Patrese guessed, when he really was junior. Rosalita in a hairdressing salon, looking comically up toward her new pageboy cut, hair turned inward to frame the delicacy of her features.

"His wife?" Selma asked, leaning forward to look at the pictures.

"Must be. Rosalita."

"Quite a beauty, huh?" Selma looked at the salon picture for a moment, looked away, and then suddenly looked back at it again. "Heavens. I don't believe it."

"What?"

"Look."

"At what?"

"Just look."

"At *what*?"

"I want you to see it for yourself. Two independent views are better than one."

Patrese picked up the photo and stared at it.

"Her hairstyle?"

"No. Nothing to do with her. Look at what else is in the photo."

The usual paraphernalia of a hairdresser's, Patrese saw. Scissors, gels, and sprays on the counter; another customer in the background; the woman who'd just cut Rosalita's hair reflected in the mirror behind her.

Look at what else is in the photo, Selma had said.

"What else" could include "who else."

Patrese looked closer. Looked at the woman in the mirror.

She was thirty years younger in this picture than she was now, but it was still unmistakably her, even without the kaftan and madras; and Patrese remembered she'd started out as a hairdresser.

Marie Laveau.

They didn't want to ask Varden about Marie while they were still here, that was for sure. Not only would he know they'd been snooping, but they were completely dependent on his goodwill to get back to New Orleans. His security men still had their passports. Yes, Patrese hoped Phelps and Thorndike would intervene on their behalf if things got sticky, but could he be totally sure of that? The very fact that he needed to ask the question gave him his answer.

They'd sit on it, dig around, ask Marie. Only when they were sure of their ground would they take it back to Varden.

About the corporate jet ride back to Louisiana, Varden was as good as his word. While one of Varden's staff took care of the Dodge that Patrese and Selma had rented in Mérida, they and the other guests were driven straight to the airport. Weather conditions for the flight home were pretty much perfect. A tropical storm was due to make landfall in Florida shortly, but they'd be flying well to the west of it.

Varden showed them on to the plane with a child's enthusiasm. It was a Gulfstream G450, he said. The line had only entered service three months before, and Varden had the very first one out of the factory. State-of-the-art stuff. No messing around with departure lounges or screaming babies wedged up against your elbow. Here, the chairs were larger and softer than La-Z-Boys, the bar was sufficiently well stocked to have kept the entire Rat Pack happy, and the flight attendants could have doubled as models rather than Soviet-era shot-putters.

The lap of luxury, or a gilded cage?

Patrese felt safer, physically safer, than he had twenty-four hours before. But as to whether or not he was being played, he still had no idea.

Patrese called Marie first thing. He had no idea whether the cell number she'd given him last month was still good; a lot of criminals changed numbers more often than they did underwear. Only one way to find out.

"Hello?"

"Marie, it's Franco Patrese." Silence. "Hello?"

"What do you want?" Her voice was stripped of even the barest hint of friendliness.

"I need to talk to you."

"I got nothing to say to you."

"Is this because of Luther?"

"You're damn right it's because of Luther. You put a man in my organization—"

"It wasn't us who put him there."

"—you have him spy on me, and then you turn around and say you need to talk to me. Uh-uh. No way. Play someone else for a fool."

"It wasn't us who put him there. Not the Bureau. It was the NOPD."

"I don't give a good goddamn if it was Hoover himself. You're all the same."

She was about to hang up; he could feel it. "Varden," he said quickly. "You know Varden. You used to cut his wife's hair."

More silence, but at least the line was still open. Patrese hurried on into the gap. "I went to Yucatán, to his place there. I saw a picture of you with her."

"So?"

"So I want to know how this fits in with what's been going on."

"The murders, you mean?"

"Yes."

"I'll tell you a hundred times: I got nothing to do with those."

"I didn't say you did. But you have links to them. So does Varden. And now I find out you have links to Varden."

When Marie next spoke, her voice seemed to rumble like approaching thunder.

"Be careful of yourself, Franco."

And she was gone.

Patrese ran Selma through his conversation with Marie, verbatim. Selma had no more idea what Marie had meant than Patrese did.

They didn't want to go back to Varden just yet, not still knowing so little. Nor did they want to confide in Phelps or Thorndike anymore. Where did those men's loyalties lie? With the Bureau and the police department, or with Varden? Patrese and Selma couldn't be sure, and even the slightest doubt was too much.

What went for Phelps and Thorndike went for the other city worthies who'd been out in the Yucatán, too: Alper the assistant DA, Dempsey the deputy sheriff, Infuhr the deputy mayor. Not that Patrese and Selma had ever had much to do with those guys.

Then there was the other guy who'd been there, the one who'd said he was an old buddy of Varden's from way back. What was his name?

Waxman. Marshall Waxman. That was it.

Patrese Googled him.

Waxman worked for FEMA, the Federal Emergency Management Agency. FEMA was part of the Department of Homeland Security and was tasked with coordinating the response to any disaster, natural or man-made, that occurred on American soil and overwhelmed the resources of local and state authorities.

In administrative terms, FEMA was divided into ten regions. Waxman was director of Region VI, which comprised Arkansas, Louisiana, New Mexico, Oklahoma, and Texas, and was headquartered in the Texan town of Denton.

Denton was where Varden had been with Cindy the day before she was killed.

The envelope Luther had sent to Selma had been logged as evidence. Patrese asked one of the uniforms to go and retrieve it from the registry.

He kept reading. It wasn't so much what Waxman was doing now that interested him, as what he'd done before. Waxman had been Varden's lawyer for almost two decades, first in private practice and then as in-house counsel. More recently, he'd taken two sabbaticals, in 2000 and 2004, both to help run George W. Bush's election campaigns in Texas. His reward had been the FEMA regional directorship; in other words, Patrese thought, the kind of political patronage that wouldn't have shamed an African republic.

Not that Waxman could have taken the post for the money or the prestige. His FEMA salary was a fraction of what he must have been earning with Varden, and FEMA's budget had been slashed to help pay for the Iraq war. Some projects had been effectively halved.

Patrese would have bet every dollar he earned that Waxman was still on Varden's payroll, at least unofficially. Waxman would also be shoving as many FEMA contracts toward Varden as possible, the cuts be damned. Half the available dollars meant half the contractors, not the same number of contractors on half the money. That was Washington math.

The uniform returned with the envelope. Patrese opened it, tipped the contents onto his desk, and fanned them out so he could see all of them at once.

Still no discernible pattern in the chaos.

His gaze landed on the American Airlines schedule for flights between New Orleans and Dallas–Fort Worth.

Was Dallas–Fort Worth the nearest airport to Denton?

There was a Rand McNally road atlas on one of the bookshelves. Patrese grabbed it and flicked through till he found the map of Texas.

From Dallas–Fort Worth to Denton was thirty, forty miles, tops. Under an hour's drive.

But why would Varden need an American Airlines schedule? He had a corporate jet. People like him didn't fly commercial.

Maybe the schedule hadn't been for Varden. Maybe it had been for someone else. Someone else coming to Denton from New Orleans.

Roger Rojciewicz had been to Dallas the day after Varden's party; he'd told Patrese and Selma that when they interviewed him following his daughter's death. Dallas on congressional business, he'd said, then back to D.C.

Could just have been a coincidence. But Rojciewicz had also just been out in the Yucatán with Varden.

Patrese had seen Rojciewicz's grief up close, and he'd been sure Rojciewicz had had nothing to do with his daughter's death. Even if Rojciewicz was mixed up in something, and even if Cindy had found out about it, Rojciewicz would never have been a party to her death.

Unless, of course, he didn't know that was why she'd been killed, which is to say, someone else involved in it had murdered her and not told him. Conspirators didn't just keep secrets from the outside world; they kept secrets from one another, too.

And if that was the case, the last place he should leave this envelope was here, where either Phelps or Thorndike could find it. He wondered why they hadn't tried to make it disappear already. Probably because getting rid of it would have caused more questions than it answered, at least while they knew Patrese was nowhere near the truth. Once he started getting closer, however, all bets would be off.

He felt he *was* getting closer, but where it was leading him, he still had no idea.

He called across to the uniform who'd brought the envelope up. "Thanks for this."

"No problem."

"Listen, when I go to hand it back, did you sign it out in my name or yours?"

"Mine. My name."

"Okay. Thanks. Just saves time with Registry, you know."

"I hear you, man. Those guys couldn't find their own assholes with a mirror."

Patrese laughed, but he was thinking. The envelope hadn't been signed out in his name, which meant he was at least one remove from suspicion if anyone came asking. Sure, it wouldn't take long to find out, but even that might be better than nothing.

Taking criminal evidence out of police premises without express authorization was very, very illegal. In this case, Patrese felt, it might also be very, very necessary.

Patrese pulled into traffic and headed toward the park. He'd take the envelope home to start with, though he wouldn't leave it there too long; it was surely the first place someone would look. Right now, though, he couldn't think of anywhere better.

He was thinking so hard about how best to fit all the pieces of the jigsaw together that it was several minutes before he noticed he had a tail. Not just one car, either; three of them, flipping positions with speed and fluency, nondescript sedans with nothing to mark them out except their very ordinariness.

They were never right on his ass; they were too smart for that. There was always another car between them and him, and only after that came the first two trackers, eyeball and backup. Then another unrelated car between those two and the third tracker, tail-end Charlie. The cars kept swapping around, but the positions remained constant. Standard mobile surveillance. Professionals.

Police? Bureau? Varden? Did it matter?

Leaving plenty of room to the car in front of him in case he had to effect a quick getaway, Patrese made an unhurried left turn onto Canal and considered his options.

He couldn't lead them all the way home, that was for sure. He could head for the interstate, but paradoxically that would cut his options right down. On an interstate, you can't make sudden turns and you can get off only at designated exits. Tailing someone on an interstate is about as hard as falling off a log.

He could try to lose them in the city streets, but he was in an unmarked car, and initiating a high-speed chase without identifying himself as a police vehicle was just asking for trouble. Asking for casualties, too. Scratch that.

He could stop, get out of the car and confront them, but there were three cars' worth of them—from what he could see, each car had at least two people inside—and he was alone. He'd have to find somewhere very public to do it; a garage, perhaps.

Traffic lights held and released them all. A streetcar rumbled up the rails on his left-hand side, almost close enough to touch. Exotic names on street signs slid past: Lopez, Genois, Telemachus.

A silver van that had seen better days cut in front of him and braked hard. Another asshole in a hurry, Patrese thought. So much for the freewheeling Big Easy.

There was another car right next to him now, hard up against his passenger side. A sedan, but not one of the three following him. Patrese tried to give himself space, but the sedan was too close to him, and he was hard up against the van's rear fender. *What the hell was this? National Drive Like a Jerkoff Day?*

He realized too late exactly what it was.

Men piling out of both van and sedan; four of them, five, all black and all armed. They swarmed Patrese's car like hornets whose nest had been disturbed; waving guns, shouting, pulling him from the driver's seat, and bundling him into the back of the van, as though this was Johannesburg or Bogotá, places with crime rates that made New Orleans look like Switzerland. As the van doors closed on him, Patrese caught a glimpse of one of the men climbing behind the wheel of his own car.

Then all was darkness and noise.

Patrese was flung around the back of the van as it drove fast and reckless through the streets, other vehicles' horns blaring in symphonies of remonstration. He wedged himself in a corner as best he could, hands tight around the envelope he'd instinctively grabbed just before the men had hauled him out of the car.

After a few minutes the van began to slow, settling into the stop-start rhythm of urban traffic. Patrese could hear voices on the other side of the partition, in the driver's compartment, but he couldn't make out what they were saying.

The dark swirled around him, an airless sauna. He took deep

breaths to steady his heartbeat. Who'd taken him? What did they want? Could he use Cindy's envelope as a bargaining tool? Or would it make them kill him all the quicker?

He wouldn't grovel or beg. Nor would he stand there blazing defiance. To be the calm man, the gray man, the reasonable man was surely his best chance.

They went over a bridge, its links reverberating under the van's wheels. Which bridge? There were plenty in the city. Not as many as Patrese had been used to in Pittsburgh, but then Pittsburgh had more bridges than Venice, as every piece of tourist literature in the city was at pains to point out.

A final right turn, and the van coasted to a halt. Engine off, footsteps on tarmac, and the rear doors opened, flooding Patrese's compartment with light.

"Let's go."

There were two of them, both with their guns trained on him. Squinting against the sunshine, Patrese clambered out of the van and onto the road. His own car drew up behind, driven by one of the carjackers, and he could see the other sedan just turning in to the street a few hundred yards away.

They were outside an enormous house that looked as though it had been styled after a Mississippi steamboat. A deep deck adorned with hanging light chains ran all the way around the outside of the building; the chimneys were shaped like smokestacks and the windows like portholes, and there was a small cupola at the top.

The men frisked Patrese; took his gun, satisfied themselves he wasn't wired up.

"Inside."

They escorted him in through the main door and across a narrow hallway. He wondered why they hadn't tied his hands. Maybe they trusted him not to try to escape. Maybe they knew he didn't have a chance of getting away.

On balance, he preferred to go with the first option.

They took him into a living room draped in dark red. Patrese smelled incense. Skulls grinned at him from an altar by the far wall.

"Hello, Franco," Marie said.

She dismissed the men who'd snatched him, and laughed at his surprise.

"You think I mean you *harm*?"

"Your men kidnap me in broad daylight. What else am I supposed to think?"

"My men *saved* you."

"From who?"

"From whoever was following you. Varden's people, I guess."

"I'm sorry. I don't understand. Those guys in the sedans—they weren't yours?"

She shook her head. "That's why we picked you up."

And why the van had driven so fast and furiously to start with, Patrese guessed: to shake Varden's men off their tail.

"I still don't understand. I spoke with you a few hours ago, you told me to get lost."

"I told you to be careful of yourself."

"Why?"

"You don't want to mess with Varden. You really don't."

"Says the biggest criminal madame in New Orleans."

"Whatever you think of me, Franco, I'm small beer compared to Varden."

"You run drugs, Marie. You kill. You have victims."

"Victims? Don't make me laugh. I have *customers*. You think I've corrupted a single person? You think I have to go out and hustle like a damn mortgage salesman? Get this: People wanna get high. Always have, always will. Why? 'Cause they can't bear reality, that's why. We all need our delusions, Franco, and it don't matter how you get them. Huxley went into the desert and took peyote. The Aztecs sacrificed humans. A billion Catholics believe the Pope's infallible. It's all the same, man. This is the underworld. Down here, supply never has *shit* on demand."

"How do you mean, compared to Varden?"

"Huh?"

"You said you're small beer compared to Varden."

"Tell me what you saw at Varden's."

Something in Marie's voice—a smear of tenderness laced with fear—pulled Patrese up short. She'd played him once before, over the whole voodoo thing. No way should he trust her this time; no way.

But it was her or Varden.

He told her what had happened in the Yucatán, right from the start: discovering that Phelps and Thorndike had hightailed it there and lied about it; interviewing all the staff; his cave diving with Junior and the photos in Varden's office.

She gestured toward the envelope in his hand. "Can I see?"

Showing a gangland boss evidence in an active criminal case was instant dismissal. But Patrese figured he was so far in now, it made no difference. He handed it to her. She opened it, pulled out the contents, skimmed through them, and shrugged.

"Makes no sense to me."

"Me neither."

"That don't mean he's not up to something."

"Tell me, Marie."

"Tell you what?"

"How you know all this. *What* you know."

"How else do you think I got started in this business?"

"Drugs?"

"Varden. I got started through Varden."

Marie and Rosalita always talked a lot, as women do at the hairdressers. They'd become friends, and that was how Marie had met Varden. She used to go around to their house now and then for supper, or lunch on the weekend. After Junior was born, she'd go and babysit quite often. It had been a world away from her life in the Lower Ninth: the poverty, the vibrancy, all the junkies just jonesing for a hit.

A few weeks after Rosalita had been killed, Varden had come by the salon himself, and asked if he could have a word.

Cut a long story short, this was what Varden had wanted. He had a place in the Yucatán, and he'd started doing some business with the Gulf Cartel; cocaine, mainly, and heroin. An international construction company like Varden's was always sending freight around the world. Easiest thing going to put some contraband in there.

Varden had needed someone on this end, in New Orleans, to arrange distribution. He hadn't wanted to use the Mafia. This was the early eighties; though the Mafia was still strong in New York and Chicago, in New Orleans they'd been on their way out. Prosecutors were all over them like cheap suits; wiseguys were breaking the omertà code and becoming informers; other gangs, from Asia and Latin America, were starting to want in on the action. The Mafia had been yesterday's men. Varden had wanted someone new, someone under official radar. Marie—lots of contacts, but no criminal record herself—had been perfect. Interested?

Of course she'd been interested. This was New Orleans. If you weren't keen to make a buck or two out of vice, the next person along sure as hell would be.

That was how it had started, and in essence that was how it remained to this day, though of course it was now a much larger and more sophisticated operation. Marie had her network of dealers and runners; the Gulf Cartel was organized more like an army than a crime gang.

Did Patrese remember the guards at Varden's estate? The ones dressed like paramilitaries with a Z on their baseball caps? They were from Los Zetas.

The name Los Zetas rang a bell. Tumblers turned in Patrese's mind.

He realized where he'd heard the name before. The man whose murder Marie had been tried for—Balthazar Ortiz, that was his name—he'd been from Los Zetas.

Yes, Marie said; he had been indeed.

She'd killed someone she did business with?

It's the drugs business, she said, not accounting. He deserved it.

Why?

Because she knew the kind of reputation he had. He'd have tried to rip her off, and the way not to be ripped off by someone was to kill them before they had the chance. If you let one person get away with it, then everyone would know you were weak, and that was the one reputation you couldn't afford to have. The Romans had a phrase for it: *oderint dum metuant*. Let them hate, as long as they fear.

And Varden? What did Varden think about Ortiz's murder?

Like she'd said, Ortiz had been a bad man. His loss was no loss.

Okay. That was Marie's connection with Varden out in the open. But why was she telling Patrese all this? It incriminated her as much as it did Varden, if not more so.

Two reasons, she said. First, Varden had been behaving weirdly lately. Hard to say exactly how, but when you've been doing business with someone for round about a quarter-century, you get to know their moods, their methods, and something wasn't right about Varden. If Marie had to put a finger on it, she'd say he seemed distracted.

Patrese needed a little more to go on than that.

Okay. Here was the second reason.

She handed him a photograph. "Found it in Luther's place after his death," she said.

Two soldiers in desert fatigues. They had their arms around each other and were grinning at the camera. In the background, plumes of flame were erupting from the ground and reaching high and exuberant for the heavens. Like everyone who was old enough to have watched CNN at the time, Patrese recognized the place immediately: Kuwait, 1991, when the Iraqis had set the oil wells on fire while fleeing ahead of the Desert Storm forces.

Fourteen years ago, but the men in the foreground were instantly recognizable.

Luther and Junior.

That was all Marie had, and that was all she knew. No, she hadn't told him earlier, as she hadn't known he was investigating Varden. She'd told him now. She could lend him a couple of bodyguards, if he wanted.

A federal agent being offered protection by the city's premier gang boss. As Yogi Berra might have said, only in New Orleans.

Thanks, Patrese replied, but he'd take his chances.

He called Selma.

"Where the heck did you get to?" she asked.

"I need to talk to you."

"Then talk."

"In person. Can you be outside the building in twenty minutes? I'll pick you up."

"Franco, what the heck?"

"Jesus, Selma. Just fucking trust me for once, can't you? Twenty minutes. And don't tell anyone, okay?"

"Okay."

Patrese's car was waiting for him out front. Almost like valet parking.

"You sure you're good to go?" Marie asked.

"Yeah, thanks. And—thanks. I'm still not sure why you're telling me this, but . . ."

"Rooster was my friend, Franco. For him if no one else, I want you to find the person who did this."

The St. Claude Avenue Bridge, which led back into town, was up, to let a barge enter the lock beneath. Patrese drummed his fingers on the steering wheel, impatient and nervous. Away to his right, the canal water reflected the sun in dull brown.

After a minute or two, the bascules came down again and the traffic moved through. Patrese deliberately made four right-hand turns, just to see if anyone was following him. If they were, he couldn't see them, which meant they were either very good or very bad. Not much he could do about it either way.

He turned on the radio—WRNO-FM, classic rock—to take his mind off things. Steve Earle was singing about the whiskey burning down Copperhead Road.

By the time Patrese got to police headquarters, Journey had exhorted him not to stop believing, Blue Oyster Cult had begged him not to fear the reaper, and Bon Jovi was wanted dead or alive.

Selma was waiting outside the building, as promised.

"What's this all about, Franco?" she asked as she got in.

He told her what Marie had said, and showed her the photo of Luther and Junior.

"And you believe her?" Selma said.

"Don't start with that. I know you can't stand her, but—"

"I didn't mean it that way. I meant 'Do you believe her?'—because I do."

"You do?"

"Sure. Why would she make it up?"

"What are we going to do?"

"Let me think."

Selma rubbed her eyes with the heels of her hands. On WRNO-FM, the news was just starting.

"Top news this lunchtime. Six people have been killed by Hurricane Katrina, which made landfall near Hallandale Beach, Florida, yesterday evening. Katrina has now moved back out to sea but is rapidly strengthening from its Category One status. Forecasters fear that further locations along the Gulf Coast may be in jeopardy. Katrina is the fifth hurricane of this year's Atlantic season, following hurricanes Cindy, Dennis, Emily, and Irene."

Patrese and Selma stared at each other.

Cindy, Dennis, Emily, and Irene.

And now Katrina.

"Kat South," they said simultaneously.

Selma called Kat.

"Wyatt Herps."

"Ms. South, it's Detective Fawcett from the NOPD. You remember we—"

"I remember very well, miss. What can I do for you?"

"Are you inside your house?"

"Sure am."

"Good. I want you to stay there. Lock all the doors, close the windows. Keep your gun with you. We're on our way."

"What's this all about?"

"Those murders we came to see you about, the ones with the snakes—we think you could be in danger."

"Me? Why me?"

"Trust me, please. We'll explain when we get there."

"Miss, I got a ton of security guards here. Those goons from Varden, the ones waiting for me to leave, they're here. Ain't no one getting past them. Hold on a sec." Selma heard her call out to someone. "I'm on the phone! Wait a sec. I'm coming!"

"Whoever that is, don't let 'em in . . ."

The line went dead.

It was forty-five minutes from town to the Bayou Barataria, where Kat South lived. Siren and lights on the roof, Patrese made it in half that.

They'd radioed ahead, trying to get cops on the scene as quickly as possible, but the bayou was in Plaquemines Parish, while they were in Orleans Parish. Different jurisdictions meant they couldn't make direct contact with the local police. Instead they had to go through the central dispatcher, which took several minutes.

Several minutes Kat South might not have.

The main gate to Kat's property was twice the size it had been before and now had a guard hut next to it. Varden's people had certainly been busy since Patrese and Selma were last here, a month or so before. The gate was already open, and Patrese could see the reflection of blues and reds up ahead. At least one police cruiser was already there.

Fast down the road, tires scrabbling for grip on a surface alternately baked hard by the heat and made mud by the rains. The car shimmied and fishtailed.

Patrese and Selma were out and running almost before they'd come to a complete stop. Into the house, screen door banging open and shut behind them.

There were two cops in the living room with Kat. One was giving her CPR; the other was using whatever he could as a tourniquet where her leg had been severed. In the corner was a rattlesnake, motionless; probably shot by one of the cops. The officer with the tourniquet looked up.

"Paramedics are on their way," he said.

"How is she?" Patrese said.

"Not good. Not good at all."

"You see him? The guy who did this?"

"Must have beat it just before we got here. Probably heard us coming, with all the sirens." He pressed harder on the tourniquet, Kat's blood seeping between his fingers.

"When was this?"

"Few minutes ago."

"Five? Ten?"

"Five, at most."

Patrese thought fast. This place was at the end of a long access road; from the main highway to the front gate was two miles, a good three or four minutes' drive. And they hadn't passed any car coming the other way since leaving the highway.

Killer must still be here.

"Let's go find him," Patrese said. "Nothing we can do here."

Selma nodded. They backed out of the room, guns held front and center.

"Through the house, room by room," Patrese whispered.

Selma nodded again.

The place was a bungalow: kitchen, utility room, bedroom, bathroom, and the monument to disorganization that was Kat's office. Patrese and Selma searched the standard way—one into a room fast and low, the other covering.

Five times they did this. Five times they came up empty.

"What about the snake house?" Selma said.

Patrese remembered the snake house from when they'd first visited. It was a little way away from the main house, and contained hundreds of Perspex cages that had reminded Patrese of a Tokyo capsule hotel. Kat had referred to all the snakes in there as her babies.

Patrese and Selma went outside. An ambulance disgorging paramedics pulled up.

"In there," Patrese said. *"Hurry."*

The door to the snake house was ajar. Patrese raised his eyebrows. Might just mean that Kat had gone in there this morning. Might mean something much more sinister.

"I'll go first," Selma said.

"I'll do it."

"You went in first to the last room we checked."

"This isn't eeny, meeny, miny, mo."

"And I ain't some little missy housewife, neither. My turn. Cover me."

Patrese took up position to the side of the door. Selma took a deep breath. Her face was shiny with sweat. If she felt anything like Patrese did, it wasn't just from the heat.

She kicked the door open and went in low and fast.

Two shots from the semidarkness inside, and Selma's chest puffed blood.

Faster than thought, Patrese aimed into the room and fired back.

A quick glimpse of Junior—my God, Patrese thought, it really was him—scampering between the cages, zigzagging so Patrese couldn't get a clear shot, and then a sudden burst of light as he opened the door at the other end of the building.

At Patrese's feet, Selma's breaths sounded like she was wading through molasses. He dropped to his knees to take a look.

Her shirt was a crimson lake. She looked at him with wide eyes.

"Selma . . ."

Footsteps coming fast behind him; the urgent voices of the paramedics. "Let me see her, sir. We'll take over, sir."

Selma gave Patrese the slightest of nods, and rolled her eyes in the direction Junior had gone: *Go get him.*

Patrese squeezed her hand and set off running through the snake house. There was a terrace at the far end, he remembered; he, Selma, and Kat had sat out there with some lemonade and admired the beauty of the bayou beneath and around them.

He checked left and right through the door. No way to be sure whether Junior was lying in wait for him, too.

Have to take a chance.

Fast through the door. The terrace was empty.

There was a jetty about fifty yards away. Moored alongside were two airboats, each of them flat-bottomed with an enormous propeller inside a metal safety cage out back; standard means of transport in the marshy shallows of the bayou. The Varden logo ran down the side of each vessel.

Junior ran onto the jetty and leaped onto the nearest boat. Patrese could hear the rise and fall of more sirens. He ran after Junior.

Junior started the engine, leaped onto the elevated driver's seat, and set off into the bayou. Patrese felt the hot wind of the propeller's backdraft as he reached the jetty and jumped onto the second airboat.

He turned the ignition key. Nothing.

Keep calm. Work it out.

The engine probably worked on the same principle as a lawn mower engine or outboard motor, which need to be primed before they start. A couple of dabs on the throttle should do it.

Patrese looked up. There was a single pedal to the right of the driver's seat. He pressed it twice and turned the key again. The propeller roared into life.

Patrese hoisted himself up onto the driver's seat. The pedal he'd just pressed was the accelerator, clearly. No sign of a brake. *Worry about that later.*

By his left hand was a vertical stick. He pushed it forward. Nothing happened. Pulled it back. Still nothing happened.

But there were no other controls visible, so how the hell did this thing steer?

He looked around. Behind the propeller cage were two large rectangular flaps, like the ailerons on an airplane's wing. Patrese pushed the stick forward again. The flaps moved one way. When he pulled back, they went the other way. *That* was how he steered, though he guessed it would work only once he was moving and there was enough airflow to change direction.

He pressed the accelerator. The airboat began to move forward.

Junior was a couple of hundred yards ahead. Patrese gave it some more gas until the boat was on a plane, skimming the surface of the bayou water. The noise of the propeller battered his eardrums, but the only protective headset he could see was on the floor, out of reach. By the time he'd slowed, picked it up, put it on, and started again, Junior would be halfway to Mexico. Patrese had to keep him in sight at all costs. The bayou splintered into mazes of tributaries. Once you lost someone here, you weren't finding them again in a hurry.

Up ahead, where the bayou channel forked, Junior was banking left.

Patrese pushed the steering stick forward, trying to balance turn and throttle. The boat began to veer to the right. He eased the stick back through the vertical and toward him. This time the airboat went left as he wanted.

Warm, stagnant water slapped against the flat hull. On a silty bank shaded by cottonwood trees, an alligator watched him pass with ferocious curiosity.

Patrese was closing in fast on Junior. My airboat must be more powerful, he thought. He saw Junior look around, slapping the air in frustrated alarm when he saw how near Patrese was. Patrese gripped his gun tight.

The front of Patrese's boat vibrated intensely as it skipped into the outer waves of Junior's wake. Patrese eased off the throttle. The boat began to slide sideways across the water, farther into the wake, where the waves were bigger. The port side, caught on a crest, began to lift, tipping the starboard beneath the surface.

Patrese realized two things more or less simultaneously.

First, that with the driver, engine, and propeller mounted so high above the transom, the airboat had a very high center of gravity. Good for skimming across shallow water. Even better for capsizing.

And second, that Junior had slowed deliberately for precisely this purpose, to catch Patrese in his wake, knowing Patrese's inexperience with airboats would do the rest.

In ghastly, inevitable slow motion, Patrese's airboat flipped over.

He arced through the air and into the thick, muddy waters of the bayou. He clamped his eyes and mouth shut just in time. The gun slid from his grasp as he went under. Blindly, he grabbed for it, half caught it, dropped it again. Gone.

He surfaced, inhaled, and looked around. The airboat was already sinking fast; not much in the way of flotation devices, by the look of it. Nothing for him to cling on to. He'd have to swim for it.

Junior had swung his own boat around a lot more expertly than Patrese and was now coming back toward him. From the look on Junior's face, and the way he was holding his gun, Patrese doubted he was going to pick him up, dry him off, and bring him safely to shore. What had happened in the Yucatán cave might still have been an accident. This certainly wouldn't be.

Patrese took the deepest breath he could manage, jackknifed, and swam directly downward. A moment later, he felt the buffeting as Junior's craft whizzed over the point where he'd just been, and heard a shot.

No point opening his eyes, even if he wanted to; visibility wouldn't be much better than it had been in the cave silt-out. Patrese flattened his body out and began to swim, keeping himself as deep underwater as possible. He didn't know which way he was heading, and didn't care. He simply wanted to put as much distance as possible between himself and the last point where Junior had seen him, knowing that the water was too muddy, and too messed up by the wake from the airboats, for Junior to spot him until he surfaced.

Patrese let the air out of his lungs little by little. The bubbles sounded like a ringing phone as they streamed away from his nostrils—keep going keep kicking work with the arms reach out beyond the pain lungs empty now just a little more that last bit might make all the difference pain across the chest going black behind the eyes—and he broke surface and gulped down the damp summer air in great chokes.

Junior's airboat was nowhere to be seen.

Maybe he'd thought Patrese had drowned. Maybe he'd figured he couldn't afford to hang around too long in case some of the cops on scene had also found a boat and come after them.

The left-hand bank was farther away, but if Patrese had gotten his geography right, it was also the quickest way back. He'd only made one left turn since setting out from the jetty, so that bank should lead unbroken to the snake farm. If he went across to the other side, he might have to swim back across the bayou.

He started to swim; breaststroke, both to keep from swallowing any water, and also to look around and see whether Junior was coming back. He headed for an oak trailing wisps of Spanish moss almost down to the waterline. Next to the oak, reeds clumped like hair tufts in the mud.

Twenty yards away from dry land: swimming strongly, and still no sign of Junior.

Up ahead, movement in the reeds; a shifting of dark green as something slid into the water. Back scaled like armor plating; eyes narrowed atop a glistening flat head.

Alligator.

Fear bubbled like lava in Patrese's throat.

He stopped swimming and began to tread water, frantically trying to push coherent thoughts through the swirling panic in his head. *Stay put or make a break for it?*

He was a Pittsburgh boy. The hell did he know about alligators?

He remembered reading somewhere that you should never swim in gator water after dark, because that's when they feed. Did that make him safer now, in the heat of the day? Was this alligator just looking for somewhere to cool off?

It was heading straight toward him. If it was going to attack, it had him right where it wanted him. This was the gator's arena; home-field advantage, in every way.

Patrese stayed very still. The only movements he made were little circles with his forearms, the bare minimum needed to keep him afloat.

The alligator kept coming. Ten yards. Five.

The death roll, that's what they call it. The gator latches on to its prey and rolls over and over until the prey is dead, either by drowning or blood loss. Appropriate enough for this case, Patrese thought.

No time to be scared. Fear will kill quicker than this brute.

Patrese was moving sideways even as the gator opened its mouth, dark water streaming from its jagged peaks of teeth. He pulled his right arm out of the water, up and around as though he were winding up for a slam dunk. He locked his middle and index fingers straight, and brought them down with vicious anger.

Straight into the alligator's eye.

The gator thrashed and screamed. Patrese yanked his fingers out and kicked for the shore as hard as he could, not daring to look back, waiting for the thousand agonies of those enormous jaws clamping around one of his ankles. Those teeth looked like they could take a limb clean off.

The attack never came. Patrese was into the shallows and through the mud before he turned toward the water again. The alligator was gone.

His legs gave way; shock, he guessed. He slumped against the oak trunk and tried to get his breath back.

Selma. Shot. Gotta go.

He set off along the bank, his shoes squelching as he walked. At least being dripping wet was helping keep him cool.

He checked his belongings. His FBI badge was still on his belt, his keys were still attached to the carabiner clipped on to one of his belt buckles, and his watch was on his wrist. His cell phone, wallet, and gun were somewhere at the bottom of the bayou.

It was a half hour before he made it back to the snake farm. Cops remonstrated with security guards, paramedics bustled around the back of ambulances. Cruisers were slewed every which way, radio chatter buzzing through high static.

Patrese unclipped his badge and walked up to the nearest cop.

"Where's Detective Fawcett?"

"Who?"

"Detective Fawcett. Black lady. NOPD."

"The one who was shot?"

"Yes, the one who was shot. Where is she?"

"They took her to the hospital, sir. West Jefferson Medical Center, in Marrero. It's about thirty minutes away. That's where they took both of them, both ladies. The detective and the snake woman."

"Okay. Thanks." Patrese gestured to his own sodden clothes. "The man who shot her, Junior Varden—"

"Junior Varden? The governor?"

"That's right."

"You gotta be kiddin' me!"

"Do I look like I'm kidding? He's out in the bayou somewhere. He's in an airboat. Get air support, get police boats, I don't care; get them, and find him."

"Yes, sir."

Patrese walked over to his car. The keys were still in the ignition: He'd hardly had time to stop the car when they'd got here, let alone pocket the keys. Selma's purse was still on the passenger seat, where she'd left it.

He bounced the car back up the road and out through the main gate. On the radio, the newscaster was talking about Hurricane Katrina again:

"The National Hurricane Center has in the past few minutes officially altered the possible track of Hurricane Katrina from the Florida panhandle to the Mississippi-Louisiana coast. Governor St. John Varden Jr. has declared a state of emergency for the state of Louisiana, and applied for federal troops to be deployed to the region."

Junior and Luther, Patrese thought; Luther and Junior. How had they worked it? Luther had served with Junior in Iraq, and had spent many years in military intelligence. At the very least, judging from the files they'd found in his house, Luther had been some kind of information gatherer, putting together dossiers on likely victims. That would explain a great deal, not least why Luther had been so reluctant to spill the beans. If Luther *had* collated the information, there was nothing he could have said without incriminating himself as well.

More than that, Luther had killed Cindy and Rooster, surely—otherwise why would he have been paid after both those murders?—

but then he hadn't been able to carry out Emily's murder when her turn came, as he'd been in the hospital. Had Junior gone along himself to kill Emily? And Irene, too? Hell of a risk, when your face was that well known, but with a baseball cap and dark glasses, under cover of darkness, no one expecting to see you there, a trained soldier . . . possible. Very possible.

And Luther? A paid assassin, or something more? Luther had been unraveling long before he'd shot himself in the leg, Patrese saw now. Perhaps he'd been on the edge even as early as the first night they'd met, when he'd come around to Cindy's apartment; perhaps he'd wanted to confess there and then, nip this thing in the bud before it was too late.

Except by then, of course, it had already been too late.

What was another layer of secrets when you were already living as many lies as Luther had been? Just a bit more to deal with, or the straw to break the camel's back?

Answers were like Hydras: Each one threw up two more questions.

Patrese remembered the note they'd found in Luther's house, about New Orleans being the new Sodom and Gomorrah, the cities God had destroyed because Abraham hadn't been able to find more than one righteous person living there.

Abraham, who had been prepared to sacrifice his own son to prove his faith.

This must be what the murders were about, Patrese thought; human sacrifices of the sinners, to try to stave off the hurricane which everyone had known would come sooner or later. He hadn't checked the dates of the previous four hurricanes, but he'd have bet everything he owned that they coincided with the murders of those people unfortunate enough to share their name with the hurricane in question. Make an offering to your judgmental, avenging God—especially an offering of one who'd fallen far from what He'd intended—and let Him spare you, at least till the next time.

Patrese had thought of human sacrifices, but only in terms of voodoo. He'd thought of Christian fundamentalism, but gotten the wrong culprit. They'd had most of the right pieces, but hadn't put them in the right order.

The West Jefferson Medical Center was well signposted. Patrese parked outside and hurried in. Summer heat and the car's aircon had between them dried his clothes to a level of dampness consistent with usual August sweating.

"Can I help you?" asked the receptionist.

Patrese showed his badge. "Two women were brought in here earlier. Kat South has a severed leg, Selma Fawcett a gunshot wound. I'd like to see them."

"Wait a moment, please." The receptionist tapped at her keyboard, frowned, picked up the phone, and dialed an internal number. "Hi, this is Cynthia. I got an FBI agent here, wanting to see those two ladies brought in . . . Yeah, they're the ones . . . Both of them? You sure? . . . Okay, I'll tell him." She hung up and turned to Patrese. "Doctor will be right down, sir."

"I want to see them."

"Sir, the doctor will be—"

"Them. *Now.* This is urgent."

"Sir. Both those ladies are dead, sir."

The doctor confirmed that both Selma and Kat had been DOAs. Kat had simply lost too much blood ever to have had any chance of survival. As for Selma, one of the shots had hit her in the aorta, and that was fatal nine times out of ten. The aorta is the biggest artery in the human body, and a direct hit is pretty much as serious as it gets. The paramedics had tried everything, but to no avail.

The doctor asked whether Patrese wanted to see the bodies.

He'd like to see Detective Fawcett's, he replied.

She was already in the mortuary; another piece of meat in a drawer, nothing more. No soul, no life, no vibrancy. She was no longer here; she existed only in his memory. If the afterlife she believed in did exist, Patrese thought, he hoped she was there. As far as he was concerned, there was nothing after this but infinite darkness. How did the poem go? *Beyond this place of wrath and tears / Looms but the horror of the shade.* That was it. That was what he felt.

He stared at Selma's corpse. It would have been too corny to say out loud that he was going to catch Junior for her, and make him suffer for her, so he didn't, but hell, he felt it. He and Selma had started this case together. He'd finish it for her if it was the last thing he did. Then, and only then, would he let himself grieve for her. There was too much to do before that.

Patrese turned to the doctor. "Do you have her personal effects?"

"Sir, I can't release them to you unless—"

"I'm a federal agent. They're criminal evidence. I'll sign for them."

The doctor came back a few minutes later with a clear plastic bag.

Patrese had already found Selma's wallet and cell phone in her purse. Nothing personal, but he needed them now more than she did. And he certainly needed what he could see in the plastic bag.

Her gun.

Patrese went first to the bank, where he emptied his account into cash, and then back home, knowing it might be his last time there for a while. He packed some clothes and personal items, bundled his laptop into its padded carrying case, and put them in his car.

Wetzel wasn't in. Pity. Patrese had wanted to see him; perhaps say good-bye.

He called Phelps, who picked up almost before the first ring.

"Franco! You okay? There's been some shootout down on the bayou; that right?"

"Junior Varden killed Selma. Tried to kill me."

"Come in, Franco. We'll talk about it."

"He killed Kat South, too. The hurricanes. Five victims, plus Selma. There's nothing to talk about. You should have a fucking statewide manhunt for him by now."

"We do. We do. We got everyone on the case. But we need to look after *you.*"

"You're part of it, aren't you?"

"Franco, don't be absurd."

Franco, Franco; using his name, trying to appeal to him.

"I tell you the state governor killed a cop, you don't even sound surprised. You're in on it. Why, Wyndham? What's it all about? What's in it for you?"

"Franco, please come in."

"You know he tried to kill me? Twice, if you include the caves."

"I didn't know he was going to . . ."

And there it was. An admission, right there. Not *That was an accident, surely*, but *I didn't know he was going to*. Very different. Very telling.

"Come in, Franco," Phelps continued. "Come in. That's an order."

"Or what?"

"Or we'll come and find you."

"You can shove your order up your fucking ass."

No holds barred now. Him against them; law enforcement officer turned outlaw.

Patrese was thinking fast, survival instinct coming to the fore. They would come to his house sooner rather than later, so that was out of bounds. They'd also be looking for his car, so he had to get rid of it.

But he needed a vehicle, and stealing one would sooner or later work its way onto the police system. He'd stolen one while on the run from the Pittsburgh police the previous winter, and the theft had been discovered within a couple of hours.

What he needed was a car he could take without the owner realizing it was gone.

And he knew the perfect place to find one.

The crime-scene tape had been removed from Irene Kolker's front door. Patrese checked that no one was watching, and then took his skeleton key, poked around in the lock until the tumblers clicked, and pushed the door open.

The place reeked of disinfectant, high and smarting. The crime-scene cleaners had obviously been in.

He went into Irene's office and opened her desk drawer. Logical place to keep a car key, and Irene had been a logical person.

There it was, the first thing he saw, as though it had been waiting for him. A Chrysler key. Patrese had noted a green Sebring on the street outside.

He left the house, locked the door behind him, and blipped on the remote. The green Sebring's central locking clicked open.

Patrese transferred his carryall and laptop bag to the Sebring's trunk.

He couldn't leave his own car here. If for whatever reason the cops found it, they'd know instantly what he'd done. And if they didn't find it here, they'd have no reason to look for Irene's car. No one was going to report it missing, after all.

Patrese took his own car, drove it back into town, left it in an underground parking lot beneath Canal Street, walked to the ferry terminal, got the ferry back across the Mississippi to Algiers Point, and walked back to Irene's house. It took him more than an hour, and he was sweating like a turkey the day before Thanksgiving; but such precautions, no matter how ludicrously paranoid they seemed, could save his life.

Now he needed somewhere to stay. Any large, anonymous motel chain should do the trick. He could pay in cash and give a false name. Those places were always full of transients, people running from or to things. With a high turnover of guests, no one would give him a second glance.

There was a whole clump of chain motels out toward East New Orleans, on Chef Menteur Highway. Patrese had driven past them several times. He headed there now.

The Super 8, hard up against the I-10 interchange, had a vacancy. The room reeked of stale smoke despite the no-smoking sign on the door, and had clearly seen better days. The surface of the table was coming unglued, some of the shower tiles had fallen away, and the bed sagged in the middle even when empty. The couple next door was arguing, loud and drunk even in early evening, and a dog barked somewhere close by, proving that the "no pets" rule was enforced about as thoroughly as the "no smoking" one.

For Patrese's purposes, it was perfect.

The room had Internet access. Patrese plugged in his laptop, waited for it to boot up, and looked up details of this year's hurricane season.

The World Meteorological Organization maintains six separate lists of names for North Atlantic tropical and subtropical cyclones, in alphabetical order and alternating between male and female both within and between years. For example, one year starts with Alberto, Beryl, Chris, and Debby; the next with Andrea, Barry, Chantal, and Dorian. Every seven years, the cycle of names begins again, though particularly damaging or notorious storms have their names retired and replaced.

This year had started with Tropical Storm Arlene, which had formed on June 8, and Tropical Storm Bret, June 28. Patrese guessed that, in Junior's warped logic, only proper hurricanes counted; a mere tropical storm wouldn't cause enough damage to merit a sacrifice.

Hurricane Cindy had formed as a tropical storm in the Gulf of Mexico on July 4, though it had only attained hurricane strength the following day. Cindy Rojciewicz had been killed the day after that: July 6.

Hurricane Dennis had formed in the eastern Caribbean on July 5—again, first as a tropical storm. It had attained Category One hurricane status on the sixth, strengthening to Category Four on the seventh. Dennis "Rooster" Richards had been killed in the small hours of the eighth.

Neither hurricane had gotten too much publicity in the U.S. Cindy had made landfall in Louisiana but as a minimal hurricane, killing only three people. Dennis had been a monster—Category Four was the strongest ever recorded in July—killing eighty-nine people and causing billions of dollars' worth of damage. But the death and destruction had mainly been in Cuba and Haiti, and therefore unworthy of the networks' attention.

Hurricane Emily had begun life as a tropical storm on July 11, but had only been upgraded to a hurricane two days later, on the thirteenth. Emily Stark had been killed the following day. Hurricane Emily had caused severe damage to the Yucatán coastline; the fallen trees, Patrese realized, that he and Selma had seen while visiting Varden. But again, nothing in the U.S. worth making a big fuss about.

Next had come three tropical storms in succession: Franklin, Gert, and Harvey.

Hurricane Irene had existed in various forms of depression and storm for more than ten days before suddenly turning into a hurricane on August 15. They'd found Irene Kolker's body on the twentieth, but the pathologist had said she'd been dead for several days by then.

Tropical Storm Jose had formed in the Gulf of Mexico on August 22 and dissipated the following day. Two days later, on August 25—yesterday, Patrese realized—Katrina had been upgraded from tropical storm to hurricane. And now Kat South was dead.

So how come, Patrese thought bitterly, *he* was the one on the run?

He was tired and hungry, and he knew the old army adage about getting your rest and chow when you could. Nothing much more he could do tonight, even if he'd wanted to. Best to recharge his batteries and get to it in the morning.

So he stuffed his face at the nearest Mickey D's, and thought about Junior.

Patrese had majored in psychology at Pitt, and he could remember enough to be able to pigeonhole Junior as a classic narcissist. Narcissists see the world in black and white: *I am good, everyone else is bad.* They can't empathize, they exploit; they feel entitled to whatever they want, they dehumanize and devalue others. Contempt and disdain are their default settings. What was murder to such people, except just another way to maintain control?

But what else could Junior have been, with a father like his and no mother beyond his formative years? To the child, Patrese remembered, the mother is not just an object of dependence, a guarantor of survival and a wellspring of love; she is a representation of the universe itself. She is the first thing the child sees, smells, touches. As the child grows, he gradually detaches himself from his mother;

338

his own self-image takes shape, and he starts to modify his view of his mother as ideal and perfect into something healthier and more realistic.

Unless, of course, she disappears from his life before that process is complete.

Patrese went back to the motel and watched football on TV; a pre-season game from the Superdome, the New Orleans Saints against the Baltimore Ravens. The Ravens were archrivals of Patrese's beloved hometown Pittsburgh Steelers, so he rooted for the Saints on principle.

The Ravens won 21–6.

After the game, the news.

"The National Hurricane Center has predicted that Hurricane Katrina will make landfall again at the town of Buras-Triumph, Louisiana, only sixty miles southeast of New Orleans. Katrina is currently a Category Two hurricane, strong enough to damage mobile homes and break small craft from their moorings. It's expected to strengthen during the next twenty-four hours. The Saffir-Sampson scale, which measures hurricanes, goes all the way up to Category Five."

A half-hour newscast, and only one topic of news. One expert explained how hurricanes need water to thrive. When Katrina had jagged out to sea again after her first landfall in Florida, she'd refreshed and replenished herself, and was now coming back for more.

Patrese thought of that old joke: Why are so many hurricanes named after women? Because they're hot, wet, and stormy, and when they leave they take your house.

Another man, white-bearded like an Old Testament visionary, looked down the camera lens. "Make no mistake, folks. Katrina's a weapon. She's a rifle, she's taking aim, she's got crosshairs. And New Orleans is slap bang in the middle of 'em."

Patrese slept fitfully, woken now and again by banging doors and traffic noise from the freeway. Every time he woke, he half expected a SWAT team to come barreling through the door and take him away, and it was a few minutes in the galloping darkness before he realized that it was unlikely. He wasn't driving his own car, he wasn't using his own cell phone, and he hadn't used his own name at check-in. Yes, the cops could be visiting every hotel in the city armed with his picture, but whoever was on the night shift at reception wouldn't be the same guy who'd checked Patrese in earlier, so a photo would mean nothing to them.

Besides, the cops had other things to do, like help keep order in a panicking city.

Patrese turned on the TV at dawn. Katrina was now at Category Three intensity: officially a major hurricane, with sustained winds of more than 115 miles per hour and a possible storm surge of around twelve feet. Category Three hurricanes, the news anchor said, were powerful enough to destroy mobile homes, peel gable-end roofs off their buildings, and cause irreparable structural damage to manufactured homes.

On the weather graphic, Katrina was a double-bladed red rotor turning lazily out in the Gulf of Mexico. To Patrese, it looked like a swastika, or perhaps a ninja-throwing star, approaching with deadly menace. Don't be fooled by the fact that it's moving so slowly, the anchor said: Slow-moving hurricanes cause much more damage than fast-moving ones when they make landfall.

Patrese went downstairs for breakfast. Coffee, pastries, and juice, all free. By the taste of them, you got what you paid for. No matter. He ate till he was full, and then went over to reception and extended his stay for at least one more night.

Yes, the receptionist said, they were staying open during the hurricane. Plenty of folks would be needing somewhere to stay. And besides, you know these things. Never as bad as the media make them out to be.

Patrese went back upstairs and showered.

What to do? He had to get Junior; he had to stay safe. Could do one or the other. Hard to see how he could manage both.

The rolling news was mesmerizing. Patrese felt he could sit and watch it all day.

Here was a spokesman for the National Hurricane Center, blinking back the explosions of flashbulbs at a hastily called, cramped press conference.

"A hurricane watch is now in effect for the southeastern coast of Louisiana, east of Morgan City to the mouth of the Pearl River. This includes metropolitan New Orleans and Lake Pontchartrain. A hurricane watch means that hurricane conditions are possible within the watch area, generally within thirty-six hours."

Quick cut over to the White House, where a press spokesman was saying that President Bush had now declared a state of emergency in Louisiana. The Federal Emergency Management Agency, FEMA, would take control of the situation down on the Gulf Coast.

Patrese sat forward on the end of his bed.

FEMA. Waxman.

And there he was on TV, Waxman himself—*live from Denton, Texas*, according to the caption—as though Patrese had conjured him into appearing purely by the power of thought.

"My name is Marshall Waxman, and I am federal coordinating officer for the Hurricane Katrina situation. FEMA is now in charge by presidential order, and we're doing everything we can to minimize the impact and allocate resources according to where they'll be needed most."

When Patrese had first investigated Waxman, he'd paid more attention to what Waxman had done *before* joining FEMA than to the significance of his current post. Big mistake. Junior killed according to the hurricanes; his father's old lawyer was in charge of the cleanup? More than coincidence. *Much* more than coincidence.

What the hell had Patrese and Selma stumbled across in the Yucatán?

Patrese turned on his laptop and linked into the Web site that let him access the surveillance camera above the front door of his home. When Lippincott had first set this up, Patrese had laughed it off as excessive. He didn't think so anymore.

The picture was black and white, but clear enough.

Right now Patrese's yard and the street outside his house were empty.

There was a rewind facility below the live feed. Patrese began to scroll through, watching the time code in the corner spool backward at many times normal speed. Cars reversed past his gate at breakneck pace. Passersby walked backward in jerky steps. Day receded into night; night receded back into day again.

A figure at the front door, right under the camera. Patrese slowed the footage back to normal pace again.

It was Phelps himself. The time code read 18:12, 08.26.05. Early yesterday evening, in other words.

Behind Phelps, Patrese could see three other men, all built like linebackers. He didn't recognize any of them.

Patrese flicked back through the footage until he saw himself arrive and leave a few hours before Phelps. As far as he could make out, therefore, Phelps had been his only visitor between then and now.

But Phelps knew about the camera. So if some of his men were still outside waiting for Patrese to return, they'd probably be parked out of sight.

Patrese didn't want to go back home, but he *did* want to know as much about the hunters as he could. Perhaps Wetzel would tell him if they were still there.

Patrese didn't want to use the hotel phone; too easy to trace. He turned Selma's cell on—he'd been charging it all night—and dialed Wetzel's home number. It rang a few times and then went straight to voice mail. Patrese hung up.

The buttons on Selma's handset were smaller than he was used to. He accidentally pressed the menu option, which took him into the pictures folder, and thumbnails unrolled across the screen; a ziggurat, a statue.

The pictures Selma had taken of Chichén Itzá.

She'd wanted to go back there one day; with a proper camera, and with him.

Grieve when this is over.

He clicked on the first thumbnail and began to scroll through. Pyramid steps; an ornate gate; a stone jaguar's head; an observatory dome; Selma herself, standing against a temple wall adorned with a plethora of stone carvings.

Patrese looked at her face for a few moments, scrolled on to the next image . . .

. . . and scrolled back again.

Not for another look at Selma, but at what he'd seen above her left shoulder, on the temple wall. One of the stone carvings. A little statue, almost.

The camera had a zoom facility. Patrese turned it up to maximum and then shifted the photograph a little until he was focused on the statue, now three times its original size. With magnification came a certain loss of resolution, but he could still make out the bits he needed to.

The statue had one normal leg and one snake leg, and on its forehead was a flat, round plate shape pierced through with an ax head.

Patrese tried a few combinations of search words in Google before hitting pay dirt.

The statue was of the Mayan god Hurakan. In Mayan mythology, Hurakan (from the phrase Jun Raqan, "one-legged") was one of the three creator deities, and presided over the whirlwind and the rumblings of the thunderstorm.

In the beginning, according to Mayan myth, everything was underwater. Hurakan lived in the windy mists above the water, and repeated "Earth!" until land emerged. Hurakan and the other gods made clay men, but these clay men were unable to speak or understand, so the gods destroyed them.

Next the gods made men from wood. These men *could* speak, but they had no intelligence, no feelings, and no knowledge of their creators. Hurakan sent a flood to kill them.

Only with the third attempt, using maize, did the Mayan gods manage to create the humans they'd always intended.

Hurakan was always depicted the way the statue showed him, the way in which all five victims had been killed. The snake and the mirror were both symbols of Mayan shamanism: The mirror opened portals to the Otherworld, and the snake presented visions of ancestors and gods, giving rulers the gift of prophecy.

From Hurakan, of course, came the word *hurricane*.

Another layer to the complex relationship between father and son, Patrese thought. Varden was the Mayan obsessive, Junior the rigid Christian. It looked like they'd both had a hand in the murders, the victims chosen for their Christian names and transgressions against a Christian god, but killed in a very Mayan manner. A perfect synthesis of two belief systems.

Varden had said that the figure of Noah appeared in Mayan mythology as much as in the Bible. Myths, like religions, borrow from one another, mutating and adapting as they do so. Most cultures have some kind of flood story deep within the framework of their shared beliefs. Noah appears in the Koran, as does Jesus. Catholic saints appear alongside pagan gods in voodoo. And pretty much every culture has made sacrifices to its gods somewhere along the line.

So that was Varden and Junior's involvement in the murders sorted. But what about the others? Phelps and Thorndike were presumably being bought off for their silence, ensuring that law enforcement never got too close. In a pinch, Patrese could apply the same logic to Marc Alper, assistant DA, and Landon Dempsey, deputy sheriff of Orleans Parish. But what about Rojciewicz, or Infuhr, and this FEMA guy Waxman? What the hell did *they* have to do with it?

In any case, what could Patrese do about it all? He couldn't call the cops. He could call the *Times-Picayune* or the networks, but they wouldn't touch the story with a ten-foot pole, certainly not without confirmation—a confirmation neither Phelps nor Thorndike would give—and certainly not at a time when they had the biggest story of the year running around the clock.

Why? Why were they all involved? That's what he wanted to find out. And the only way to do that was to get one of them to tell him.

Who was the weak link?

Rojciewicz.

Rojciewicz, because Patrese had something to trade with him. *I tell you who killed your daughter, you tell me what this is all about.* Not very subtle, perhaps not even very ethical. But Patrese was way past caring.

He tried Rojciewicz's number. No answer. An electronic voice invited him to leave a message. He thought about it, decided not to. The last thing he wanted to do was leave prior warning of his intent.

Patrese couldn't sit around the motel anymore. He had to go and do something, feel like he was being useful.

He'd go down to St. Charles Avenue and see what was happening at the Brown House; Varden's house, where Patrese had gone for the Fourth of July, and where this whole thing had started.

Foolhardy, to put his head in the lion's mouth again? Perhaps. But he wouldn't get too close. He just wanted to feel like he wasn't letting this lie. Maybe his next move would come to him while he was there.

Patrese hid the laptop under the mattress—not a great hiding place, but better than nothing—made sure the door was locked, and went down to the parking lot. Traffic was backed up a quarter of a mile or so eastbound on Chef Menteur. He looked for an accident, or roadwork, but saw neither, and then noticed that the front of the line was turned toward a gas station.

Gas. They were all lining up for gas.

Patrese got in his car and headed the other way, back uptown. The radio was no longer background noise; it was constant companion, lifeline.

"Following mobilization by the state governor, the Louisiana National Guard has called four thousand troops into service. This is almost all the manpower available to them, a spokesman said, even though it represents only just over half their capacity. A further three thousand of their men are currently serving in Iraq, along with many of their high-water vehicles and heavy equipment. Federal coordinating officer Marshall Waxman has confirmed that the troops will be deployed in Louisiana according to the terms of the 1878 Posse Comitatus Act, which prevents military personnel from acting in a law enforcement capacity within the United States. Troops will principally be tasked with humanitarian and search-and-rescue duties."

Some people were loading up their cars as though they were going camping for a month; a mass summer vacation, all booked at the last minute. Others strolled the sidewalks as though they didn't have a care in the world, as though they'd heard it all before. Maybe they had. Maybe they thought this was just another false alarm.

Patrese didn't know a whole lot about hurricanes, but he knew enough to be sure that they weren't like earthquakes. Once you'd suffered an earthquake and ridden out the aftershocks, the pressure was released, and everything was safe for a while. Not so with hurricanes. With hurricanes, the gun was reloaded every time.

Patrese could hardly see the Brown House for the number of men there. There must have been twenty workmen, swarming over the place like giant ants in fluorescent vests and hard hats, boarding up windows, carrying plants and trash cans inside, securing roof tiles. Patrese also counted six men wearing mirrored shades and black T-shirts. These six had biceps the size of Patrese's thighs, and they were all armed to the teeth: automatic assault weapons in hand, pistols strapped to their belts. Security guards. Private military contractors. Mercenaries.

Patrese drove by on the other side of the road as slowly as he dared. One of Varden's men was keeping a constant eye on traffic going up and down St. Charles, and Patrese knew that even parking, let alone getting out of the car, would attract attention he could do without.

Just as Patrese was almost past the house, he saw Junior come out of the front door and stop to talk with a couple of the men. Patrese clamped his teeth together so hard that he felt the muscles in his cheeks stand out like walnuts.

F. Scott Fitzgerald said that the rich are different because they have more money. No, Patrese thought. The rich are different because they can get away with murder.

He tried Rojciewicz again. No answer.

He drove back to the Super 8. He wanted to watch the city on TV rather than in the flesh, to maintain the sense of disconnect without which he feared he might go insane.

The news networks reported the impending apocalypse with a relish that only just stopped on the decent side of pornographic. Airlines had begun to close down services into and out of Louis Armstrong. All lanes on Interstate 10 had now been designated outbound from New Orleans, and traffic was backing up by the minute as people in the thousands got the hell out. Building supply stores had run out of plywood. Supermarkets were low on perishables—bread, water, nuts, fruit. Convenience stores looked as though a swarm of locusts had been through them. Gas stations and ATMs were running empty. The city aquarium was killing its piranhas for fear that they'd get into the Mississippi and breed.

"Preparations to protect life and property should be rushed to completion," said the man from the National Hurricane Center.

Mayor Nagin came on TV, shaved head shiny above his man-of-action frown. He declared a state of emergency in New Orleans and advised people to leave the city, though he stopped short of calling for a mandatory evacuation. Legal reasons, Patrese knew: If by some miracle Katrina passed by and left New Orleans unharmed, City Hall would have the shit sued out of it by every person and every business that claimed to have lost earnings.

The Superdome was being opened to those in dire need, Nagin added. This time yesterday, the stadium had been gearing up to host a football game. Now it was being press-ganged into service as a giant campsite. Folks who went there, he said, should take food, water, and something to keep them comfortable: folding chairs, air mattresses. They should not bring guns, bullets, knives, razors, ice picks. They would be searched.

"Ladies and gentlemen, this is not a test," Nagin concluded. "This is the real deal."

Another night of fractured sleep, this one with the TV as a constant companion. Patrese dozed between ghoulish updates of Katrina's progress across the Gulf of Mexico and toward the Louisiana coastline.

By four A.M., Katrina had reached Category Four: sustained winds of 145 miles per hour. Three hours later, she was up to Category Five, the highest there was: sustained winds of 175 miles per hour, gusting up to 215 miles per hour. Patrese had to check he'd heard right—215!

Talk in the motel's breakfast room was of nothing else. People moved slowly and spoke in murmured whispers, as though the funeral had already started.

Patrese ate, went back to his room, and continued to watch the rolling news.

At ten o'clock, Mayor Nagin announced a mandatory evacuation of the city after all. Patrese reckoned Nagin's lawyers must have advised him that not telling people to get out was now going to attract more lawsuits than telling them to, which in turn meant the chances of Katrina missing the city were somewhere between zero and zero.

There would be a curfew in the city from six o'clock tonight, Nagin added. That was it. Statement over, no questions. Evacuation meant evacuation, curfew meant curfew. Now, if the press would excuse him, he had work to do, and off he strode.

"We've just got this in from the National Weather Service," said the anchorman, holding up a sheet of paper, "and I'm going to read it to you in full, as it's one of the most extraordinary, frightening things I've read in years . . . To those folks out there still pondering whether to stay or go, this might help you decide."

He began to read. "Devastating damage is expected. Hurricane Katrina is a most powerful hurricane with unprecedented strength, rivaling the intensity of Hurricane Camille of 1969. Most of the area will be uninhabitable for weeks, perhaps longer. At least one half of well-constructed homes will have roof and wall failure. All gabled roofs will fail, leaving those homes severely damaged or destroyed. The majority of industrial buildings will become nonfunctional. Partial to complete wall and roof failure is expected. All wood-framed, low-rising apartment buildings will be destroyed. Concrete-block low-rise apartments will sustain major damage, including some wall and roof failure. High-rise office and apartment buildings will sway dangerously, a few to the point of total collapse. All windows will blow out. Airborne debris will be widespread and may include heavy items such as household appliances and even light vehicles. Sport utility vehicles and light trucks will be moved. The blown debris will create additional destruction. Persons, pets, and livestock exposed to the winds will face certain death if struck. Power outages will last for weeks, as most power poles will be down and transformers destroyed. Water shortages will make human suffering incredible by modern standards. The vast majority of native trees will be snapped or uprooted. Only the hardiest will remain standing, but will be totally defoliated. Few crops will remain. Livestock left exposed to the winds will be killed. Once tropical-storm and hurricane-force winds onset, do not venture outside!"

The anchorman put the piece of paper down and looked at the camera. "'Human suffering incredible by modern standards.' That's what it says. What it means is this: Get. Out. If you *can* go, then *do* go. *Please*."

What could Patrese do here? What the hell difference to anything did he think he could make? He was stupid, that's what he was, hanging around a doomed city because he couldn't think of a way past the impasse in his head.

Of all the people who knew that Junior had murdered five victims, Patrese was pretty much the only one who wanted that knowledge put out there. When Katrina hit, people would die. If Patrese was one of those people, Junior would have gotten away scot-free with what he'd done. He'd have sacrificed five innocent people without punishment, and without reward—the hurricane was still coming, wasn't it?

If Patrese left New Orleans now, he'd be better placed to fight another day.

He didn't know where he'd go. There'd be somewhere; some lousy motel would have a spare room. And if he had to wait, he'd rather sit in traffic and know he was going somewhere than sit in this room and know he was going nowhere.

He packed his carryall, zipped the laptop into its case, and, more in hope than anything else, dialed Rojciewicz's number for what felt like the umpteenth time.

"Hello?"

Patrese caught his breath. "Congressman?"

"Who's this?"

"I know who killed your daughter."

"Agent Patrese?"

"Meet me, tell me what the hell's going on, and I'll tell you who killed Cindy."

A pause. Then:

"Can you get to my house?"

Trap. Must be a trap. "Don't be stupid."

"I guess so. Sorry. Shall I come to you?"

And let everyone know where I am? Equally insane.

"No. I'll meet you at the Museum of Art. Out front, by the blades. One hour."

The Museum of Art is situated in the city's main park, and the blades—an endlessly rotating sculpture, a Swiss army knife in motion—are located out front. By the blades, you can see people coming from some distance away. That was why Patrese had chosen it.

He was there early, and walked around the perimeter of the entire museum twice. No one there, not that he could see: none of Varden's men, no state troopers.

Rojciewicz was right on time. Alone, and looking like he hadn't slept in a week. They didn't shake hands. It didn't seem appropriate.

Rojciewicz held up a flash drive, a couple of inches long. "It's all on here."

He was a man way, way past lying; Patrese saw that clearly. Patrese had lost his parents, Junior his mother. That was bad enough. Losing a child was of an entirely different magnitude.

So Patrese told him everything, and Rojciewicz listened in a silence punctuated only by the occasional nod.

When Patrese had finished, Rojciewicz stared at him for what seemed like hours.

"Do you have any idea what it's like," he said finally, "to fail your little girl?"

He reached into his pocket and pulled out a gun. Patrese didn't flinch, not for a second. He didn't feel alarm. He knew the gun was not for him.

He was right.

He took the flash drive from Rojciewicz's dead hand, went back to the motel, and inserted it into his laptop.

A disk icon appeared. Beneath it was the caption *Removable Disk (E:).*

Sweet Jesus, Patrese thought.

He clicked on the icon. It opened to reveal another icon, this time of a document, captioned *Project N.O.A.H.*

Patrese opened it and began to read.

PROJECT N.O.A.H.
(NEW ORLEANS AFTER HURRICANE)

INTRODUCTION

This position paper sets out the background to, aims of, and plans to execute Project N.O.A.H. It supersedes all previous position papers on the topic.

In August 2001, the Federal Emergency Management Agency (FEMA) published a report detailing the three most likely catastrophes to occur on American soil within the next 25 years. One was a major terrorist attack against New York City, which of course came to pass, tragically and prophetically, a month later. The second was a massive earthquake in San Francisco.

The third was a direct hurricane hit on New Orleans and the subsequent flooding of the city as canals, Lake Pontchartrain, and possibly even the Mississippi itself overtopped their levees and walls. The FEMA report estimated that up to 250,000 people could be stranded in New Orleans, and up to one in ten of those would be killed in the flooding.

Project N.O.A.H. was initialized in response to two concurrent beliefs:

- that such a hurricane is inevitable
- and that when it does come it will provide an unparalleled and unrepeatable opportunity to reshape New Orleans drastically, permanently, and for the better. We have no idea when the hurricane will come; but come it will.

This paper is divided into three sections: before, during, and after the hurricane.

The first section, "before," details the background of the project and the conditions that make New Orleans particularly susceptible to such action.

The second section, "during," details the action to be taken by the various parties to this project during the hurricane and subsequent flooding.

The third section, "after," details measures to be implemented in the weeks, months, and years after the hurricane.

PERSONNEL

The project's personnel are as follows:

- St. John G. Varden, Chairman, Varden Industries
- St. John G. Varden Jr.; Governor, State of Louisiana
- Roger P. Rojciewicz, Congressman, First District of Louisiana
- Wyndham S. Phelps, Special Agent-in-Charge, New Orleans Field Office, Federal Bureau of Investigation
- R. Ken Thorndike, Assistant Chief, New Orleans Police Department

- Erskine B. Infuhr, Deputy Mayor, New Orleans
- Landon M. Dempsey, Deputy Sheriff, Orleans Parish
- Marc J. Alper, Assistant District Attorney, New Orleans
- Marshall T. Waxman, Director, Region VI, Federal Emergency Management Agency

1. BEFORE

1.1. THE WETLANDS

The destruction of much of the wetlands south of New Orleans, particularly in the parishes of St. Bernard and Plaquemines between the city and the Gulf of Mexico, has made New Orleans much more vulnerable to flooding than it would otherwise have been.

Hurricanes produce offshore rises of water called storm surges, when strong winds press on the ocean's surface and cause the water to pile up higher than the ordinary sea level. The hurricane then pushes this surge ahead of itself. Wetlands create friction, absorbing and slowing storm surges like a sponge. Scientists estimate that every 2.7 miles of wetlands absorbs one foot of storm surge.

The wetlands have been greatly diminished over the past decades by the construction of manmade channels and canals, many of them in connection with the oil and gas industries. These channels and canals have encouraged saline water to flow inland, killing vegetation and fueling erosion. Many of these channels have been dredged for the installation of pipelines. In environmental terms, dredging is far more damaging than other installation methods such as push-pull or directional drilling.

Varden Industries has undertaken a high percentage of all such construction work in the St. Bernard and Plaquemines wetlands.

One of the largest construction projects across the wetlands, the Mississippi River-Gulf Outlet Canal (MRGO), should also help funnel storm surges into the heart of New Orleans. MRGO was originally completed by the U.S. Army Corps of Engineers (USACE) in 1965 to provide shipping with a shorter route from the Gulf of Mexico to New Orleans's Industrial Canal via the Intra-coastal Waterway. It is currently used by less than one ocean-going vessel per day.

A recent report described MRGO as a "hurricane highway" and stated: "If a team of top-flight engineers had been assigned to build an instrument for the quick and effective flooding of New Orleans, they could not have come up with a better design than MRGO."

Varden Industries' own modeling systems concur with this assessment.

1.2. FLOOD DEFENSES

The state of New Orleans's flood defenses is poor.

Responsibility for their maintenance is split between several different bodies: USACE, the Orleans Levee District Board, private contractors (of which Varden Industries is by far the biggest), and subcontractors. This leads to bureaucratic confusion, exacerbated by the recent 44 percent drop in federal provisions for USACE's flood and hurricane protection projects in New Orleans; from $147 million in 2001 to $82 million in 2005. Diversion of resources to the war in Iraq accounts for the shortfall.

As a result of these factors, routine maintenance is often left partially or totally undone. Many of the defenses are old, inadequate, and unfit for purpose. Varden Industries' own engineers have identified more than 100 separate locations where the structures will withstand at most half the force built into their design thresholds. Some of these structures were built to lower tolerances than officially stated.

That many of the levees and canal walls will be overtopped in the event of a storm surge is a given. However, overtopping by itself will cause limited damage. Once the surge is spent, the water will recede back over the flood defenses.

Holes in the flood defenses, however, will present an entirely different proposition. If the canal walls and levees fail outright, water from Lake Pon-tchartrain will flow unchecked into the city. The holes could not be repaired while the water flowed, as the pressure will be too great, and the water will be coming in much too fast to be pumped away, even if the pumping stations were still working following the hurricane (unlikely in itself). The flow will only stop once water levels in the lake and city are equalized; in effect, once New Orleans and Lake Pontchartrain have become one.

To this end, and to be sure the canal walls will fail at their weakest points, Varden Industries has moored three cargo barges in strategic locations.

- *Holly Oakdale* is moored in the 17th Street Canal, opposite Fleur de Lis Park between 38th and 40th.
- *Shannon Bell* is moored in the London Avenue Canal opposite Warrington and Filmore.
- *Teresa Crawford* is moored in the Industrial Canal opposite the 2200 block of Jourdan.

These barges will inevitably break their moorings in hurricane-strength winds. The impact of them against the canal walls will destroy the immediate section of the walls.

The integrity of the structure of the Orleans Avenue Canal is so compromised that no barge is deemed necessary here.

There is a historical precedent for the deliberate destruction of flood defenses. During the Great Mississippi Flood of 1927, the city fathers used 30 tons of dynamite to blow up a river levee in Caernarvon, St. Bernard Parish, in an effort to protect the city itself from dangerously high waters. They did not do so in secret; they even invited the press along to witness it.

Ever since then, the black community has distrusted levee breaches. During Hurricane Betsy in 1965, a breach in the Industrial Canal flooded the Lower Ninth Ward, and allegations persist to this day that the breach was made deliberately. The black community will believe the worst of any breach of the flood defenses, irrespective of the truth.

1.3. DEMOGRAPHICS

Decades of "white flight" to the suburbs have meant that two-thirds of the population of metropolitan New Orleans is black.

Forty percent of the population is illiterate. Nearly half of all children begin kindergarten without standard vaccinations. New Orleans public schools, which are 93 percent black, are among the worst in the nation: 47 percent are deemed "academically unacceptable" and another 26 percent are under "academic warning."

New Orleans's crime rates are also among the highest in the United States, particularly in homicide, in which no other city has a higher per capita figure. Homicide rates in New Orleans run at ten times the national average. Senior law enforcement personnel have come to the conclusion that no amount of arrests will staunch the murder rate. Violence is entirely normalized in this city. Many criminal cases collapse because witnesses, fearful of reprisals, refuse to testify. The police and judicial systems are seen as institutionally corrupt, prompting citizens to take the law into their own hands.

New Orleans is also one of the poorest cities in the United States. More than 25 percent of residents, and 40 percent of children, live at or below the poverty line. In 65 percent of families living in poverty, no husband is present. These people, the poorest, are mostly black; they also tend to live in the lowest parts of the city, the ones most vulnerable to flooding. Property prices in New Orleans are largely (though not exclusively) proportionate to height in regard to sea level.

The vast majority of the city's poorest residents are unlikely to leave in advance of a major hurricane. Many do not own vehicles. Some will have health problems mitigating against long journeys in stressful conditions. Some will not want to leave their properties for fear of looting. Some will want to stay with friends and neighbors. Some will believe that the hurricane warnings are false alarms.

The majority of white people will leave. Many black people will stay, at least until they are forcibly removed for their own safety and the greater good of the city. Those who do not leave, voluntarily or otherwise, are at considerable risk of death.

2. DURING

The approach of a sufficiently high-category hurricane will prompt President Bush to declare a federal state of emergency, giving FEMA responsibility for managing the situation. Mr. Waxman will take personal charge, and afford any and all assistance, to the other signatories as he and they deem fit. He will also ensure that all emergency responders, assistance and relief personnel are registered with FEMA, preventing the deployment of any unauthorized personnel in accordance with the Emergency Management Assistance Compact.

Congressman Rojciewicz will ensure that all necessary channels are kept open to power bases in Washington, D.C., and that all decisions needing approval in the capital can be expedited quickly and without problem.

Mr. Varden will oversee the construction of a temporary holding facility at the Amtrak/Greyhound terminals, where both bus and rail services will have ceased. This facility will be known as Camp Greyhound.

Mr. Varden, Jr. will use emergency legislation to mobilize as many members of the National Guard of Louisiana as possible. These soldiers will be authorized to carry weapons and use deadly force where they deem appropriate.

Mr. Phelps will ensure the deployment of all available and necessary FBI enforcement officers.

Mr. Thorndike will ensure the deployment of all available and necessary NOPD enforcement officers. All law enforcement personnel will be authorized to shoot to kill.

Mr. Infuhr will liaise between City Hall and law enforcement. It is anticipated that City Hall will order evacuations and impose curfews.

Mr. Dempsey will take charge of all inmates of the Orleans Parish Prison.

Mr. Alper will take charge of Camp Greyhound, ensuring the suspension of due process for the duration of the state of emergency. Miscreants and felons will not be entitled to hearings or trials.

Looting and civil unrest is probable, and must be contained at source. Maintenance of public order is critical at all times. Food and water must be rationed and if necessary withheld to keep the population quiescent, weak, and helpless. Those who remain in flooded homes must be forcefully removed and relocated.

3. AFTER

The flooding of New Orleans, as expedited according to the measures set out in section 1.2., is projected to leave 80 percent of the city underwater, with flood levels varying from a few inches to in excess of 15 feet. All areas, whether flooded or not, are also expected to have suffered severe wind damage from the hurricane.

This will almost certainly constitute the biggest single civil disaster in American history. The bill for the reconstruction of New Orleans is impossible to calculate accurately, but even the most conservative estimate begins at $100 billion and goes north from there. Rebuilding the levees and canal walls alone is expected to cost $20 billion. In addition, the following will need to be repaired or rebuilt:

- roads
- bridges
- transport hubs
- commercial property
- residential property
- municipal buildings
- power lines
- sewage facilities
- communications facilities

The urgency of the tasks, and the relative paucity of firms with the capacity to undertake them, means that the majority of reconstruction contracts will be no-bid. Given its extensive international experience, most recently in Iraq, and its unique place in the social, economic, and political fabric of New Orleans, Varden Industries anticipates picking up a high proportion of such contracts, whether as sole, main, or part signatory. Contracts are anticipated to contain cost-plus provisions.[1]

Reconstruction is not anticipated to be like for like.

Post-hurricane reconstruction provides an opportunity to drastically re-

---

1 Cost-plus provisions guarantee contractors a certain profit regardless of how much they spend.

duce or even eliminate some of the most serious of New Orleans's problems. Instead of a city beset with crime and poverty, New Orleans can be a safer, wealthier place, where tourists need not feel that venturing beyond the French Quarter after dark is a death sentence. The benefits of such remodeling are not hard to see: increased tax revenues, reduced welfare payments, more attraction to businesses, more luxury condos, and so on.

To achieve this, criminals and welfare claimants must be removed from the city without the option of return at a future date.

In the first instance, criminals will be incarcerated in various penitentiaries across the state of Louisiana and elsewhere. The city of New Orleans will be unable to incarcerate them while its jailhouses need reconstruction, and the criminals cannot simply be set free. They will therefore be transferred to other institutions.

In the second instance, people will find that they do not have a home to return to. This will not necessarily be because their homes have been destroyed, though this may often be the case. It will be because the city of New Orleans has requisitioned the properties under eminent domain.[2]

The recent Supreme Court ruling *Kelo vs. New London*, No. 04-108 (June 23, 2005) has vastly expanded the powers of government to take property under eminent domain in situations where it is arguably for a private, not a public, purpose.[3] The decision allows governmental officials to condemn private property for the purpose of increasing tax revenues and promoting development.

It is anticipated that New Orleans's notorious public housing projects, where many residents have criminal records, will all be destroyed and replaced. More than 5,300 public housing units, including the sprawling low-rises of the St. Bernard, C. J. Peete, B. W. Cooper, and Lafitte developments, will be replaced by units for people with a wider range of incomes. Public schools and health care services will be reduced.

In the immediate aftermath of the hurricane, low-income residents will

---

2   Eminent domain applies when property is sold to local, state, or federal government at the official assessed value for public purpose; in this case, to be rebuilt as homes for low-wage workers primarily serving the expanded tourist industry.

3   In Kelo, the Court by a 5-4 majority upheld the city of New London, Connecticut's condemnation of 15 homes in the Fort Trumbull neighborhood for the sole purpose of furthering economic redevelopment around a planned pharmaceutical research facility.

be rehoused wherever there is space available. They should be dispersed as widely as possible throughout the country to prevent the formation of a critical mass who might challenge the eminent domain ruling. Kept in small pockets, they are likely to decide that it is better to stay in their new locations than risk everything by returning "home."

It is anticipated that the political demographics of a city reconstructed on the above lines will be drastically altered. A richer, whiter, older New Orleans is likely to become a Republican city. It may even tip the balance of power in the entire state of Louisiana toward the GOP.

FURTHER ITEMS

This paper is merely a summary of our aims and methods. Each individual has his own detailed plans. These plans are subject to change and review when necessary. Regular meetings between the participants will take place outside the New Orleans metropolitan area for safety purposes. The two favored locations are Denton, TX, where the FEMA Region VI offices are located, and the Varden residence in the Yucatán peninsula, Mexico.

Given that Mr. Varden stands to gain the most in financial terms from reconstruction contracts, it is only fair that Mr. Varden remunerates the other eight signatories to this project for their cooperation. Mr. Varden Jr., Mr. Rojciewicz, Mr. Phelps, Mr. Thorndike, Mr. Infuhr, Mr. Dempsey, Mr. Alper, and Mr. Waxman will each receive the following:

- $500,000 per annum until the hurricane strikes
- $1,500,000 after the hurricane strikes, subject to the successful execution of the operations tasked to them
- a holiday home worth in excess of $1,000,000 in Paradise Valley, AZ

This is our chance to make history. We must not let it slip.

Patrese read the document three times—the second time because he couldn't believe what he'd read the first time, the third time to properly appreciate the full demented, bureaucratically euphemistic, warped-logic horror of the thing.

Several things struck him more or less at once.

Though first Luther and then Junior had killed the five victims as sacrifices, they hadn't done so to stave off the hurricane and spare New Orleans. They'd done so to bring the hurricane on and destroy the city.

Callous though it sounded, those five murders were small beer in comparison to what they were intended to presage. This was no longer the murder of a few individuals. This was the murder of an entire city. It was the logical endpoint of disaster capitalism, be it war in Iraq or a hurricane in New Orleans; the corporate looting of public resources under conditions that were effectively martial law.

New Orleans was a black city. Not only was most of its population black, but so, too, its most senior elected officials. The mayor, the police chief, the district attorney, the sheriff—they were all black. But their deputies were white, and it was these men who sat around the table with Varden, where the real power lay. It was white families who dominated the city's professional and executive classes. Lawyers, bankers, industrialists—most of the ones who mattered were white.

And the city they imagined being resurrected from the floodwaters was a corporatized, sanitized, gentrified pastiche of what had made New Orleans so special in the first place. It would be Disneyland-on-the-Mississippi; an X-rated theme park, Six Flags Over Bourbon Street; a place where white folk would come to spend, drink, gamble, get laid, blow off steam, and where black folk would wait on them, make their beds, clear their garbage, or perform dead-eyed jazz routines like minstrels.

This wasn't reconstruction, Patrese thought.

This was ethnic cleansing.

It was several minutes before Patrese moved; just too much to take in.

He took several deep breaths and forced himself to think. *Concentrate; prioritize.*

First things first. He had to get this information out.

He attached the document to an e-mail and addressed it to . . . who? Selma was dead; he didn't have an e-mail address for Marie; he had no idea where Wetzel was; and everyone else he could think of was part of the Noah Project in the first place.

He typed in his sister Bianca's address, wrote a brief cover note— *Dear sis, please just keep this safe, open it and send it on if you haven't heard from me in a week or so, love franco*—and pressed Send.

The machine flashed a system error at him. Could not find server. Patrese called down to reception.

"I'm trying to send an e-mail, and it tells me the server's down."

"That's right, sir. Everything's crashing. Overuse before the hurricane comes."

So now what? Keep this flash drive safe, that was what. The hotel had a safe, but what would happen to the hotel in the next twenty-four hours? No, the drive would stay with Patrese at all times.

Next, he had to try to do something about those barges.

He scrolled back up through the document till he found them, and wrote down their names and locations.

- *Holly Oakdale* is moored in the 17th Street Canal, opposite Fleur de Lis Park between 38th and 40th.
- *Shannon Bell* is moored in the London Avenue Canal opposite Warrington and Filmore.
- *Teresa Crawford* is moored in the Industrial Canal opposite the 2200 block of Jourdan.

Patrese stared stupidly at the notepad, amazed that he hadn't realized before. Then again, he'd had so much to process that it was hardly surprising.

- *Shannon Bell* is moored in the London Avenue Canal opposite Warrington and Filmore.

In other words, about fifty yards from Patrese's house.

He stopped by the nearest drugstore and bought himself a money belt and some waterproof sealable freezer bags. The flash drive went in a freezer bag; the freezer bag went in the money belt. He also bought some bottles of water and energy bars. Then he drove up to the London Avenue Canal, taking the long way around so he could come at it from the lakeside and see any watchers outside his house before they saw him.

And there they were, clear as day even from almost a quarter-mile away: two cars, just up the street from his place. Two cars that Patrese had never seen on this street before; a quiet residential street, at a time when most everyone with a vehicle was getting the hell out of the city. The cars could therefore hardly have been more obvious if they had ten-foot-high neon letters spelling out *FBI* on their roofs.

Patrese turned down a side street, out of the watchers' line of sight, and parked his car. He couldn't drive onto the canal wall, so he'd have to get there on foot. It was only a short climb up a grassed bank.

Shannon Bell had a covered top with a steel hull. It was dark red, rusting, and enormous, at least a couple of hundred feet long, Patrese guessed, and perhaps a fifth of that across. It wasn't that tall, but even a layman like Patrese could see how heavy it must be, especially fully laden.

There were men walking around the outside of the deck. Varden's men, as heavily armed and intimidating as the ones Patrese had seen outside Varden's house. There was no way Patrese could even get onto the barge.

He walked along the top of the wall, away from the barge. The security men were unlikely to be on the lookout for him specifically, as they didn't know Patrese had uncovered the significance of the barge. He figured it was less risky walking along the wall away from them than instantly ducking back down to street level, which would have aroused suspicion in a moron, and whatever else Varden's men were, Patrese doubted they were stupid.

Maybe the other barges would be less well defended. Unlikely, Patrese thought, but he had to give it a go, anyway. He returned to the car.

In a few hours' time, a wall of water's going to knock my house clean off its base. It's going to drown this entire neighborhood—a middle-income, mixed-race neighborhood at that, far from the insanity of Project Noah's ethnic cleansing. But destruction means reconstruction, and reconstruction means money.

He headed uptown toward the park and, beyond that, the 17th Street Canal. WRNO-FM was cranking up the gallows humor, playing back-to-back Scorpions tracks—"Rock You Like a Hurricane" followed by "Wind of Change"—and then Billy Joel's "Storm Front."

Patrese made it across to the 17th Street Canal in double-quick time. Nobody on the roads, nobody at all. They were all most probably stuck on I-10 outbound. Sensible people, Patrese thought. He must be out of his mind not to be going with them.

Holly Oakdale was a little smaller than *Shannon Bell*, but no less heavily guarded.

One of Varden's men was staring him down. Even as Patrese felt his stomach lurch, he put his fingers in his mouth and whistled, as loud and piercing as he could. "Ginger! Ginger! Come on, girl!"

He made a show of looking for a dog; not Oscar-worthy, but good enough. Varden's man turned away, uninterested.

Patrese headed back toward the car. It wasn't just his dog that was nonexistent, he realized: There were no animals around, no birds in the sky. They must already have gone to seek shelter. They *knew* something wasn't right.

Patrese got back into his car and pointed it down toward the river. "Here Comes the Flood" sang Peter Gabriel. Katrina and the Waves were "Walking on Sunshine."

The city flashed vistas at Patrese's window as he drove. Outside the Superdome, a snake of people unrolled down the ramp, around the stadium, and along the street. Uniformed police officers swarmed a Cadillac dealership in the CBD and drove the vehicles straight out of the parking lot. On Canal Street, a man stripped to the waist walked along the streetcar line, his arms raised while he shouted: "Flee for your life. Do not look behind you lest you be consumed in the iniquity of the city. The righteous will be destroyed along with the wicked." In the French Quarter, bars were selling hurricane cocktails like they were going out of fashion.

Patrese kept his windows all the way up and his doors locked, as though to stop the madness from infecting him.

He drove across the St. Claude Avenue Bridge. Half a mile or so up the Industrial Canal, he could see the *Teresa Crawford* squatting in the water, dirty and menacing as her ugly sisters. He made a left and began to follow the canal bank toward the barge.

Varden's men were on board *Teresa Crawford,* too; of course they were. He'd make sure they stayed till the very last minute, till the roads were almost undrivable, before standing them down, knowing by then it would be too late for anybody to do anything about it, anyway.

There was no way Patrese could take them on single-handedly. Nor could he rely on the Feds or the cops; even if they didn't arrest him on sight, they wouldn't pick a fight with a bunch of ex-soldiers specially authorized by FEMA. Besides, if what Patrese had seen at the Cadillac dealership was anything to go by, half of the cops would be hightailing it out of there as it was. Little wonder they came in for such criticism. NOPD? No PD, more like. No PD at all.

If Patrese wanted to have a shot at disarming those barges, there was only one person he could turn to. He pulled his cell phone out and dialed.

"Franco! You okay? You take my advice to look after yourself?"

"I need your help, Marie."

She was waiting for him at the front door to her steamboat house. A couple of the guys who'd snatched Patrese from out of his car the other day were there, too; Marie's own personal phalanx of muscle.

Patrese told her everything he could remember from the Project Noah document. When he'd finished, she pursed her lips and whistled softly, shaking her head.

One of the young men stepped forward. "Man, that's gotta be bullshit."

"You wanna see it? You wanna see the document?"

"This whole thing is bullshit. They been singing the same song for years, you know? Those forecasting guys, half the time they can't even predict sunrise. So I ain't believin' them now, you know? You workin' for them, huh? You here to kick us out, whitey? Take our homes?"

"*I'm* not. *They* are." Patrese turned to Marie. "You believe me?"

"Oh, yes. I believe you, Franco. Like I told you before, with Varden, you don't know what you're dealing with." She gave a short laugh. "Well, you do now."

"Then let's stop it. Give me as many men as you can spare. There can't be that many guards on board. We can take out at least one barge, the one nearest here."

She thought for a moment, working out her options. Patrese didn't know how many gang members were still around, but he guessed quite a few. Most of them were young and single, which meant they wouldn't bring themselves to leave for fear of looking scared. Family men could always say they were going to take care of their wives and kids. Single men, too cowardly to admit their fear, had no such get-out.

Marie turned to the man who'd squared up to Patrese.

"Darnell, get everyone you can."

"But—"

"*Do it.*"

He hurried off, pulling two cell phones out of voluminous pockets.

Marie ushered Patrese inside the house. The TV was on. They sat and watched.

In the CBD and on Canal Street, people were streaming into hotels, claiming space wherever they could find it—makeshift cots in the lobby, on the staircases, along the corridors. Solid structures and safety in numbers, Patrese thought; better to be with people than alone at a time like this.

Around 400,000 people had evacuated by now, the news anchor said. There were still 100,000 left in the city, and they'd probably stay, despite the mandatory evacuation order. Why weren't people going? Some didn't have transportation; some were too sick; some wanted to protect their property; some wouldn't abandon cherished cats and dogs (no pets were allowed in the Superdome); some wanted to be Good Samaritans; some just simply enjoyed the thrill of shooting craps with Mother Nature.

Patrese turned to Marie. "Why are *you* staying?"

"Like I told Ortiz just before I shot him, the second Marie Laveau—daughter of the original—she was conducting a ceremony on the waters of Lake Pontchartrain when a storm came up. Swept her out into the middle of the lake. She stayed in the water five days. When they found her, she didn't even have exposure."

"That's not an answer."

"Yes, it is."

Darnell was back after half an hour, eight other gangbangers with him. Most of them were dressed in jerseys and outsize shorts, and carried a hodgepodge of weapons: M16s, P99s, .357s, SW1911s, AK-47s. If a single one of these weapons was legally registered, Patrese would have been amazed.

The gangbangers lined up. They looked like a basketball team that had taken a wrong turn and found itself in a war zone.

"I can't do this," Patrese said.

Marie raised her eyebrows. "What?"

"We'll all get killed. These guys on the barge, they're trained soldiers."

"We're soldiers, too, man," Darnell said.

"No, you're not."

"The fuck you know about it?"

"You're not soldiers in the way they are. They're trained. This . . . we don't stand a chance. We're lambs to the slaughter."

"You think we gonna die?"

"No. I *know* we're gonna die. We go like this, none of us are coming back."

"Then I got some news for you, white man. We all gonna die, anyway. You know how many of my friends I've buried? Do you? No, you don't. And here's the thing. Nor do I, man. Too many to count. It don't bother me no more. It don't bother none of us no more. You tell us that barge gonna flood this whole place because we all niggers, then we gots to do somethin' about that. We don't go there, this place is history. We do go there, it might still be history. But shit, man. At least we'll have tried." Darnell turned to the others. "Y'all with me?"

They all reached forward and made a hand tower.

Patrese thought back to a visit he'd made the previous fall to Muncy women's prison in Pennsylvania. He'd gone to see a woman who was scared her teenage son was going to fall in with one of the Pittsburgh gangs.

You seen them toolin' up for a rumble, ain'tcha? she'd asked. *They goin' to war, man. They goin' to fuckin' war, and it's bullshit, like every war ever is. Some of those kids wanna die, Franco; they wanna be re-membered as a goddamn fallen soldier, they wanna be put out of their misery, but they sure as hell don't wanna do it themselves, 'cause that's the coward's way out, ain't it? So they go to war hopin' they catch a bul-let. They're scared, but they ain't allowed to be scared. So what do they do? They dress it up into bullshit about retaliation and honor.*

The gangbangers barreled out of the room. Patrese got up to fol-low them.

"Stay," Marie said.

"I've got to—"

"This ain't your fight, Franco."

"They're doing it to my neighborhood, too."

"Then you go fight there."

"No. I came—"

"*Listen.* Darnell and the others, what do they look like to you? A buncha hoodlums, that's what, a buncha guys who gone hurricane crazy and just want to rob something. They just gonna go in there and start shootin'. Ain't like *that* never happens 'round here, you know. But if *you're* with them, those assholes on the barge gonna know it's somethin' else. You want that?"

"I should be with them. I was the one who told you about it."

"Yeah. And you done a good thing. But let them handle it now."

The barge was only a few minutes' walk away. Patrese and Marie sat in silence, listening to the sounds of a city on the move. Engines growled in the distance. Children shouted in high-pitched delight.

A sudden eruption of gunfire, crackling and spitting like firecrackers on the Fourth of July.

Then silence, and then the screaming.

The ambulances came, and the police cars, and the black pickup trucks with Varden's operatives spilling out of the flatbeds as though this was Baghdad. They came quick enough when their project was threatened, Patrese thought. Would there have been such a response to a shooting—even a multiple shooting—in the Lower Ninth under normal circumstances? It was hardly even a question.

The ambulances took away the bodies of Darnell and the others. The police kept people back and blocked questions with officialese. Varden's men stood around doing their best to look intimidating. Their best was plenty good enough.

Patrese stayed inside Marie's house. Even if he'd wanted to go outside, which he didn't, she wouldn't have let him. It would have caused a whole host of problems, and helped precisely no one. If Patrese couldn't do anything about Project Noah now, so be it. Better to keep him as safe as possible and hope he could somehow bring the participants to justice afterward.

By the time the cops and Varden's goons had gone, it was well past dark, which also meant well past the six P.M. curfew. For Patrese to try to make it back to the Super 8 would be madness. All he needed was to be stopped once, and then what? Yes, he had his Bureau badge; and yes, all was confusion out there on the streets. But did he really want to risk it? He didn't know how far down the line Phelps's search for him had penetrated. One zealous officer might recognize him, or get suspicious, and then what? Camp Greyhound? Worse?

So he stayed in the Lower Ninth, at Marie's home.

This was the kind of neighborhood that usually got together only in weary huddles up against the billowing yellow and black of crime-scene tape. But tonight folks gathered in the street to have a hurricane party, cooking up all the food before it spoiled when the power went off. They cracked open bottles of Abita and toasted Darnell and his buddies, and wondered what the hell they'd been doing up there on the canal wall, and why the hell all those cops and the other guys had turned up. Even though Patrese was pretty much the only white guy present, everyone knew he was there on Marie's say-so, and that made him cool.

No one could get reception on their cell phones, not because of the weather, which wasn't that bad yet, but because the system was overloaded with people calling to check on one another, report their progress, say good-bye and God bless, see you on the other side.

This one was big and bad; everyone knew that now. With the excitement came the dread, but to Patrese there was something curiously, stupidly noble about standing in the middle of a Lower Ninth street rather than taking to the freeway. The folks here weren't running. They accepted their place in the universe, whatever that may be. Whatever happened tomorrow, they'd face it with their heads high and their chins up.

The rains from Katrina's outer bands began to fall.

Marie called for quiet and, swaying slightly, began to sing. Through the pricking of tears, Patrese stomped and whooped with the rest of them.

It felt like the last night on earth.

Katrina came barreling into town with the dawn; banshee howling, volcano rumbling, wailing like a mother seeking her children. She scudded angry clouds ahead of her in fast-forward; bomblike, she ripped windows from high-rises and left blinds in tattered ribbons. She pulled mobile homes inside out, pushed traffic lights back and forth, shook palm trees like pompoms, and spun fast-food signs like weather vanes. She peeled roofs off buildings as though they were Saran wrap; she pulsed walls till they seemed to breathe; she bent back billboards like limbo dancers. She churned the Mississippi into froths of primal madness and sent it flowing in reverse—yes, the mighty river that flows out at a million gallons a second.

White noise, an endless freight train underlaid with the percussion of the *Teresa Crawford* smashing into the canal wall. Even from well inside Marie's house, as far away from the windows as possible, Katrina was so loud that she physically hurt Patrese's eardrums, as though he was sticking screwdrivers into them.

And yet he knew it could have been worse. The eye of the storm was passing forty miles to the east. What they were getting here was something down from maximum.

Patrese had no idea for how long Katrina raged around them, but eventually she continued her stately march northward and away, fading through dull roar to strong breeze. He opened the front door and went out onto the street.

Roof tiles and shards of glass crunched beneath his feet, but houses and cars were all still pretty much in one piece. People were coming out of their houses, blinking in surprise and relief as they looked around. They high-fived and hugged one another.

"Good to be alive!" someone shouted.

"Man, that weren't so bad," someone else said. "That weren't so bad at all."

And then a hissing explosion as the wall of the Industrial Canal finally gave way.

A maelstrom of water barged its way through the hole, throwing the wall's concrete blocks aside or dragging them along as it surged hungrily down the bank. The barge was skewed across the opening, filthy brown waves spewing around and beneath it, and suddenly it came free, riding the surge into the streets like a grotesque surfer.

Patrese ran. He ran for his life. He sprinted back inside Marie's house. She was standing in the hall, eyes wide. He grabbed her as he jumped for the stairs.

"Upstairs! Now!" he yelled, only just audible above the crashing of the water.

They were halfway up the flight when the entire house was smashed sideways, sliding as though a giant hand had pushed it across a skidpan. Patrese was thrown against a wall. Marie bounced against and off him. He kept climbing, pulling her with him. Below them, the canal water knocked the front door flat and rushed in, a living thing, a predator seeking victims.

Patrese looked out of the landing window. Houses were playing bumper cars. Cars and trucks were shaken and tossed like snow in a globe.

The house finally came to a stop. Marie joined Patrese at the window. She looked left and right, and laughed.

"This is the next street up," she said.

"What?"

"We've moved a block."

"Jesus."

Patrese looked down. The water was already lapping halfway up the stairs; seven or eight feet high, he guessed, and rising all the time. Marie followed his gaze.

"You think we need to get higher?" she said.

"Can we?' "

She nodded upward to a trapdoor. "Got the cupola up there."

"Room for both of us?"

"Just about."

Born with a caul, Patrese remembered. Not going to drown.

Patrese reached up and opened the trapdoor. An extendable ladder lay flat against the inside. Patrese pulled it down.

"You go first," he said. "I'll pass the stuff up to you."

The cupola was shaped like an upturned bell; about eight feet in diameter, and the same in height, with glass panes all the way around and a narrow bench next to the opening hatch. Marie climbed the ladder. Patrese collected all their essentials and passed them up.

"Got everything?" he asked.

"Think so."

"Okay."

The water was beginning to lap around his feet. He remembered what the Project Noah position paper had forecast: that with catastrophic failures of the canal walls, the water would only stop flowing into New Orleans once it had equalized with the level of Lake Pontchartrain. The water could keep rising for hours, even days. This part of town was one of the lowest in the whole city, many feet below sea level; that's why they'd shoved the poor here. In New Orleans, topography was destiny.

He climbed the ladder into the cupola. It was as hot as a Hopi sweat lodge. He gestured to the glass panes. "There any way to open these?"

"Not without breaking them."

"Then that's what we'll do. If everyone else is drowning, I don't want to be the asshole who dies of heat exhaustion." He took off one of his socks and filled it with four of the heaviest batteries he could find. "You better duck down. This space is pretty tight. Watch your face."

Marie turned away and put her arms around her head.

"Okay?" Patrese said.

"Yup."

He swung the sock around his head a couple of times to build up speed, and then smacked it against the nearest pane of glass as hard as he could. A spider's web of hairline cracks rippled across the surface. Patrese hit it again, and this time made a jagged hole at the point of impact. He took off his shirt, wrapped it in a ball around his fist, and punched the shards away until the frame was more or less clear.

"Take care not to catch yourself on the way through," he said. The tiny stalactites of glass around the edges were viciously sharp.

Again, Marie went out first; again, Patrese passed all the stuff out to her before following. Out on the roof, he looked around, and caught his breath.

The Lower Ninth was no longer a residential district. It was an archipelago. A rooftop here, a tree's upper branches there, poking out of the water like tropical icebergs. Sweaty, frightened faces appeared up from roof windows like jack-in-the-boxes.

Patrese turned the radio on. Without it, this patch of drowned world was all they had. He wanted to know what was happening elsewhere.

"More news just in," said the announcer. "I tell you, every bit's more terrible than the last. All four main canals in the city, the walls have failed. A massive breach in the Lower Ninth by the Industrial Canal. The Orleans Avenue Canal, water's flowing into the city park. A levee failure on the Seventeenth Street Canal, and Lakeview's drowning there. London Avenue, too, east side, water rushing into Gentilly. The whole city, people."

That was Patrese's own home gone. Lucky it was a rental, he thought.

More people appeared on their rooftops. Some of the less tall houses were all but underwater already. If no one had emerged from them, it meant either that they'd left town or that they were still inside; but few people around here had left town.

Patrese could hear muffled shouting and banging from inside one of these houses.

"Stay here," he said to Marie.

"Honey, where the fuck you think I'm gonna be goin'?"

The house in question was about twenty yards away. Patrese looked down at the water. It wasn't water at all, he knew, not really;

it was a witches' brew, a toxic sludge of diesel, shit, asbestos, piss, benzene, lead, gasoline, battery acid, and God alone knew what else. The smell was bad enough; what it would taste like if he accidentally swallowed any hardly bore thinking about.

Marie's house was higher than most of the others, so Patrese was still a good six or seven feet above the water level. He went to the edge of the roof, gripped the gutter, and gradually lowered himself over the edge until his feet could just about touch the water. Then he screwed his eyes and mouth as tight shut as he could and let go, spreading his arms wide to ensure that his head would remain above the surface.

He'd hardly got going when he barked his shin against something hard. Could have been a car, a lamp post, a street sign, a floating chair or table; he didn't know, and he wasn't going to stop to find out. He made himself as horizontal as possible while keeping his head up and kept going. This water was a microbe's paradise. He hoped he hadn't drawn blood.

He reached the roof of the other house without smacking into anything else, and pulled himself out of the water.

"Hello?" he shouted. "Can you hear me?"

An old man called out from inside. "Help us, man. Help us, for the love of God. We drowning in here."

Patrese looked around. The roof had no window, no skylight. The people inside were presumably jammed up hard against the eaves. Patrese looked back at the water level and tried to judge it against what he imagined was the geography of the attic. The people inside would have a foot or two of air at most.

The roof was shingled and had clearly seen better days, even before this morning. If Patrese had an ax, he could break a hole in it and pull the people inside to safety.

He didn't have an ax. What he did have was his gun.

"Listen up!" he yelled. "I'm standing right in the middle of your roof. I want y'all to go to the sides, far away as you can. I'm gonna shoot some holes in it and kick it in. You got that?"

"Don't shoot, man! You're crazy. You shoot, you'll kill us."

"Where's the water level at?"

"Round about my neck, man."

"Then if I don't shoot, you're gonna die. Move to the sides. *Now.*"

He heard some scuffling inside as they did so, and then a woman's voice: "Jesus, help me now."

"Ready?" Patrese shouted.

"We ready."

He fired six shots to make a circle about four feet wide, and then stamped down on the circle as hard as he could. No movement; the roof held firm. Patrese stamped again, and this time felt it give a fraction.

"Hold on!" he shouted.

"Hurry up, man!"

Patrese stamped again and again and again, working with a blind rage. His foot stung, but he paid it no mind, focusing every ounce of strength he had on punching through this roof and getting them to safety.

The circle sagged, cracked, splintered, and finally gave way so suddenly that Patrese almost fell in after it. He regained his balance, got down on his front, and thrust his arm in for them to grab hold of. "Come on!" he shouted.

The water lapped around his shoulder. He peered inside and saw the old man and his wife floating silently in the filth.

Patrese rolled away from the hole and looked somewhere more comforting, like straight into the sun.

After a while, he slid back into the water and swam back to Marie's roof.

"They won't be the last," she said.

"Ain't that the truth."

"So, you got any plans for the day?"

He laughed; what else was there to do? "Thought I might just hang out here. Take a dip from time to time, you know. Otherwise, just chill. Work on my tan."

Which was, as it turned out, pretty much exactly what happened. They were there all day, and no one came for them—not a boat, not a helicopter, no one. Patrese and Marie debated whether or not he should hide if any rescuers did appear, balancing his need to keep out of the authorities' way with the likelihood that a white man in the Lower Ninth was more likely to be rescued, but in the end it was academic. The only craft of any variety they saw was a news helicopter. Even given what Patrese knew about Project Noah, it was woeful.

"This is a FEMA gig, right?" Marie asked.

"That's right."

"They really are the sorriest bunch of jackasses I ever came across."

The water stabilized a couple of feet short of the gutters. Dragonflies chased mosquitoes across the surface. The sun crawled across the sky. Time ceased to mean anything; either Patrese and Marie were alive, or they were not. The radio brought news from the rest of the city, though it may as well have been outer space. The hurricane had torn off a section of the Superdome roof. Prisoners from Orleans Parish prison were being held at gunpoint on the highway. Help was on its way. The looting had begun: a grocery store in Tremé, a sporting goods warehouse in Mid-City, a hardware store uptown. Vigilante posses were forming.

At some point in the afternoon, a red permanent marker pen floated past. Patrese reached down and plucked it from the ooze.

"Here," he said. "Write your blood group on your arm."

"Huh?"

"Who knows how long we'll be here, or what state we'll be in when they find us. You need a blood transfusion, and you're not conscious . . . Soldiers do it. Sensible."

She nodded, pulled the cap off the pen, and wrote *B+* on the inside of her left forearm. The red ink glowed against the coffee color of her skin.

"That's how she died, you know," Marie said as she passed the pen to Patrese.

"Who?"

"Rosalita."

"She died in a car crash."

"They could have saved her, if they'd had enough blood. But it was

Mexico. Back then, at least, made New Orleans look like the most advanced place in the world. What's the universal blood group?"

"O."

"Yeah, O. That's what she was. Any transfusion would have done . . ."

"That's not exactly how it works, you know."

"Whatever. All I know is, any transfusion would have done, but by the time they got round to it, it was too late."

"That's shocking."

"It was deliberate, Franco."

"Huh?"

"You think it was a random accident?"

"I've seen the way they drive over there."

"She was *murdered*."

"What are you talking about?"

"When Varden asked me to help out with distribution, that wasn't long after Rosalita's death. You remember?"

Patrese thought for a moment. "Yeah, I remember."

"That's why she was killed. The Gulf Cartel wanted Varden to help them. So did a rival gang called the Sinhaloa. The Gulf were more persuasive."

"By killing her?"

"In Mexico, that's persuasive."

"Someone killed my wife, last thing I'd do is go into business with them."

"You would if they threatened your son next."

Junior had been nine or ten at the time, Patrese realized. Yes, he thought, Marie was right; he'd have done exactly what Varden had. Any father would have.

"Nothing more powerful than blood," she added.

"They ever find who did it?"

"Who? The Mexican police?"

"Yes."

"They knew, of course. Did nothing about it."

"So the man who killed her, he went free?"

"For a while."

"And now?"

"Now? He's dead."

"How do you know so much about this?"

She smiled. "'Cause I killed him. That's how."

Gulf Cartel. Los Zetas. "Balthazar Ortiz?"

"Clever boy."

Patrese looked out across the water. "There's a lot I don't understand about you."

"That's the way I like it, honey child."

The sun burned down the west. The night was hot, and darker than Patrese had ever seen in a city. Katrina's winds had chased away the clouds and knocked out every power station for miles around. The only lights were the candles on other roofs, flickering like votive fireflies. No streetlights, no house lights, no office blocks lit up like Christmas trees, no cars with twin headlights slicing through the blackness. The stars were so clear and shining, Patrese could have been camping in the Rockies. He couldn't even tell there was a city out there.

And through the darkness came the joyful croaking of thousands of frogs, rejoicing in a city made swamp once more. Patrese had a sudden memory of Kat South the second time he had gone to see her, when Junior and his men had already started moving in down on the bayou.

There's a frog chorus, she'd said. *Loud as all hell, raucous, discordant. Most beautiful thing you'll ever hear. Enjoy it while you can, 'cause it won't be here in a few months' time, not once those asswipes put up their damn rigs and pipelines.*

Patrese smiled. Kat had fought to her last against the city taking over her bayou. She'd have laughed her ass off that the bayou had taken back the city.

The boats began to come for them shortly after first light. No official vessels, of course; heaven forbid. Instead it was a ragtag flotilla of dinghies, airboats, canoes, launches, and tenders. New Orleans had been the birthplace of the Higgins boat, the flat-bottomed landing craft that had delivered many thousands of Allied troops onto the beaches of Normandy. Without the Higgins boat, Eisenhower had said, the war would have been lost.

Now the best the city could do was a motley Cajun navy. Nothing against the fishermen, water-skiers, and tourist captains picking their way through the sunken houses, Patrese thought—quite the opposite, they were damn heroes in his eyes—but they shouldn't have had to be doing it in the first place.

A speedboat glided toward the eaves of Marie's house. An old couple were already sitting in the back, and the driver called out to Patrese and Marie.

"Y'all wanna lift?"

"Sure," Patrese said. These guys were clearly no danger; they weren't FBI, NOPD, or Varden.

As the speedboat drew closer, Patrese started, not in fear, but recognition. The driver of the speedboat was Tony Wattana.

"Agent Patrese," Tony said. "What are *you* doing here?"

Patrese helped Marie into the boat. "Long story. Listen, if you don't want to take me, then . . ."

"Why on earth wouldn't I take you?"

"Well . . . we had our differences, didn't we?"

"You been on that roof since yesterday?"

"Yup."

"Then don't be a damn fool. Get in."

Making sure he had everything with him, Patrese climbed aboard. "Thanks. Appreciate it."

Tony opened the throttle and nosed between the houses, looking for anyone else still marooned. Patrese glanced at the old couple. The woman was asleep. Her husband gestured toward her.

"She don't have a drop of water in her lungs. I'm proud of that, you know? I got her to safety, kept her above the water. Heart attack. Not drowning. Means a little."

Not asleep, Patrese realized; dead.

"I'm sorry," he said.

"Young man, I survived Guadalcanal. I survived Korea. I survived Vietnam. Hell, I even survived disco. I can handle a measly old flood."

"No thanks to FEMA," Tony said. "Wouldn't let us launch yesterday."

"Why not?"

"Said we weren't authorized."

"And now?"

"Why do you think we're out here so early? Those assholes are probably still asleep. Damn fools."

They passed beneath traffic lights and overhead road signs, so close that Patrese could have reached up and swatted them. Tony slalomed adroitly past floating bodies, their skin already greenish-blue and blistering across swollen tissue. Fallen power lines sprawled across the surface like outsize water snakes.

"I'm gonna drop you at the bridge," Tony said.

"Which one?"

"St. Claude Avenue. The water starts there; it's a good slipway, it's where we're all launching from. From there, it's dry ground all the way, long as you stick close to the river. Lot of folks heading for the Convention Center, that's what I heard."

The Ernest N. Morial Convention Center, named after the first black mayor of New Orleans, ran for eleven blocks along the riverfront. On a normal day, it would have been about an hour's walk from the St. Claude Avenue Bridge. Today Patrese felt so dislocated that he'd have been surprised even to see the Center in its rightful place.

"Convention Center?" Patrese said. "What about the Superdome? I thought people were going to the Superdome."

Tony shook his head. "Superdome's full, man. And from what I hear, it ain't no place to be neither."

"How do you mean?"

"You got twenty thousand folks in there, hot as all hell, no running water, restrooms backed up, floodwaters coming in at lower levels . . . I've been hearing assaults, drug abuse, even rape and murder."

I've been hearing. In situations like this, rumor spread twice as fast as fact and was four times as damaging. But Tony had just plucked him off a rooftop when he could easily have left him there, so Patrese bit his lip.

The St. Claude Avenue Bridge looked about as busy as Hartsfield-Jackson; an endless stream of boats disgorging passengers before casting off again into the ooze. Patrese perched in the bows of Tony's speedboat until they were near the makeshift slipway, then vaulted over the edge and pulled the boat in as the water lapped around his waist. He helped Marie and the old man ashore; then he and Tony carried the old woman's corpse onto the road and laid her down as gently as they could.

"Thanks again," Patrese said.

A statue of the Virgin Mary bobbed in the swell.

"Agent Patrese . . ."

"Franco."

Tony curled his hand into a light fist and bumped Patrese's knuckles. "One love, Franco. One love."

If Patrese and Marie had thought that reaching dry land meant their ordeal was over, they were very much mistaken. In some ways, it had only just begun.

Hot morning, not enough food, not enough water, not enough sleep. They walked through the sliver of dry land by the river as though treading nightmares. Folks with their skin flaking off, swollen in the heat as they sobbed arid tears, all dried out in a city of water. Severe dehydration made some people foam at the mouth;

diabetes untreated by medicines lost in the flood left others confused and disorientated.

Patrese and Marie passed a convenience store, doors flung wide to the world. People hurried out lugging as much as they could carry; didn't seem to matter much what, as long as it was free. Inside, half obscured in the darkness, Patrese could see young men squatting on countertops with their pants down. The big dump, psychologists called it; Patrese had seen it at homicide and robbery scenes. You hate, you exult, you transgress; you take a shit in celebration of your empowerment.

A news photographer snapped pictures of the looters—a white couple clutching milk and Gatorade, a black man with crackers and processed ham. They paid him no mind. Marie gestured angrily toward the photographer.

"Vulture," she hissed.

"They're looting," Patrese replied.

"They're *surviving*, same as we are. Food in this heat's gonna go off, so take it while you can. The store will be insured up the ass, so they won't lose. But I tell you how it'll play in the papers tomorrow, Franco. They show the white couple, they'll say they were being resourceful. They show the black guy, he's a thieving nigger."

Patrese couldn't argue, because he knew it was true. He was acutely conscious of his whiteness: The couple with milk and Gatorade were pretty much the only other white people he'd seen since yesterday morning. If this was Boston, would the authorities have left tens of thousands trapped in the city? Not a chance.

Marie continued. "To white America watching on TV, it'll be a surprise that a whole heap of black folks were left out to rot like trash sacks on garbage day. Not a surprise to anyone in the Superdome or the Convention Center, I can tell you that. You know what it'll look like on TV? Like something from the Third World; stranded refugees. And you know what? It'll look like that 'cause it'll *be* that. Banana republic, here on the Mississippi."

The nearer they got to the Convention Center, the more the atmosphere seemed charged with a jittery belligerence. A Varden SUV sprouted juiced-up freaks in mirrored shades and bandannas. In the back of a flatbed, another Varden operative with an M-16 scanned the roofs for snipers. Radios chattered in squelches of static, disembodied voices advising that residents could be evacuated against their will.

Varden's men on foot now, patrolling in squares, backs to each other so they could all look outward. Patrese saw that one of them was wearing his company ID around his neck in a carrying case emblazoned with the words *Operation Iraqi Freedom*. Another was muttering about wanting to "get back to Kirkuk where the real action is. Get paid three times as much there, that's for damn sure."

Although Project Noah had set a great deal of store by Varden Industries' experience in Iraqi reconstruction, it was only now, on the streets the day after Katrina had created a new Atlantis, that Patrese appreciated the extent to which Iraq and New Orleans seemed to be morphing into a single entity; New Oraq, perhaps. First came the shock and awe, whether from hurricane or cruise missiles; then followed the feeding frenzy. Varden had sown the wind; now he was reaping the whirlwind.

But this wasn't a war zone, Patrese thought. There were no insurgents with machine guns and mortars, no sweaty-fingered teenagers burying makeshift bombs by the roadside. Sure, there were looters; probably a few gangbangers taking potshots here and there, too. But that was hardly the same thing. Lyndon Johnson had declared a war on poverty. These guys had kept those words but twisted the meaning 180.

A stand-up row was taking place on the sidewalk outside the Convention Center. A young woman in a yellow top was yelling at four guys. "The *fuck* you think y'all are? Y'all ain't real men! Y'all pieces of *shit*, you know?"

"Fuck this, bitch," said one of the men. "Y'all think we so shit, see how you do without us. Come on, fellas."

The men started to walk away. The woman grabbed the man who'd spoken to her.

"Don't leave me!" she screamed.

He backhanded her without even looking. She clawed at his face, and suddenly they were all on her, pushing her to the ground, flashes of color as they ripped at her shirt and shorts; a wildlife documentary made real as gang rape on the streets.

Patrese sprinted over and pressed his gun against the ear of the nearest man.

"Back off!" Patrese yelled.

The man was pulling the woman's shorts below her knees. He didn't even seem to have noticed that Patrese was there, let alone pointing a gun at him. "Fuck you, bitch," he was snarling through ragged breaths, "you gonna be sorry—"

"Back off!" Patrese yelled again. "Back off, or I'll kill you."

The man glanced at him, wild-eyed, and then turned away and started to pull his own shorts off. "Hold this bitch down," he shouted. "Hold her the fuck down."

Patrese pressed his pistol against the man's temple and fired.

The man jerked once, fatal parody of an orgasm, and lay still. The other men looked at Patrese and took off down the road. The woman pulled the scraps of her clothes around her as best she could and staggered to her feet. Marie took her by the arm. "Come, child. Let's get out of the heat."

Three of Varden's men came over, all in tight corporate T-shirts, all with their blood groups marked on the upper part of their left arms. Two of them started directing people back inside the Convention Center, while the third held out his hand, palm open and upturned. "No unauthorized firearms."

"Excuse me?"

"No unauthorized firearms. Give me your gun."

Patrese thought fast. The only way to keep his gun was to show his Bureau badge, but showing his Bureau badge might alert them to who he was. Then again, there were hundreds, perhaps thousands, of Varden's operatives on the streets. Even if they had all been told to look out for Patrese, they presumably had more on their minds than simply him. *Might* get recognized, *would* lose the gun—put in those terms, it wasn't a tough choice.

Patrese pulled out his badge. "FBI."

Varden's man seamlessly converted the give-me-your-gun gesture into a handshake, and nodded toward Patrese's clothes. "You okay, man? How come you look like them?"

Them. The niggers. In Baghdad, *them* would be the ragheads. *Them.* Not us.

"Been doing S and R out there."

"You want some water or something?"

"Sure. Thanks."

"This way."

Varden's men had set up a makeshift command post just across the street from the Convention Center; a few pickup trucks parked in a circle like an Afrikaner *laager*. Crates of bottled water were stacked high in one of the flatbeds. An operative with a machine gun was watching over them as though they were liquid gold.

In these conditions, Patrese thought, that was exactly what they were.

The bottles were passed around. The water was warm enough to have been virtually undrinkable in normal circumstances, but Patrese couldn't care less. He gulped down the first bottle in one go and only surfaced for air halfway through the second.

"Thirsty, huh?" said the man who'd originally demanded Patrese's gun.

"You bet." He gestured toward the Convention Center. "What about the people in there? They got enough?"

"Hey, man, we look like the Red Cross to you? Our job is to keep order. That's it. We have enough water to drink, enough food to eat, enough ammo for our weapons, then we can keep order. Rest of it ain't my problem."

Behind Patrese, someone clapped loudly for attention, and shouted, "Okay, people, listen up!"

Patrese recognized the voice even before he turned.

Junior.

Patrese ran as though the hounds of hell were at his heels, jinking left and right so they couldn't get a clean shot, that old scatback rush hardwired into him from years on the football field. *Run to daylight,* his coaches had always told him; run toward the glimmering chinks through the darkness.

Now he ran from light into darkness, from the glaring sledgehammer sunshine into the gloom of a Convention Center without electricity.

He heard two shots above the shouts, neither of them close. They'd want him alive, Patrese thought; want to know what he knew, who he'd told, before they killed him.

He burst through one of the Convention Center doors and immediately retched. The stench; dear God, the stench. All the TV footage and all the pictures in the papers couldn't begin to convey the horror of that smell—the superheated gagging foulness, the cadaverous mephitis. Judging from the piles of vomit around the doors, Patrese wasn't the only one whose stomach had gone into involuntary revolt.

He headed farther inside, neither knowing nor caring where he was headed, so long as it was away from Junior and his men. Sweat sprang in great beads from his skin. People were crying—no, they were *wailing,* a great collective biblical lamentation. They stewed in their own filth and fear while wearing looted sneakers and hats with the price tags still on. The floors were slick with piss, the stairs were smeared with blood. Feces piled up like molehills. Clothes sprawled in muddy wetness. Dogs chewed on dirty diapers; dead cats adorned piles of debris. Bodies lay unmoving on the floor, either dead or unconscious, Patrese thought, as no one in their right mind would lie in that filth, and surely no one could sleep in this heat.

Clattering and shouting behind him as the chasers burst in.

"Franco!" Junior yelled. "Give it up!"

Patrese pressed on, pushing his way past people and up a stationary escalator. A man with breath like a sewage works grabbed Patrese by the collar and thrust his face close. "If I died right now and went to hell," the man hissed, "I'd think I had it made."

Patrese took half a pace forward and, using all the force he could muster, drove the crown of his head into the bridge of the man's nose.

Yelping, the man let go of Patrese's collar and pressed his hands to his own face. Patrese shouldered him aside and kept climbing.

Easier to become feral than retain your humanity.

People were crying out for their medication. Insulin for the diabetics, Zyprexa for the schizos, Coudamin for those with a bad heart. Goya could have redone his Black Paintings all over again just from five minutes in this city, Patrese thought: a witches' Sabbath at the feet of a goatlike devil; a dog looking skyward for divine intervention that would never come; a toothless, grimacing old man eating soup alongside a skull-faced cadaver. They were all here in one form or another.

"Franco!" A voice ahead of him, not behind. A woman's voice. Marie.

She was still with the girl in the yellow top. They were surrounded by six or seven young black men, all of them armed. Patrese wiped his palms on his shirt and gripped his gun as tight as he could.

"Move the fuck away from those women!" he shouted.

"Franco, these are my boys. They're protecting us, not threatening us."

He raised his palms in apology. "Sorry."

A couple of the youths stepped aside to let Patrese into the circle.

"We gonna restore some order round here," she said. "There are other gangs out there, and we gonna get together, assert some damn authority. No one's gonna get raped, no one's gonna hurt old folk or children, not while I'm here."

"Listen, Marie, those assholes out on the street, the mercenaries . . ."

"I know."

"How do you know?"

She nodded back in the direction from which he'd just come. "'Cause they're here."

Patrese turned. Junior was at the head of a dozen or so men. A crowd was forming behind them, eager to see something—anything—kicking off.

"Come on, Franco," Junior said. "Come with us."

"What do you want?"

"You know what I want. We need to talk."

"Then let's talk here."

"No. Let's talk where I say. Come."

Marie looked at Junior. "Don't do this, Sonny."

"This has nothing to do with you."

Marie turned to the gathering crowd. "If these men take him away, they'll kill him. He's a good man. I can vouch for him. Don't let them do it."

Murmurs in the crowd; a spark of angry defiance arcing from person to person. Varden's men fanned out in a circle, instinctively positioned to maximize their sectors of fire.

The AB+ markered on Junior's arm stretched as he flexed his bicep. "You try and stop us, there'll be a massacre," he said. "We'll kill whoever we have to. Don't be a fool, Franco. Don't make us kill everyone."

"Fuck you!" a man shouted from the crowd. "You come here with no food and water, and you put guns in our faces? This ain't Kent State no more, motherfucker."

The crowd roared their assent. Patrese saw one of Varden's men twitch. One way or another, this was all going south, and fast. The crowd would swarm Varden's men, Varden's men would open fire. They'd be overwhelmed eventually, but how many would they have killed first? Patrese knew that, even when vastly outnumbered, a small number of soldiers could triumph if they were well organized, and these guys were nothing if not that.

No, Patrese thought, there was only one way to defuse the situation.

He stepped past Marie's men, toward Junior.

"Okay," he said. "Let's go."

"You don't have to do this, Franco," Marie said.

"Yes, I do."

They removed his gun and took him to Varden Tower, a few blocks away. The building's generators were providing auxiliary power for essentials, but those essentials did not include elevators or aircon. Varden's office was on the fifty-fifth floor, and they had to take the stairs. Junior led the way, apparently unbothered by either the heat or the exertion; then again, Patrese thought, Junior hadn't spent last night on a rooftop in the Lower Ninth.

Varden was in his ballroom-sized office. He was wearing slacks and a polo shirt, and even he had taken no chances with the blood group: A+. Patrese felt the faintest of breezes as they entered, and he took a moment to work out where it was coming from. The room had floor-to-ceiling windows on three sides, and several had been blown clean out by the force of the hurricane.

Patrese wondered idly how Varden had managed to climb fifty-five stories in ninety-five-degree heat, and then realized that of course he hadn't. There was a helipad on the roof. Varden would have flown in by chopper and walked down a flight of stairs.

Strange, inconsequential thoughts, the kind you have when your life expectancy is suddenly being measured in minutes.

They'd find out what Patrese knew, and then they'd kill him. And if he wouldn't tell them . . . if he wouldn't tell them, Junior knew his way around a few interrogation tricks, Patrese was sure of that.

"Agent Patrese," Varden said. "Good of you to come." He made it sound absolutely, wholeheartedly sincere.

"I didn't have much choice."

Varden looked at the small posse of men standing behind Patrese. "No. No, I suppose you didn't." He nodded to the operatives. "You can go now, gentlemen. Thank you. Junior, you stay here."

The men left. It was just the three of them.

"Tell me what you know," Varden said, as though this were a fireside chat.

"Everything," Patrese replied.

He'd considered this on the way over; to reveal or not to reveal that he'd found Cindy's flash drive. They knew he knew about Luther and Junior, which in itself was reason enough to want him dead, so why not up the ante? The more they knew he knew, the better his bargaining position would be. And if it didn't work out—well, might as well be hanged for a sheep as a lamb.

Varden cocked an eyebrow. "Everything?"

"Project Noah."

The eyebrow went higher. "You mind telling me how?"

"Cindy found out."

"And she told you?"

"She gave it to Luther."

"'It'?"

"The position paper. Supporting documents."

"Which you will hand over."

"I don't have them on me." They hadn't searched Patrese for anything other than a gun. If he kept up the impression that Cindy had left physical documents rather than electronic ones—documents they could clearly see he didn't have on him—he might get away with keeping hold of the flash drive.

Not that it would do him much good if he was dead, of course.

"Then where are they?"

"Somewhere else."

"Come, come, Agent Patrese. You can only have found them very recently, or else you'd have either gone public with them or come to us to strike a deal. Wyndham is positive you didn't know on Friday after all the excitement at the bayou, so you must have discovered them since then. Since you're unlikely to have left the city and come back to it in that time, those documents must still be in New Orleans. Not in your house, though, because you haven't been back there since Friday afternoon."

"My house is under ten feet of water, by the sound of it."

"That's true. So, again: Would you like to tell me where they are?"

"Not really."

Junior took a step toward Patrese, but Varden stayed him with a raised palm.

"Don't think he won't hurt you," Varden said.

"I don't think that at all."

"Good."

"If I tell you where they are, will you answer a few questions first?"

Varden laughed. "Agent Patrese, I don't think you're in any position to be making demands of me."

"I have something you want."

Varden thought for a moment, a sultan amused by the fawning request of a courtier. "You ask if you want. But I may not answer."

And if you do, and if you answer honestly, it means you're going to kill me anyway, and who's going to notice one more corpse in a city of thousands? You'll dump my body somewhere and say I was caught looting, or I killed myself, or I refused to comply with an evacuation order.

"Okay. First question. Why Luther?"

"Why Luther? Why *not* Luther? He was just what we needed. Great at gathering intelligence, enough skeletons in his closet to make him a perfect patsy. He needed money. He did what he was told."

"But why put him undercover with Marie if he was already working for you?"

"Ah. That was, er, *unintended*. Hiring Luther was something Junior and I did unilaterally. We didn't tell the others, not until the murders had already begun. Listen, Agent Patrese. Project Noah has been around for several years. Each year, hurricanes raged across the Atlantic, and each year, New Orleans dodged the big one. So eventually we decided to do something to try and make it happen. We were discussing religion one night, and the role of sacrifice, and the idea grew from there. We needed victims, but not just any old victims. Victims who *suited*. Victims the gods would savor. Luther had just been discharged from the army, and he got in touch with Junior, looking for work, wondering if I had any job opportunities. So we gave him this instead. We gave him lists of names, the hurricane names, go and find people in the New Orleans area with these names, and build up a dossier on each one. Name, address, job, lifestyle, all that."

"You tell him why?"

"Of course not."

"And he never asked?"

"He was a soldier. He followed orders and he respected need-to-know."

"Even to killing?"

"He was a soldier."

"And when the murders began, he could say nothing without implicating himself."

"Exactly."

"But he wanted out, didn't he?"

"Yes, he did. Right from the start, he wanted out. Even with the money we were offering. He was becoming a liability. What else?"

"Excuse me?"

"You said you had a few questions. That's only one. Any more?"

"Yes. Why?"

"Why what?"

"Why all this?"

"Come."

Varden led Patrese over to one of the intact windows. From this high up, Patrese could see the entire urban panorama. An ocean of black slime sat still and stinking in the sun. Where the streets could still be demarcated by lamp posts, they seemed some diabolical Venetian parody. Cloverleaf interstate junctions rose twisted from the sludge. Smoke from burning buildings reached high and mocking into the sky; a city of water, but the fire trucks couldn't get around and the hydrants had no pressure. Choppers swarmed in the sky as though unleashed from a hornet's nest.

"What do you see?" Varden said.

"A city in ruins."

"You know what I see? The *future*."

Patrese glanced across. Varden's face was rapt, contemplation of the new Jerusalem he envisaged emerging from the flood; a man in love with his own vision of the world.

He doesn't see, Patrese realized incredulously. He really doesn't see.

The kind of cases the police deal with every day—the robberies, the rapes, the assaults, the murders—everyone knows they're crimes. Many of them are done by bad people; many, too, by those just trying to survive. For those crimes, people get punished. But there are some crimes that society isn't equipped to punish; instead the perpetrators of those crimes are rewarded.

This was one of those; *this,* this genocide, which Varden portrayed as a public service, a regrettable but necessary staging-post on the march to the promised land. And he portrayed it that way because he honestly believed it that way. It wasn't that he could tell right from wrong but went ahead, anyway. It was that he was so corrupted that he could no longer tell the difference. In his mind, the only distinction was between getting caught and getting away with it, and when you were Varden there was no distinction, because you got away with everything.

It was evil on a scale so far in excess of anything Patrese had ever known that he could hardly comprehend it. People think evil lurks and skulks in the shadows. It doesn't, Patrese realized; not true evil. True evil walks tall and proud in the sunshine, dressing itself up as success, profit, expansion, ambition, sliding into primal madness.

Patrese had a sudden memory of walking into this office with Selma when they'd come with a warrant to take Cindy's computers. As they'd come in, Varden had been talking on the phone, but had shut up the moment he saw them.

What had he been saying? Something about a Joe. Joe Zee, that was it. *Remember what Joe Zee said.*

"Who's Joe Zee?" Patrese asked.

"You ever seen *The Godfather*?"

"I'm Italian."

"You remember Joe Zaluchi?"

"Boss of the Detroit syndicate. Sure."

"You remember what he says about drugs?"

Patrese couldn't remember the exact words, but he knew the gist: something about keeping drugs in the black areas, about blacks being animals and losing their souls.

"I remember."

"You look at what's happening in this city and tell me he was wrong."

"Enough of this." It was Junior's voice from behind them. Patrese had almost forgotten he was there. "Give us the documents."

"I've sent copies of them—" Patrese began.

He stopped suddenly, knowing he'd made a mistake, but the words were out, and he couldn't bite them back. Copies meant electronic, as he couldn't have photocopied and mailed the documents in a city fleeing for its collective life. Electronic meant something small enough to carry.

Junior was on him in a second, patting, frisking, searching. Money belt, waterproof bag, flash drive. Varden held out his hand. Junior gave him the flash drive.

"This it?" Varden asked.

"I've sent copies," Patrese repeated.

"Who to?"

"People." It sounded weak even as he said it.

"Then why haven't they done anything about it?"

Junior stepped back behind Patrese, grabbed him around the neck, and pressed a gun to his temple.

"This is your own gun," Junior said. "It'll look like you committed suicide; right angle, right placement." He looked at his father. "Say the word."

"I've sent copies." Patrese fought to get the words out of his constricted throat.

"*Who to?*"

"My sister."

"You're lying."

"I told her not to open the attachment, but if she hadn't heard from me by—"

"You're lying. You wouldn't put her in danger like that. Blood ties run deep."

Junior's arm was still around Patrese's throat. His blood-type marking was about six inches from Patrese's eyes.

Blood ties. Blood types.

Junior's blood type was AB. Varden's was A. Rosalita had been an O.

But an O mother and A father can't make an AB child. They can only make an O child or an A child.

So Rosalita couldn't have been Junior's mother.

And even as Patrese wondered who *was* Junior's mother, he knew the answer.

A woman who'd just called Junior "Sonny" in the Convention Center.

A woman who'd explained a decision to go into partnership with a drugs cartel by saying, *You would if they'd threatened your son.* She'd been talking about Varden, of course, but also about herself.

A woman who'd written her own blood group, B, on her arm with a pen Patrese had given her.

Patrese turned his head as far as he could toward Junior.

"You're Marie Laveau's son," he said.

Astonishment and horror fought for supremacy on Varden's face. None of his ruthless calm now; for once, he'd found a situation he couldn't bully or buy his way out of. By the time he composed himself, it was too late to dismiss Patrese's statement as bunkum. Junior had seen his father's reaction. He *knew.*

"How did you know?" Varden seemed to physically shrink before Patrese's eyes, the wizard laid bare behind the curtain. "How on earth . . . ?"

"Fuck that." Junior let go of Patrese and stepped toward Varden. "It's true, isn't it? Tell me it's not. Tell me it is."

"Your . . . your mother and I . . ."

"*Tell me!*"

"Your mother couldn't have children. We tried everything. Nowadays, it would be much easier, medicine's a whole lot better at these things, but then . . . Everything, you hear? But in the end, even I had to accept defeat. We wanted a child more than anything. And I loved her, I really did. People told me to leave her, find someone else, but no, that wasn't why I'd gotten married. So we talked about it, and she said, maybe someone could carry a baby for us. Cut a long story short, we asked Marie. She didn't have a husband, but she still didn't want to do it. I persuaded her."

"You paid her."

"Of course. So she and I . . . and then she was pregnant. Your mother started putting pillows under her blouses at about four months, and the pillows got bigger and bigger. And then out you came, and Marie handed you over, and . . . there you were."

"So Marie goes into the hospital and comes out empty-handed. How does she explain that to everyone?"

"She said it was stillborn."

"*I.* She said *I* was stillborn."

"It was a cover story. We took you back home, your mother and I . . ."

"Except she wasn't my mother, was she?"

"She always thought of herself as your mother."

"She *wasn't.*"

"And I've always been your father."

Junior, still holding Patrese's gun, was right up in Varden's face now. Varden took a step back, and another, until he bounced lightly off the window frame. He raised his hands; surrender, self-defense. The flash drive dropped to the floor. Neither he nor Junior noticed. Varden began to inch along the wall, trying to get away from his son.

"I did it for you," he said.

"Were you going to tell me?"

"Of course."

"When?"

"I never found a good time."

"How about now? Is now a good time?"

"I'm telling you now."

"Only because you have to."

And there was the irony, Patrese thought. It was the blood groups that had given it away, and the blood groups had come to his attention only because of the flood. Varden had been hoist by his own petard.

"Listen, Junior . . ."

"*Don't call me that!* I hate it. I've *always* hated it. Junior. Like I'm still in high school. Like I'm nothing except an appendage of yours. Fucking *hate* it."

Varden was still moving along the wall, always backing away from Junior. Patrese scuttled in behind Junior and picked up the flash drive from the floor. Junior carried on talking:

"This is the way it ends, huh? This is the way. It. *Always*. Ends. Humiliation, betrayal, abandonment. The one constant in my life, the one pure memory. *Gone*. You know, all the time I was killing those people—"

He stopped, as though what he was about to say was too far beyond the pale, and if that was the case, Patrese thought, that could only mean one thing.

All the time I was killing those people, I really wanted to kill you.

A dress rehearsal? Projection? Diversion? Maybe all of them. Put all your energies into keeping a man safe, and suppress your most basic desire to do just the opposite.

"Don't." Varden's voice cracked. "Please don't."

"Don't plead. Don't be fucking *weak*."

Varden had gone so far along the wall that he was almost at the next window . . . except this window was one of the ones Katrina had torn out. There was no glass. Just a hole between floor and ceiling, and 750 feet down to the sidewalk.

Junior had the gun in Varden's face now.

Varden turned his face away, toward the gaping void.

"No," he said. Fear-saucered eyes swiveled toward Patrese. "Stop him."

"Remember when you taught me Nietzsche, Father?" Junior hissed. "The will to power, yes? Master over slave, *yes*? Superman over man, *yes*? You remember?"

"Of course."

"You told me Nietzsche was the only philosopher who'd ever made sense to you."

"Yes."

Junior grabbed his father's face and twisted it outward and down, forcing him to make the vertigo stare; down, down to the hopeless streets.

"When you look into the abyss," Junior said, "the abyss also looks back into you."

And he pushed.

Patrese walked out.

Junior was still looking out of the window, down to where Patrese could hear the first stirrings of commotion: a woman's scream, a man's rough shout. He wondered whether Junior would jump after his father, and found he didn't much care either way.

He walked out, and Junior didn't seem to hear, let alone try to stop him.

In the antechamber, a couple of Varden's goons barred Patrese's way.

"In there." Patrese jerked his head back toward Varden's office. "Give them a few minutes. They said they'd call for you when they're ready."

The goons looked at each other. Patrese was unarmed, unshackled, and unaccompanied, and they didn't dare incur the wrath of either Varden by entering unannounced. How could Patrese not be telling the truth? They let him past.

He went back down the fifty-five flights of stairs and out onto the street.

He walked. Didn't know where he was going; didn't care. Just walked along the edge of the high-water mark.

Coffins floated in the sludge, burst free from their crypts by the floodwaters. The tangles of power lines seemed to truss the city hog-tied tight. Staircases rose and stopped, the buildings once around them now all gone. Stray dogs howled like hoarse coyotes. Adults tugged plastic laundry tubs full of children through the waters. People huddled in the paltry shade of interstate overpasses. First responders went from house to house, spray-painting crosses on the doors with strange alphanumeric codes in the interstices as though daubing on lamb's blood for the Passover.

It was an end-of-the-world movie, an African war zone, something filtered through the cameras of Paramount or CNN, not something in real life.

An SUV emblazoned with a news network logo crawled past. Patrese pulled out his FBI badge and held it out. The SUV stopped. A brunette with more makeup than Baby Jane dropped her window a fraction.

"Where you going?" Patrese said.

"Baton Rouge."

"You want to make a deal?"

"Depends what it is."

"You give me a lift."

"And?"

"And I'll give you a story that'll win you a Peabody."

Epilogue

Thanksgiving

Patrese sat at the edge of the sinkhole and looked down. *Cenote*, he remembered, that was what the Mayans had called it. *Cenote*. Door to the underworld.

He considered this place to be where it had really started. They'd already been four murders into the case, sure, but it was here that Junior had tried to kill him, here where Patrese had first really felt that the murders were the tip of something more.

More to it. That was an understatement, to put it mildly.

He'd given Baby Jane the flash drive and let her interview him. No voice masking, no face pixeling, no silhouette in a darkened room with an actor's overdub. Just him, Franco Patrese, telling America—telling the *world*—about Project Noah.

Varden had already been dead, of course, killed by his own son. Of that son, there was still no sign. Junior had skipped out of New Orleans a few hours later, and no one knew for sure where he'd gone, though he'd been "sighted" more often than Elvis—usually in countries that had no extradition treaty with the U.S.

Phelps, Alper, and Infuhr had all committed suicide before the cops had gotten to them. Thorndike and Dempsey had been shown on every news program from Tremé to Timbuktu performing the time-honored walk of shame—hands cuffed behind their backs, unsympathetic police hands pushing wonky-blanketed heads down while flashbulbs popped and bored ghouls hurled abuse.

Waxman had offered to testify against Thorndike and Dempsey—and against Junior in absentia—in return for witness protection.

Patrese had been given indefinite leave from the Bureau while it came to terms with the extent of Phelps's involvement in Project Noah. His sister Bianca had invited him to spend Thanksgiving with her and her family back home in Pittsburgh, and he'd wanted to go, but he'd figured this was more pressing.

He'd come back for three reasons, all of them interlinked: salute to the start of his discovery; determination to return to a place where he'd seen death's beady eyes; and cleansing in ancient cave-water of the filth that had swamped him in New Orleans.

The sensible thing to do with cave diving was to go in pairs. Patrese knew that, but he knew, too, that this was something he wanted to—had to—do alone.

He adjusted his mask and slid into the water.

No problems with silt-outs or tangled lines this time. He was calm, and his air gauges read what he expected them to. He passed through the bottleneck, left a spare tank in the alcove, and hovered in weightless ecstasy as he passed through the cavern with the flow-stone wall.

When the marker line ran out not long afterward, he pulled a nylon rope from a pouch on his belt. He tied one end to a rock and spooled the line out as he swam.

Light played in the water up ahead. It took Patrese a moment to recognize it: the entrance to the chamber with the air hole high above. He'd stopped there on his previous visit, after Junior had left him for dead.

For the first time since immersion, Patrese shivered.

He began to turn, to swim away from that place, and heard a voice through the monotone of his bubbled breathing.

Come and see.

He spun all the way around, eyes wide behind his mask.

There was no one there. Just him.

Come and see.

Impossible, of course, but Patrese was swimming toward the chamber even before he realized it. Up to the opening, squeeze through it—chest flat against the rock to give the air tanks space to clear, he remembered that bit—and then the water drained away from around his mask and mouthpiece as he surfaced back into natural air.

Junior was lying on the ledge. The white wet suit gave away his identity; his face was so decomposed and bloated as to be more or less unrecognizable.

Patrese looked around. Two air tanks were laid neatly on their side next to each other. Both were light to the touch; empty. No food packaging anywhere to be seen. Junior would have had air to breathe and water to drink, but nothing to eat.

A slow, agonizing starvation. It was almost three months since Junior had gone missing. Hunger strikers had been known to survive for two months.

Most people would have swum back up the tunnel and let themselves drown. Not Junior. Nothing to eat. Nothing to read, nothing to watch, nothing but the torture of his own demon-raddled company, but still he'd stuck it out, narcissist to the end, unwilling or unable to destroy the only thing over which he still had control: himself.

Above and around the ledge, covering an area the height and breadth of a man's reach, the rock face was gouged with strange markings. Patrese looked closer. Junior had tried to write, perhaps to draw. Hieroglyphics of nonsense; the workings of a delirious mind transcribed by failing hands.

He must have gone totally insane before he died, Patrese realized; *totally insane*. Those whom the gods would destroy, they first drive mad.

There was only one section that was legible. Ten words carved into the heartless limestone with such frenzy that perhaps the effort alone had finally done in Junior.

It is finished.
It is finished.
IT IS THE MERCY.